D0596003

DON'T BE A
HERO

**CHEEKY
MINION**

ALSO BY CHRIS STRANGE

The Man Who Couldn't Be Bought (Short Story)
The Man Who Crossed Worlds

www.chris-strange.com

**CHEEKY
MINION**

Originally published by Cheeky Minion 2012

First Edition

Cover art by Kitty Gunn

ISBN: 1479341096
ISBN-13: 978-1479341092

For Eleanor

PART ONE

Now I am become Death, the destroyer of worlds.

— J. Robert Oppenheimer, also known as Dr Atomic

CHAPTER 1

NO ONE CAN STOP ME NOW

DR ATOMIC

REAL NAME: *J. Robert Oppenheimer*

POWERS: *Super strength, flight, energy beams, impervious to most conventional weapons. All abilities derived from his immense psychic powers.*

NOTES: *The first superhero. Originally the lead physicist for the US atomic bomb development program, dubbed "The Manhattan Project". Gained his powers in an explosion at Los Alamos and became the leader of scientist-superhero group the Manhattan Eight. Disappeared from the public eye in 1951. Died of oesophageal cancer in 1954.*

—Notes on selected metahumans [Entry #0001]

Somewhere over Northern Russia
October 1969

Morgan Shepherd leaned against the airship's expansive windows, drinking in the light from the sun. Below, the powdered Siberian tundra rolled past. Pine trees and brown grasses dotted the landscape, clinging to patches of exposed earth. The airship's heating system kept out the cold, but when he pressed his forehead against the glass, he could almost smell the dry air outside.

"I saw him once, you know," Morgan said without taking his eyes from the landscape. "Dr Atomic. The Americans brought him to London to show him off to Parliament. I must've been about ten at the time. They had a parade through the streets, all confetti and flags. Mum brought me and my brothers to see. We lived in a little town outside

Birmingham. Did I tell you this?"

"Yes, sir." John's voice quavered a little. He seemed a nervous man.

Morgan smiled out the window at the past. "I spent all my pocket money on Dr Atomic comics. I liked the ones about his real adventures the most, the ones where he and the rest of the Manhattan Eight were fighting for freedom, fighting the Nazis, pushing them through Belgium and all the way back to the Fatherland. I knew every story by heart, every little bit of trivia. But there was nothing like seeing him in real life."

He rubbed a white-gloved hand across the tan and pale patches on his cheek. He'd shaved an hour ago. It was important to make good impressions. He wore a white suit and tie as pure as the snow. A series of gold buckles ran up the jacket, and a pair of cuff-links engraved with starbursts clung to his cuffs. The black domino mask he wore over his eyes wouldn't do a thing to hide his identity, but that didn't matter. He wanted them to see his face. If he had his way, he wouldn't wear a mask at all. But traditions had their place.

"At the parade I snuck away from Mum and my brothers to get to the front. I was tall for my age, but skinny, so I easily slipped through the crowds. I got to the front just as Dr Atomic came past." He closed his eyes to picture it better. "He was magnificent. That yellow suit was a hundred times brighter than in the comics. And his royal blue cape, blowing behind him in the London wind…." He tried to find the right word. "Remarkable. The Americans were never afraid to use colour. Not like we English. We were always obsessed with browns and greys, treating metahumans like soldiers to be camouflaged. But soldiers are just boys who point rifles at other boys because their government tells them to. No, the Americans understood. Those men weren't soldiers. They were heroes."

The airship hummed and started a slow bank to starboard. Morgan glanced behind him, where Navigatron's skeletal, half-naked body sat hunched over in the pilot's chair. His eyes glowed with green light and his mouth hung half-open, tongue twitching within. If Morgan concentrated, he'd be able to sense the packets of information travelling from the airship's control panel into Navigatron's palms. That particular metahuman had been a good find. Morgan had picked him up just eighteen months ago in New Delhi. He couldn't walk or talk without assistance, but the improvements he'd made to the airship's rocket engines alone were enough to speed up Morgan's plan by months. Morgan's father had worked developing electronic appliances during the Depression. It would boggle his mind to see what Navigatron could do when he made friends with a machine.

"You're awfully quiet, John," Morgan said, returning his gaze to the wastelands below. "Can I get you something to drink? Eat?"

"No," John said quickly. "Thank you."

"Did you eat before you came aboard?" He turned without waiting for an answer. "Obsidian," he called.

Obsidian glanced up from the map she was studying. Or at least it seemed she did. With her eyes, it was sometimes difficult to tell where she was looking. Her black body shone and glinted as she drew herself upright, sunlight reflecting off the crags of her shoulders. She wore no clothes, and he had no reason to think someone made of rock even had any genitalia to cover. Her chest certainly had no hint of bosom. It reminded him more of a cliff face.

"Yes, my lord?"

"John is hungry. Do we have any more of that mashed potato?"

"I believe so, my lord."

"Excellent," Morgan said. "Do you like mashed potato, John? We've got some in tubes, like toothpaste. I'm told it's what the cosmonauts eat."

John Bishop sat huddled in the corner of the command deck, a notebook open on the wooden table in front of him and a stub of a pencil in his hand. He was a portly fellow, in his mid-twenties if Morgan remembered correctly. The man was supposed to be a rising star in investigative journalism, and he was pegged to get one of the lead jobs at the BBC in the next couple of years if he played his cards right. Morgan hadn't expected to find a fellow Englishman in Moscow, but it had been a serendipitous meeting.

"Please," John said, "I'm fine."

"Nonsense." Morgan straightened his jacket and waved to Obsidian. "Fetch Longtooth and tell him to bring John something to eat after we disembark. And a glass of wine." The man needed his nerves calmed.

Obsidian bent her neck and stomped out the rear hatch. The airship shook a little with every step.

Morgan shot John a toothy smile. "There, no problem. Are you getting everything you need?"

John looked puzzled, so Morgan pointed at his notebook.

"Oh, yes, sir," he said. "Very good, sir."

"Excellent." Morgan turned his attention back to the window as a rectangular black blotch on the landscape appeared from behind a snow-covered hill. "Ah, here we are. Good work, Navigatron."

The husk of a man didn't give any indication that he'd heard. Morgan knew his ears worked fine, but his mind would be occupied with the running of the ship. Still, Morgan believed in giving credit where it was due.

"Yes, those were the days," he said, watching the compound slide slowly closer. "The days when a hero knew who he was, what he stood for. Where men and women all across the world could go about their business without fear. Because they knew that no matter how dark the world got, no matter who was threatening nuclear annihilation or genocide, there were heroes to stand against the darkness. The Manhattan Eight. The Light Brigade. Liberty Corps. Mr October. Kingfisher. Future Girl. Battle Jack. Dr Atomic." He touched his mask. "People who knew what the costume stood for."

As the airship floated closer, he could make out the twenty-foot high walls surrounding the compound, with guard towers set in every corner. A windowless concrete building dominated the centre. The compound had started its life as one of Stalin's gulags, before he was toppled. Now it served a different purpose.

"Navigatron, disable the cloak. They'll be able to hear us by now anyway. We may as well give them a fighting chance."

The cripple said nothing, but a throbbing noise faded away, leaving only the sound of the rocket engines. A few moments later, a low wail echoed across the tundra from the prison. He squinted and made out dozens of tiny figures scrambling across the snow-covered yards. On the walls, a pair of huge black anti-aircraft guns began to swivel into position.

"You're probably too young," he said to John. "You don't remember. You don't understand. You're not alone. Most people have forgotten. But it's time they remembered."

He took a breath and adjusted his white suit one last time. Clothes didn't make the man, they just magnified him. His father taught him that.

"Arm the cannons," he said.

A high-pitched whine, just on the threshold of perception, went through the airship. He thought he heard John whisper a prayer to himself. He didn't understand yet, but that didn't matter. It only mattered that he saw what happened here. "Come, John," Morgan said.

There was a pause, then the rattle of metal as John got to his feet and shuffled over. Morgan had chained John's ankles together as a precaution, but he'd left the man's hands unbound. He would need them to record what he saw.

John stood next to him at the window and stared down at the prison, clutching his notebook in thick hands. His cheeks quivered. Morgan could smell sweat on him. He put a hand on the small of the man's back to keep him from backing away.

Last chance to back out, Morgan told himself. No. It was too late for that. Some things just had to be done. "Give them a volley," he said.

Yellow light bright enough to make Morgan squint cut through the air, accompanied by a screech like a boiling kettle. An instant later, the first anti-aircraft gun exploded into a cloud of molten metal. The laser's ray swept along in an arc from the airship, making the concrete crack and crumble wherever it touched. John pressed his hands to his ears and his eyes narrowed into slits, but Morgan could tell he was still watching. *Good.* Steam rose from the compound as ice and snow sublimed, turning to vapour instantly.

A pair of figures on the ground tried to run from the laser. They sprinted from the wall to the central building, throwing their rifles to the ground in a desperate bid to gain more speed. It didn't help. Morgan forced himself to watch as the beam swept across them, burning the flesh from their bones. Their blackened skeletons toppled onto the snow.

God forgive him.

A low moan escaped John's throat. He'd turned pale, as pale as the patches that covered Morgan's skin.

"Remember this," Morgan said. "Remember what I did here. And write your story." He swept away from the window, leaving John to stare at the carnage. "Obsidian," he shouted as the stone woman reappeared in the command deck doorway. "Prepare to disembark."

He could swear he saw a smile on her expressionless face. "Yes, my lord." Her voice was smooth, like water over polished stones.

The screech of the ray gun became a pulse as it started picking off targets. The weapon he and Navigatron had designed would punch them a hole, but the real prize was deep inside. To get to it, he'd have to do the butcher's work, up close and personal.

He followed Obsidian's jerky, clockwork movements through the spartan corridors and down a narrow spiral staircase, stooping to avoid the low ceiling. A low throbbing started in the base of his skull. It always happened these days whenever the adrenaline started flowing. The ache was comforting, somehow. Familiar. As he walked, he pulled his medicine bottle from his pocket and swallowed a couple of white pills.

The two of them emerged into a wide loading bay with bare metal grating for a floor. Amongst the equipment crates lashed to the floor and walls, a dozen metahumans milled. They were dressed eclectically; Sand Fury was in full-body desert camouflage while Tinderbox wore nothing but the flame that licked across his bare skin.

They grew silent and still the instant Morgan stepped through the door. This was no military group. No one came to attention or saluted when he came on deck. He'd already briefed them on the building's layout and what they'd find. But they all straightened and turned towards him, waiting for him to speak.

He drew up before them and cleared his throat. "It's time. Ground defences are down, but expect heavy resistance. Each of you is here of your own free will. You have no obligation to fight today. If you have no wish to face death, I suggest you return to your quarters."

No one moved.

Morgan nodded, heart swelling. Of all of them, Obsidian and Morgan were the only ones who had the ability to sustain serious small arms fire. Even then, an anti-tank round or a rocket-propelled grenade would do them serious damage. But still they stood here.

Courage. Loyalty. These things still existed. "Open the bay doors."

Obsidian punched a button on the control panel, and the floor at the rear of the cargo bay began to slide away. Cold air rushed in, and goose bumps spread across his skin. The pulses of the ray gun became deafening. The ship vibrated with each shot.

He led the way to the open bay doors and took hold of one of the ropes hanging on a winch from the ceiling. He tossed the other end of the coiled rope out and watched as it dropped to the ground.

"With me," he shouted over the noise, taking hold of a pair of handles on the electric motor connected to the rope. And then he stepped out over the abyss. With his thumb he pressed the red button, and the motor kicked into gear, wheels spinning.

His stomach lurched with sudden weightlessness as he plunged out of the airship. He wrapped his feet around the rope as the motorized wheels drove him down along the line. Icy wind cut through his clothes, freezing him to the core. The speckled plains spread around him in all directions, not a city or town in sight. It was almost peaceful, aside from the hiss of stone cracking and the screams of the ray gun.

Ropes dropped down beside him, cutting through his view. He could just make out the sound of a dozen more little motors whizzing to life. The ray gun finally fell silent. The risk of hitting his own people was too great. But the exterior of the prison was already shattered and stripped of life. The walls were cracked, the anti-aircraft guns were disabled, the guards were dead.

As the ground rushed to meet him, Morgan released the speed control and applied the brakes. Another lurch of his stomach as he slowed, and then his white leather loafers crunched on the rocky courtyard made slippery with melted snow. He was inside the compound.

He was already moving by the time the other metahumans touched down behind him. The single windowless building stood like a huge black monument in the centre of the compound, gleaming in the sun. A well-placed ray gun blast had cracked open the sole door. Figures moved in the shadows. As he sprinted across the courtyard towards the soldiers, he drank in the harsh Siberian sunlight. He seemed to recall a song about a flower clinging to life in the snow, but the words escaped him.

Morgan shifted his energy inside himself, just like he did every day during his personal training. Flashes went off in his head, like a horde of over-eager cameramen, and he brought his hands together in front of him. Light bloomed around him, oozing out of every pore as though it were liquid. To other men, it would be almost blinding. But to him, it was like opening the curtain onto a beautiful summer's day.

Russian shouts reached him, and nine or ten men poured out of the building's doorway. The soldiers dropped into crouches and aimed their Kalashnikov rifles at him. Some glanced up nervously as his airship, *Hyperion*, passed over them, its rocket engines idling. It had cost him a fortune, but money was easy to come by. And no one could say it didn't have a touch of class.

Then the soldiers returned their attention to him. Muzzles flashed and the clatter of automatic fire burst through the air. Morgan didn't stop. The light around him hardened in response to his thought, and an instant later he was peppered with a dozen rounds. Sparks flew around him. Bullets ricocheted off the solidified light he'd drawn up. Each round set his teeth chattering, sending little ripples of force through him.

But his shield of light held. His own heavy breathing echoed inside his head, loud enough to drown out even the gunfire. His footfalls crunched across the courtyard, and bullets kicked up fragments of snow and packed soil all around him. The shouts became desperate. He was close enough to see how young these soldiers were.

And then he was amongst them. He leapt, slamming his shield of light into one and kicking the rifle out of another's hands. With another switch of energy, the light changed shape again. A sword bloomed into life in his hand. A sword with an edge the size of an electron.

He swung in a wide arc, and blood flew. He'd learned fencing at university, but there was no art to what he did now. He slashed out again and again, relying on speed and the protection of his shield. He wasn't cold anymore.

The stink of death was everywhere. The three surviving soldiers pulled back into the doorway. They abandoned their rifles for their handguns in the tight quarters. He swept in after them, stepping over the bodies of their comrades and using his shield to keep the blood from staining the white fabric of his trousers.

Tinderbox was the first of Morgan's people to arrive. He skated in on feet of flame and projected a narrow jet of fire at a soldier. The flesh of the man's face bubbled where it hit him. He fell, screaming. Morgan forced himself to listen. No blocking out the screams. He would live with them. He had to.

Morgan and Tinderbox had secured the doorway by the time the others caught up. Obsidian observed the carnage with the only face she was capable of making, and said nothing, like the rest.

"Sand Fury will cover our exit. Screecher, take B team to the upper floors and crush anyone you find. The rest of you, with me."

They were two floors underground, fighting one minor skirmish after another in the cramped concrete corridors, when the Russians launched a full counterattack. Morgan got his light shield up just in time to deflect a hail of bullets from a machine gun mounted behind a thick concrete wall. Rounds hammered him, sending ricochets sparking into the walls.

"Scramble!" he ordered, and the rest of the metas scattered behind him. Obsidian kicked open a door and led the rest of his metahumans into an intersecting corridor.

Morgan planted his feet and gritted his teeth against the oncoming barrage. The machine gun was perhaps sixty feet away, with a clear line of sight down his corridor. Behind it he could make out groups of soldiers massing, and behind them, the static purple glow of Unity Corporation shielding systems. The prison cells.

He ducked back into the doorway Obsidian and the others had retreated into. The colourful array of metahumans crouched or stood, poised like jungle cats.

"This is it," he yelled, struggling to make himself heard over the gunfire echoing through the corridor. "Obsidian, a little help would be very much appreciated."

"As my lord says." She jerked a nod and turned her diamond eyes on Haze. "Cover."

The thick-set Haze unzipped the mouth area of his full-face mask and showed his teeth. "About fuckin' time." Smoke trickled from his lips as he spoke.

Morgan moved aside and made room for Haze to step up to the doorway. Tracer rounds from the machine gun flew past, tearing the corridor to shreds. Haze took a few deep breaths in and out, waiting.

The gunfire suddenly stopped, leaving Morgan's ears ringing. The machine gunner swore in Russian. He needed to reload.

Haze's eyes rolled back in his head. The meta took one last breath in, held it for a moment. Morgan could hear boots stomping on concrete and a few bursts of suppressive fire as the soldiers moved to support the machine gunner.

And then Haze exhaled. Smoke and wind blew through the corridor. In an instant, Morgan was blinded by a wall of grey smog.

The ground shuddered as Obsidian dashed out into the clouded corridor. He could imagine her raising her fists into the air, poised above her head.

"Brace yourselves," her smooth voice said.

Morgan pressed himself against the wall as she brought her fists down on the ground. The earth screamed and shook like a meteor had hit. He heard the concrete groaning as the wave of energy flowed through the ground ahead of her.

Haze braced himself against the doorway and sucked the smoke screen back towards his mouth. The rumbling of the earth slowly died away, leaving nothing but shouts and the tinkling of crumbling masonry.

Morgan was first out of the corridor, racing across the cracked ground before the last shakes had vanished. Obsidian came close behind him, breathing heavily, and the others followed, whooping and shouting.

Morgan drew up a blade of light and slashed at the machine gunner's neck while he struggled to get back to his weapon. Without slowing, Morgan leapt over the chest-high wall. Thirty or forty Russian soldiers lay scattered across the main prison chamber, trying to regain their feet. His metahumans fanned out beside him, kicking and slashing and biting and burning the soldiers who tried to get to their guns. One soldier fell with swarms of insects crawling down his throat, choking him. Obsidian hurled another at the wall, and Morgan could hear the man's neck crack. The throbbing in his skull grew as the soldiers died, but he pushed it aside. He couldn't worry about that now. He wasn't done yet.

Behind the dying soldiers, twenty prison cells sat nestled in the walls. Twenty prisoners for this prison in the middle of nowhere. Each cell was closed over not with bars, but with purple, half-transparent shields. Behind the shields, twenty sets of eyes watched their guards being butchered.

"Enough!" Morgan shouted. His people grew still. He glanced around the room and found a soldier still breathing in the corner, his arm broken and bleeding.

The man watched with a grimace painted across his face. He was older than the others, with a thick black moustache resting on his upper lip. An officer.

"*Vy govorite po-angliyski?*" Morgan asked.

The man sneered. "Yes," he said in a thick accent. "I speak English, dog."

Morgan crouched in front of him, careful not to get blood on his shoes. "The controls."

The soldier spat. Morgan suppressed a flash of anger and pulled a handkerchief from his pocket to wipe the saliva from his cheek.

"There are only two ways this ends," Morgan said. "Both ways I get what I want. I'm trying to help you. Please. The controls."

The soldier's eyes were filled with fire. Then the light dimmed, and he jerked his head to his right. Morgan glanced up and found the panel the man indicated. He pointed it out to Obsidian, then turned his attention back to the soldier.

"Get word to your Premier. Tell him what happened here. Tell him I found your prison. Tell him I destroyed it. Tell him I took what he thought was so carefully hidden. And tell him it took me less than an hour. *Vy panimayete?*"

"*Da.* I understand, dog. Do you?"

Morgan stood and nodded to Obsidian. She pressed a series of buttons on the wall panel. A light blinked green, and Morgan smiled. It had been ten years since the last breakout attempt. The guards had grown complacent. They didn't change the codes as often as they should.

The purple shields of every cell flickered and disappeared.

The prisoners slowly shuffled out of their cells. One man floated out a foot above the ground, his legs crossed beneath him. Another woman sniffed at the air before emerging and let a long, snake-like tongue dart from her mouth.

Morgan stepped in front of Obsidian and his other metas and studied the prisoners. They were malnourished, and some bore old, untreated injuries. But their eyes were strong. A few of them he would need to put down, but the rest....

He smiled.

"My name," he said, "is Quanta." He paused for a moment, letting his words echo around the chamber. "I'm looking for the one who calls himself Doll Face."

Silence answered him. His head continued to throb, like the pulsations of a rocket engine. Despite his self-control, a crack of doubt appeared in his mind. No. It would work. It had to work.

Something sharp pricked his throat.

"What does the pretty man want with me, hmmm?" a voice whispered in his ear. It was girlish, yet obviously a man's voice. Spindly fingers wrapped around Morgan's shoulder. He froze, trying not to breathe. He could feel a drop of blood trickling down his neck where the jagged blade pressed. "Does it want to hurt Doll Face? Or does it just want to play?"

"Neither," Morgan said, moving as little as possible. "I'm recruiting."

CHAPTER 2

THERE'S NO I IN HERO

Even today, after two decades of research, the mechanism behind the formation of so-called "metahumans" is unclear. There is no single mutation that causes the condition, and in many cases, multiple gene loci appear to be affected. What is clear, however, is that the nuclear radiation that leads to these mutations is a danger to all mankind. Even if only one in ten thousand exposed individuals develop superpowers, the selection pressure could well be enough to drive non-powered humans to extinction. The only solution is control of the metahuman population.

—From the notes of Professor Gloria Becker

The outskirts of Neo-Auckland, New Zealand
One month later

Niobe Ishii tapped out a Pall Mall cigarette, glanced around the dark, empty street, then rolled up the fabric of her mask to expose her mouth. That was the worst thing about a mask. She didn't mind not eating or drinking until she got somewhere private, but sometimes she just needed a goddamn smoke. When she'd spent the last hour being interrogated by her girlfriend, she *really* needed a smoke. Her utility belt's auto-lighter set the cigarette tip glowing, and she slowly inhaled.

The smoke drifted through her, and the nicotine started to calm her nerves. Gabby would've cooled off by the time she got back. The woman just worried too much, that was all. But Niobe had work to do. It was time to get moving.

She set off down the dark street. While she walked, she pulled her goggles over her eyes and put her bowler hat on. The goggles and utility belt were Gabby's work, along with the heavily modified .455 Webley revolver in her shoulder holster. The rest of Niobe's costume was already in place: a black and grey bodysuit, full-face mask, gloves, combat boots. A trench coat went over the whole thing. She could never pull off spandex alone, and she liked that the trench coat hid her shape. Anything that helped her stay anonymous was worth it.

The night was scattered with clouds. A breeze cut through the air, washing an old newspaper down the street. To the south, a police dirigible floated. She doubted they'd be able to see anything with their spotlight off. She turned her back on it and made her way through what used to be the suburb of Epsom.

The occasional light shone in a window, but she was the only one on the streets. She expected that. You weren't likely to get mugged in the Old City, not with the police dirigibles and the curfews. But people here had grown afraid of the dark.

She made her way through the shadows, passing a yowling pack of stray cats clinging to a fence. A one-eyed tortoiseshell tom twitched his ears as she slid past. She was already beginning to breathe easier. Walking the streets at night was calming. She was invisible here, just the way she liked it.

Most of the apartment buildings she passed were simple and clean in design, just rectangles with white or grey walls. The blackened shell of a townhouse stood on the corner next to a stop sign. A long time ago, she'd known the people who lived there. The boy was her age, a friend from school. Most of her friends were boys. But his parents stopped him from seeing her because she was Japanese. It was okay. That was just the way things were in those days. Now the boy and his parents were all dead, and their house was home to rats.

She paused for a moment, then dropped her cigarette to the concrete, stamped it out, and walked on. She didn't want to think about the bomb, or the fire that consumed her city. Not tonight.

Niobe stopped outside a townhouse in a cul-de-sac. In the narrow yard outside was one of the only gardens anywhere in the Old City.

Even in the darkness, she could make out the tangle of wild flowers leading up the short path. A morepork called its own name twice before falling silent. She caught a glimpse of the owl's eyes high in the tree, and then they disappeared.

The house itself was an old weatherboard villa, one of the few that survived, sheltered from the worst of the blast by One Tree Hill. It had seen better days, but compared to the buildings on either side, it was a palace. The windows were dark. She cast another look around the street, found it empty, and made her way up to the front door. The door was a good one—thick, solid—so she reached into her pocket for her lockpicks.

Wait. She screwed up her nose and returned her hand to her side. He'd been upset with her last time she came in uninvited. Not that she worried much about his feelings, but he'd been careful to impress upon her his annoyance. Very careful.

Reluctantly, she tapped the frosted glass with her middle finger. There was no answer for a few minutes, but she didn't knock again. Solomon was a light sleeper.

She was just about to light up another smoke when she heard the squeak of footsteps on floorboards. A light came on and the door creaked open.

"We've got a job," Niobe said.

Solomon Doherty rested his head against the door frame and squinted at her through puffy eyes. His tree-brown hair was mussed and flattened on one side. Deep crevices ran down the sides of his cheeks. On a softer man that would've made him look old, but on him they gave an air of dignified permanence. A kind of inevitability, maybe.

"Good evening to you too, Spook," he said. "You ever think of visiting during the day? Or at least calling ahead first?"

"And wake your kids?" Niobe pulled another cigarette from her pack, adjusted her mask, and lit up. "For a family man, you sure are inconsiderate."

"That's rich coming from you, mate." Solomon wore a set of holey grey pyjamas with the Wardens logo embroidered on the breast. They'd given Niobe a pair as well, back when Battle Jack brought her into the fold and gave her the terrible alias of Gloomgirl. She never wore them. Like hell she was going to announce her supergroup membership while she slept.

He wrinkled his nose and shot a look at her cigarette. "The doctors say that'll kill you, you know."

She plucked it from her mouth. "Cancer's coming for us metas whether we smoke or not." She took another draw. "Might as well have fun first."

Something creaked inside the house. Solomon glanced back inside and lowered his voice. "So what's this job you had to get me out of bed for?"

"Gabrielle picked it up on the wire. Missing persons case."

"In the Old City?"

She shook her head. "Neo-Auckland proper. Mangere Central."

Solomon's bushy eyebrows rose and he whistled quietly. "Pay?"

"Dunno yet. I thought we could go find out."

"Does our potential client know we're visiting him at two in the morning?"

She shrugged. "The man's got a missing person. I'm sure he's not sleeping too heavily."

"Point."

"So you'll come?" she asked.

He appeared to consider it for a moment. It wasn't a very convincing show. She knew he'd made up his mind the moment he opened the door. He was like a kid that way, never mind that he had a good ten years on her. Something about the old days still called to him, she knew, the days of heroes and villains.

"Lord, give me strength," he muttered to himself, but a smile played at the corners of his eyes. "Come in and let me get changed."

She stubbed out her cigarette, wiped her boots carefully on the doormat, and followed him inside. The house was cluttered with books and pot plants. She liked that. It made it seem lived in. Gabby always kept everything clean and ordered. It drove her crazy.

Solomon left her in the living room and disappeared down the hallway. She'd once made the mistake of sitting on the couch. A loose spring had sliced a hole in the thigh of her suit and left her needing a tetanus shot. So instead she stood and eyed the mementos scattered through the room.

A floppy, wide-brimmed hemp hat had pride of place, mounted on the wall above the grated fireplace. One side of the hat was blackened and melted. Beneath it hung a small hatchet with a wooden handle, the blade chipped and nicked in a dozen places. A trio of front pages from old copies of the *New Zealand Herald* had been framed and fixed to the wall alongside, each showing the triumphant Wardens at the site of some crisis or other.

Solomon had been one of the first generation Wardens, along with Battle Jack and Drillman. Ever since the bomb hit, New Zealand had always had more than its fair share of metas, so supergroups were always springing up. The Wardens modelled themselves after the groups springing up across America and Europe, but with a greater focus on integration with regular law enforcement.

One of the newspaper clippings on the wall had a photo of Solomon looking bruised but smiling anyway, with a pair of giant black insects dead at his feet. *NAGASAKI HORRORS CRUSHED*, the headline proclaimed. That had been the group's biggest fight, and it had taken place before Niobe's time. The Wardens and the Māori crime-fighting group Te Taua had shipped out for Japan to push back the monsters. All those heroes—Grim, Madame Z, Battle Jack—they'd saved the world. And Solomon too, of course, but she didn't know his real name then. To her and the rest of the world, he was simply the Carpenter.

No one had predicted what the atomic bomb at Nagasaki might do to the fabric of our universe. When the black mantis-like creatures came crawling into our dimension seven years later, destroying everything in their path, there were a few red faces. It scared the hell out of Auckland and Warsaw. If a nuke could do that in Japan, it could do it anywhere. The rebuilding of old Auckland halted, and the construction of a new city a dozen miles south began in earnest. But Niobe and the other heroes remained in the Old City. Those were proud days. The heroes waited there, ready in case the Horrors returned. They waited for years. Until the world changed, and no one trusted superheroes to protect them anymore.

"He's going out, I suppose?" a woman's voice came from the doorway.

Niobe turned away from the old superhero memorabilia to find Kate watching her from just inside the doorway. Solomon's wife clung to beauty even in her forties. Despite the late hour, her blonde bombshell hairstyle was perfect. She had her arms crossed over her nightgown, with a small silver cross around her neck. The look she gave Niobe was the one she'd come to expect, a kind of cold disapproval.

Christ. Niobe had just wriggled out of one argument. She sure as hell didn't want to wind up in another.

"Yes," Niobe said. With her goggles in place, Kate wouldn't be able to see her eyes, and she was glad for that. Most people would be creeped out if they saw that Niobe's eyes were charcoal black all the way across, but Kate wasn't most people. The woman had a gaze that could crack rocks, even if she wasn't a meta.

The silence stretched between them. Niobe could never work out if Kate disliked her because she put Solomon in dangerous situations, or because she thought Niobe was shagging him. She didn't suppose it would help to tell her she found him about as attractive as she found any man. Kate probably wouldn't be any happier to know her husband was running around with a lesbian. It had taken Solomon long enough to come to grips with that himself. He was old-fashioned that way.

Kate opened her mouth to speak, and it didn't look like it was going to be pleasant. But by some miracle, Solomon chose that moment to come back into the room. "Oh, there you are, dear," he said to Kate. He must have sensed something, because his back stiffened. He glanced at Niobe, then back to his wife.

Kate turned her icy stare on her husband. Niobe recognised that look. It was the same one Gabby gave her during their argument an hour ago. Kate's lips twisted as she studied his new attire. He'd exchanged the pyjamas for full costume, and Niobe wondered if he was as grateful for his mask as she was for hers.

The Carpenter's outfit was all forest greens and autumn reds. A new hat—sleeker and more modern than the tattered one on the wall—sat low across his eyes. A brown half-mask left his mouth uncovered, and a cloak hung over his left shoulder, stretching down to his elbow. Poking out the bottom was the handle of his hatchet, hanging from a loop in his belt.

The costume still fit well. For some reason, it was the only thing she saw him in that ever seemed to suit him. Anyone else would look ridiculous in something so damn rustic.

Too bad his appearance did nothing to improve the mood in the room. It was lucky Kate's looks couldn't kill. More than one person had lost limbs from their superpowered spouse's misdirected eye beams.

"I'll get the car warmed up," Niobe said. She shoved her hands in her coat pockets and squeezed past the couple, while Solomon did his best to look anywhere but his wife.

Superpowered combat and interdimensional alien attacks she could handle. But there was no way in hell she was putting herself into the middle of a marital spat. She'd had enough of that already.

CHAPTER 3

THE NIGHT BELONGS TO ME

THE PILGRIM

REAL NAME: *Gordon Whitman*

POWERS: *Teleportation.*

NOTES: *The youngest member of the Manhattan Eight. When the radiation of the Los Alamos explosion struck him, he became metahuman and instantly teleported to Santiago, Chile. He was consequently assumed dead until several weeks after the incident when he returned to the US. Although he occasionally engaged in direct combat, his main role in the Manhattan Eight was to insert other members into danger zones.*

—Notes on selected metahumans [Entry #0008]

Solomon finally emerged from the house a few minutes later, looking calm but walking a bit too briskly away from the front door. He got in the passenger side and glanced at Niobe behind the wheel.

"I don't know if it's a good idea to let a woman drive," he said.

She pushed back the lapel of her trench coat to reveal the butt of her gun. "Try feeding me that line again. Try."

He grinned and pulled his hat low over his eyes. Niobe took a swig of water from her canteen, then pulled the choke out and gave it some pedal.

The car was a black 1949 Ford two-door sedan. Or it had started out that way. Gabby had made so many modifications to the thing Niobe doubted there was an original piece left. The dashboard was outfitted with a dozen knobs and levers for gadgets that might come in handy. A police radio scanner was tucked under the dash on the passenger side, tuned to the local Met Div frequency. It was silent now. A little strange, but not entirely unexpected. Few metas got themselves into trouble with the law these days. They must've been smarter than her.

The streets were deserted. They made their way out of the Old City the usual way, taking the barely-policed route through the bomb-damaged streets to the east and then travelling south past the Mangere Inlet. The roads looked worse than they were. The cracks and collapsed buildings that remained in place nearly two decades since the bomb hit turned the route into a maze if you didn't know where you were going. But it was navigable, if bumpy, and kept them free of checkpoints.

Officially, metas weren't forced to stay in the Old City. They were still human after all, and could go where they pleased. But probable cause wasn't hard for the coppers to manufacture, and if Niobe and Solomon got caught driving around after nightfall where they weren't welcome, a quick search would turn up a dozen things that weren't strictly legal. Her gun, for one, not to mention the road tack deployment system in the boot of the car. But the checkpoints and police dirigibles were well to the west, so the law didn't bother them.

The Neo-Auckland skyline cut a jagged line through the night. The guys who'd designed it had been fond of tapering towers and spires that glimmered even in the darkness. Above the streets, the upper highways and monorail tracks swooped between apartment buildings and offices, suspended on the impossibly thin support struts originally conceived by the metahuman Green Tornado. Billboards dotted the skies as well, advertising Coke or the new electric Toyotas or rocket-plane trips to the sunny Gold Coast. And in the middle of it all, the Peace Tower stood tall, its spire piercing the sky; a monument to the destruction of the Old City, and a promise of something greater.

Thinking of the Old City brought her mind back to Gabby, and the argument. Gabby always worried when she went out on a job, and lately it had been getting worse. Niobe tried not to bring her work home with her, but it was never enough to keep the pain out of Gabby's eyes.

"Are you all right, Spook?" Solomon's voice snapped her back to reality. "You're quiet, even for you."

Niobe blinked and cleared her throat. "Yeah. Fine." She nodded outside, to where the lawns and trimmed hedges of the Neo-Auckland suburbs gave way to a pair of three-storey department stores and a long shopping mall. Past the dress and shoe shops, a sleek white tower stood between elevated monorail tracks. "That's our man's hotel."

"Hotel? He doesn't live here?"

She shrugged. "Maybe he doesn't want us to know where he lives."

A row of manicured trees divided the road in two. They drove beneath coloured banners that stretched across the street, proclaiming a Christmas sale at a toy store. It wasn't even December yet.

The shops were all shut, of course, and the moving footpaths had been switched off for the night. Niobe pulled the car off the main street and parked it down an alley a block from the hotel. Even the alley was spotlessly clean. It looked like some poor bugger had scrubbed each green rubbish bin until it shone.

Niobe activated the car's security measures—you could never be too careful—and they strode down the footpath together, Solomon's shoulder cape billowing in the breeze.

A tall silver birch stood guard beside the Starlight Hotel, the base of its trunk ringed by a low brick fence. The hotel's revolving door faced the street. It'd be locked at this hour. Through the glass came dull orange light, probably from a lamp. She touched the lever at the side of her goggles, switching the magnification. She could just make out the silhouette of the night-shift clerk at the front desk, her head nodding.

"Our man's in four-oh-eight," she said in a low voice. She stepped back and counted off the fourth floor balconies. "That one there."

"I take it asking politely isn't an option?"

She buttoned up her trench coat and smiled beneath her mask. "Race you there."

She sucked in a lungful of warm night air, held it, and relaxed her body.

Then she spread out in all directions like an ice cream melting in double time. Everything became thin, two-dimensional. Sight disappeared, replaced by a sense of position and an awareness of the minutest traces of light reflecting off surfaces.

She never really liked becoming a shadow. It made her feel so flat. Incorporeal. She was a slave to every bump and crack on the surface.

Still, it had its uses.

She shot along the ground and turned ninety degrees as she hit the wall. There was no sense of up or down as a shadow. There was only the surface. She flitted up along the outer wall of the Starlight hotel, passing balconies and feeling the roughness of sealed paint beneath her.

Dimly, she registered the noise of the silver birch creaking and groaning as the sound waves generated tiny vibrations on the tower surface. She paused for a moment to turn her attention back to Solomon. She could just make him out, a fleshy surface against a concrete one, gripping the end of a long low-hanging branch of the tree with one hand, his feet spread wide on the ground. Then, with another crack of groaning wood, the branch swung upwards, sending Solomon flying into the air. Another branch further up rotated and bent down like a friend offering Solomon a hand. He grabbed it and let it pull him back up, flinging him to the next branch.

If Niobe still had a mouth, she would have smiled to herself. He was getting on in years, but he still knew how to move. She raced up the side of the Hotel, matching him inch for inch.

The Carpenter could bend wood to his will, use it as a weapon if he wanted. But his real control came over trees and bushes that still had life in them. While a pure telekinetic meta was limited to bending things and hurling them around, Solomon had a kind of kinship with wood-based plants. He said he could sense things from them, talk to them in a limited capacity. Occasionally it came in useful, but trees didn't tend to be very coherent or observant. They could tell you what the weather was like a few days ago, or when something blocked their light, or if a possum was stripping their leaves. But if you wanted to know if a bad guy had been past, they were as silent as a mobster in a film noir.

She slipped under a balcony to avoid the light from a street lamp and crossed to the opposite side. She could feel Solomon's heavy breathing as he heaved himself up in one last leap.

She got to the balcony of 408 and drew herself back together. Her body and clothes reformed and her normal senses returned. It took less than a second. Quietly, she let out the breath she'd been holding.

Solomon landed next to her a moment later. "Call it a draw?"

"You wish, Carpenter." She peered through the double French doors, but the inside was dark. No movement that she could see. She tried the handle with a gloved hand. Locked.

Her set of lock picks were nestled in her inner coat pocket, but she didn't need them. The doors didn't sit well in their frames. She ran her fingers down the crack between them. It was enough.

She held her breath and shifted back into shadow form. In an instant, she'd slipped through the crack and reformed herself on the other side. A minor thrill ran through her heart as she crouched and peered around the hotel room. The teenager in her had never got over the excitement of being where she shouldn't be.

She could make out a couch and a dining table with four chairs, but only a single one was out of place. Next to the table, a room service trolley sat. She sniffed. Roast chicken. Better than the beans and stew she'd cooked for dinner. A television rested in the corner. Supposedly the Americans all had colour TVs by now, but New Zealand was still broadcasting everything in black and white.

Satisfied they were alone, she unlocked the balcony door and let Solomon in. He hesitated before entering. She knew the part of his brain trained in Sunday School got anxious whenever he trespassed with her. He preferred the straight-up-and-down fights. Too bad there weren't many of them going round anymore.

Still, Niobe was no criminal. You had to have a code. Breaking in to a place was all right, as long as you didn't take anything or do any actual breaking. You couldn't own the space inside a building, not really. The night belonged to the shadows, and the shadows belonged to Niobe.

Niobe signalled with her fingers and crept forwards. Solomon's footsteps came behind her, only slightly louder than hers. Battle Jack would've been useless in this line of work. He tended to get confused when confronted with a situation he couldn't either punch or shag his way out of.

Bed springs creaked. Niobe threw out a hand, gesturing for Solomon to stop, but he already had. Something scraped against carpet in the next room.

Niobe padded silently to the corner of the hotel lounge. *We were so quiet.* She'd once had an entire fist fight with Black Collar five feet from two of his security guards, and they'd never heard a whisper. So how the hell had this guy heard them?

A walking stick appeared from the open bedroom door and rested on the carpet, followed a moment later by a foot.

"I know you're there," the man said, "so your options are to leave or try to fight me."

The accent was American, educated. Interesting. Not many Americans came out to this part of the world. Not since the AAU was formed, anyway. She breathed, calming her heart.

The man took another step out. He saw the Carpenter first, silhouetted as he was against the balcony doors.

"Well?" the man said. He spread his legs and raised his cane.

Niobe flicked on the lamp in the corner of the living room. The man squinted and blinked against the sudden glare, but he didn't let his guard down. His hands didn't even shake. Doubly interesting.

She put him in his sixties. His cheeks sagged and the top of his head held nothing but liver spots. The little hair he did have clung to the sides of his head, a ring of black and grey. He hunched a little as he stood, but not, apparently, from fear.

"You've got keen ears, Frank," Niobe said from the corner, recalling the name Gabby had given her. "Or is it Mr Frank?"

The man kept his walking stick aimed at the Carpenter. Solomon could rip that stick from the man's hand and beat him round the head with it, but he wouldn't. Not unless the man attacked first.

Frank's startlingly blue eyes caught a flash of light. "What is this? Have you come for me too, now?" He was soft-spoken, but his voice didn't tremble.

"We haven't come for anybody," Solomon said. "We hear you've got a missing person."

Niobe nodded. "We're in the business of finding missing people. Amongst other things."

Frank narrowed his eyes a little, his gaze darting between them. "You're metas?"

"Nah," Solomon said. "We're a pair of wandering freelance circus clowns. You don't like the outfits?"

"I'm Spook," Niobe said, "and the smart-arse is the Carpenter."

"The Carpenter," the man said. He lowered the stick a fraction. "I remember your name."

Solomon grinned at that, but she cut him off before he could get too excited. "Time's an issue here, Mr Frank."

"Frank," he said. "Just Frank. Frank Julius." He dropped the cane to his side, but he didn't seem to put much weight on it.

"Frank, then," she said. "We like to stay under the radar. That means we want to be gone before dawn. Now, do you have a case for us? Or were we mistaken?"

He studied them for a moment, then turned his gaze to the purple veins running across the backs of his hands.

"The people I talked to said they would get the word out," Frank said. "I just expected a little more notice."

"And miss all this fun?" she said.

The man frowned. "Couldn't you have called first?"

"That's what I keep telling her," the Carpenter said. "But does she listen?"

"What my partner means to say," she said, shooting him a look, "is that we like to know who we're dealing with. Keeps us safe."

The man nodded slowly. He seemed to be weighing his options. It didn't surprise Niobe. He looked out of his element, conducting shady business like this. This hotel was nice, and sure as hell not cheap. Offering them a job might be the most illegal thing he'd ever done. It might be the *only* illegal thing he'd ever done. But there was desperation in his face. She knew there would be even before she got here. If he was coming to them, it meant the police wouldn't or couldn't help him. He could have even gone to a normal private eye, since he seemed to have cash to burn. But there were some things only a meta could do.

They didn't get job offers from normals very often. The crackdowns in the early '60s still lingered in people's minds, when offering jobs to metas could get you a prison sentence if you were unlucky. But maybe he was old enough to remember the days when superheroes kept the world safe. Maybe that was what she could see stirring behind those blue eyes.

"My nephew," he finally said. "My nephew is missing."

His voice was steady, but his eyes were focussed on something else.

"You got a picture?" she asked.

"What?" he said.

"A photo. Of your nephew."

"Oh. Yes. Yes. It's in my suitcase." He turned went back into his room.

Niobe shot Solomon a glance. She pulled him aside and lowered her voice. "Does he seem familiar to you?"

"Can't say he rings a bell." He grinned. "Maybe you saw him at the pictures or something. All Yanks are film stars nowadays, right?"

She wasn't sure. It was just a feeling, but she couldn't place him. She shrugged. "You wanna keep an eye out while I do the interview?"

"He likes me more," he said.

"Men never talk to men. Not about stuff like this." She didn't want to mention that she needed to stay busy to keep her mind off her fight with Gabby. Being lookout would only give her time to brood. Besides, the Carpenter's eyes were sharper than hers, and he could stand look-out for hours at a time, never growing bored. Sometimes he was more tree than man.

He must've seen something in her face, because he pulled his hat down and didn't argue. "Be careful. That walking stick doesn't have as much wood as it should. It's hollow."

She glanced back towards the bedroom. "Sword-cane?"

"Maybe."

Perhaps Frank Julius wasn't as innocent as he looked. The Carpenter patted her on the shoulder and made his way back to the balcony.

She found Frank standing over his suitcase in the expansive bedroom. The soft glow of a wall-mounted lamp cast his face into shadow. The cane was on the bed, and he held a small colour photograph.

"You're close?" she asked from the doorway. "You and your nephew?"

He nodded without looking up from the photo. "My brother died without ever seeing him. I raised the boy like my own son. I never had children of my own."

She entered the room and stood next to him. She held out a gloved hand, and he passed her the photo. "You can keep that," he said.

The boy was handsome. His face was narrower than his uncle's, but he had the same blue eyes. He couldn't have been older than twelve or thirteen. The picture had him against an ocean background, smiling a toothy, made-for-photography smile.

"His name's Sam," Frank said.

"Before, you asked if we'd come to take you too. You think someone took Sam?"

He nodded.

"Do you know who?" she asked. She pocketed the photo and went to the bedside table. A couple of unlabelled pill bottles caught her attention. She picked them up, rattled them, and returned them to the table. A thin wad of clean New Zealand twenty dollar notes sat there too, but she left them untouched.

"Thugs, probably," he said after a moment. "Someone looking for a ransom. I was out when they came. Two days ago, sometime between three and five in the afternoon. They turned the place over."

"Not this place, apparently." There was a single suitcase in the room, and no sign anyone else had ever been here. She turned over an old gold watch that had been sitting on the chair in the corner. Nothing engraved on it. The time matched her own watch: 3:58 a.m.

"No," he agreed. "Not this place."

She waited for him to elaborate, but he said nothing more. She wasn't sure if the man was being deliberately tight-lipped, but something about this whole thing was beginning to grate. Her instinct tugged at her, telling her to walk away. But she didn't like to make decisions without having the facts.

She put the watch down and pursed her lips beneath her mask. "Was there a note?"

"No."

"No one called with ransom demands?"

He shook his head.

"I take it you haven't been in the country long?" she asked, and he shook his head again. She fiddled with the cigarette packet in her pocket. "Who knew you were here? Family? Friends?"

"We don't have many of those. It's just me and Sam these days."

"You came to New Zealand for a purpose, presumably."

He gave a noncommittal inclination of his head. "Just travelling. We've never been down under."

She studied his face as he spoke. He wasn't a good enough liar. Goddamn it. She couldn't help him if he didn't talk.

"Could someone have marked you?" she asked, trying to keep the frustration out of her voice. "At the airport, maybe? Recognised your name, or seen you flashing money around?"

He hesitated and rubbed a hand across his forehead. "We…travelled under assumed names."

She suppressed an annoyed sigh. The rich ones were always a pain in the butt. "Any enemies?"

"None that I know of."

He was lying again. This job was getting worse by the second. "Frank, we don't take jobs that smell funny, you understand?"

He met her eyes and nodded.

"Then understand I'm about three seconds from walking out of here," she said. "Is there anything else you can tell me? There's a reason you contacted us and not the coppers."

His hand went to his forehead again, brushing through his remaining hair. Now that she was closer, she could see he wasn't as old as he looked. His hair was thin, but it was the bags under his eyes that really aged him.

"It might be unrelated," he said slowly, "but Sam, he's been showing signs. I don't think he's even noticed yet. He's lived a sheltered life. But his father—my brother—was a metahuman."

The way he said it, she could tell he didn't just mean any old meta. He meant superhero. Or supercriminal.

No enemies my butt.

"Who was Sam's father?" she asked. "Anyone I'd recognise?"

Frank nodded and said nothing.

"Hero?" she asked. "Villain?"

"What's the difference?"

She ground her teeth together. This added a whole new layer of complicated. But she understood now why he was being so evasive. She was no different. A few metas managed to operate off-grid since the Seoul Accord crushed the rights of metahumans across the world. Niobe was one of them. By law, the children of metas had to be tested and monitored. It was a public safety measure, and the carrot they waved at the metas was the healthcare they offered when the inevitable lymphomas and leukemias arose. Now that there were no more battles to fight, the leading cause of death in metas was cancer. Dr Atomic himself had died of throat cancer.

But there were costs to being a legal and duly-registered meta. And they were costs not everyone was willing to pay. That must be why he refused to contact the coppers.

Half the puzzle pieces were missing, but she had to work with what she had. This kid's father was a meta. That meant revenge was a possible motive. There were plenty of folks still around that'd been put in prison by heroes. And plenty more that had been betrayed or hurt by a supercriminal. Was someone looking to take his anger out on the kid? But why would they be in New Zealand, of all places? And how did they know where Frank and Sam were going to be? Was Frank a meta as well? She'd assumed he was a normal, but now she wasn't sure. Most metas with this much cash to throw around now lived where the normals couldn't persecute them.

Frank's idea of giving her a lead seemed to raise more questions. He was hiding a lot from her, but she got the feeling that asking more questions would get her nowhere. That was okay. She had enough to get started, and there were other ways of getting information. But they didn't come cheap.

"Our fee—"

He waved a hand. "Never mind your usual fee. I have fifty thousand dollars in a New Zealand bank account. Get my nephew back and it's yours."

Niobe's mind ground to a halt. She opened her mouth to speak, but the words were stuck. *I misheard him*, she tried to convince herself, but she knew it wasn't true. He wasn't looking at the ground anymore. His eyes were fixed on hers, filled with icy intensity.

"Please," he said. "He's all I have. Please."

"Fifty thousand?" she finally said. What the hell was his game? It made her hackles rise, even as the number sang to her. It was absurd. It had to be a ploy. But what kind, and for what purpose? She wanted to help him. She wanted to help the kid. But what else did he know about this job that he wasn't telling her?

"Spook." A hand gripped her shoulder from behind. She glanced back to find the Carpenter staring at her, his lips downturned. She recognised that look. He cocked his head at her, the brim of his hat flopping to the side. "You okay?"

She refocussed her gaze on his stubble and nodded. She could just make out the scent of his cologne through her mask. "What is it?"

He jerked his head towards the balcony and led her out through the French doors, leaving Frank standing in silence.

"There," he said, pointing into the night, but she'd already seen it. The northern highway was choked with a convoy of black vans, sedans, and station wagons. They raced into and out of view through the gaps between buildings. Blue and yellow lights flashed on several roofs, but no sirens pierced the night.

"They're not coming for us," she said, though she knew he already knew that.

Frank's footsteps pattered behind them. "What's going on?"

She ignored him. "The radio," she said to Solomon, hands gripping the balcony rail. "The police radio in the car. On our way here…."

"Nearly silent," Solomon said.

"Yeah. Shit." She turned to Frank. "You're staying here the next few days?"

"Yes, but—"

"Good," she said. "We have to go. We'll call you about the job. We might have a few more questions before we decide whether we're going to take it. And if you're lying about that money…."

He nodded, frowning. "Of course, of course. What's going on?"

Niobe readied herself to return to shadow form. A tree branch stretched out over the balcony, groaning as it moved. Solomon took hold of it and stepped up onto the railing. He tipped his hat at Frank. "Always nice meeting a fan." He jumped, letting the tree carry him down.

Niobe put a hand on Frank's shoulder and gently pushed him back. "Go inside, Frank. We'll be in touch."

"What is it? What's happening?"

"It's a raid. The cape coppers are raiding the Old City."

She sucked in a lungful of air, dropped into shadow, and left Frank Julius alone on the balcony.

CHAPTER 4

FIGHT DIRTY

You don't believe me. No one ever believed me. I came to terms with that many years ago. You lock me in this asylum and call me a lunatic, a madman, but it is of no consequence. You ask me again who I am, so I will tell you. I was the pilot of the HMS Cheetah in 1701. We had narrowly escaped attack by pirates when a storm took our mainmast and wrecked her off some uncharted island in the Caribbean. Only I survived. To this day I cannot explain the effect the island had on me. Perhaps there was some radioactive substance there. All I know is that I prayed to the Lord God to survive, and I did. I survived for two hundred and fifty years.

—Transcript from psychiatric evaluation of [NAME REDACTED]

Niobe gunned the engine. The road peeled away in front of them as they pulled out. The police were taking the Northwestern highway, the one constructed to maintain a line to the ports after the bomb hit. So Niobe pulled back onto the same route they'd taken to get here, cutting through side streets and making their way north.

"How many do you reckon?" Niobe said as she pulled sharply around a corner.

Solomon gripped the dashboard and wedged his legs in place to keep himself upright. "Gotta be half of Met Div out there. I saw a bunch of Tactical Unit vans."

"Crap."

"Tell me about it."

A lone early-morning driver leaned on his horn as Niobe brought the old Ford sweeping past, missing by inches. The Ford was older than most, but she still had some guts left in her. The streetlights flashed above as they raced down the street.

She squinted north and made out the police dirigible floating over the main checkpoint to the Old City. It had its spotlight on, guiding the ground teams in. She couldn't see the coppers now. Too many miles and buildings between them. The police had a head start, and their road was easier. The coppers would beat them there. Damn it, damn it, damn it. The Metahuman Division of the police weren't known for friendly community policing.

She didn't have a clue what the raid was about, but that didn't matter. To Met Div, one meta was the same as another. If they were going in with numbers like that, they were doing something that was going to cause trouble. And Gabby was home alone. Bloody hell. She glanced over and saw the lines running through Solomon's stubble. He'd pushed his mask up to massage his forehead. His wife wasn't a meta and his three kids hadn't starting showing signs yet. But that might not be enough to protect her from Met Div. It just meant his family had no way to defend themselves.

While they drove, she filled him in on what Frank had told her, more to distract herself than anything else. It seemed to loosen the tension in Solomon's back as well. He whistled when she mentioned the dollar figure Frank had given her.

"He must be some kind of business tycoon to have that much cash to throw around. Or a bank robber. Were you there that time that math whack-job tried to rob the Reserve Bank? What was his name, again?"

"Captain Calculus. No, that was before my time."

"Oh yeah," he said. "Kate doesn't like that I still run around in a costume. But that might change if I can bring home enough to get the kids through uni and have enough left over for a colour TV or fifty."

She nodded and shifted gear to take another tight turn. "It's not the money I'm worried about. I don't like the feel of this. He's keeping too much back."

"So do most of the people we deal with. Secrets are part of the game.

Hell, I'm your partner, and I don't even know where you live."

That was true. It wasn't personal. It was just reasonable caution. He never pried, though, which she was thankful for.

"Tell you what," he said. "We see what we can fish up. If it stinks, we throw it back. It it's clean, well, we've got ourselves a nice juicy pay-cheque wriggling on the end of our hook."

She chewed her lip. She wasn't convinced. Could they really walk away from the money when they'd already put time and sweat into it? It'd be better to break away now, leave it clean. If Frank Julius was telling the truth, he'd find another way to get his nephew back. Someone with the resources to do the job proper.

"I can see police lights," Solomon said, cutting through her thoughts. She saw them too. The road had opened up, and now it was a straight line all the way home. Back into the Old City. Blue and yellow flashed off the buildings. They were in Epsom. Her neighbourhood. *Shit.*

"Shall I press the button?" he said, clearly trying to suppress a smile. Bloody man-child. "Do it."

He stabbed the central button on the dashboard, and the car let out a groan. She held the steering wheel tight as weight shifted in the back. Solomon flipped the switch next to the button.

The miniature rocket engine in the back of the car screamed to life. It felt like someone had punched her in the chest. The car roared and leapt forwards, throwing her back in her seat. Her stomach churned. The road markers on either side became a blur, and she struggled to keep the car from skidding off the road.

Solomon whooped and grinned. She would've hit him if she was willing to take a hand off the wheel.

The first of dawn's fingers were clawing their way over the horizon, streaking the sky with pink. She guided the rocket-propelled car down the increasingly narrow street as buildings streaked past. It gained them a few minutes. Maybe, maybe they'd be in time.

They were back in the Old City now, and the contrast between here and Neo-Auckland was staggering. She flew past the made-in-bulk apartments that took up half the street. They were built after the bomb hit, when the government in Wellington wanted to get the city back on its feet. Of course, after the Nagasaki incident, they changed their minds in a damn hurry.

Funny how things turned out.

"Now."

At her signal, Solomon disabled the rocket, and the pressure on her chest eased as the car slowed. They topped a small rise and looked over the neighbourhood. People were emerging from their homes, staring at the Met Div lights a mile or two away. They kept driving.

Niobe pulled over before they were close enough for the coppers to spot them, parking inside the garage of an abandoned villa they sometimes used as a safe house. If someone recognised the Ford, she didn't want them to track it back to Solomon's family. Or to her and Gabby, either.

They trotted the rest of the way on foot, keeping to the dawn shadows. People milled outside their homes and apartment buildings, most dressed in pyjamas and robes. Some pulled on costumes as they emerged from their buildings. Those who used to work as heroes were required to wear their costumes when interacting with the authorities. It made them easier to identify. Occasionally, a meta would make the sign of the First Heroes and utter a quiet prayer. It was a stupid religion. Dr Atomic was long dead, and he wasn't going to be saving anyone anymore.

Solomon tugged on her coat. "I'll scout ahead." She nodded and he jogged away, moving amongst the growing crowds with ease.

Niobe jumped a broken fence and passed across two abandoned properties, coming out on the street alongside. Nearly there. A group of coppers were a couple of hundred metres behind her, pushing the crowds along the street. Niobe fell into line and nudged a woman with a child in each hand. "What do the coppers want?"

The woman scowled at Niobe, her eyes narrowing as she looked over her costume. "How the hell should I know?" the woman said. "They've got warrants, they say. Registration violations. That's all they've said." She hurried away, dragging the gawking children with her.

"Bloody hell," Niobe said to herself. She glanced around to make sure none of the coppers were watching her, then slipped away from the crowd.

She found the Carpenter perched on the branches of a half-dead tree a block away, using the vantage point to see over a series of fences. A tui whistled, then took off and fluttered past him, paying him no more attention than if he were part of the tree himself. He descended when he saw her. "I count fifty cops altogether. They're gathering everyone out of the apartment buildings at this end of the street."

She looked where he pointed, and the knot that had been forming in her stomach suddenly tightened. It was her building.

"Come on." She made her way along the street running parallel to hers, trying to stay inconspicuous while her heart hammered. Solomon jogged behind her, boots pumping on the footpath. They came to an abandoned architect's office she knew gave a good view of the street outside her building, and she clambered through the long-broken window. Solomon grumbled as he followed, and together they climbed the darkened stairwell and reached the windows on the upper floor.

Solomon was right. There must've been about fifty Met Div coppers out there. The street was cordoned off, with Met Div vehicles at either end. They operated in units of four or five, splitting up groups of people and comparing them against rosters.

The process looked ordered, clean. No one made a fuss. The coppers were all in uniform, with dark blue, silver-buttoned tunics and round-topped custodian-style helmets. Most standard New Zealand coppers were unarmed apart from a nightstick. That wasn't enough for taking down metas. In addition to the pistols at their belts, each Met Div officer carried an L1A1 self-loading rifle. The black plastic frames shone in the early morning light. Few metas were bullet-resistant. A few rounds from one of those guns would put most down easy.

Niobe scanned the crowd, looking for familiar faces. She could make out several people who lived in her building. But she couldn't find Gabby. She had to be safe. Damn it, Niobe should've been there to protect her.

"We've got the ringmaster himself out to conduct today's circus," Solomon said in a low voice. He pointed with two fingers.

She saw who he was pointing at. Senior Sergeant Raymond Wallace was speaking into a car radio while he watched the proceedings, his free arm gesturing as he spoke. He wasn't a tall man, but he was built like a rugby player, with broad shoulders and a thick, muscled neck. His handlebar moustache hid whatever limited facial expression he was capable of showing, and a scar cut through the thick brown hair on his head. She'd had cause to conduct her own investigations into Senior Sergeant Wallace before. He was a veteran of the war, took a bullet in the arse in Italy. He still limped a bit. Clean record, for the most part. Like that meant anything.

A shout cut through the ordered hubbub, and her heart rate kicked up again. A pair of coppers appeared in the doorway of her apartment building, escorting a skinny man in his late twenties. The man hollered and tried to twist away from the coppers, but they met him at every turn with a nudge and a gun barrel to the back.

For a moment, all she could feel was relief that it wasn't Gabby. Then she looked closer.

"Son of a bitch," she whispered.

The Carpenter shot her a look. "You know the kid?"

"That's the McClellan guy."

He rubbed his chin for a moment. "McClellan? You mean the stretcher? Amorph?"

She nodded. They'd encountered him a few times back in the old days. The guy had had a complicated life, living on both sides of the law. But when he met his wife-to-be he'd settled down and gone straight. He was a hell of a sportsman, and he'd even been on track to get into the Black Capes, New Zealand's metahuman cricket team. He'd been out of trouble for years. What were the coppers doing with him now?

And then it dawned on her. *Oh, shit.* "His wife gave birth last week." She scrunched her cigarette pack in her pocket. "It's a goddamn cradle-snatch."

McClellan screamed and twisted. Niobe knew what he was about to do before the coppers did, and her heart went to her throat.

The stretcher wrenched his arm away from one of the coppers, slammed an elbow into the man's nose, and grabbed his rifle by the barrel. Instantly, the surrounding coppers raised their weapons.

"Idiot," Niobe whispered. "Stop it."

McClellan pointed the rifle at the coppers and shouted loud enough for Niobe to hear. "Leave her alone, you goddamn pigs. She's just a baby!"

Out of the apartment doorway came more coppers. Two escorted a hysterical red-headed woman. McClellan's wife. The other copper carried a swaddle of white cloth in his arms. Niobe could just make out the pink flesh of a baby.

Senior Sergeant Wallace snatched his helmet from the top of his car and approached McClellan, making soothing gestures with his hands. The other coppers fingered their rifles nervously.

"Spook," Solomon said, "we gotta get lost. This is going to get crazy."

She ignored him. She couldn't move away if she wanted to.

Everything happened in slow motion. McClellan made a grab for the baby as the officer passed. A single gunshot rang out. She couldn't tell who fired. A spray of red flew from McClellan's flank. He dropped the rifle and screamed.

McClellan spun, his arms stretching like a rubber band. A moment later, they were ten times their normal length. They flew out and knocked a group of coppers from their feet. McClellan continued to scream as his body stretched, flattening out like putty. He tried to envelop the officer carrying his baby with both rubber arms, but the officer broke into a sprint. The rest of the coppers opened fire. The morning rang with the thunder of gunfire.

The crowd of metas screamed and scattered, running for shelter. A stray bullet pinged off the wall a few feet from Niobe, but she just stared out at the carnage, throat constricting. What the hell was the idiot doing?

McClellan kept going despite the bullet wounds. She didn't know what the anatomy of a rubber man was, but they couldn't have hit anything vital. Yet. Screaming, he wrapped a pair of coppers in his arms and flung them across the street.

Niobe scanned the street for the officers with McClellan's wife and baby, but there was too much chaos. All she could make out was Senior Sergeant Wallace sprinting back to his car, shouting orders as he moved. He ripped open the passenger door and pulled something from the glove box. It looked like a hand-held radio. Gunfire ripped around him as he twiddled the knobs and jabbed two buttons at once.

It took her a few moments to pick up the smell of sulphur in the air. It must've been strong for her to smell it from here. McClellan's screams grew louder.

"They flipped his kill-switch," she said. The Carpenter just nodded.

McClellan's movement slowed. As the smell of sulphur became stronger, his stretched limbs grew stiff. The flesh cracked like a super-heated car tyre.

Senior Sergeant Wallace had a megaphone to his mouth. "Cease fire," he boomed. "Damn it, cease fire." The officer's gunfire dropped off.

McClellan grew still, frozen, a silent scream still fixed on his face. For a moment, there was no movement in the street. Then he toppled backwards, limbs still stretched out in every direction. Everyone went quiet.

A bang cut through the silence. The back of McClellan's head blew out, flinging fragments of solidified blood to the concrete. The small explosive charge would've been planted near his brainstem, along with a small package. Niobe knew the mechanism. At a particular radio frequency from Senior Sergeant Wallace's box, the package had released sulphur and exothermic chemicals into his bloodstream. It was clever, in a way. They'd vulcanised the rubber man.

She swallowed back vomit and forced herself to breathe.

"He didn't have to do that," she said. "The bloody idiot could've gone quiet."

The Carpenter didn't seem to have anything to say. He took his hat off and pressed it to his chest. His lips moved. A silent prayer. She didn't follow suit. She didn't have anything to say to God.

"All metahumans will clear the area," Wallace's voice boomed from the megaphone. "Return to your homes." His voice held no malice, but no regret either. *Son of a bitch. Murderer.*

Wallace handed the megaphone to one of the other coppers and gave more orders. At the officers' insistence, the metas that hadn't fled shuffled back into their buildings. Most didn't look at McClellan's stretched body, still lying stiff and cracked in the street.

"They're taking the woman as well as the baby," the Carpenter said. He'd finished his prayer, apparently. Niobe followed his gaze and found McClellan's sobbing widow in the shadow of the building opposite. They were leading her around the corner. "What the heck are they doing that for?"

"She's an accomplice. That's prison time."

The Carpenter muttered something under his breath, his eyes dark behind his mask. "She'll have a rough time of it."

"Yeah," Niobe said. She studied the dead man stretched across the street. "You know, for a while, Amorph was one of us."

The Carpenter nodded.

Niobe made up her mind in an instant. She reached into her pocket and tossed the car keys to the Carpenter. "Do you think you can get the baby?"

He didn't hesitate. "I'll try." He turned and jogged back down the stairs, and she followed. "What are you going to do?"

"I'll get Mrs McClellan away from the coppers," she said. "If I can. Sound good?"

"Sounds stupid."

"You always liked stupid."

She emerged into the morning light and followed the Carpenter towards the corner. The metas were slowly dispersing, refusing to make eye contact. Even the ones in costume walked with shuffling steps and bowed heads. No one spoke above a whisper. Niobe checked her goggles and started to move.

The Carpenter's head snapped around to follow one meta making his way down the street. She followed his gaze.

"Hey!" Solomon called. "Hey, Brightlance."

The dark-skinned man was dressed in a yellow bodysuit with a tattered red cape pinned to the sunburst in the centre of his chest. He glanced back and kept walking.

"Piss off, Carpenter. Now's not the time."

Niobe kept one eye on the coppers as the Carpenter caught up to the ex-hero. Bloody hell. They didn't have time for this.

"Just give me a second," the Carpenter said, loud enough for her to hear even a few steps behind. "We need your help with something."

"I know what you want. Piss off."

"You knew Amorph better than we ever did."

"Only because I was the one giving him a hiding whenever he tried to shoplift from Mum's store."

The Carpenter grabbed Brightlance by the shoulders. "He turned it around. You turned him around. He got himself a family. Now you want to let the coppers take them away?"

Brightlance planted his feet and shoved the Carpenter away from him. His palms glowed threateningly with blue light.

Niobe reached into her coat and took a step towards them, but the Carpenter put his hand towards her, waving her back. Goddamn him. Grinding her teeth, she stopped and returned her hands to her side. She could see Mrs McClellan being escorted away. The woman had nearly disappeared from sight. Bugger this.

"You really want them to take Amorph's wife?" the Carpenter said, his voice low. "You really want them to have his baby? They'll put a killswitch in her."

Brightlance's palms didn't stop glowing. "She won't be the only one. You think they'll hesitate to flip my kill-switch if I try something? Go home, Carpenter. Take your pension, keep your head down, and go home. No one wants bloody superheroes running around anymore."

The Carpenter tried to take him by the shoulder again, but Brightlance shrugged him off and turned away, his cape fluttering in the breeze. He didn't look back as he strode away with the rest of the metahumans.

Niobe tried to see the Carpenter's face, but his hat cast him into shadow.

"We're out of time," she said.

He watched Brightlance's back for another moment, then turned and nodded. "I'll do what I can. Meet me behind the old museum in an hour."

She slapped him on the arm, nodded, and broke into a run. She'd lost sight of McClellan's widow, but she couldn't be far. Sweat soaked into Niobe's mask as she made her way through dirt-filled backyards and slipped over fences. She kept one hand on her bowler hat to keep it from flying off. Her heart started to thump, spurring on her legs even as her brain told her to stop and think. She hadn't acted like this for years. Police raids weren't that uncommon in the Old City. People got arrested. So what? Brightlance was right. These weren't the old days. Justice died along with the superhero.

But the McClellans were decent folk. Hotheaded, sure, but decent. They'd probably never seen her in the building, but she'd seen them. This was their first kid. Metas going into labour were supposed to present themselves to one of the Neo-Auckland hospitals. Newborns were typed and gene-tested for any signs of metahuman mutation. Tier two and three metahumans had kill-switches implanted before they turned ten. And if parents were unlucky enough to have a tier one metahuman for a baby, they didn't even get a chance to name them. The Seoul Accord stated that metahumans with the strength of Mr October or Kingfisher presented too great a risk to be allowed to live.

The McClellans had tried to hide their baby. They'd failed. The cape coppers were good at their jobs.

Niobe crouched and peered around a low brick wall. The officers were dragging Mrs McClellan to their Black Maria police van. The woman was hysterical, barely able to walk. Her powers had no combat use. All she could do was read auras to determine someone's mood and personality.

The woman collapsed to her knees a few feet from the van. The coppers exchanged a look. "Get up, damn it," one of them said. He slapped her across the face with his open hand.

The sun was slowly rising, but the coppers were in the shadow of the building. In full light, Niobe's powers were useless. It'd kill her to turn to shadow in full sunlight. But there was still enough darkness here. She took a deep breath, held it, and slipped into shadow.

It was harder to make out figures during the day when she was in shadow form. Everything was bright, almost painful. But it wasn't hard to follow the vibrations as the coppers stomped their boots and gave the woman a few good whacks.

"Bloody freak," one of the coppers growled. "You'd think these bitches would learn to keep their legs closed." He gave her another half-hearted kick. "Get the fuck up."

The other one pressed his hand to his nostrils for a moment. "God-damn it. I think the rubber man broke my nose. It won't stop bleeding."

"It ain't broken. You just got smacked around a bit."

"No, it's broken!" He raised his rifle, aiming the butt at the woman. "Your fucking husband broke my nose!"

Niobe reformed behind him, wrapped her arm around his neck, and pressed the barrel of her modified revolver against his temple.

"I wouldn't do that," she said, and aimed her revolver at the other officer's head. "Not if you don't want me to break some more bits off you, anyway."

The copper she held stank of sweat. The other one snarled behind a thin moustache, hand moving to the rifle slung across his shoulders.

"For the love o' God, don't!" the one she held yelled at his companion. "She'll kill me."

The copper was taller than her, so she kept her knee pressed into the back of his leg, bringing him into an unbalanced half-crouch. The moustachioed copper scowled, eyes narrowed. He let the rifle slip from his shoulder and clatter to the ground.

"Freak," he said through gritted teeth.

"Spare me," she said. She nodded to the red-haired woman still sob-bing on the ground. The woman didn't seem to know what was hap-pening. Blood trickled from the corner of her mouth. "Pick her up—

gently—and put her on the bench over there."

He paused. Niobe pulled back the hammer of her revolver. That got him moving. Grudgingly, he took her under the arms and led her to a rickety bench on the side of the road. *She's walking all right,* Niobe confirmed. *No serious damage. Thank God.*

Niobe put her gun arm across her whimpering hostage and gestured to the apartment building they were using for shade. "Into the stairwell."

He hesitated at that.

"I could've shot both of you already," she said. "And I really, really wanted to. Don't make it any more tempting."

He backed away and opened the stairwell door. Niobe held her hostage tight and followed.

"Cuffs," she said. "Get them out."

Officer Moustache's frown deepened, but he pulled the handcuffs from his belt and made to toss them to her.

"No," she said. "Cuff yourself to the rail."

He did so.

Keeping one eye on him, she took the other set of cuffs from her hostage, put one bracelet around his wrist, and cuffed him opposite his partner. She took both their sidearms, unloaded them, and tossed them as far up the stairs as she could reach.

"Why do you hide behind that mask, eh?" The moustachioed man sneered as she turned to leave. "To hide your identity? Or do you just get scared when you look in the mirror and see a freak?"

She holstered her revolver and turned her back on the cape coppers. "I don't cream my pants beating a widowed woman senseless. Tell me again who's the freak."

She went back to the officers' car and ripped a handful of wires out of the police radio. Just in case.

Mrs McClellan hadn't moved from the bench. Her sobs had quietened, but her freckled face still ran with tears. Niobe wordlessly put an arm under her shoulders and helped her to her feet. Her cheek was red and angry where she'd been hit, and she'd probably have a black eye.

But Niobe knew her real hurts ran deeper.

Most of the coppers must have already pulled out, because Niobe didn't see anyone as she made her way to the museum. She'd move faster if she could envelop the woman in shadow and slip through the shaded areas, but subjecting the poor woman to that would do nothing but traumatise her further. A few curtains moved as they walked, but the streets were deserted, and no one came to help them.

It took her half an hour to get to the museum. The edges of the obelisk-shaped war memorial were worn and rounded. Dead trees and bracken surrounded the hill, and what little grass remained was mostly brown. The Carpenter was waiting there, leaning against the bonnet of the car. When he spotted them, he ran down through the abandoned car park and took the woman's other side.

Niobe nodded her thanks. "Did you get the...?"

She could already see the answer from the shape of his mouth.

"Too many coppers," he said. "Most of the convoy went with the kid. I trailed them as far as the checkpoint, but there were no openings. If there were more of us, maybe, like the old days...." He shrugged.

She felt deflated, empty. It had been a long shot. The coppers were always going to take more care with a high tier meta baby than some woman whose powers weren't worth a damn. Solomon was right. The Wardens, as a team, would've got that baby back no problem. But the Wardens didn't exist anymore. It was just the two of them now, doing what they could to scrape a few bucks together.

Frank Julius wanted them to save his kid. He thought they were worth fifty grand. But they couldn't even rescue a goddamn baby. What the hell use were they anymore?

The two of them got Mrs McClellan into the back seat of the car. She didn't say a word. Niobe used the corner of her coat to wipe the blood from the woman's mouth.

"You said most of the convoy went with the baby." Niobe slipped a hand under her goggles to rub her eyes. "What about the rest?"

He shrugged. "I think the boss man left eight or ten coppers to take doors in the apartment building. I guess they figured other people in the building knew. Maybe some helped with the birth. So they went cracking heads."

Niobe's guts turned to ice. *Gabby.*

"Spook?" Solomon said. "What'd I say?"

"Can you get her somewhere safe?" she said, nodding at Mrs McClellan.

"You're running off again, aren't you?"

She pulled her goggles into place. "I'll call you later." She turned and sprinted back through the car park.

She should never have left the neighbourhood. She could've found someone to get Mrs McClellan away, or....

She didn't know. She wasn't a hero anymore. She had Gabby to protect. Panting, she raced through the empty streets, trying to suppress a rising panic.

The Met Div vehicles were gone by the time she reached her street. McClellan's body had been carted away somewhere, but fragments of rubberised human flesh still littered the concrete.

She kicked open the door to her apartment building and ran up the stairs. People sobbed in the apartments she passed. Her legs burned. Her mask was humid and her clothes stuck to her as sweat coated her back. She reached her floor and slipped silently down the hallway.

The door to her apartment was splintered, the lock kicked in. Her vision blurred and her throat clammed up. She drew her revolver and entered. Her breathing echoed in her ears.

She found Gabby sitting on the bedroom floor in her robe, leaning against the bed. She held a wine glass with a few dregs of red wine sitting in the bottom. Her hands shook as she gripped it. Blood dripped freely from a cut across her forehead, matting her frizzy blond hair. She flinched when Niobe came into view, then started crying.

Niobe tore off her mask, dropped to her knees in front of Gabby, and wrapped her arms around her. Gabby shook against her shoulder. Niobe tried to swallow back the lump in her throat. Her fingers kept slipping into shadow as she tried to hold back the tide of emotion.

After a few minutes, the crying stopped, and Gabby told her what happened. The coppers must've banged on the door, but Gabby was in bed. She'd lost her hearing years ago, when she was still the Silver Scarab. When she didn't answer the door, the coppers kicked it in and hauled her out of bed. The first thing she felt when she woke was the corner of the bed slamming into her forehead. The coppers turned the place over and shouted at her, but she was too dazed to lip-read. They hit her a few times before they finally worked out she was deaf and left her alone.

—*How can they do this?* Gabby signed, arms still trembling. Her arms moved in small, jerky motions. *We're not animals.*

Niobe blinked back tears and nodded.

—*I know. Come on, let's get you up.*

Gabby didn't move.

—*You went after that job.*

—*Yeah,* Niobe signed.

Gabby's face twitched. Niobe knew she was remembering their argument just as vividly as she was.

—*Are you going to take it?*

She thought about it, even though she'd made up her mind the instant she walked in the door and saw Gabby sitting there. They didn't belong here. None of them did. The world didn't want them, so they had to leave the world.

One night a couple of months ago, when Niobe was huddled in bed with Gabby listening to another raid from the police Metahuman Division, Gabby told her she wanted the two of them to pack up and go to the Moon. Niobe couldn't blame her. This was no way to live.

Frank Julius's money would be enough. Fifty thousand dollars. The two of them could get a plane to Adelaide. And from there, one short rocket ride to the Moon. To freedom. The Alpha League were the first metas—the first humans of any kind—to establish a lunar colony. The place was supposed to be a metahuman utopia. Niobe wanted to keep Gabby safe. She wanted it more than anything.

—*Yeah,* Niobe signed. *But it's an easy job. It'll be over in a couple of days. Don't worry.*

Gabby chewed her lip, her grey eyes clouded. Then she nodded.

—*I love you,* she signed.

A smile flickered in her eyes and she buried her face back in Niobe's shoulder. Niobe kissed her forehead and cradled her until she fell asleep.

CHAPTER 5

AND YOUR ENEMIES CLOSER

GREEN TORNADO

REAL NAME: *Miguel Valdés*

POWERS: *Superspeed, air manipulation.*

NOTES: *One of the few Argentinian metahumans to achieve international fame and recognition. He chose to work on civilian projects rather than fight crime, using his powers and background in architecture to build numerous bridges, monorail networks, and towers that were not practical for normal humans to construct. Valdés later aided the Alpha League in the construction of the lunar colony.*

—Notes on selected metahumans [Entry #0239]

Bangkok, Thailand

Morgan Shepherd rolled up his sleeves and lounged in the bar's booth. He'd picked a spot near the window, where a breeze did nothing to alleviate the pervasive humidity. The instant he'd left his airship, he was almost crushed by the steamy Bangkok night, and now the back of his shirt was damp and sticky. Even so, he wore a fitted, snow-white shirt and trousers, along with his white gloves. They helped cover the worst of the patchy, non-pigmented skin on the backs of his hands. And he didn't want to leave fingerprints.

He smiled and raised his glass at a pair of Thai girls in miniskirts who had been shooting him glances since he came in. They giggled and blushed, turning away. They were pretty enough, he supposed, but that sort of thing no longer held any interest for him. It had been years

since he was in love, and it had happened just the once. The world became brighter, so bright his heart nearly burst. For months they flitted
through Europe, taking coffee in a little café in Marseilles, making love
in a villa outside Tuscany. Those had been the happiest days of his life.

Killing her was the hardest thing he'd ever done. *Lisa.*

Morgan shook his head. He wasn't in Bangkok for the ladies. He
nursed his beer—a local lager that was too watery—and kept one eye
on the door, watching the motorcycles and tuk-tuks buzzing past outside. The bar wasn't big, but it was popular with both locals and foreigners. It had been slowly filling up in the hour since he arrived. A
couple of blocks away, the Chao Phraya River would be humming with
ferries and longtails even at this hour. He'd flown over the river further
upstream—with the stealth cloak on, of course—while they searched
for a suitable place to set him down. By river standards, it was nothing
special. It was no Danube, or even a Mekong. But the constant movement and the industriousness of the people who worked on it touched
him.

Morgan popped a couple of pills into his mouth and washed them
down with another sip of beer. He silently toasted himself once again
on the successful recruitment drive in Siberia. Only two of the supercriminals he liberated had declined to join him, and they were killed
without too much resistance. Another was too weak from malnourishment to be of much use, so he had to put that one down too. But the
rest were turning out to be fine specimens. They were still adjusting to
their life outside the prison walls, and their training would have to be
shorter than he'd like, but that was unavoidable. Time was short, and
he could brook no delays.

His star prize, of course, was Doll Face. The man—creature, almost—had seemed delighted with the task Morgan had in store for
him. Granted, with the plastic mask stitched to his face it was difficult
to judge Doll Face's true emotions. The creature seemed to delight in
painting on makeup each day. He always gave the mask some fresh red
lipstick and a coating of mascara for the synthetic eyelashes. At Doll
Face's insistence, Morgan had picked up some new fishnet stockings

from a market stall earlier in the evening. The man was undoubtedly insane, but that was of no consequence. In fact, crazy was just what he needed.

News of the boy's capture in New Zealand had reached him a few days ago. Julius was the name they were travelling under now, apparently. The old man had slipped the net, but Morgan had contingencies in place for such an event. As soon as they were done here, they'd be making their way to New Zealand to deal with that situation. Doll Face was bursting with glee.

A large shadow filled the bar's doorway for a moment, and Morgan brought his thoughts back to the matter at hand. He affected a bored disinterest while he took another sip of beer and surreptitiously studied the giant of a man who came through the door. Yes, it was him. William Hayne's pug-nosed face was not one that could be easily mistaken. The broad-chested American wore a faded blue T-shirt and baggy shorts. The man once had hair, but now the top of his head more closely resembled a bowling ball. Morgan scrunched his nose a little at the state of Hayne's attire. True, the weather here was unforgiving, but appearances were still important.

Hayne lumbered up to the bar and waved to the short Thai barkeep. He got a big smile in return, and the small Thai man rushed over with a beer. In a glass, no less. Morgan hadn't received a glass with his beer.

Morgan relaxed and continued to nurse his beer while he let Hayne settle in. His information had said he was a regular here, and that appeared to be the case. Good. That would make everything go much smoother.

Hayne's bulk flowed over the narrow barstool. The two Thai girls made their way to the bar a few minutes later. Morgan watched Hayne's eyes tracking them. When they had their drinks, the bald man made no pretense about watching the girls' wiggling backsides as they returned to their table. When they sat down again, he immediately leaned over and tried to strike up a conversation with the young woman sitting next to him. Yes, Hayne hadn't changed a bit.

Hayne had polished off two beers and a glass of top shelf whiskey by the time Morgan took the last sip of his lager and weaved through the crowd towards the bar. Amongst the people, the air was so thick he could barely breathe. The Thai girls fluttered their lashes as he passed. He gave them a smile.

"Do you ladies speak English?"

They giggled. "A little, yes," the slimmer one said. "You are new here. Will you sit?"

The other one was pulling her white singlet down to give him a better look at her cleavage. Something about it repulsed him. They were most likely whores.

"I'm honoured," he said, smiling broadly. "I have to see a friend first. Maybe a little later."

The slim one pouted, and he stilled a sudden urge to slap that silly look off her face. He noted what they were drinking—a screwdriver and a daiquiri—and he gave them a wink and a polite goodbye. "*Laaeo phohp gan mai.*"

The barstool next to Hayne was vacant now. He must've scared the poor woman away. He was probably twice the poor woman's age, but in Bangkok, that wasn't always a handicap for a white man. Unfortunately, Hayne's charm didn't seem to have improved since his retirement.

Morgan slipped into the seat alongside Hayne and pulled a worn Thai phrasebook from his pocket. Without glancing at Hayne, he tentatively raised his hand at the short barkeep. "Ah, excuse me. Ah...." He consulted his phrasebook. "Ahh...chan kaw..." he said in butchered Thai. His thumb flicked through the pages. "Beer..." he muttered to himself. "Beer...."

Out of the corner of his eye, he could see Hayne watching him struggle. Then the man slapped the bar with his meaty palm. "Kiet! This man needs a beer." He turned to Morgan. "What are you having?"

"Oh, thank you," Morgan said, smiling politely. "I had some Thai beer before." He pointed at a bottle in another patron's hand. "That one."

"You don't want that shit. Kiet! Give him one of the German imports."

The smiling barkeep bobbed his head and obligingly poured a tall glass with just the right amount of head. He slid it over to Morgan on a cardboard coaster, bobbed his head again, and left.

"Thank you for the help," Morgan said. He took a long sip. Hayne was right, it was much better than what he was having before. "I just flew in this afternoon and these people may as well be speaking Martian."

A grin grew on Hayne's face. "Where's that accent from? You British or something?"

Morgan nodded. "An Englishman walks into a bar...."

"And can't even order himself a drink. That's grim." Hayne winked. "But you seemed to do okay with those girls over there." He jerked his beer towards the two Thai girls.

"Ah yes, lovely girls," Morgan said. "They seem a little young to be in here, though."

"This is Thailand, friend. Age don't mean the same thing here that it does in the West." He held up his glass, and Morgan clinked it with his own. "Not too many white folk come in here. Lots of other Orientals, but not many whites. What're you here for, anyway?"

"Business," Morgan said. "I have to meet a client about an investment tomorrow."

Hayne screwed up his face as if the very idea of work bored him. He held out his hand. "The name's Will."

"Morgan."

They fell silent for a while, sipping their beers amongst the rapid Thai conversations. Morgan studied Hayne over the lip of his glass. A foul man. Even in his prime he was the same. During his divorce in '49, the press had spread rumours of extramarital affairs and domestic violence. They didn't know the half of it. Hayne was the sort of man who'd let the world turn to ruin. He was the sort of man who'd turned the world against metas.

Morgan stretched and leaned back in his barstool. "I should thank you for your help. Would you like to help me buy those two girls a drink?"

The grin hadn't changed either. It was the grin that had graced thousands of newspapers across the world. The grin of Iron Justice, comrade of Dr Atomic, and the hero who'd slaughtered more Nazis than anyone else in the Manhattan Eight.

"I thought you'd never ask."

Two hours later, they were drinking rice wine in a private room at a small tourist hotel. Of course, Morgan had arranged the room to be free several hours previously. Morgan, Hayne, and the two young Thai girls lounged on the tattered couches in the glow of several lamps, laughing uproariously. The room already stank of Hayne's sweat.

"What I'm saying," Morgan said as he topped up Hayne's chipped glass, "is that there must be something that makes someone become a metahuman."

Hayne tottered a little, red-faced, and waved his glass at Morgan. Even after all these years, his biceps looked like mountains. "'Course there is, everyone knows that. Don't they teach you about the nukes back in England? No wonder we had to save you in the war."

Morgan put on a polite smile. "Obviously the nuclear radiation is a factor. Countries that have been exposed to nuclear radiation have the greatest number of metahumans per capita. Japan, Poland, New Zealand, anywhere the bombs hit. And of course the Manhattan Eight were a result of the accident at Los Alamos. Dr Atomic would attest to that. He was a scientist first, just plain old Robert Oppenheimer."

He stared at the drunken Hayne while he spoke, but the man gave no sign that he'd even heard, let alone realised that Morgan knew who he was.

Morgan poured some more wine for the girls as well, even though they were half-unconscious already. "I wonder sometimes," he continued, "what Einstein and Bohr and Oppenheimer and all those other scientists thought when they realized the true power of nuclear energy. Not just to power light bulbs and disintegrate enemies, but to truly create. To make new forms of humanity, people that could be pillars of their community like never before. I wonder what it was like for Oppenheimer, one day being in charge of creating the very first atomic bomb, and the next, becoming the world's first superhero."

Hayne fondled the slimmer girl's breast over her singlet. She moaned and writhed on the couch, eyes closed.

"But don't you think it's strange the number of metahumans that became heroes?" Morgan said.

"There were more than a few supercriminals too, as I recall," Hayne said as he pulled the girl's top down to expose her breast. She giggled and tried to bring the glass to her lips, but spilled most of it. Hayne pinched her nipple, and her giggle turned to a gasp. Her friend was dozing, head nodding.

"Yes, that's my point," Morgan said. He put the glass to his lips while he watched Hayne's groping hands, but he didn't take a drink. "The US government commissioned a census in the early fifties to find out what occupations metas held. Of the tier four and higher metas, over twenty per cent were professional superheroes or crime-fighters. They estimated another five to ten per cent were supercriminals. And so many of the rest were designing hyper-advanced technology or trying to build cities the likes of which had never been seen before. So the question is this: do metas gain these powers, and then decide to do great or terrible things with them? Or was there something in those people already, something that was just waiting for the chance to make a difference? Something that took the catalyst of nuclear radiation and gave metas the power to change the world."

Hayne tightened his grip on the girl's nipple, and she tried to slap his hand away. Laughing, he gave her one last squeeze before releasing her. She rolled away from him, dropping her glass to the wooden floor.

Hayne let out a noise that was half-grunt, half-sigh, and drained his glass. Holding his hand up in front of him, he frowned. "That's a hell of a wine," he slurred.

"Think about it. No animal has ever been discovered with super-powers. Only humans are affected." He swilled his wine. "Hero or crim-inal, I believe all metas became metas because they have something in common. No meta's subconscious—his id, as it were—is content to just let life happen, to 'go with the flow', as they say. They shape themselves, and then they shape the world around them. They all share one deeply-held belief, a belief so buried they might not even know they possess it." He pushed himself to his feet. "Carpe omnia."

Hayne doubled over, clutching his head in both hands. "Carpey what? Morgan, I ain't feeling so good."

"I know." Morgan lifted up the couch cushion and pulled out the object he'd concealed there before he went to the bar. It was white and shaped somewhat like a small handgun, with a needle encased within a cage in the barrel. "Although sometimes I wonder whether you were ever truly 'good', William."

"What you talking about?" Hayne tried to stand up, but he collapsed to the floor on his hands and knees. The two Thai girls were motionless now, aside from the slow rise and fall of their chests. They would have bad hangovers for a day or two, but the drug he'd slipped into the rice wine wouldn't do them any serious damage.

"Never mind," Morgan said. He flipped the safety switch on the gun, and the needle protruded out of the protective cage. As he brought the injector gun down towards Hayne's bulging neck veins, he exhaled. "Just remember what you used to be."

But before he could make the injection, his muscles froze. *What? What's happening?* Dimly, the realisation came to him. His disease. *No! Not now.* Morgan's limbs tensed of their own accord, sending little bolts of electricity through his body.

Then white hot pain shot through Morgan's head. A scream tore through him as his vision went red and spotted. *For the love of God, not yet.* His head swirled like a merry-go-round, and the injector dropped from his hand. His hands and arms curled, muscles seizing. *No!*

He wrenched his eyes open, and a metal-plated fist collided with his jaw. A new wave of pain crashed through him. He flew back and smashed into a table, breaking it in two. His brain scrambled to deal with the twin assaults, both internal and external.

"You son of a bitch," Hayne's voice growled through the fog. "What the hell did you do to me?"

Morgan forced his eyes into focus. The pain in his brain was receding, the nausea passing. Cold sweat poured from his face. He'd thought that was the end of him. The final gasp of his illness.

Time. He had none left, and so much more to do. So much more to set in motion before the end.

He locked his gaze on the man stumbling through the room towards him. Hayne was still going, still moving, despite the incredible dose of the drug racing through his system. Only it wasn't Hayne anymore, not really. The man who stood before Morgan bore scales of steel across his entire body, like they'd grown from his skin. His eyes glowed red, and his knuckles were slick with Morgan's blood. He was a human tank, built for destruction.

He was Iron Justice.

Every muscle screaming, Morgan forced himself to his feet. He'd miscalculated how much sedative he needed to slip into the wine to immobilize Hayne. The man had got fatter and, if possible, more muscled since his retirement. There was a tranquilizer in the injector gun to finish the job. But first he had to get the needle into three hundred and eighty pounds of steel-plated metahuman.

So be it.

Iron Justice charged, swinging his armoured fist again. Morgan was ready for it this time. He swung to the side and brought up a shield of solid light. The punch glanced off, and Iron Justice overbalanced, falling forwards. If the ex-hero had been sober, Morgan knew, that blow would've killed him.

Morgan kicked off a couch to change direction and slammed back into Iron Justice, using a wall of light to shove the man further off balance. Justice stumbled, groaning, and went back onto his knees.

No time to stop. He wouldn't stay down long. Morgan leapt back and snatched up the injector from where he'd dropped it. The needle and vial were still intact. As Iron Justice lurched back to his feet, Morgan snatched up a lamp that had escaped the carnage.

"Who are you?" Iron Justice growled.

Morgan ripped the wires from the lamp and spread his legs. "I'm the man who's going to damn the world."

Justice swung. He was too slow. Morgan ducked, dodged, and pressed the live wires against Iron Justice's metal neck. Sparks flew and blue lightning arced across the steel scales. Hayne screamed.

The metal plates of Iron Justice's neck seemed to liquefy and retract as they fled from the electricity. A patch of skin a few inches wide emerged. It was enough.

Morgan plunged the injector needle into Hayne's neck and squeezed the trigger. The gun silently released its contents into the man's bloodstream. His red eyes bulged. Morgan tossed the wires aside as Justice fell. The ex-hero didn't even groan as he slipped into unconsciousness.

Morgan panted, sweat pouring from him. That had been too close. His disease had nearly cost him everything. He shouldn't have delayed all those years. So long he'd been healthy, content to plan and plot. But now, when it came down to it, he had no time.

Haze and Tinderbox pounded into the room a moment later. They stared at the carnage for a moment, and Haze leered at the unconscious girls.

"My lord Quanta," Tinderbox said. "Are you all right?"

Morgan stepped over the unconscious Hayne and adjusted the Thai girl's singlet to cover her exposed breast. "I'm fine. Contact Obsidian. I think we'll need her help to carry this one out." He gave Hayne a light kick.

Head pounding, Morgan picked up the bottle of rice wine. By some miracle it had survived the battle. Before he'd started drinking, he'd lined his stomach and oesophagus with solidified light. Later, he'd have to deal with the unpleasantness of vomiting the rice wine up so he could remove the light lining. But for now, neither the sedative nor the alcohol would affect him.

Morgan stared at Iron Justice and raised the nearly empty bottle in a toast to the defeated hero. "Carpe omnia."

Tinderbox frowned. "My lord?"

"Carpe omnia," Morgan said again, almost to himself.

Seize everything.

CHAPTER 6

A WORD BETWEEN FRIENDS

MR OCTOBER

REAL NAME:	*Joseph Yager*
POWERS:	*Psy-blasts, telepathy.*
NOTES:	*Acted as the Manhattan Eight's main spokesman and media representative. Yager was the only non-scientist member of the Manhattan Eight. Before the explosion, Yager was a soldier stationed at Los Alamos. Reportedly died of bowel cancer in 1951 and was buried in an undisclosed location. To this day, some claim his true cause of death was covered up.*

—Notes on selected metahumans [Entry #0004]

Niobe hung up the payphone and stepped out of the booth. They'd had to drive for twenty minutes to reach the last working payphone in the Old City, but she wasn't willing to use her home phone. It was this or drive back to the Starlight Hotel in the middle of the afternoon to talk to Frank Julius in person. That was out of the question. The coppers were still on high alert after the raid that morning. She supposed they feared a retaliatory attack for the death of McClellan, and a few years ago, that might've been the case. But the Old City metas had just gone back to their homes to gossip over what happened. All except Niobe and Solomon.

"How's our old friend?" Solomon leaned against the phone booth, munching on an apple he'd brought from his tree at home. "He get any more talkative?"

"No," she said. To be honest, she hadn't even tried to pry more information out of him. Anything she got would be half-truths and mis-information. She learned long ago, before she became a superhero, that if you wanted the truth, you had to hunt it down yourself. "But the job's ours. I charged him our standard retainer. We get the balance when we get the kid."

"I can already taste that caviar and lobster. What are you going to spend your share on, Spook?"

Niobe shrugged and lit up a cigarette. She hadn't told Solomon what happened to Gabby, or her plan to leave Earth. It was easier that way. Solomon was a good friend, but he still believed in the world. He thought there was still a place for metas here. But Gabby was right. The longer they stayed, the worse it would get. A one-way trip to the Moon was just what they needed. It was the only place they could be free.

After Gabby had run out of tears, she'd plunged herself back into some radio scrambler she was working on. The cut on her head was superficial, nothing serious. But that didn't mean she was okay. She'd been mumbling in her sleep again, one of the few times she spoke. Whenever it happened, Niobe pulled her close and stroked her hair until the nightmare left her. It was the same nightmare Gabby always had. The day she lost her hearing.

It happened before the Seoul Accord, when Gabby had moved to Sydney for a couple of years to do some part-time crime-fighting work as the Silver Scarab. Occasionally, she went into the field wearing a suit of armour she'd crafted herself, but mainly she provided logistical sup-port. There was no machine in the world that she couldn't coax into doing her bidding, no matter how badly damaged. Every machine had a soul, she insisted, a soul she could talk to.

She'd been working late one night when the anarchist supercriminal Kiloton attacked her group's base. The group was just a local initiative, poorly funded. They had no bomb-proof doors or advanced security systems, except for what Gabby had cobbled together. Kiloton and his flying bombs tore through the place. Gabby barely had time to suit up before he hit the main hall. A few civilians were inside, doing routine cleaning and maintenance work. Gabby tried to cover their escape. But she didn't know Kiloton had maneuvered motorized bombs into position at the rear exit.

She was in combat with Kiloton when she heard the bombs go off, followed by the screams. For a moment, Gabby had frozen.

Kiloton saw his chance and tossed a grenade at her face. The armour prevented damage to her face, but the detonation blew out her inner ears. Kiloton left her for dead and continued his rampant destruction.

It was months before Gabby could stand without falling over. The balance centres in her inner ears were damaged, but with rehabilitation, she improved. Her hearing never returned, though, and neither did her desire to be a hero. And then the world changed, and she wasn't the only one who didn't want to be a hero anymore.

Niobe stubbed out her cigarette on the wall of the phone booth. She hadn't told Gabby where she was going, just that she had to get onto the job. She couldn't let her worry. The job was just something that had to be done. Otherwise, sooner or later, they'd end up like McClellan, dead at the hands of cape coppers. Niobe had avoided getting a kill switch, but Gabby had one. All it would take was one overzealous copper with the right radio frequency and Gabby would be lying in the street, the back of her head blown out, her blood leaking into the storm water drain.

Niobe couldn't let that happen.

Solomon seemed to have picked up on her mood. With the help of some old friends, he'd got McClellan's widow out of the Old City with a couple of hundred dollars. Hopefully the coppers wouldn't have the resources for a full man-hunt. Anyway, they had what they wanted. Chances were the baby was already dead or kill-switched. Niobe swallowed. She had to save who she could. That was just the way things were now.

Niobe got behind the wheel in silence, Solomon in the passenger seat, and they started on their way. Frank Julius hadn't been willing to give them the answers they needed to track down his nephew. Usually they dealt with stupider people, ones who'd give information away while they thought they were being secretive. Photographs on the mantelpiece showing lakeside cabins where they kept their important documents, or an extra pair of shoes at the door that could only belong to a jilted lover. The clues were there.

But Frank Julius was careful. Niobe tried to weasel some information out of the clerk at the Starlight Hotel when she called. After a sob story where she claimed she was Frank's niece and his sister was sick, the clerk gave up the information he had. But it turned out to be little more than she already knew. The same name he'd given her—probably fake—and an American passport—another fake—was all the identification he'd left with the hotel. He'd paid in cash, and he was the only one staying in the room. That meant the kid had already been snatched before he took a room there. But other than that, they were in the dark.

So now they had no choice but to go to more extreme measures to get information. The plastic bag in her pocket creaked every time she shifted gears. It contained a single hair, taken from the gold watch she'd examined in Julius's room. The hair was short and brown, probably an arm hair. Frank's body hair had gone prematurely white, and besides, the watch was too fancy to be something he'd wear. Despite his high-class accommodation, the man seemed to travel light and unornamented. Everything he'd brought with him had been simple, functional. The watch belonged to Sam. And so did the hair. Or so she hoped.

The roads grew more damaged as they drove. They weren't going south this time. They made their way east, deeper into the Old City. Through Greenlane and Remuera, and on towards Meadowbank. There was someone they needed to see, someone who could point them in the right direction. For a price.

The surviving buildings became fewer and farther between, and uncleared debris lay scattered across the road. After the nuke hit Auckland back in '51, not much remained standing. That was nearly a decade before the Seoul Accord, when the Americans were still in Korea eyeing up the Commies. The supercriminal Red Bear was flying around causing trouble when someone got the bright idea to fire a nuke at him. But they miscalculated. Red Bear deflected the bomb. Right into Auckland.

The rest of the world seemed to think it was no big deal. Everyone was getting nuked in those days. Warsaw got it worse. That didn't make it easier.

As Niobe and Solomon drove closer to the sea, she spotted gulls perching on the surviving lamp posts. Solomon was as quiet as her. She knew him well enough to recognise his moods even behind a mask. He'd never say it, but the McClellan thing had rocked him. It had rocked both of them. They hadn't been able to get the baby back. Hell, they couldn't even convince Brightlance to help them out. *We couldn't even save one damn baby.*

She drove on in silence.

They had to abandon the car after a few miles. The roads became impassable except on foot, so Niobe activated the car's security measures and they continued on.

She kept her eyes on the ruined houses around her as they walked. She didn't like moving during the day. Too exposed. The Carpenter kept his wide-brimmed hat low as well, casting glances out from under his half-mask. He'd brought along a wooden quarterstaff that he kept half-concealed by his shoulder cape. It didn't look like much, but she'd seen the broken bones sticking out of supercriminals after Solomon's fights.

"The wife'd kill me if she knew I was out here," he said after a while.

"Where'd you tell her you were going?"

"Didn't." A small smile grew on his face. "We've got an understanding. She doesn't ask what dumb place I'm going, and that way she doesn't have to beat me over the head with a rolling pin. It'd be a bad example for the kids."

Niobe shook her head. "You've got a screwy family, Carpenter."

"Not their fault. I'm just a bad influence."

They walked in silence. Packs of stray dogs watched from the shadows, sniffing the air. Her neck prickled. What she wouldn't give for some darkness. But they couldn't wait for night. The man they were meeting was powerful, but he couldn't work miracles. The longer they waited, the colder the kid's trail would become. They'd already failed one child today. She wasn't going to fail this one too.

"I'm not enamoured by this idea of yours, Spook," Solomon said after a while. "You know how I feel about psychics. You can never be sure the thoughts you're thinking are your own."

Niobe cast a look around. The wind was picking up, and there were fewer surviving buildings here to shelter them. "Technically, you're a psychic."

"That's different," he said. "Trees don't tend to have much in the way of private thoughts. But there's all sorts of things in my head that shouldn't see the light of day."

"Why do I get the feeling you're talking dirty?"

"*Moi*? I'm just an innocent old man."

"A family man," Niobe said.

"Pillar of the community."

She smiled in spite of herself. To be honest, she wasn't keen on the psychic idea either. She didn't trust information she didn't obtain herself. But the job demanded what the job demanded.

A shadow flickered in the window of a ruined townhouse. She gave no outward sign that she'd seen it, but she lowered her voice and spoke to Solomon. "We're being watched."

"Yep. I can sense wood moving behind us." He adjusted his mask and pointed with the barest movement of his pinky finger. "Probably from rifles. Three of them."

Niobe adjusted her shoulder slightly to feel the weight of her revolver in its holster. It was set to stun rounds at the moment. She could draw and fire in 0.7 seconds. She'd timed it. But she still wished it was dark.

Something crunched on concrete. A gull took flight.

"Spook…" Solomon said.

"They won't attack without a challenge. Probably."

"Confidence," he said. "That's why you never made an inspiring leader. You need more confidence."

"Shut up and keep your eyes open."

Movement at the corner of her vision.

Solomon's free hand moved slowly to the hatchet at his side. "Plan?"

She ran through the items in her utility belt. "If they attack, I'll deploy smoke pellets while you disarm them. No deaths."

"Us or them?"

"We can't afford enemies. We play it clean."

He grunted. "I can deal with any gun-toting normals. But the Blind Man has metas."

She didn't have an answer for that.

"How set are you on doing this job?" he asked.

"Very."

He nodded. "Just making sure."

A streak of white flashed along the road towards them. It was the only warning they had.

Something slammed into Niobe's shoulder as the streak collided with her. She was on the ground before she knew it, her bowler flying off in the thing's wake. The streak flew down the street and disappeared.

"Speedster!" she yelled as she grabbed her hat and scrambled back to her feet, but Solomon was already in action. He turned, spread his legs, and cast his arms out to the side like some pagan shaman. Shouts of surprise came from the buildings around them and three bolt-action rifles came flying from the windows. The wooden stocks of the weapons snapped in mid-air and floated there.

Niobe came up with her gun drawn. Her ears were ringing, and her shoulder stung like all buggery where the speeding meta had struck her. Bloody hell. This wasn't part of the plan. She touched a button on her goggles and slipped a coloured filter into place to try and see where that damn speedster had got to.

"You see him?" the Carpenter asked. The broken fragments of the guns swirled around him. The brim of his hat billowed in the breeze, and beneath, she could make out the darting shadows of his eyes.

The streak flashed back into view. "Two o'clock, incoming." She tracked it down her gun sights.

The Carpenter thrust his hands forwards, and the rifle fragments followed. The wood hurtled at the speeding figure, slamming into it.

The streak wavered like a spinning top losing momentum.

Niobe turned and sprinted for the narrow shadow of a ruined building, tossing down a smoke pellet as she moved. She glanced back as the wobbling speedster swept past Solomon and hurtled towards her.

She spun, brought the gun up, fired. Blue light flashed, accompanied by an electric crack that split the air. The shot went a foot wide of the streak. *Calm*, she thought. She brought the sights up again and focussed. *Calm.*

She squeezed the trigger.

The shock round struck the speedster full on. The only sign the meta gave was a strained scream, and then he was toppling, still moving at top speed. Right towards Niobe.

She sucked in air and dived into the shadow. The figure hit the ground where she'd been standing moments before. His white bodysuit took most of the punishment as he finally slid to a halt. In her shadow-state, she could feel the thick elastic fabric scraping along the concrete, shredding the top layer of the suit.

Niobe shifted out of the shadow and ran to the downed speedster, revolver raised. "How's it looking, Carpenter?" she yelled.

"Peachy. Made some new friends." Solomon still stood in the road, facing away from her. His shoulder cape billowed in the wind. Broken pieces of wood whirled down the street, prodding other figures out of hiding in the ruined buildings. There were five young men, three Caucasian and two Māori. Swirling fragments of wood kept each of them in his own temporary prison. They scowled at Niobe and Solomon.

Niobe reached the speedster as he lay groaning on the ground. She put her boot under him and rolled him onto his back.

"Be still," she said. She couldn't tell if he was conscious enough to hear her.

The white suit covered him head to toe. A pair of black lenses covered his eyes, and a streak of red ran down each side of his bodysuit. *Racing stripes. Cute.*

She didn't recognise the costume. Metas with super-speed weren't uncommon, but they rarely survived long enough to make effective use of their powers. Getting yourself killed was a lot easier when you could run a hundred miles per hour. This guy was probably young, too young to have been a hero. *And too hot-headed.*

A swooping sound came from behind her. Niobe spun, heart pounding. Then she lowered her gun. A Māori woman progressing into old age hovered in the air behind her, a few feet off the ground. An elaborate *moko* was tattooed on her chin, and her lower lip was completely black. The woman's grey hair was tied back in a bun, and her clothes were simple woollen garments, but no one would be fool enough to mistake her for a simple woman.

"*Tena koe*, Spook," the woman said.

"G'morning, Hine-nui-te-pō." Niobe nodded at the woman and holstered her gun. "Are these some of yours?"

"Mmm, unfortunately," she said, shaking her head at the speedster. "This stupid boy calls himself Quick-fire. He *will* be on fire when I'm finished with him."

Quick-fire groaned something unintelligible. The stun round was starting to wear off. Niobe stepped away from Quick-fire and allowed him to recover himself. He put a hand to his head, groaning, then slowly pulled himself off the ground.

Hine-nui-te-pō floated forwards and positioned herself in front of the speedster. The hovering gave her a good few inches on the boy, despite his height. Niobe didn't know what her real name was. The original Hine-nui-te-pō was the goddess of night and death in Māori mythology. Few would argue with this woman's resemblance.

Quick-fire seemed to shrink as Hine-nui-te-pō stared at him. Under her gaze, he grew thinner, almost transparent. He didn't cry out, he just shivered. The Carpenter was herding the other young men he'd captured towards them. The boys were all turning pale. They kept their eyes on their feet.

Finally, Hine-nui-te-pō ceased her deathly stare. Quick-fire gasped and stumbled. Instinctively, Niobe reached out to steady him. The burn mark of her stun round sat squarely in the middle of his chest, but there was no sign of the round itself. Gabby had designed them to disintegrate on impact to better deliver the stunning charge. Niobe didn't pretend to understand how it worked; her mind was for clues and patterns, not advanced physics. What mattered was that it did its job.

Thinking of Gabby drew the spectres of several confusing emotions out of her heart, so she turned her thoughts aside. *Later. I'll deal with it later.*

"Carpenter." Hine-nui-te-pō nodded at Solomon as he drew close. "I'm sorry about all this. The children have been on edge since we saw the raid this morning. Every year the police get more brazen." She shot a look at the young men. "But that is no excuse for unnecessary violence."

Solomon grinned and shrugged. "Kids."

"The young ones don't have respect anymore." She turned to Quick-fire. "This is Spook and the Carpenter. They are friends."

"Friends" was pushing it, but Niobe wasn't going to split hairs. They needed her. The woman was on their side for now, but that would change bloody fast if Niobe or Solomon got in her bad books. Hine-nui-te-pō was big on respect. And family.

"Sorry about breaking your guns," the Carpenter said, sounding anything but. "Want me to let the kids go?"

"Please."

The wooden fragments of the rifle stocks stopped circling the young men and flew into a ball in front of Solomon. Niobe could swear she saw a few of the larger pieces whack the boys on the legs and backside as he drew them together. They yelped, but said nothing.

"We're looking for your husband," Niobe said.

Hine-nui-te-pō nodded as if she'd been expecting it. "You brought *koha*?"

Niobe patted her pocket. The Blind Man wasn't dumb. He was the best, and he wouldn't work for every Tom, Dick, and Harry that came knocking. Not without an offering.

Hine-nui-te-pō nodded again. "The boys will stay here." Her gaze swept over Quick-fire and the others. "Hopefully they learn to tell friend from foe before the police come around again. They'll probably invite the pigs in to have tea with us."

The boys slinked away. A couple of them shoved Quick-fire as they walked.

Hine-nui-te-pō watched their backs until they were out of sight, then turned her gaze back to Niobe and Solomon. "Come. My husband is looking forward to this *korero*."

Yeah, Niobe bet he was. Solomon met her eye, shrugged, and slapped her on the shoulder.

They followed the floating woman through the ruined streets to see a blind man about a kidnapped boy.

CHAPTER 7
IN ANOTHER'S SHOES

BALLISTA

REAL NAME: *Amy Duncan*

POWERS: *Enhanced vision, pinpoint accuracy.*

NOTES: *Acted as an independent crime-fighter throughout New Zealand in the late 1950s. Her powers led her to favour an oversized modified crossbow as her weapon of choice. Most famous for breaking up the child prostitution ring led by former Attorney-General Julian Radcliffe. Accepted registration and kill-switching after the Seoul Accord was signed, then retired.*

—Notes on selected metahumans [Entry #1894]

The Blind Man sat alone in a straight-backed chair in the middle of what had once been a hotel pub. The Māori man had too much skin; it sagged around his chin and cheeks, but there was an air of dignity around him. His eyes were clouded, constantly shifting. He was blind to this world, but he could still see things no one else could. He cocked his left ear towards them as they came into the room.

Hine-nui-te-pō hovered in first, announcing herself and her guests to her husband. Niobe followed. Solomon came in last, but when the Blind Man beckoned them forwards, Hine-nui-te-pō silently urged Solomon in front of them. It was a nod to the old ways, where the men's duty on entering another's meeting place was to protect the women and guard their retreat. That irked her; she was capable of taking care of her own damn self. But she did what she was told and stayed behind the Carpenter. She was a guest. She'd abide by their rules, for now.

They stopped just inside the doorway, and for a moment, there was silence in the room. The old pub had long been stripped of fixtures and wallpaper, if they had even survived the bomb. In their place were portraits of ancestors and wooden carvings of *taniwha*. They lacked the skill of a professional, but had a life all of their own.

A familiar policeman's uniform hung in the corner. She smiled at that. Back when she was a member of the Wardens, they'd investigated a disturbance in a small town to the north of Neo-Auckland. Police had been trying to evict the Blind Man's people from contested land. Fifty coppers had stormed the makeshift settlement the Blind Man had established there, but within minutes, the police guarding the perimeter lost radio contact with the team. Half an hour later, all the officers marched out like clockwork dolls, stark naked except for their helmets. Not one of them could recall what had happened after they entered. The coppers wanted the Wardens to show the Blind Man and his people the business end of their fists, but Niobe, Carpenter, and Battle Jack decided some battles weren't worth fighting.

"Husband," Hine-nui-te-pō said, finally breaking the silence, "the Carpenter and Spook want to speak to you."

The Blind Man's face was fixed in a small smile. He wore a black double-breasted suit that'd seen better days, and his left hand gripped the handle of a ceremonial walking stick carved with outlandish faces. The eyes near the haft of the stick were set with paua shell, giving them a rainbow sheen. The Blind Man remained motionless except for his mouth.

"What do you seek?" He spoke quietly, but his deep voice resonated.

"Knowledge," the Carpenter said. "To know what we do not know, to see what we have not seen."

Solomon always got a kick out of the ceremony. Niobe was just thankful the Blind Man didn't draw it out any more than he already did.

The Blind Man's smile did not move, but the crinkles around his shifting eyes deepened. "Come," he said.

Solomon led them forwards. At a gesture from Hine-nui-te-pō, they drew up chairs in front of the man. Silence reigned for a few moments while Hine-nui-te-pō retreated and returned with drinks. It was sauvignon blanc for the Carpenter and Niobe, and a tall glass of lager for the Blind Man. She pulled her mask up to uncover her lips and they sipped in silence. The wine wasn't bad.

The Blind Man turned his ear to his wife. "Thank you."

Hine-nui-te-pō floated from the room, leaving them alone. When she was gone, Niobe pulled the small package from her pocket and laid it at the Blind Man's feet. It was filled with twenty dollar notes, but it was only part of the *koha*. The rest would come later.

The Blind Man didn't reach for the package, but he gave a small nod and raised his head. "You are seeking something. Someone."

The Carpenter nodded even though the Blind Man wouldn't see it. "An American boy. He's got himself lost. His uncle thinks he was taken."

Niobe reached into another pocket and pulled out the small plastic bag. Inside was the photograph Frank Julius had given her and the small brown hair she'd pulled from the watch. She placed them on the floor alongside the bag of cash. That got the Blind Man's attention. His milky gaze shifted slowly down to the photo, and he cocked his head to the side as if listening to it.

"Hmmm," he said after a few moments. "The trail is faded. You were slow."

Niobe moistened her lips. Smug bastard. "Can you still read him?"

"Yes," the Blind Man said. "Barely. But the price is high."

She met the Carpenter's eyes. His mouth was in a tight line; no grins from him now. She could make out the wrinkles at the edge of his eyes where the mask didn't quite cover. He bowed his head. "What's the damage?"

The Blind Man took a long pull on his beer, smacked his lips, and smiled. "Two years of childhood."

She balked. Two years? He'd never taken more than a few months from Solomon before. The bastard was insane. He had to be pulling their legs. But his face was fixed in that same half-smile that betrayed

nothing.

Solomon seemed to be having trouble speaking. His eyes were bugging, and she could see the wheels turning. Her own mind was doing the same thing.

"Carpenter," she said, "forget it. It's too much. We'll find another way."

He blinked a few times, then shook his head. "No. I'll do it. We're blind here, Spook." He glanced at the Blind Man. "No offense."

"Carpenter...."

"You know we have to. The kid's been gone for what, two days now? We don't have time to do this the slow way. There hasn't been a ransom, there hasn't been anything. That's not good."

He was right. The longer they took to find him, the more likely they'd find a corpse. It wasn't just the cash driving her, not just the chance to escape this hell. She wanted to save him. She *needed* to save him. *He's only thirteen.*

But the price.... "It's too expensive," she said. "It's not the old days. You can't take everything on yourself."

"Yeah?" he said. "You took on the coppers this morning, didn't you?"

"That's different and you know it. This is a job. You've got kids to look after."

"So has Frank Julius." He pointed at the smiling boy in the picture. "The kid needs our help. Where else is he going to get it?

Bloody hell. Solomon was so determined to be a superhero. There was no point trying to change his mind. She sighed and looked away. *Goddamn hero.*

The Blind Man's smile hadn't shifted. "I'm sorry," he said, "but I wasn't clear. I already have all I want from you, Solomon Doherty."

Solomon flinched at the sound of his real name. "What do you mean?"

"The price is two years of Spook's childhood. Ages ten to twelve should do it."

Her blood chilled. The Blind Man had never taken her memories before. Solomon never spoke about what'd happened, but there was always something in his eyes afterwards, a kind of suppressed grief. An irretrievable loss.

The Blind Man wouldn't just read the memories of her childhood. He would take them. All she would have left was a hole, a vacuum. Another quiver ran through her. Her parents died in the nuke blast when she was thirteen. She'd been away at a boarding school in New Plymouth at the time. When the bomb hit, nothing they owned remained. Nothing except Niobe. Her memories of them were few as it was. And the Blind Man wanted to take most of what still remained.

"No way," Solomon said. "That's never been the deal before. Do me again."

The Blind Man just smiled.

"Do me," Solomon said.

She snapped out of her reverie. "Shut up, Carpenter. Let me think."

"Have you made your decision?" the Blind Man asked.

Solomon stared at her and gave the smallest shake of his head, but she ignored it. He'd been right before. Something bad was going to happen to Sam, she felt it in her gut. It didn't matter if his uncle was the target, the boy would pay the price. He was only thirteen.

Don't think about it like that, she told herself. *It's just a job. We need the cash. That's all.* Fifty thousand dollars. And then she could get Gabby away from this place, before it killed them both.

She made up her mind.

"Deal," she said.

Solomon lowered his head so his hat covered his eyes. The Blind Man nodded. There was hunger in his face. She didn't know what he did with the memories. Were they some sort of energy to him, or did they just fulfil his desire for knowledge?

It doesn't matter, she thought. *They're just shadows of the past. I've got the future to worry about.*

"Payment will come later," the Blind Man said. He put down the empty beer glass, levered himself out of the chair with the aid of his staff, and lowered himself until he sat cross-legged on the ground in front of the photograph of Sam Julius. He beckoned. "Come."

She didn't meet Solomon's eyes as she got out of her chair and sat on the floor opposite him. Her heart started to hammer. *Do it for Gabby.*

The Blind Man's left hand hovered over the photo and the arm hair. He extended his right arm towards her, palm extended. "Spook."

She'd seen this done to Solomon before; she knew the drill. Still, her stomach clenched. She searched the room with her eyes, but it was just the three of them. That didn't make it any less uncomfortable to pull off her hat, goggles, and mask in such an exposed place. Her short black hair came free and tumbled around her cheeks, and she suppressed the urge to cover herself like she was naked. Solomon had seen her face before, and the Blind Man was, well, blind. But if someone came in....

She shook her head slightly. Some things had to be risked.

The Blind Man's palm found her forehead. His skin was cool, or maybe she was just warm. She was conscious of the dried sweat on her skin. Distantly, she registered the ache of her shoulder where Quick-fire had hit her.

"Open your eyes, Spook."

The voice came from far away. She didn't realise she'd closed her eyes. But yes, it was dark now. When had that happened?

The dark was comforting, as it always was. Darkness and shadows. She was drowsy. Thoughts swirled and collided with each other in her head, but she couldn't hold onto them long enough to make sense of anything. Where was she?

"Open your eyes."

There was that voice again. It was deep, familiar, but she didn't want to obey it. Her eyelids were so heavy, and it was warm here.

No, she thought. *You can't stay. You have a job to do.*

"Open your eyes."

Wake up, hero.

She opened her eyes, but they weren't her eyes. She was standing in a small room with wooden panelling. Below her feet, the floor rocked slowly back and forth. She moved with it, maintaining her balance.

A faint banging, wood against wood, came from somewhere outside. Where the hell was she?

She tried to move her arms, but they wouldn't budge. Her eyes wouldn't do what they were told either. Then they started moving by themselves. The sensation sent a ripple of panic through her, but she quickly suppressed it. Her gaze darted around the room without any input from her brain, giving her a strange sense of motion sickness that had no root in her gut. Instinctively, she began taking in details: the ticking of a numberless clock on the wall to her left and the faint smell of salt in the air. *I'm taller,* she thought. *And heavier.* Her proportions were all wrong.

A pile of old paperbacks sat on a shelf next to her, all well worn. A quick glance revealed titles like *The Adventures of Sherlock Holmes* and *Gods of Mars.* None of the books looked like they'd been published in the last few decades. As the gaze passed across them, she felt something comfortable and familiar wash over her.

Her vision lurched as the head that wasn't hers swivelled to take in the narrow bunk beds in the corner. The covers of the higher one were thrown back. Had she just got out of bed? And why was the roof so low? The smell of salt hit her again, mixed with petrol this time, and she felt the slow rolling of the floor beneath her. Then it clicked. She was on a boat.

"Uncle?" The voice that left her mouth wasn't hers. It was younger and deeper. And was that an American accent?

Where is he? The thought came from another part of her brain, so faint it was almost an echo. Something else lurked beneath it. A kind of chronic desperation. Loneliness?

That was it. She remembered the Blind Man now. He'd done something to her. The photo and hair she'd given him were what he needed to make a link to Sam Julius. She was in the boy's head.

She tried to probe the unfamiliar mind. She could detect curiosity and unease, but no fear. The boy hadn't been taken. So where was he?

The body lurched again and she lumbered out of the cabin, moving through the space with practised familiarity. Niobe had no choice but to go along with it.

Sam climbed a narrow set of stairs and emerged into daylight. He shielded his eyes against the glare. The boat bumped against the wooden marina with the slow movements of the swell. She took in the sight of the boat's exterior while she could. It had another two floors above the deck, and thick white fabric covered the top, acting as a sun shade. The boat was big enough to use as a house, if the close quarters weren't a problem.

Sam turned on the spot, giving Niobe a view of the ocean and marina. The skyline was instantly recognisable. He was within sight of the Old City. That nailed his position down to somewhere in Waitemata Harbour. A few dozen private boats rocked in the marina, deserted. Half a mile or so away, a container ship buzzed with the hurried movements of dock workers, but she couldn't spot anyone closer.

Through the echoes of his consciousness, a dull longing called. *He wants to talk to someone,* she realised. *Anyone.* An image drifted into her head, like another channel coming through the static of a TV set. A pretty dark-skinned girl, maybe fourteen or fifteen, was swimming in the ocean beside a sandy beach. She began to wade out of the sea, her shoulders glistening while she squeezed the water from her hair. In the memory, Sam's heart pounded as he watched her from the boat. He wanted to talk to her so badly. Maybe even kiss her, if she liked him too. But he couldn't do any of that. He wasn't allowed to talk to anyone. Not even a pretty girl he'd never see again.

Sam shook his head, and the image disappeared. But the longing remained, so strong Niobe almost felt like she'd fallen in love with the girl too. She thought back to the cabin with the two bunk beds. His uncle said he was sheltered. But just how sheltered? Was it really just the two of them? He had no friends at all?

She tried to tap his memories further, but she got nowhere. Everything was too different, too far away. It was just noise, and she could only pick out the strongest signals. Giving up, she tried to identify a landmark to further pinpoint the boy's location. But before she found anything, he turned again and made his way back inside. His feet trudged through a different door and up a narrow flight of stairs.

"Uncle?" he said again. His stomach churned with growing unease. He passed a mirror, and Niobe confirmed the boy's identity. It was clearly the same kid from the photo. Narrow face, but with strong cheekbones. His short dark hair was cropped close in a serviceable fashion. Maybe he cut it himself. His clothes were unremarkable: a T-shirt and jeans that looked like he'd slept in them.

How long did I sleep for? The boy's thoughts intruded again. *If he went out, why didn't he leave a note?*

Something creaked on the deck outside. Niobe shifted into a state of hyper-awareness, but the boy just turned, the muscles of his face relaxing. He didn't notice that the creak was made by someone heavier than Frank Julius. She tried to tense her muscles and suck in a lungful of air, but the boy's body didn't respond. Why didn't he hear it, goddamn it?

"Oh, there you are," Sam called out, walking back towards the stairs. "Where were you? I looked—"

A shadow filled the doorway. Big, broad-shouldered. She could make out the shape of a pistol in his hand.

Run, Niobe willed the boy. *His eyes haven't adjusted to the dark in here yet. Take the back exit, improvise a weapon, circle back, use the space, neutralise him. Bloody hell, move!*

But Sam remained stock-still. His heart lurched, and his thoughts stopped. Time slowed.

"Who—?"

The figure dashed forwards and slammed his elbow into Sam's throat. A desperate pain exploded inside him, like his entire world was shattering. The agony drove straight into Niobe's soul. The room grew fuzzy.

The man came forwards as Sam toppled. Even through the pain, Niobe picked out weaknesses. Knees. Eyes. Throat. But Sam could do nothing. He crumpled, adrenaline coursing through him. He'd never known fear like this. She could taste vomit, and she felt his throat close up, cutting off his air.

For a moment, something sparked inside Sam. It shot through him like bottled lightning. The pain dulled and his muscles rippled. Strength flooded him. Even though it was different from anything she'd felt before, she recognised it. The awakening of a superpower.

But before Sam could act, the man came at him again. She caught the glint of the silver buttons of the man's tunic as he drove his fist into Sam's side. The lightning disappeared and a new wave of pain crashed through him. She couldn't see the man's face. Her vision was fading in and out. Something was pulling her away from Sam's consciousness. *Or am I being pushed out?* She couldn't tell.

The last thing she saw was a thick burlap sack being pulled over Sam's head. Then the world lurched once more, and there was nothing.

Niobe's mind crashed back into her own body. She flung herself backwards, away from the Blind Man's cold palm. Sweat soaked her costume, and strands of hair clung to her cheeks. She was back in the refitted bar. She sucked in air like a drowning woman and tried to still the hammering in her chest. The details were burned into her mind, right down to the smell of the attacker's sweat.

The Carpenter was at her side in a second. She bent over and swallowed down her queasiness. "I'm okay." She brushed off his hand. "My mask."

"Spook, take a second, let it wear off."

Her vision was coming right now. She took a long, slow breath. "My mask."

Solomon shook his head, but he passed her the goggles and mask. She pulled them back on without wiping the sweat from her face, then picked up her bowler hat and gripped it tight. She tried to get her thoughts straight. Where were the answers she'd been hoping to get? She'd been through all that, and what did she have? Bugger all, that's what.

"The guy who took the kid," she said, "I didn't get a good look at him." The bloody boy should've run. Poor stupid Sam. "But he wore a uniform. He was Met Div."

The son of a bitch didn't need to be that rough with Sam. The kid didn't stand a chance. The fear running through him had been so dense she practically bathed in it. She knew what it was like to feel terror like that.

Solomon grunted, but said nothing. She tried to get up, but her knee buckled, and she was only saved from falling by Solomon's grip on her shoulders. *Goddamn it.*

She expected the Blind Man to have his smug half-smile in place, but his face was slack and his eyelids drooped. He looked like he'd aged a decade while she was in Sam's head. The old man was bent over, drawing deep, wheezy breaths. He looked nothing like the wise and treacherous wizard he usually resembled. Had he ever looked that knackered before?

The trail must've been fainter than she'd assumed. He'd only been able to give her a snippet of Sam's past. Niobe felt a twinge of sympathy for the Blind Man. She and Solomon had come asking for help, after all.

"I hope you got what you came for," the Blind Man said, using his stick to support himself while he returned to his seat.

Niobe shook her head and winced at the pain that shot through her brain. "It was only a fragment. The past. A few minutes."

The Māori man exhaled noisily. "Something parted the flow. Some sort of barrier prevented me from channelling the boy's present."

"He's not…dead, is he?" the Carpenter said.

"No," the Blind Man said. "Something would still linger on. The spirit is not a thing that just vanishes. If the boy was dead, I would have broken the connection immediately. Communing with the recently deceased brings uncleanliness into the soul."

Niobe didn't hold much belief in spirits. But it wasn't worth arguing over. Her legs felt steadier now, so she took her own weight and brushed off Solomon's arm.

They didn't have much, but it was a start. The man who attacked Sam wore a Met Div uniform, but he didn't have any backup. And that attack was nothing close to a lawful arrest. She didn't put it past the cape coppers to pull something like this, but her gut told her this wasn't official. A rogue element, maybe, or someone hired by an outside party. She'd seen what passed for internal affairs in the Metahuman Division.

The Carpenter watched her, his mouth turned down in a frown. She gave him a short nod to let him know she was okay. "Come on. I'll fill you in on the way back. I'll even let you drive."

The grin he gave was forced, but he slapped her on the back anyway. "You know, you're a lot more agreeable like this. I may have to make arrangements to have your head messed with more often."

She turned towards the doorway.

"I believe you're forgetting something," the Blind Man said. "Or rather, there's still something you need to forget."

She froze, stomach tightening.

"Hey, wait a minute," Solomon said. "You said you couldn't give us the full picture. I think she's entitled to a discount."

The Blind Man pushed himself up to his feet, still wheezing. Niobe faced him as he shuffled towards them.

"I gave you all there was about the boy," he said. "Now comes payment."

"It's okay, Carpenter," Niobe said as Solomon opened his mouth again. Her guts twisted as she spoke. "It was my deal to make."

She stepped forwards to meet the Blind Man. He reached out again with his large palm, but this time he gripped the base of her neck and gently pulled her forwards until they were inches apart. He pushed up her mask to expose her mouth and nose, and brought his own shriveled lips close to hers. Their faces touched, nose-to-nose and forehead-to-forehead.

Don't you dare die, Sam, she thought. Even now, she could feel the boy's soul imprinted on hers. In those few minutes, she'd been closer to him than she ever had to any other human being. She'd come to know a sad, lonely boy who loved his books and wanted to kiss pretty girls. *We'll get you out of this. I promise.*

The Blind Man's breath had no smell. It came slow and whistling against her nose. She ran through the memories of her childhood one last time, knowing it was hopeless. She couldn't remember the internment camp on Somes Island she'd been born in during the war, but she remembered the insults and the hatred that came after. Even though her parents had been in New Zealand for a decade before the war, they were still Japs, still the enemy. But they worked hard, built a life for Niobe and her little brothers. She remembered when she was eleven and her mother was teaching her to play piano at a public library. She'd been so happy to find the old piano. Her mother always had the most beautiful fingers.

Forget it. Do it for Sam, and do it for Gabby. Save them.

"Hurry it up," she said. "We've got a job to finish."

The Blind Man inhaled sharply. The image of her mother's fingers on ivory keys crawled out of her inner eyes and turned to smoke inside her. Memory after memory flashed before her eyes, then slipped away like a dream upon waking. The Blind Man continued to inhale, sucking in the memories while his eyes twitched in wild pleasure.

Then he stopped. There was no hole gnawing at her mind, not even a shadow of the memories she had lost. She was still the same person. But when she tried to summon the event she'd been recalling before the Blind Man began, she found nothing. Just a vague sense of loss.

The Blind Man smiled. He looked refreshed, almost youthful. She shoved her hands in her pockets to stop herself punching him.

"You have fine memories," he said. It was almost a sigh. "So full of life. *Haere rā*, Niobe Ishii. Find the boy you seek."

She didn't trust herself to speak, so she turned on her heel and walked out of the pub, leaving the Carpenter to trail her. *Just shadows of the past,* she reminded herself.

The sky was red when she emerged. She stopped on the cracked footpath, trying to make sense of the time. "How long was I out?"

"A few hours, maybe," Solomon said. "Time doesn't seem to work the same way when the Blind Man's doing his thing."

Hours. Now that she thought about it, her stomach gnawed with hunger, and she needed to pee. A few of the Blind Man's people were milling around the street, smoking or talking. She spotted the white-suited Quick-fire prodding at the burn mark on his suit. He glanced at her, saw her watching, and quickly shuffled away.

"That boy's father used to be a hero." Hine-nui-te-pō glided up behind them, arms folded in front of her. She followed Quick-fire with her eyes. "Now the man starts drinking when he wakes and doesn't stop until he passes out at midday. It's not good for a boy, growing up in a house like that." She shook her head sadly, then sighed and turned to Niobe and Solomon. "It's still early. Won't you stay for *kai*?"

"No time to eat," Niobe said, ignoring her rumbling stomach. She wasn't going to stay here a minute longer than she had to.

The woman nodded and looked up. Her *moko* made her look bestial in the sunset. "A bloody sky before a long night. Violence is coming. Do you feel it? Do you hear the Earth singing her last songs?"

Niobe pulled a Pall Mall from her packet and lit up. She glanced at the sky again. The Moon was out early, nearly three-quarters full. She couldn't see the lunar colony, but it was there at the northern pole, nestled between the craters. Metahumans had beaten both the Americans and the Soviets there and built themselves a new home. McClellan and his baby wouldn't have been killed if they'd been there. Sam wouldn't have been taken. And when Niobe and Gabby got there, they'd be safe. Free.

"No," she said to Hine-nui-te-pō. "I don't hear anything. The Earth stopped singing a long time ago."

She turned away and gestured to Solomon. He nodded at her, and together they strode back down the ruined street, the night closing in around them.

CHAPTER 8
A Crooked Man

Miss Knuckleduster smashed through the wall of our island lair and started crushing robots and genomorphs like they were toys. Steel Skull had left me in charge of the defence. He figured he'd escape while I was getting my teeth kicked in. He figured wrong. While Miss Knuckleduster tore through the last robot, I disabled the auto-airlocks and set the island to sink. She panicked as soon as she saw the sea pouring in through every opening. So did Steel Skull. I locked his cabin door before he could get to a diving suit and watched as the water slowly engulfed him. I didn't need a suit, of course. Everyone always laughed at the meta with gills. They didn't laugh so hard when I drowned them all.

—Shrimp to Shark: An Autobiography of Mako, Supercriminal

Sam ached to see the sun. Being confined to a small space didn't bother him. He'd lived on the boat with his uncle for years, after all. The cell—or whatever it was—was a little bigger than the cabin he shared with his uncle, but there was no window here. God, how he wanted to feel the sun again. He was starting to forget what colours looked like, what the sea smelled like. All he had here were the concrete walls and the light that stayed on all day and all night.

He sat curled up on the mattress and tapped the back of his head against the cool concrete wall. How long had he been here? Three days? Four? A month? Time had no meaning. He slept most of the time now, if you could call it sleep. He had no blanket to shield himself from the cold and the light, so he did little more than doze. Sometimes—he had no idea how often—a hatch at the bottom of the thick steel door would open and someone would shove in a bowl of porridge or watery soup. The first couple of times, Sam raced to the door and begged to be let free. Then he begged for whoever it was to talk to him, to say something, anything. But the hatch always closed in silence and the footsteps faded away, leaving him alone again. His last meal had come an hour or so ago—it was hard to tell—and now the remainder of it sat beside him. Something in it tasted strange this time, but he couldn't put his finger on it. Maybe he was just forgetting how things were supposed to taste.

He didn't move from his bunk much anymore. Sometimes he wondered if he was even still alive, or whether he was a disembodied ghost. He wasn't hungry and he hardly drank anything, so he didn't need to use the steel toilet in the corner very often. His heart still pounded whenever the hinges of the food hatch creaked, but he forced down the excitement. He didn't know why he was here, what they wanted from him, but they weren't going to let him go. Maybe he'd be here until he shrivelled up and stopped collecting his food, then they'd come and clean out his corpse to make room for the next prisoner.

While he tapped his head against the wall, a memory dredged itself up from the swamps of his mind. A few months ago, while he and his uncle sailed slowly south through the Indian Ocean, he reread *The Count of Monte Cristo*. In it, the protagonist Dantès was imprisoned for fourteen years. Would Sam be imprisoned that long? He wouldn't survive. At least Dantès had a Mad Priest to keep him company. Without contact, without the sun, Sam would just stop existing.

Of course, Dantès had escaped. Sam had thought about escape when he first woke here. He studied the creaking, noisy pipes that ran across the ceiling, and he tried to pry the toilet away from the wall. But all he got was bloodied fingers and broken nails. He cried that day. He didn't have the strength for that anymore.

But maybe there was still a chance. He'd felt something back on the boat when the man attacked him. He couldn't describe it, even to himself, but he could feel the residue of it sticking to his skin, like seaspray on a windy day. He pressed his hand to the bruise on his throat.

In that brief second when the man elbowed him, strength cut through the pain. It was some sort of energy, maybe even electricity, as stupid as that sounded.

He'd felt the energy once before, when he'd had a shouting argument with his uncle over something he couldn't even remember. The energy was fainter then, and he figured it was just anger. But his uncle got quiet all of a sudden, and backed down just as the energy went through him. *Did he see something in my face? Why wouldn't he talk to me about it?* Afterwards, they made up and had fresh fish for dinner. But his uncle wouldn't meet his eye for days.

He held his palm under the light. He swore he could feel traces of the energy tingling in his fingertips. But it was just childish, naive hope. Wasn't it?

Footsteps clicked outside the cell. Sam snatched his hand back and crossed his arms over his knees. *It's just mealtime. You lost track of time again.* But there was another sound along with the footsteps. A voice.

"There was a crooked man," the high-pitched voice sang, "and he walked a crooked mile."

Sam pushed himself to the end of the bed as the footsteps came closer. His heart thudded.

"He found a crooked sixpence upon a crooked stile." The voice giggled.

He'd heard that nursery rhyme before, but never in that lilting, off-key tune. The footsteps came to a stop.

"He bought a crooked cat, which caught a crooked mouse."

The door's lock groaned and clicked, and the hinges creaked slowly open.

"And they all lived together…" Spindly fingers appeared around the door. Sam backed into the corner. "…in a little…crooked…house."

It took Sam's tangled mind a moment to take in the slender man in the doorway. He wore a skin-tight black leotard and torn fishnet stockings. One of his long, pale arms held the door open, while his other hand rested against his face, fingers splayed. *No*, Sam realised. *That's not a face.* He tried to force himself further into the corner, but he couldn't take his eyes off the man. Leather string held a plastic mask shaped like a doll's head to the man's face. Crusted, dead flesh surrounded each of the stitch-marks in his skin. Crude make-up covered the face, with a grin of lipstick and thick pink blush across the cheeks. Mad eyes stared out of jaggedly carved eyeholes. Goose bumps ran down Sam's arms.

The man cocked his head to the side and took a step into the room, a high-heeled woman's shoe clicking on the concrete. "Is it scared?" His voice was high, girlish. Sam couldn't see the man's mouth move behind the mask, which only made things worse. "Doesn't it like Doll Face's singing?"

"Who are you?" Sam tried to keep his voice from trembling. His feet were frozen in place. *Oh my God, what is this thing?*

The man giggled and took another step forwards. "It doesn't know Doll Face. The Pretty Man said it wouldn't know, but Doll Face didn't believe him. Everyone knows Doll Face."

Sam had to get out of here. This guy was crazy. *Uncle, where are you?*

Doll Face slowly pushed the door closed behind him. Sam watched the narrowing crack, mind spinning. He was gripped with a sudden urge to run. He was nearly as tall as Doll Face; maybe he could rush him. But Sam couldn't make his feet move. There was something dangerous in the man's stop-start motions. *He's killed people,* Sam thought, and he knew it was true. *Uncle, why didn't you tell me the world was like this?*

The door closed with a sickening thud. Doll Face cocked his head to the other side and skittered forwards. Sam shrank down as small as he could make himself.

"It shakes," Doll Face said, bending towards him. "Is it scared? Yes. It understands. It might not know Doll Face, but it *knows* Doll Face." His head twisted and jerked as he spoke, inspecting Sam from every angle. He nodded. "Yes. Yes, it knows Doll Face."

"What do you want with me?" Sam whispered.

"Pretty Man says it is a bad boy. He tells Doll Face a story. Would it like to hear the story?"

Sam could smell the rotten flesh around Doll Face's stitches when he came close. It made him want to puke. "Please. I just want to go home."

"Well it can't go home!" Doll Face screeched. He threw up his arms and screamed in Sam's face. "It can't!"

Sam cowered at the creature's rage. *Oh God, let me go.*

Doll Face stared at Sam for a few seconds, neck twitching. Then he jerked away and continued in a sweet voice like nothing had happened. "Once upon a time, there was a powerful wizard. He went all around the world." Doll Face bought his spindly fingers up in front of Sam's face and mimed walking. "Some people loved the wizard, and some people hated him. He hurt a lot of people. People he loved. Wizards do that, you know." He leaned forwards conspiratorially and winked behind his eyeholes. Sam shivered.

Doll Face's fingers started moving again. "Lots of people wanted to get back at the wizard for all the people he hurt. But one day, the wizard just vanished. Poof!" His fingers jerked open then curled closed again. "Years go by, and without the wizard around, the world is much safer. No one is getting hurt anymore. Everyone is happy, hmmm? Does it understand so far?"

Sam swallowed and jerked a nod.

"The world changes. The Pretty Man comes along, plotting his plots, planning his plans. One day, a little birdie speaks to the Pretty Man. 'Cheep cheep,' it says. 'I know a little secret. Would you like to know a secret?' The Pretty Man says he does want to know a secret. 'You remember that powerful wizard that hurt everyone?' the birdie says. 'He had a son.'

"The Pretty Man is shocked. A wizard's child is a dangerous thing. He needs to be controlled. He can't be allowed to hurt people like his father. So down comes Doll Face, down to the dungeons. To see how dangerous the child is. Because Doll Face is magic too, hmmm?"

The girlish voice stopped, and all Sam could hear was the blood pounding in his ears. Doll Face was talking about him. And if he was the child, the wizard must be his father. His uncle always refused to speak about his father. The only thing Sam had of him was an old photo he kept in his drawer. It showed his father and uncle side by side when they were much younger, in front of some cabin in the woods. But beyond that, he knew nothing. Not even his father's name. Could this man…this thing…really know something?

Doll Face cocked his head to the side. "Does it like Doll Face's story?"

Sam said nothing. He wanted the sun, and his uncle, and to see that beautiful island girl swimming one more time. He wouldn't be scared to talk to her now. He wouldn't be afraid of his uncle's scolding. He'd dive off the boat and swim over there and say hello. Because nothing she could say, nothing his uncle could do, nothing in the world could be worse than this. Not even the thought of learning about his father was enough to overcome the dread that swam through his veins.

"It is silent," Doll Face said. "It doesn't like Doll Face's story. Doll Face is sad. But Doll Face is not hired to talk to bad boys. It doesn't know about Doll Face's *special skills*." He covered the mask's mouth with his hand and giggled. "It's been so long since he got to use them. So very long."

His fingers crawled like a spider around to the side of the mask and tugged on the leather cord that threaded through the crusted skin. Sam tried to close his eyes, but he couldn't look away. His nostrils were filled with Doll Face's stink. *God, Uncle, anyone. Please.*

Doll Face's nimble fingers undid the knot in the cord and slowly began to unlace it. Pus oozed from the festering sores as the cord slipped out of his flesh.

"Doll Face was a little boy once." Another stitch came undone. "He doesn't remember where, or when, but he remembers being a boy. The other boys were mean to him. They called him names and said he smelled. Little Doll Face went home and cried every day, but the teachers didn't help him. Mummy didn't help him. He was so alone. Except for his toys. Little Doll Face loved his toys. He was crying one day, and a teddy bear spoke to him. It told him how to make the boys stop being mean."

One side of the mask was completely free now, and Doll Face held it in place while he went to work on the cord on the other side. Sam panted rapidly, heart vibrating. His fingers tingled.

"Teddy bear was right," Doll Face said. "Doll Face had *special skills.* If he got very close to the boys, he could do something magical. He could see into their minds." Only two more stitches remained. He tapped the mask's forehead with the hand that held it in place. "And he could do things to their minds. He could play with them, hmmm?"

He undid the last stitch and let the leather cord drop to the floor. Sam gave one more thought to trying to overpower the creature, but every muscle in his body was frozen.

"The boys became his toys," he said, slowly withdrawing the mask. "Just like Doll Face's little dolls."

A scream built in Sam's lungs, but his throat had closed up tight. Doll Face's naked face stared at him, and he couldn't help but stare back. *Oh God, what is this thing?*

From the eyes up, the face was that of a normal man, filthy and with a misshapen forehead. But it was the lower half of his face that Sam couldn't take his eyes off.

Out of every pore, thin, twisting strings crawled across his skin. Wherever they touched, they left trails of slime. Several longer ones emerged from Doll Face's nose as Sam watched. They seemed to sniff at the air. *They can smell me.*

"It is sickened," Doll Face said. His lips twisted as he spoke. The strings wormed their way out, growing longer. They stretched towards Sam. One brushed his cheek. He could feel the ooze it left behind. A scream got caught in his throat.

"It still doesn't understand," Doll Face said. More strings crept towards Sam, brushing his hair back, crawling across his eyelashes. "But it will. Oh yes, it will."

Sam finally screamed as the strings entered his mouth.

CHAPTER 9

IT'S TOO LATE FOR ME

FUTURE GIRL

REAL NAME: *Carla Owens*

POWERS: *Able to change the speed of her personal timeline.*

NOTES: *Only female member of the Manhattan Eight. Disputes between her and Iron Justice were well publicized. After Dr Atomic retired, Owens claimed that Iron Justice made unwanted sexual advances towards her, but she never pressed charges. Shortly after the Manhattan Eight disbanded, she was trapped in a time loop by the supercriminal Chronoburner. Chronoburner was later captured and sentenced to death, but Future Girl was never recovered.*

—Notes on selected metahumans [Entry #0007]

Morgan did his best thinking when he was staring into space, and now was no exception. To anyone else he would seem to be studying the map fixed to the wall of the office, but he'd memorised it weeks ago. Everything was ready. Well, almost everything. He didn't relish the thought of the coming days, but he couldn't pretend his heart didn't quicken when he ran through the plan in his head. Once again, he rubbed his forehead with a white-gloved hand. His head ached a little—it hadn't let up since Bangkok—but everything was on track. Just a few more days, and he'd be done.

A muffled crack brought him out of his thoughts. His chair squeaked as he swivelled to look through the office window. In the abandoned warehouse below, his people went through drills amongst the old machinery and shipping crates. They moved swiftly, and they were learning to complement one another. The first team would advance and secure cover under the protection of Haze's smokescreen, while Screecher probed for hidden enemies. Obsidian had set up several of Navigatron's target drones throughout the warehouse to try to ambush the metas.

Morgan's man had sourced this warehouse to act as a base while they were in Neo-Auckland. *Neo-Auckland. A stupid name for a city.* The New Zealanders should have given the newly constructed city its own name, instead of basing it on the crumbling husk of the old bombed city. If it weren't for the name, no one would know they were even related. He'd never visited New Zealand before the bomb hit, but he'd seen photographs of old Auckland—a city clinging to its English roots, embarrassed by its youth.

Neo-Auckland, by contrast, was like a tacky American theme park. It abandoned the narrow gardens and English villas to fully embrace modern suburbanism and technology. His flight over the city in *Hyperion* had revealed street after street lined by freshly-mown lawns and trimmed hedges. The old city's tangled road networks had been replaced by swooping highways, monorail tracks, and grid-like street layouts. Shopping malls and department stores were the new churches. Not that this was a bad thing in itself. At least the civilians he'd seen had improved their dull English fashion sense.

According to Morgan's man, the warehouse had been used as a front by a trio of minor supercriminals back in the late '50s. It explained the row of prison cells downstairs behind a false wall. His operative said the supercriminals who built it were trying to run a kidnapping racket, but they'd got picked up by the police. It didn't sound like they were experts. The trio managed to get ambushed when they were out collecting a ransom. After the trial, the warehouse was sold at police auction for a steal. And the owner had been keeping it for just such an occasion ever since.

Two of the cells in the basement were occupied now. The boy was already there when Morgan arrived, and they secured Iron Justice in the cell he'd had specially prepared. Morgan hadn't looked in on the boy. What he had arranged for Sam was necessary, but that didn't make it pleasant. He preferred not to think about what Doll Face was doing.

"My lord," came Obsidian's voice from the doorway. Her black, rocky body had a strange sheen in the office light. "The boy has been given the first dose."

"He didn't notice anything?"

"No, my lord. Doll Face is with him now."

Don't remind me. He nodded and said nothing.

"You wanted to see the reporter," Obsidian said.

"Ah, yes," he said, pushing aside thoughts of Doll Face. "Bring him in."

Obsidian shifted her bulk from the doorway and the young, portly reporter came into view. John Bishop was red-faced, with a few drops of sweat clinging to his forehead, but the young man was clearly doing his best to hide his fear. He'd improved remarkably in the last few days. You had to respect a man who could remain stoic in company such as this.

Morgan had arranged for the man to be given fresh clothes when they arrived, since his abduction in Moscow hadn't left time for John to pack a bag. Now he wore a pair of grey trousers and a vest over a white buttoned-up shirt. Obsidian had done a good job choosing clothes that fit the man, especially since she didn't wear any herself.

"Obsidian," Morgan said. "The cuffs. John won't be needing them."

She inclined her head and worked a key into the handcuffs that bound the reporter's wrists in front of him. John rubbed his wrists as they came loose. A chain remained in place between his ankles, just as a precaution. Obsidian bowed her head once more and stiffly retreated from the room, closing the door behind her.

"Thanks for coming, John," Morgan said.

The reporter shuffled on the spot. "The stone woman didn't give me much choice."

Morgan smiled and gestured to the seat across from him. Like the desk and the filing cabinet in the corner, it was well made and barely used, though it was getting a little dated. "Please."

John Bishop shuffled to the chair, keeping his head high, and sat down without much difficulty. He was only in his twenties, but his hairline was already beginning to recede, leaving a V of dark hair pointing to his forehead.

"How are your new quarters?" Morgan said. "Comfortable?"

"Yes, sir." His voice was clipped, probably hiding his nervousness.

"How's the story coming?"

"Good, sir."

"You've been able to talk to my people? They haven't given you any trouble?"

John shook his head. "Most have been eager to tell me their stories." He licked his lips. Perhaps John wasn't so eager to hear some of what his people had to tell. Many had killed before, and some had done worse. But it was necessary.

Morgan smiled to try to put the man at ease. "I understand this is a difficult time for you. Truly, I do. I was taken against my will once myself. This is a dangerous world we live in. Though I'm sure you knew that already. You've done some war correspondence, correct?"

"Yes, sir. I covered the last coup d'état in Syria. There was fighting in several major cities."

Morgan nodded. "A young man, to have seen that. What you do is important. A single soldier is nothing to anyone, but a single reporter can change the world."

John nodded, but said nothing. His mouth was in a tight line, and he would only make eye contact with Morgan for the briefest moment before shifting his gaze.

"Cigarette?" Morgan asked. He produced a packet of Rothmans from the desk drawer. John hesitated, then nodded. He leaned over, took one, and allowed Morgan to light it.

"Aren't you going to…?" he said when Morgan returned the packet to the drawer.

"I don't smoke." Morgan smiled and leaned back, resting his hands on his white trousers. "You've been with us a few weeks now. So I suppose you're wondering why I want you to write this story."

John looked more comfortable with a cigarette in his hand. He brought it to his lips and inhaled. "It's not unheard of. My editor once had an exclusive with Suicide Prime. Sometimes supervillains want—" His eyes widened and his mouth slammed shut with an audible click. His gaze met Morgan's, then darted away again.

Morgan laughed. "It's all right. I'm not going to dangle you above a pool of acid because you called me a supervillain." He leaned forwards and put his elbows on the table. The poor man looked like he was going to drown in his own sweat. "The media doesn't like to use those words anymore. Supervillain, supercriminal. Even superhero. It's like society has tried to forget its past, don't you think? All around the world, metahumans are pushed to the fringes of society. The Alpha League went so far as to leave Earth entirely. And now the world treats nearly two decades of metahuman activity as if it never happened."

The cigarette slowly burned down in John's fingers. He held it inches from his lips, but he made no attempt to take another drag. The cigarette trembled as Morgan let the silence draw out between them.

"You're right," Morgan said. "I am a supervillain. But I didn't bring you here just to show off. Without you, everything I'm doing, everything I'm going to do, will be worthless. Without you, I'm just another madman."

He stood, opened the filing cabinet behind the desk, and pulled out a series of folders bound together with rubber bands. He tossed them down and they hit the desk with a thud. John jumped, but stayed silent.

"It took me nearly a decade to put that together. Years of planning and tracking down fragments of information. That file contains everything. Every operative's report, every piece of tech I had specially designed. You can read it, all of it, if you want. Everything will become clear soon, anyway."

Smoke drifted from John's cigarette, but he hardly seemed aware of it. He licked his lips, staring at the file. "Why?" he finally asked.

Morgan smiled. "That's always the best question. And that's the one thing you won't find an answer to in there." Now that he was standing, he didn't want to sit down again. *I'm getting restless,* he realised. He was so close to the end now, so close. Years of setting up the chessboard. Months of moving his pieces into position. Checkmate in two moves. He wanted to act now.

But the timing had to be perfect. If he made his move now, he'd bring retribution down on him and his people. He paced back and forth, hands clutched together behind his back.

"I'm not in this for money," he said. "I have no desire to rule anything. I don't want revenge, at least, not in the usual sense. No doubt others will challenge my motives in the coming weeks, but I need you to understand."

He stopped pacing and faced the reporter. Part of him bristled at the idea of sharing information with this man, laying out his plot like a moustache-twirling villain. But he had to make John understand. The reporter's eyes were still nervous, but he leaned forwards slightly now, brow furrowed, interest piqued. He'd stubbed out his cigarette, but the aroma remained.

Does he see? This was the weakest link in Morgan's plan. The realisation that he needed someone like John only came to him two months ago, during a nightmare. He dreamed his plan unfolded perfectly, every cog meshing with the next. But a decade afterward, the world began to forget. It had all been for nothing. He woke in a cold sweat that night. It was only by chance that his people found John in Moscow, an English journalist trying to peer behind the Iron Curtain. *If John fails, everything fails.*

Straightening his white jacket, he continued. "My plan would have stayed just a plan, never acted upon, if my life had remained the same." He gestured to the file. "Back then, all this was just—excuse the expression—academic masturbation. I realise that now. But of course, things never stay the same, do they?"

He resisted the urge to massage his forehead. The ache was building again. "I have a condition. Oligodendroglioma. A type of brain tumour. Surgical resection is too risky. The tumour will kill me, eventually." He'd accepted that. He'd always been a logical man, and having your cause of death presented to you with such stark certainty had a certain beautiful logic all of its own. Most metas died of cancer, of course. He'd just never truly considered that he might be one of them. "I take medication to control the seizures, but it won't be long until I can't function at the level I need to. I suppose I should have carried out my plan years ago, when I was still healthy. But I never would have, of course. No one ever acts until they're forced to, supervillain or not."

Turning away from John, he fell silent. He wasn't a robot. He feared death like any man. But more than that, he feared leaving the world as it was.

"Who…" John said. "Who are you?"

Morgan watched his people fight the training drones in the warehouse. Only Obsidian knew about his cancer. She knew almost everything. The others had their own reasons for being here. But regardless of their motivations, they were serving a noble cause.

"My name is Morgan Shepherd. I went to school in Birmingham, and in nineteen fifty-five I left home to attend the University of Cambridge to study law and politics. My powers were known only to me at that stage. I assume they were a result of the atomic bomb tests in the North Atlantic Ocean, but of course, I cannot be sure. You can't imagine how excited I was when I first discovered I was a metahuman. After years of collecting Dr Atomic comic books and watching the exploits of the world's superheroes at the pictures, I was becoming one myself.

"I practiced in private, training for the day when I'd take a cape for myself. I wasn't content to just be a superhero. I was going to be a hero to make Dr Atomic himself proud." He turned back to John and gestured to the blotches of pale skin on his face. "My skin started to change at the same time. I didn't mind. Why would I? The last thing I wanted to do was hide." He paused. "And then the protests started. You know of the Cambridge protests?"

John nodded. "Nineteen fifty-seven. Students Against Metahuman Control."

Morgan smiled. He knew he'd picked the right man for this. "We couldn't stand idle while governments across the planet restricted metahuman rights more and more. Registration, compulsory medical checks. The introduction of kill-switches was immoral beyond reason. We clashed with other protesters on more than one occasion. The student body was divided into pro- and anti-metahuman. Other students across the world protested in solidarity with us, but it was strongest at Cambridge."

He could tell the reporter knew what was coming next; he would have heard of the day, but Morgan kept speaking. It had been a long time since he spoke about it with anyone.

"In June of fifty-eight, our group was marching through campus. There were dozens of openly meta students amongst us, and several more that we all assumed had powers as well. Our protests had mostly been peaceful, but times were changing. We tried to continue our march out of campus, and found our way blocked by officers of the new Metahuman Control Unit of the police. They attempted to force us back, and some of our more extreme members retaliated." The day was seared into his memory. "I couldn't believe it when the police opened fire. My people—my friends—all crumpled. Other people's blood coated me. I couldn't hear; I couldn't see through the smoke. This wasn't how it was supposed to be. We were going to be heroes.

"The practice I'd been doing saved me. Without thinking, I brought up a shield of light to protect myself against the gunfire. It was the first time I'd ever used my powers in public. But my people were still dying. My best friend, a meta I'd known since school, took a round in the throat. I watched him drown in his own blood. All thought fled from me."

He flexed his gloved hand into a fist behind his back. "Next thing I knew, I had sliced a police officer's head from his shoulders with a blade of light. I can still see the blood pulsing from his neck as the body slumped to the ground. I kept moving, kept cutting. A few of the surviving metas saw what I was doing and tried to stop me. Others attempted to fight as well. But most of the killing I did alone." He sighed and bowed his head. "You know the event I speak of?"

"Yes," the reporter said. He paused as if debating with himself, and his fingers tapped on his knees. Finally, he appeared to make up his mind. "They were rounding up the survivors of the riot for months." His voice barely quavered. "How did you escape?"

"Luck, mostly. I made contact with the Erasers, and they helped me out of the country. I made my way through Europe under several false identities. It wasn't hard to stay ahead of Interpol and anti-metahuman squads. They were overwhelmed in those days. I moved every few weeks, never spending more than a couple of months in a country at a time." *Until I met Lisa.* He shook the thought from his head.

"Even if this is all true," John said, "it doesn't explain any of this." He waved his hands at the office, but the gesture seemed to encompass much more. He'd fully transformed into the reporter now. "You said this wasn't revenge. You've freed criminals and kidnapped people, but for what?"

Morgan relaxed his hands and pushed his plan file across the desk to the reporter. "Read. And think. I hope you'll understand now." He caught a glimpse of movement through the office window, and he sensed a kind of darkness approaching. His heart sank a little, but he steeled himself. Doll Face was coming. He must be done with the boy, for now. *A necessary evil,* he told himself, but it wasn't convincing.

"We're done for now," Morgan said. He picked up the file and pushed it into John's hands. "Read."

The man nodded jerkily. Morgan held out his hand, and after a moment, John shook it. A strong grip. *Yes,* he thought, *he'll do it. He's the one.*

He showed John to the door. Obsidian was waiting outside, ready with the handcuffs, but he waved her away. "John won't be needing those. He has writing to do."

Something giggled in his ear. "What's it writing? Is it writing a story?"

Morgan forced himself not to shudder at Doll Face's stench. How did he move so quietly? The makeup on Doll Face's mask had been recently reapplied. The crooked lipstick smile sent shivers down Morgan's spine. John was almost cowering behind Obsidian.

"Take John back to his quarters," Morgan said to Obsidian. She bowed and escorted the shaking man away. The reporter cast fearful glances back at Doll Face as he went. Doll Face cocked his head to the side and watched the reporter until he was out of sight.

"It's done?" Morgan asked shortly. The less he had to deal with this creature the better.

Doll Face returned his attention to Morgan and leaned close. "Doll Face enjoyed playing with the boy's mind. So many secrets. So many dark places to explore. When can Doll Face cut him?"

"Not yet. You have more…playing…to do."

The creature's head jerked to the other side. "Doll Face is patient. Doll Face likes to play." He glanced around, leaned in, and whispered. "But the best bit is making a toy cut its own eyes out."

Doll Face turned and slipped away, making no sound as he went. That was a good sign. He only made footsteps when he wanted his victims to be afraid.

Morgan realised he'd been holding his breath. He exhaled and massaged his aching head. *A necessary evil,* he told himself again as he watched Doll Face disappear.

Just like me.

PART TWO

Both the victor
and the vanquished are
but drops of dew,
but bolts of lightning -
thus should we view the world.

—Japanese death poem by Ôuchi Yoshitaka

CHAPTER 10
WHAT SHE DOESN'T KNOW

Signed and ratified by 87 member countries in 1960, the Seoul Accord granted governments strict controls over metahuman rights in the interests of public safety and economic stability. Use of superpowers became heavily restricted, and many member countries also prohibited the employment of metahumans to protect the jobs of non-metahumans. The most controversial component of the Seoul Accord was the granting of governments the right to fit metahumans with so-called "kill-switches". These could be activated by authorities to terminate the metahuman in case of violent criminal activity that could not be contained by conventional means.

—A Concise History of Metahumans, George Walters, PhD

Niobe greeted the dawn by pulling the curtains of her apartment's kitchen shut and sitting in darkness. She couldn't think clearly with sunlight streaming down on her. Everything became clearer in the shade.

She wore an old blank T-shirt and the same panties she'd slept in. A mug of instant coffee sat in front of her alongside a newspaper, but she made no move to drink it. The bitter aroma was all she wanted, really. Gabby had built a machine like the ones in new Neo-Auckland cafés, one that brewed fresh coffee directly from beans, but Niobe never used it. The smooth liquid it produced didn't taste like coffee should.

She'd woken half an hour before dawn and slipped out of bed without waking Gabby. Her sleep—or what passed for it—had done nothing to leave her refreshed. All night she was tormented by images of uniformed figures striking at her throat and shoving bags over her head. Other shapeless creatures crept through her mind, stealing away with her memories. Again and again she woke drenched in sweat, until she finally gave up. She was probably just overtired. That was all it was.

She sighed and inhaled the scent of the coffee on the table. What she really wanted was a photo album. That was what other people had, right? Photos of their families and themselves growing up. Maybe if she had something like that she could patch over the hole left in her memories. The memories the Blind Man took had been the clearest ones she had of her parents. Now she could barely remember their faces. All she had was the smell of the coffee her mum used to make for her dad before he went to see his patients.

Bugger it. She pushed the coffee away from her and folded her arms. She'd made the trade willingly. She had a lead on the kid, no matter how small. If she could get him back, maybe it'd be worth it. Maybe.

Solomon had made a call to the bloke he knew at the cape coppers' headquarters. The guy wasn't a meta; all he did was mop the floors. But the coppers had a habit of flapping their jaws when he was around. A cleaning guy was invisible to them, she guessed. Piss-poor security. That sort of thing wouldn't have been tolerated in the Wardens. But those days were different. You could never be sure someone wasn't a doppelgänger or the mind-controlled slave of some psychic supercriminal. It was a matter of survival to make sure no one was eavesdropping on a sensitive conversation.

Solomon's man hadn't heard any goings on about a kid being subdued on a boat in the harbour. No prisoners that matched Sam's description were being held there either, as far as he knew. It was what she expected. The man she saw in the vision was acting outside normal protocols. Either he really was a copper, and he'd been wearing the uniform to get close enough to the Juliuses without attracting attention, or he was an impostor, and the uniform was designed to throw her off the trail.

She'd put out her own feelers, but nothing had come back yet. There weren't many people willing to work with her and Solomon, but if metas were being snatched, maybe there were rumours her informants could trace. The information would cost. *But not as much as the Blind Man*, she thought. She scowled into the darkness and wiped her resentment away.

Soft footsteps padded behind her, and a second later the kitchen light clicked on. She didn't turn around, so Gabby came and sat at the table opposite her. Niobe's stomach clenched when she saw the bloodstains on the shoulder of Gabby's robe. The cut on her forehead had begun to scab over, but the purple, raised bruise disappearing beneath her frizzy blond hair was still vivid. Niobe's mood softened. Gabby's eyes were puffy and tired, but she still looked beautiful. She was always beautiful. *You should have protected her better*, a voice in her heart whispered.

Gabby's lips twitched in a small smile that didn't reach her eyes.

—*That coffee smells terrible,* she signed.

"Bourgeois pig." Niobe spoke slowly, signing at the same time. Gabby gave the smile another try, but Niobe couldn't bring herself to return it.

—*What's wrong?* Gabby signed.

Niobe shook her head and said nothing. She couldn't see how she could explain it. She couldn't even explain how she felt to herself. Was it really a loss when you couldn't remember it anyway?

Gabby waited and watched, but Niobe didn't meet her eyes. After a few minutes, Gabby reached across the table and took Niobe's hand. Niobe returned the squeeze. *For her,* she thought. *I'm doing this for her.*

With a final squeeze, Gabby released her hand and pointed to the newspaper.

—*Did you see that?*

Niobe nodded, glad for the change of subject. Splashed across the front page was a blurred photograph from at least eight years ago of a man in a plastic mask.

NOTORIOUS SUPERCRIMINAL DOLL FACE ALIVE!
Soviets Admit Breakout

She wasn't sure whether to believe it. Everyone was sure the psychopath was killed after a few hundred Soviet soldiers cornered him in Ukraine. They even had a body to prove it. He'd single-handedly taken a school hostage and turned the place into his own personal house of horrors. It was never reported in the media, but she heard through the Wardens that most of the surviving children were missing their ears and noses. The investigators found those missing body parts in the stomachs of the kids who'd died. The soldiers had shown no mercy when they got a clear shot at Doll Face.

She'd never gone toe-to-toe with Doll Face. No one in the Wardens had. For the best part of a decade he'd terrorised Europe and parts of Asia. Vindictive parents would tell their children that if they didn't be-have, Doll Face would get them. He was a psychopath, maybe, but no one could cause that much devastation and evade capture for so long without some kind of twisted, instinctive intelligence.

She shook her head, dismissing the thoughts. "Even if he is run-ning around, the Reds can deal with him," she said. "Serves the stupid bastards right for keeping him alive all these years."

She stood and tipped the coffee down the sink. It was lukewarm now anyway, and it hadn't helped her remember a single damn thing. She had to focus. Find Sam, get him back to his uncle. Make this damn hole in her head worth it.

Gabby followed her back to the bedroom and sat on the bed, hug-ging herself. Niobe tried to pretend she couldn't feel Gabby's eyes on her while she dressed. She was too restless for a shower, and besides, the hot water had been acting up in the old building lately.

—*Where are you going?* Gabby signed.

—*Out,* she replied, and clipped her utility belt on. She wasn't going out in full costume, not in the daylight. Today was strictly detective work. Still, she strapped her gun on and covered it with a pale, loose-fitting jacket that she picked up at a seconds sale in Neo-Auckland a couple of seasons ago.

Gabby frowned. Her nose always wrinkled when she did that.

—*It's not even seven yet. Have breakfast with me.*

—*Can't,* Niobe signed. *I have work to do.*

Gabby grabbed her arm as she tried to brush past out of the room. "Please." Her voice came out quiet, distorted. It embarrassed her, so she didn't speak often.

Niobe stopped, looked at her feet, then met Gabby's eyes. They shifted colour in the light, but now they were grey and rough like a stone wall. Niobe hadn't forgotten the first time she saw those eyes. The coppers had raided her place back in '61, trying to force her into the metahuman registration programme. She had to make a run for it, abandoning her cash and all the equipment she had. As a parting gift, the coppers kindly gave her a bullet in the upper arm. In the days that followed, she slept where she could, avoiding patrols, trying to stay clear of trouble, hoping the infection in her wound didn't kill her. But then she heard a rumour about a master gadgeteer operating in the outskirts of the Old City. If she was going to survive, Niobe needed supplies, equipment. Maybe the gadgeteer could help.

It took her a week, but she found the gadgeteer's workshop. She scoped the place out, waited for nightfall, then tried to sneak in. But she was so sick and starved by then she didn't notice she'd triggered the silent alarm. Not until she felt the barrel of a pulse rifle pressed against the back of her head.

And when she turned around, she found those silver eyes looking down at her, and those cheeks tinged with pink, and that soft golden hair. Over time, they became friends. And then more than friends.

It was strange. She'd had relationships before, but she'd always thought she was too cynical to feel like this.

They'd been through so much together. They'd watched the world change. But she knew it upset Gabby when she went out, just like Solomon's wife worried about him. She couldn't quit this job, but she loved Gabby, and she wanted her to be happy. Niobe couldn't let the best thing in her life slip away.

She touched Gabby's cheeks with both hands. Then she slowly pulled her close, close enough to make out the little downy hairs at the edge of her hairline. She kissed her. Gabby's lips were hard for a moment, but they softened, and her tongue slipped out to touch Niobe's.

Niobe breathed in the scent of her.

Gabby melted into her arms. Niobe's hands drifted down over her back, down to the sash of her robe. She wanted to untie it, let the robe fall from Gabby's shoulders, run her fingers over her. The first few times they'd had sex it had been a nervous exploration, each touch like a little electric shock, each inch of flesh new and exciting and scary. But over time they'd become comfortable with each other's bodies. She'd learned the spots that made Gabby sigh and the ones that made her gasp. She'd learned how Gabby's back would arch when Niobe let her fingers turn to half-shadow and creep along the crease where her leg met her pelvis.

But she couldn't do those things now. There was a thirteen-year-old boy out there somewhere, in the hands of God knows who. She'd wasted too much time already. When their kiss ended and Niobe opened her eyes again, she returned her hands to Gabby's cheeks. Gabby's face was flushed with pink. Niobe drew her close again, kissed each of her eyelids in turn, and released her.

—*I have to go*, Niobe signed, *but we'll talk tonight. We'll go up to the roof, look up at the Moon, and we'll work this out together.*

The colour slowly faded from Gabby's face. She smiled, but it was strained.

—*I promise*, Niobe added. She kissed Gabby one more time, took her hand, and squeezed. "Love you."

She buttoned her jacket over her gun and went out of the room, ignoring the tightness in her chest.

She thought about contacting the Carpenter and bringing him along, but in the end she decided not to. They were due to meet with his informer at Met Div on the guy's lunch break. Solomon might as well sleep in and spend some time with his family. Besides, her mind was a mess right now. What she really wanted was to throw herself into the investigation and forget the past and relationships and Doll Face and the Moon.

She slipped on a pair of over-sized sunglasses to conceal her black eyes. The traffic was light as she drove towards Waitemata Harbour.

Most of the people who worked the ports would already be there, and few other normals travelled so close to the Old City. In the old days, metas with minor strength or technology-related powers could make a good living loading and unloading the ships that came here. The more powerful metas usually set their sights higher, preferring to build entire structures or design machines so advanced they ran competing industries into the ground. But now the ports were run on a skeleton crew, with a large proportion of incoming cargo ships diverted to Tauranga and other parts of the country.

She wound down the window and let the sea breeze blow the swirling thoughts from her head. The few scattered cargo ships rolled past, crawling with workers while cranes shuddered and turned. She kept on driving until they fell behind and the private marinas emerged near Herne Bay. Most were new, built in the last couple of years. If Neo-Auckland residents took the Northwestern Highway, they could get there while bypassing the Old City completely, but this part of the city was still out of the way and suffering from neglect. Still, there were a lot of rich folks in Neo-Auckland, and having your own boat had become the new status symbol. It'd probably stay that way until the Germans finally made personal rocket-planes commercially viable.

She slowed the car, keeping one eye on the boats and the other on the surrounding streets and buildings. Her mind automatically started comparing the scene to the images burned into her retinas. Spatial and visual inputs were what her mind liked best. When she was a kid, she loved solving her dad's mechanical puzzles, the ones where you had to work out how to assemble or disassemble the wooden pieces. She begged her dad to give her a new one for her tenth birthday, she remembered. Had she ever gotten it? The date was sheared off in her mind by the Blind Man, neatly excised like a tumour under a surgeon's knife.

She shook her head and returned her attention to the marina. *There.* She spotted the houseboat rocking in the water, in the same place it had been in her vision. She looked around at the streets to confirm her position. A row of abandoned shops and offices faced the sea. Yes. This was definitely it.

She drove on, watching the surroundings, but there was no one to be seen. No cars parked on the side of the road, no one out for a stroll. It made her uneasy. She wouldn't look so out of place if she wasn't the only one here. She parked around the corner, activated the car's security measures, and walked back to the marina.

No gates or security guards protected the marina. She lit up a cigarette and tried to look like a tourist while she used the time to analyse the place. The marina consisted of four long floating walkways with refuelling stations at the end. Seagulls squawked atop yachts' masts.

Exits were limited. Either take the platform back to shore or jump into the sea. Maybe steal a boat, if necessary. It'd have to do. Satisfied that no one was around, Niobe took a long drag of her cigarette, plucked it from her mouth, and made her way to the old man's boat.

She wasn't much of a boat person, but it looked expensive. The motorboat was white, maybe forty foot long, with a tall cabin that didn't look very aerodynamic. The name *Wanderer* was painted on the side.

If Sam's attacker had left any obvious signs of his presence on deck, they'd been cleared away. A pair of plastic deck chairs were folded up neatly near the entrance to the cabin, and a coil of rope sat next to the ladder. Niobe gave one more glance around and stepped down onto the deck. She stayed near the edge of the boat and gave it a quick sweep. No obvious bloodstains, and no stray hairs. She couldn't see any damp shoe-prints, but it was hot enough that any sea spray quickly dried.

Satisfied there was nothing to see on deck, she worked the handle on the heavy door and stepped into the cabin. Sam had been upstairs when he was attacked. She felt a sense of déjà vu as she ascended the same narrow stairs as in her vision. She took off her sunglasses and emerged into a small kitchen and living area. A mirror hung on one wall, and a fridge and kitchenette unit occupied the opposite wall. But Niobe's focus went straight to the centre of the room, where the boy had been standing when the man incapacitated him.

She crouched and inspected the linoleum floor. A single speck of blood was all that remained of Sam. The blood had gone brown and hard in the last few days. Maybe the kid had scraped his knee when he fell, or maybe he spat up some blood after the hit to the throat. Niobe's vision had been so filled with pain and fear that the details after the first strike didn't register. It didn't matter. She breathed a sigh of relief that there wasn't more blood.

She sniffed the air, but detected no scent of gunpowder. A glance at the walls and ceiling revealed no bullet holes either. Good. The kid had most likely been alive when he left the boat. Something loosened in her chest.

Sam was okay, but his attacker had been careful. She took her time, inspecting every inch of the kitchen floor, but again, no shoe-prints. He hadn't left so much as a hair. No plates or cutlery had been left out on the kitchen bench. A worn paperback copy of *The Count of Monte Cristo* sat in a chair in the corner. There were two exits from the kitchen: the door she came through, and another stairway leading down on the opposite side of the room.

She went and followed the other staircase down. It had a kink halfway down, turning back on itself. It was narrower than the other stairway and led out to starboard, away from where the boat nestled against the marina walkway. The attacker probably wouldn't have used this staircase to take the kid out.

She returned to the kitchen and examined the stairs leading down the other side. The guy was big, so it would've been easiest to carry Sam over his shoulder down the narrow stairway. She closed her eyes and pictured the events she'd seen in the Blind Man's vision. The man had been holding his gun in his right hand, making him right-handed, so she'd assume he had Sam over his right shoulder. The stairs were steep; maybe he'd need to grip the handrail to steady himself. Was he wearing gloves? They weren't part of the Met Div uniform, but it had been too dark to see in the Blind Man's vision.

She pulled her powder and brush from her utility belt and gave the whole handrail a light dusting. Nothing, not even prints from Sam or Frank. Wiped clean. So was the door handle. She chewed her lip and looked around. Okay, he came down the stairs, put Sam down outside, came back in and wiped the handrail and the door handle. Sam must've been unconscious, but the man couldn't leave him for long. It was daylight; someone might see.

Her eyes fell upon the doorway. It was small, with the bottom raised nearly a foot to keep water from getting in. Sam's attacker was big. Maybe....

She got out her powder again and dusted the metal door frame on both sides, starting at about shoulder height. She worked slowly, methodically, enjoying the work. This was honest, down-to-earth investigation, with not a psychic in sight. Then she smiled to herself.

"Gotcha," she said.

The two fingerprints were almost perfect. Judging from their position and size, she'd guess index and middle fingers. A partial palm print accompanied them, but it was too distorted to be much use. They were on the top left-hand corner of the door frame. Frank Julius wouldn't be likely to reach up there, not with his walking stick and shuffling gait, and the palm looked far too big to be Sam's. Perhaps the attacker had tripped on the raised lip of the doorway and had to steady himself, or maybe he was just manoeuvering himself through the tight space with Sam over his shoulder. She put away her powder, got out some clean plastic tape, and carefully retrieved the fingerprints.

Technically, she didn't have access to any fingerprint records. But she'd learnt long ago that technicalities were just excuses for people who didn't know where to look. If the guy was a cape copper, his prints would be on file. The coppers were meticulous about that sort of thing. If a doppelgänger was impersonating a copper, prints might be the only way to confirm it. Doppelgängers struggled with details like that.

Of course, the records would be at Met Div headquarters, surrounded by a few dozen coppers. She should probably wait until nightfall if she didn't want to catch a bullet or ten.

She continued her inspection of the attacker's probable exit, but he'd made no more mistakes. No prints on the rail on deck, no clothing fibres. All right, that was as good as she was going to get on that front.

But there were still questions surrounding Frank Julius and his part in all this. Who was he really? Someone had gone to a lot of effort to kidnap his nephew, and then they'd forgotten to make any ransom demands.

She went down into the sleeping cabin where the Blind Man's vision had begun. It looked as she remembered it: a set of bunk beds, some shelves with a few old paperbacks, and some drawers.

Strange, using a boat as home and transport. Why not just take a rocket-plane like everyone else who wanted to travel internationally? The most obvious answer was to stay under the radar. Policing the oceans was like trying to stop kids smoking pot. No matter how hard you tried, you'd never do anything but scrape the surface.

She tried to imagine spending weeks at a time confined to this boat. She couldn't handle it.

She did a walk-through of the room and came up empty. The top bunk appeared to be Sam's, and the bottom Frank's. No cash under the mattress. She found a few folded wads of assorted currency—American dollars, British pounds, a few pesos—in Frank's underwear drawer. Probably just day-to-day money, since it wasn't enough to live on long-term. He'd mentioned bank accounts when she talked to him at the hotel, but she couldn't find any bank statements or account numbers. Maybe he committed them to memory. Or maybe he'd cleared them out when he found Sam missing. Either way, it wasn't really the mark of someone with nothing to hide.

A search of Frank's drawers revealed clothes and little else. The only thing of note was an address book, but each entry was only signified by initials and a phone number. At a quick flick through she guessed there was nearly a hundred numbers there, most of them international. It didn't take a genius to work out that anyone unwilling to be listed by their full name wouldn't reveal information over the phone. She pocketed the address book, but her gut told her it was another dead end.

Sam's drawers painted a similar picture. She was about to give up—she'd be meeting Solomon soon—when the corner of a slip of paper caught her eye sticking out from under a pile of T-shirts. *No, not paper,* she realised as she pulled it free. A photograph. Now that she thought about it, it was the only photo she'd found on the whole boat. If Frank had any copies of the photo he'd given her, he kept them well-hidden.

The photo showed two men in front of a log cabin. Forest stretched behind them in great sweeping valleys. She pulled a small torch from her belt and held the picture up to the light. It was black-and-white, faded, most of the detail lost. One of the men was a younger Frank Julius. His hairline was already receding. Who was the other man? Sam's father?

Frowning, she took a miniature hand lens from her belt and used it to magnify the photo. The other man's features seemed familiar, but she couldn't place him. A roguish grin was plastered to his face and a pork-pie hat sat atop his head, casting shadow over his eyes. He was slimmer than Frank, with an easy demeanour to him. Probably fancied himself a ladies' man.

She pocketed the photo and returned her tools to her belt. She gave the room another quick once-over, then paused. Her gut gnawed at her. There was something she'd missed. Then she saw it. One of the wooden panels in the corner near the bed was slightly askew, not quite flush with the wall. A few narrow scratches ran along one end, like it'd been scuffed a few times. She'd been in enough supercriminals' lairs to recognise a hidden compartment.

She crouched and studied it. It didn't seem to be booby-trapped. Why did he need a compartment like this? Maybe it just held his cash. Maybe. One way to find out. She retrieved her pocket knife from her belt, flipped out the blade, jammed it into the crack, and levered the panel open.

No cash, no diamonds. Not even a gun. She shone her torch into every corner of the compartment, but there was only one object in there, sitting in a foam cut-out. A ring.

It was a simple ring. Probably only silver-plated. It had lost its shine, and the large green stone didn't look precious. She picked it up and turned it over. No inscription. It didn't look like an engagement ring. It looked more like…a signaller.

When Niobe joined the Wardens, they gave her a small button

disguised as a pendant. She'd kept it around her wrist since she didn't like the feel of things around her neck. She turned it in when she quit. Something about this ring reminded her of it. The device was designed as both a simple transmitter and receiver. If you had an emergency, you pressed the button and the group would assemble, or you could hook it up to a radio transmitter to deliver a message. Likewise, if someone needed help, the thing would flash or start playing a message.

She thought back to her first meeting with Frank. He said Sam's father was a metahuman. Logic would suggest this was the signalling device his group used. That didn't necessarily put him on the side of superheroes; some of the more organised supercriminal groups had adopted the method. But for argument's sake she decided to assume he was a hero. If Sam was around thirteen and never knew his father, that gave her a time-frame for when he was alive. Superhero organisations were already crumbling thirteen years ago. Maybe Gabby would be able to have a look at the ring and track down who manufactured it. She wasn't eager to bring Gabby into this mess, but the sooner they solved the damn case and got the kid back, the sooner they could be off this planet.

Niobe was no thief, but she pocketed the ring anyway. If it turned out to be nothing, she'd return it. For now, it was one of the few leads she had.

She exhaled and checked her watch. Time to get back to Solomon and the informant. She closed the hidden compartment and turned her back on the room. The ring felt strangely heavy in her pocket. She went back out onto deck, replacing her sunglasses as she went.

Only a few scattered clouds marred the blue sky. The shore was still deserted, but a couple of yachts were off sailing in the distance. She took a few more deep breaths of the sea air. At least she had something. The gulls squawked at her again as she climbed back onto the marina walkway and started making her way towards land. She was ready to get somewhere that didn't smell like fish.

If she hadn't stopped to light up another cigarette, she would have missed it. Sunlight glinted off something small in the second-story office directly opposite the marina. A curtain fluttered.

Her mind spun. Sniper? No. No, of course. Someone was watching to see if Frank Julius came back. That wasn't a scope. It was a telephoto lens.

And someone had just got a clear photo of her face.

Stupid, stupid, stupid! She tossed the cigarette and broke into a sprint, pumping every bit of energy she had into her legs. Her bloody civilian shoes flopped as she ran, slipping on the damp walkway. How could she have been so dumb? She should've come last night, when she could use the darkness, but she'd stayed with Gabby. Damn it!

She reached into her jacket and grabbed her mask. Without slowing, she pulled the mask on and replaced her sunglasses. She wasn't going to give them another shot of her face.

A figure darted out the side entrance of the building and fled down the alley. It looked like a woman, but something about her arms was misshapen. She disappeared around a corner, and Niobe pounded after her. Niobe needed to get her to talk. And she needed to destroy that film.

Panting into her mask, she tore across the deserted street and into the alley. Maybe she should go back to the car, radio for Solomon. No, no time. She reached under her jacket for her gun as she emerged into a vacant plot of land strewn with litter and covered in grass bleached by the sun. She searched the debris with her eyes. Where was the woman?

Movement flashed. Not on the ground. Above her. *Oh, crap.* A screech ripped through the air.

She drew her gun, but too slow. Something black and feathered came crashing into her. Talons raked her cheek, tearing her mask and missing her eyes by an inch. She tried to turn her tumble into a roll, gritting her teeth against the pain that seared through her face.

Her gun was on the ground somewhere. *There!* She grabbed for it, but a huge, bird-like claw snatched at her arm. For the first time, she was able to get a clear look at what had attacked her.

The form of a lithe, naked woman crouched above her. Grey skin was littered with patches of unkempt feathers. Her legs and feet were almost human, muscular, but her arms were twisted and thin, with elbows that bent the wrong way. Each wrist ended in a set of talons. Now those talons grappled with Niobe, drawing blood wherever they touched. The woman was bald with a pointed nose, and when she opened her mouth to screech, she revealed a dry, pink tongue. A pair of black-feathered wings stretched from her shoulders, beating at the ground around Niobe.

No. It can't be her.

Niobe hesitated for a moment. Another claw raked at her, tearing her arm. That snapped her out of it. She kicked at the creature's stomach and rolled out of her grasp. A small bag dangled from the bird-woman's shoulder. *The camera.* Still on the ground, Niobe made a grab for it, but the woman swiped at her again with her talons. Her wings beat at the air with tremendous force, and the woman kicked Niobe's gun away as she struggled against the wind.

Clouds of dust flew up in Niobe's face. Her sunglasses and mask did nothing to stop the burning in her eyes. She stumbled back, groping for the wall, trying to maintain awareness of her surroundings. Something collided with her chest and she fell, gasping for breath. Her eyes were on fire. Where was her bloody gun? She felt at her belt for her mini-stunner while she pushed her glasses out of the way and tried to wipe the grit from her eyes.

The woman screeched once more, and the wind gusted up again. Niobe clambered to her feet, half-blind, certain that the woman was about to tear her throat out. *What a fucking stupid way to die.*

But the blow never came. The wind died away, and silence returned. When Niobe could finally see again, she was alone in the vacant lot. She searched the skies, but there was no sign of the bird-woman. Breathing heavily, and with her cheek and arm burning from the deep scratches, she found her gun, stumbled out of the alley, and headed back to the car.

Logically, she knew how close she just came to death. But as she walked, she could only think one thing.

They have my face.

CHAPTER 11

AN INSIDE JOB

BRIGHTLANCE

REAL NAME: *Edward Hardy*

POWERS: *Palm-fired energy beams.*

NOTES: *Hardy was offered membership in the Wardens in the early 1950s, but he preferred to remain independent, focussing on local crime-fighting. His relationship with the Wardens remained amicable, and he assisted them on several missions. When the Seoul Accord was passed, he tried to resist mandatory registration. In the ensuing battle with police he was shot three times and suffered a skull fracture from a blow to the head. While unconscious in hospital, he was fitted with a kill-switch. He remains in forced retirement.*

—Notes on selected metahumans [Entry #0820]

"You're an idiot," Solomon reminded her as he drove. "And I don't go throwing that word around. I keep it nice and safe like good china, ready to bring out for those occasions of extra-special idiocy."

Niobe scowled and dabbed at the scratches on her cheek with tissue paper. She'd requisitioned the rear-view mirror to see how bad the damage was. Three deep gouges ran from her ear to her chin. She'd only just got them to stop bleeding. After driving back to the Old City, she'd changed into her bodysuit and trench coat. Her jacket and blouse were a write-off. She'd never get the bloodstains out. *Oh Christ, how am I going to explain this to Gabby?*

"Thanks for the constructive criticism." She dipped the tissue paper in a bottle of antiseptic and touched it to the wounds. Bloody hell, it stung. "I'll stick it straight in my suggestions box."

"What the heck were you thinking?"

"I was working." What did they make this antiseptic out of, acid? "I was trying to get us closer to payday."

Solomon scoffed and shook his head. Like her, he was in costume apart from his mask and hat. Anyone glancing at the car would probably assume he was a man taking his young wife out for a drive. His cloak was pushed back over his shoulder, and both hands were gripped tight around the steering wheel as they made their way towards Neo-Auckland. "What's got into you, Spook? Why didn't you call me? You could've been hurt!"

"I *am* hurt."

"Exactly!" he said. "You got carved like a roast chicken and no one was there to back you up. Heroes have to work together."

She slapped a gauze pad from the first aid kit onto her cheek harder than she intended, and a new wave of pain shot through her face. "Should I call up the Wardens next time, then? Get the old gang together? That's what you want, right?"

His eyes narrowed, but his voice took on an infuriating calm, like a teacher scolding a foolish child. "I want us to keep doing what we chose to do. What we *have* to do. Wardens or not."

"You're delusional."

"Back then, we did what we did because of what was in here." He jabbed his chest with his finger. "Not because someone gave us permission. They took a lot of things from us. But this…" He pointed to his heart again. "…this is still here."

"Not for me." Niobe stared out the window as the suburbs of Neo-Auckland came into view. "You're the last damn hero, Carpenter. It's time to grow up and leave the fantasy behind."

They fell silent. The car rattled its particular rattles while Solomon guided it onto the upper highway. The green suburbs and brick houses stretched out below them as they headed for the centre of the city.

She shouldn't have snapped at him like that. There was just something about this case that had her on edge. Being inside Sam's head was part of it. She'd never felt that connected to anyone before. But it was more than that. Maybe Hine-nui-te-pō was right. There was something in the air. Met Div was stepping up its raids, Doll Face was alive and at large. Maybe the world really was about to end.

Her guilt grew in the tense silence, but she was spared from having to apologise when Solomon reached over, popped open the glove box, and handed her a paper bag from inside. "Lunch?"

The sandwich had three slices of bread, and it was stocked with lettuce, slices of boiled egg and tomato, roast beef, and a thick layer of butter. She was already devouring it by the time she remembered to offer her thanks.

"Did you see who jumped you?" he asked after a moment.

She nodded and swallowed. "It was Avin."

"Avin." He sounded skeptical.

"Avin," she confirmed.

"Bird-woman, doesn't fancy a lot of clothes, ugly as all get out?"

"How many metas named Avin do you know?"

He frowned. "She's one of us."

"I don't have any feathers."

"Har har. You know what I mean," he said. He looked like he'd taken a bite of an apple filled with cigarette butts.

She did know what he meant. Avin had been a Warden. Well, a reservist, more accurately, and only for a few months. She'd only done a couple of missions with them before she left and joined up with the Patrolmen. But still….

Niobe stared out the window. A rocket-postman was up early, delivering the mail to the upper floors of a nearby apartment building with the help of his backpack-mounted rocket engine. Niobe idly watched him work while she polished off the sandwich and picked the crumbs off her gloves.

"She was straddling the line even in the old days," she said. Last she heard, Avin had become a prominent member of the anti-Seoul Accord group Heroes for Freedom. Those were ugly days. More than once the group had made veiled threats against international legislators. "It's not a stretch that she'd go over to the bad guys."

Solomon didn't look convinced. "I talked to her once after she left us. It was a superhero conference. Great spread. You should've seen how many crayfish they had. It was when everyone was starting to get jumpy. She was fiery, sure, but she wasn't cut out to be the brainless sidekick of a two-bit supercriminal. Snatching kids? I don't see it."

To be honest, Niobe didn't either. Even in the old days, not many supercriminals did kidnapping gigs. Too risky. But things were tight for metas now. Maybe she got drawn in by money. It didn't ring true, but the scratches on Niobe's cheek didn't lie. And she had no sympathy for the woman. The bitch had her picture. She'd compromised her identity. Niobe had never liked her anyway.

They got off the highway in the central city and rode the exit down to the streets. All around, sleek towers of white and satin-red stretched to the sky. The moving footpaths were packed with shoppers, mostly fashionable young people. It was just after noon, so the cafés were crowded. Most of the cars that ambled down the street were new Japanese models. Still, their old Ford wasn't so unusual as to stand out. No one paid them any mind as they drove past and took the main road out to Metahuman Division headquarters.

Met Div had its own building a few blocks from the central police station. It was more functional than the city's commercial towers, just a simple, four storey orange-brick building. Behind it, a large section was fenced off for a car park. She could see Met Div vans peeking between the chain links and barbed wire as they approached. Most of the building's windows showed no movement. The division had slowly shrunk over the years as less and less supercrimes were committed and the metahuman population slowly succumbed to their new destiny.

While they drove past, Niobe checked the place over for any new security measures installed since her last visit, but nothing stood out. In any case, that was a worry to file away for later, like Avin's photo. For now she had to focus. Their meeting with Solomon's informant would be taking place in a local park, where the guy took his lunch breaks. It suited her fine. Meeting at a bar or restaurant brought all sorts of complications. At a park, you could get a bit of privacy and be certain no one was eavesdropping.

They pulled over in a secluded area, put on their masks and hats, and got out of the car. The park was big and densely populated with trees, and the monorail track only ran past the northern end. Niobe kept alert, but it wasn't difficult to make their way through the park without anyone spotting them. They'd attract less notice in civilian clothes, but she wasn't going to let anyone else get a look at her face today.

They found the cleaning guy on his usual bench, finishing off a sandwich. He was small and frail-looking, even though he was only in his early fifties. His hair and moustache were streaked with grey, and his skin had a dark tan to it. Maybe he had some Māori blood in him.

A smile broke across his face when he saw them approaching. Solomon returned the grin and they warmly shook hands. The man's narrow cheek twitched every few seconds. He had some sort of nervous disorder.

"Carpenter, Spook," he said. "Been too long."

"Sure has, Marvin," Solomon said.

At the man's gesture, they sat down next to him and faced the trees. A pair of sparrows bathed in the dust in front of them. Since this morning Niobe wasn't so fond of birds, but she pushed the irrational feelings aside.

"How's Sara?" Solomon asked.

Somehow, Marvin's smile got even wider. "She's great. Good as gold. She's at uni now, did I tell you?"

"You're kidding," Solomon said. He held his hand out about four feet off the ground. "She was only this big last time I saw her."

"Eighteen already. Studying to be a nurse, can you believe it?"

Niobe remained silent while they chatted. Marvin's daughter had got caught in a school fire along with a bunch of other kids back in the fifties. The Carpenter had been first on scene, beating the fire department by a good ten minutes. He never talked about it, but the old war stories always came out. It was the height of summer and the classrooms were all made of wood. The place went up like a gas oven. The

Carpenter broke down the door and went room to room, manipulating the burning wood to keep the ceilings from collapsing while he opened safe exits for the staff and kids. He'd gone in with only basic equipment, so he inhaled a lot of smoke and took a few nasty burns. He spent the next couple of days in hospital. But he got Sara and every other kid out safe.

"About this Julius kid," Solomon said after a couple of minutes. "Has anything come up?"

Marvin shook his head. "Not on our end. After you called, I managed to sneak a peek at the prisoner logs and transfer requests. No one younger than twenty-five. We don't have him."

"Could it be off-record?" Niobe asked. "Something too secret for the foot soldiers?"

"I don't think so," Marvin said. "Ol' Wallace is a hard-arse, but he's pretty straight-laced. I don't think he could keep something like that a secret."

"All right," Solomon said, "so maybe our kidnapper is a copper who found himself a part-time job. Moonlighting, you know? Using his uniform to give him credibility and get close enough to nab the kid."

Marvin shrugged. "Could be. Pay's not that flash for a sworn officer, considering the risks. I hear them sometimes, grumbling about it. It's getting worse lately. A bunch of them got knocked about in their last raid, so I hear. And it's not the only thing making them jumpy."

Once more, her mind was filled with the image of McClellan's super-stretched body hardening, his brains splattered over the concrete.

"Say," she said, a thought occurring to her, "No one's mentioned Avin lately, have they?"

He screwed up his face in thought, and his cheek twitched again. "Is that the harpy lady?"

"That's the one," Solomon said.

Marvin spread his hands and shook his head. "Not that I know of. I haven't heard that name in years."

Damn it. When were they going to catch a break?

There was a pause, and Niobe found herself thinking about Hine-nui-te-pō's words again. *Violence is coming*, she said. She wasn't wrong. Anyone could see the signs.

"You said the coppers have been getting nervous lately," she said. "What about?"

"You've seen the papers?" he asked. "This Doll Face thing has got every joker talking. There'd been rumours going around headquarters for a week or two before the story hit the news. Apparently this was no ordinary breakout. One of the guards survived. Said a meta named Quanta led the attack."

"Quanta?" She frowned and glanced at Solomon, but he shrugged and shook his head. The name didn't ring a bell.

"Yeah. The word is he attacked from a zeppelin."

"Bit theatrical, isn't it?" Solomon said.

Marvin nodded, twitching. "Thing is, the coppers in Thailand started picking up rumours of an airship near Bangkok a couple of weeks later. Some Thai farmers thought they saw it for a moment, but then it suddenly disappeared."

"Coincidence?" Solomon said.

"Not likely. And that's not the worst part."

He opened his mouth to say more, but the words seemed to be stuck in his throat. A gust of wind blew through, and the sparrows left their dust bath to flutter away.

"Don't string us along," Solomon said. "You know how I hate suspense."

Marvin's smile wasn't so big now, and something in his eyes made Niobe's stomach tense.

"I shouldn't know this," he said. "But I saw the report on Wallace's desk." He didn't seem to be able to keep his hands still. "There was another sighting of the airship a few days ago. A fisherman was out in his boat when he spotted it."

"Where?" Niobe said.

Marvin licked his lips. "The west coast. A few miles out from Muriwai. The coppers think it…they think it's…."

She met the Carpenter's eyes, and she saw the realisation go through him.

"He's here," she said.

Marvin nodded. Her spine turned to ice. Maybe it had nothing to do with Sam. Maybe it was nothing more than the rumours of over-excited farmers. Maybe. *Bloody hell, who am I kidding?* They weren't that lucky.

Doll Face was here. The Breaker of Souls, the Great Puppetmaster, he was in New Zealand. And he wasn't alone.

"Thank God you two are still around," Marvin said. He looked at the two of them, the tension draining from his face. "At least we still have heroes to protect us."

She tried to speak, but she'd forgotten how.

CHAPTER 12
And Now, A Message From Our Host

As in many Asian-Australasian Union member countries, the Metahuman Division (colloquially known as Met Div) of the NZ Police was formed in 1959 in response to increasing public concern around metahumans. Met Div is tasked with controlling metahuman activities and responding to superpowered threats, although their methods for doing so are controversial. The division operates outside traditional police structure and combines both investigative and response elements to form an almost entirely self-contained organisation. In recent years, many branches of Met Div have been downsized due to decreased resistance from the metahuman community. Today, one of Met Div's major roles is ensuring that all metahumans are registered and fitted with kill-switches if above a certain power level.

—Metahumans in New Zealand: Past to Present, Herbert Gutman

Morgan was finishing the briefing on the evening's upcoming raid when the right side of his vision went dark.

He paused in mid-sentence, facing the men and women who would be fighting alongside him tonight, and tried to get his heart rate under control. The air was stuffy in the requisitioned warehouse. He blinked, hoping the black splotch would go away. It didn't.

"My lord?" Obsidian said in a low voice. She stood beside him; as his second-in-command, she would be in charge of securing the building's perimeter and dealing with any external threats. Her sharp, stony face betrayed nothing, but her eyes dimmed.

It had come on so suddenly. He didn't even have a headache at the moment, and the pills were controlling his seizures. How was he supposed to fight with this blind spot in his vision? *Damn it all!* His gloved hands curled into fists. He could feel sweat dripping from his forehead and rolling around the corners of his domino mask.

Perception is all that matters.

"This is not going to be like Siberia," he said to the group, channelling his anger into his voice. "Our target is easier, yes, but do not let your guard down. We are in a city that is hostile to us. Any counterattacks will be rapid. Those of you holding the perimeter will need to be prepared. You cannot fail."

He stared at them, trying to ignore the black spot, but his mind was already calculating scenarios in which it would be a fatal weakness. Why now, of all times?

"Make your preparations," he said. "We leave in an hour."

The metas bowed as one and wandered away, chatting and joking with one another. Only Obsidian remained at his side. He turned his back on her and faced the maps and building blueprints he'd marked with routes and extraction points. The spot was like a black ghost, haunting him. Every time he tried to look at it directly, it shifted away. It was infuriating.

Obsidian shifted her weight and the floor rumbled. "My lord—"

"It's nothing," he said.

"Very well." She paused. "Avin approaches, my lord."

Avin? Oh, the harpy. He turned to find the naked bird-woman making her way towards him. Her wings were folded around her shoulders, but they were still tall enough to brush the top of the doorway. The feathers weren't enough to cover her flat breasts. She walked unnaturally, like she was unused to it, and her twisted arms gave her a somewhat demonic appearance.

She stopped before him, and gave a small bow of her bald head. That was enough for him; his people didn't need to treat him like a god. The "lord" business was all Obsidian's doing. It was only important that they believed what he believed. Or that they knew little enough of the darker parts of his plan that they didn't actively oppose him.

Wordlessly, the woman passed him a pair of enlarged colour photographs, each about the size of a leaf of legal paper. He forced himself to ignore the black spot and focussed on the pictures instead. "This is the woman?"

"Yes."

The pictures seemed to have been taken a few seconds apart. They both showed a short Asian woman—he couldn't narrow down her race any further by sight—dressed in an unfashionable jacket and blouse and wearing a pair of large sunglasses. She wasn't pretty, really, but she was a long way from hideous. In the first picture she was stepping off a boat onto the marina walkway, and in the second she was lighting a cigarette and staring directly at the camera.

"Do you recognise her?" he asked.

"I didn't at first," Avin said. Her voice was sharp, almost painful to listen to. "But the way she fought reminded me of someone I worked with once. A Warden called Gloomgirl."

"A Warden?" He stroked his chin. *Interesting.* He didn't realise there were any Wardens still around. He vaguely remembered the hero's alias, but he couldn't recall anything else about her. He studied the photos closer. "Do you know her real name?"

Avin shook her head. "She was always careful, more careful than the others."

"What was your impression of her?"

"She was a frigid bitch. Always had to do things her own way. I'm not surprised she was there alone."

"And how did she act this morning, before she saw you?"

Avin shrugged. "Calm. Careful. She took her time, scoped out the place. I didn't see where she came from, but she must've had a car somewhere. She was on the boat for one hour and twenty-two minutes. What she did there, I have no idea."

Interesting. Morgan had posted Avin and two other metas there on rotating shifts on the off chance the boy's uncle showed up. Instead, he had this mystery woman.

"Did she use any powers?" he asked.

"No. If it's who I think it is, she's a shadow-shifter. But either way, she's well-equipped. The gun she pulled on me wasn't stock, and she had a mask on by the time she came after me. I would probably have had to kill her if I stayed to fight."

A friend of Frank Julius's? Unlikely. Maybe she was just working with him. But in what capacity? Mercenary? Or hero? The question intrigued him. He'd expected that if anyone came after him this quickly, it would be Frank Julius himself.

He touched a gloved finger to his cheek. "You did well. I know you didn't want to kill anyone. I don't either. Moral quandaries aside, her body would have been a complication we could do without." He passed the pictures back to her. "I want you to work with the research team. See what you can find out about her. A name would be a good start."

"Why?"

"You seem to know more about her than anyone here. And she intrigues me. I like to know all the variables."

The muscles of her wings rippled, and she jerked a nod. Without another word or gesture, she turned and left.

So someone was following the breadcrumbs. It wouldn't be a problem. Things were in motion now that couldn't be stopped. But perhaps the metas here weren't as downtrodden as they first appeared. The ones his people had picked out to aid them had been like tightly wound springs, just waiting for someone to lift the weight from their shoulders so they could jump into the fray.

That reminded him of something. "This Avin," he said to Obsidian. "She doesn't know everything, does she?"

"No, my lord."

He nodded. "Have her watched while she tracks down the Asian woman. Just as a precaution."

Obsidian bowed and left Morgan to his thoughts. He turned back to the maps, imprinting them on his memory. Always, the black spot stayed in his vision. It wasn't that terrible a disability, he supposed. And he probably wouldn't have to deal with it for long. If his plan didn't kill him, the tumour would.

So be it.

———•———

At 9:37 p.m., a white van screeched to a halt in the centre of Neo-Auckland. Morgan jumped from the passenger side. All around him, metas unloaded from the four vans that arrived seconds later. They were all dressed in their respective costumes; a dizzying array of clashing styles and colours. None bore firearms. He'd chosen them for their skill with their powers alone.

Other cars came skidding along the road, blaring their horns. A few passers-by gasped, eyes wide. The area was heavily trafficked even at this hour. An unfortunate fact. With luck, none of his people would need to kill anyone. But luck was a fickle whore, and he never relied on it.

By the time night had fallen, he'd adapted his fighting style to cope with the vision impairment. As long as he kept his eyes moving and kept up his guard to the right, he didn't anticipate any serious issues. Even so, he'd transferred control of the prisoner over to Haze and Screecher.

It was strange. He still had the same fluttering in his stomach every time he had to fight.

"Let it begin," he said, and the metas moved into action. The ones who had been involved in Siberia were calmer this time around. Many of them had been in supercombat in the past, so they were familiar with matters of violence. Now they were getting back into the groove. He just prayed that confidence didn't become cockiness.

Tinderbox clapped his hands, and the street around the vans burst into flames. The heat scorched Morgan's face, but he didn't flinch. Civilians screamed. The street was filled with movement as people fled, shielding their faces. The flame chased them, licking at their heels, until it reached the opposite side of the street and exploded through a jewellery store window. Somewhere, a fire alarm screeched.

Obsidian and her team were already fanning around the building ahead of them. A pair of fliers took to the skies as watchmen. When the Police Metahuman Division responded, the fliers would know.

The TVNZ studio was almost quaint. It had the same tacky design as the rest of the Neo-Auckland towers, but it was diminutive compared to the commercial office buildings that surrounded it. The size was unimportant. By morning, the world would know his name.

They would remember what they had forgotten. And they would tremble.

"Bring the prisoner!" he boomed over the roar of Tinderbox's fire. Haze gave a half-hearted salute and disappeared into the centre van along with Screecher. Navigatron had outfitted all the vans with simple armour and engine modifications in case a swift exit was needed. The centre van also had a folding ramp that extended on a hydraulic mechanism. A moment later, Haze and Screecher emerged, dragging a wide cage on wheels. The bars crackled with the purple sheen of a Unity Corporation shielding system. William Hayne, the great Iron Justice, sat folded up inside, howling.

Morgan's earpiece hissed to life. "Secure, my lord," a voice said.

"Thank you, Obsidian," he said. He turned to the others and raised his voice. "With me!"

His team whooped and broke into a run. He kept pace with them, eyes fixed on the building's double glass doors.

Sand Fury fired a high-powered blast of sand from the glowing centre of his chest. The doors crumpled inwards against the onslaught. For a moment, the shattered glass sparkled under the light of the entrance-way, and then a cloud of dust obscured everything.

Morgan was second through the broken doorway. The building's layout was imprinted on his memory, so he had no need to slow. He brought up his shield and blade. He didn't expect resistance, but he was nothing if not cautious. Besides, if someone was watching, he wanted them to understand what he could do.

A single security guard was in the lobby, struggling to extricate himself from a pile of sand. The eyes of a pretty blond receptionist peeked over the sleek metallic desk. The dilated pupils fixed on him, then she ducked down out of sight and offered a pitiful moan.

Morgan swept his blade of light down in an arc that stopped an inch from the security guard's throat. The man swallowed and immediately stopped moving. Sand enveloped his legs and lower torso.

"Are you armed?" Morgan asked him.

He shook his head rapidly.

"I believe you," Morgan said. He swung a light-covered fist. It connected with the side of the man's head, and a cry left his mouth before he slumped, unconscious.

Without being asked, Sand Fury closed his eyes and arched his back. The centre in his chest glowed again, and he sucked the sand back towards himself. The grains bounced against Morgan's light shield in a miniature sandstorm, and then as quickly as it had been filled, the lobby was free of sand.

Haze and Screecher pushed in the cage with the shouting Hayne, followed by the two other metas in his team. Hayne's words were unintelligible. Every few seconds, the huge man would pound his fists against the glowing sides of the cage, to no avail. He'd long since given up trying to form the metal skin that gave him his superhero alias. Every time he did, the shields on the cage would deliver a strong electric shock to him. Crude, but effective. Morgan had modified the Unity Corporation technology himself. Everyone needed a hobby.

He could hear shouts and stamping feet from the floors above. The building was filled with a restless energy. No doubt they'd already discovered that the fire exits were barred by Obsidian and her crew. Did any of them understand what was happening?

He jabbed the lift call button, and the doors slid open with the ring of a bell. They loaded Hayne's cage in first and crammed in around it. Morgan pressed the button for the eighth floor.

"You goddamn son of a bitch!" Hayne shouted. "I'll make this place your grave, you hear me?

Morgan ignored him.

"You made a tactical error, coming here," Hayne continued. "This building's a death trap."

Morgan straightened his white suit and watched the numbers on the elevator dial count up. "We know our exits."

"Ha! Exits! We stomped little fucks like you into the ground three times a week back in my day. They're gonna come for you, and I'm gonna make sure you don't get no cushy prison cell."

Morgan spun and slammed his fist against the bars. Blood pounded in his head, and his lips peeled back in a snarl. "No one's going to come. No one. You and your precious heroes let the world walk all over you. Now there's no one. No one but me."

Hayne must have seen something in his eyes, because he backed away in his cage. Turning away, Morgan forced himself to breathe. *What was that?* The rage had come from nowhere. The red mist still lingered at the corners of his consciousness. Since the day of the protest at Cambridge, he always held himself in check. Cold logic kept him alive. *I can't get emotional. Not now.*

A bell dinged, and the elevator doors slid open. The studio lights were on, aimed at the news desk on the far side of the room. Crew members screamed and hammered on the fire exit doors. It did them no good. One of the newsreaders—a middle-aged woman in a red jacket—was the only person that hadn't fled her post. She spoke rapidly into the unmanned cameras.

"They have reached the studio. There appears to be four, no, five of them. Ladies and gentlemen, if you're just joining us, our building has been attacked by what appears to be a team of supercriminals. We can only pray that this broadcast is still transmitting, and that the police are on their way. God save us all."

Morgan let his blade and shield fade, and drew light around himself to make his body glow. He strode from the elevator, taking his time, and looked into the eyes of everyone with the courage to meet his gaze.

Perception is all that matters.

"My name is Quanta," he said. Silence fell in the room, and all eyes turned to him. He let an easy smile cross his face. "I have a message for the people of Earth."

CHAPTER 13

GENTLY, GENTLY

IRON JUSTICE

REAL NAME: *William Hayne*

POWERS: *Super strength, able to transform skin into metal armour. Metal skin renders him impervious to small arms and low-grade explosions.*

NOTES: *Reported to have survived several direct hits from the Astral Bomber. Faced numerous accusations of physical and sexual assault, but was never formally charged. Left the Manhattan Eight under a cloud of controversy.*

—Notes on selected metahumans [Entry #0003]

Night fell on Neo-Auckland. Niobe stubbed out her cigarette in the car ashtray, readjusted her mask, and switched her goggles to high contrast.

"Play it clean, mate," the Carpenter said. He pulled his own mask into place and put on his wide-brimmed hat. He couldn't come with her; there was no way to get him inside without bringing all of Met Div down on them. He'd be on the outside, guarding her escape.

"Always do," she said. She wouldn't be stupid this time. No one would get another look at her face.

The side road they'd parked in was nearly empty, so she pushed open the door and got out. The Carpenter leaned over and stuck his head out the window. "Did I ever tell you you look like Rick Blaine in that coat?"

"Rick who?"

"From *Casablanca*."

She shrugged.

"You haven't seen *Casablanca*?" He affected an American accent. "'Louis, I think this is the beginning of a beautiful friendship.' That doesn't ring a bell?"

She turned away, shoved her hands in her pockets, and slipped silently across the road. She didn't have time for Solomon's nonsense.

His voice called out after her. "'Of all the gin joints in all the towns in all the world, she walks into mine.'"

With a shake of her head, she disappeared into the shadows and made her way down the alley to the rear of Met Div headquarters.

Time was ticking away, and they were no closer to finding Sam. If this was a simple kidnapping, she wouldn't be so worried. Kidnappers who wanted ransom generally didn't let harm come to their captives. But something weird was going on here, and every day that passed decreased the chances they'd ever find him alive. If they found him at all.

Bloody hell, she needed another cigarette.

The fenced-off car park at the back of the headquarters was deserted. Behind the chain-link fence, cars and vans were lined up in neat rows. She stayed in the shadows and watched for a moment, then something caught her eye. A little white box perched on the brick wall above the rear door. No, not a box. A video camera. That was new.

She touched the side of her goggles and increased the contrast to its maximum, then tried to gauge the camera's line of sight. It looked out over the car park, probably to stop the division's vehicles being pinched. But there was a blind spot directly beneath it. Too easy.

She breathed in a lungful of air, held it, and pulled darkness around her. The world flattened out as her body slid into a puddle on the concrete. The rough surface of the alley pressed against her, and her thoughts became flat.

She slipped through the gaps in the fence and sped silently along the dark ground. There weren't many lights around, but it was still more comfortable to move under the cars, using their shade. As she moved, she became aware of the shadows of cape coppers moving in the building's windows. Met Div headquarters were never completely deserted, so she'd have to be cautious. Always cautious.

Her shadow form slid up the three stairs at the rear exit and stopped in the darkness beneath the camera. Releasing her breath, she reformed her body and looked around, letting herself readjust to three dimensions. With a glance at the camera to make sure it couldn't see her, she pressed her ear to the door. Silence. The door was heavy and well-sealed at the edges to protect against gas attacks—no one had forgotten Colonel Mustard's assault on the New South Wales Met Div back in '61. Unfortunately for Niobe, it also left no room for a shadow to slip under. She pulled her pick set from her jacket pocket and worked the torsion wrench and pick into the lock. Eyes closed, she let the tips of her fingers fade into shadow and dance along the length of the tools. A hazy picture of the surface of the lock's pins formed in her mind, adding to the tactile sensations as she jiggled the pick.

She worked the pins as swiftly as she dared. Her heart maintained a steady rhythm, keeping her alert. She'd broken in here before, but it sure as hell wasn't a cakewalk. Even at night, the hallways were lit and coffee-fuelled coppers huddled over paperwork. Luckily, the higher-ups pulled rank, leaving many of the offices dark and empty after nightfall. If she had to hide, they were her best shot.

The pins gave in to her touch, and she smiled into the darkness. With a twist of the torsion wrench, the lock clicked and the door opened a crack. She returned the tools to her pocket, checked through the crack for any coppers roaming the hallways, and slipped inside.

Her shoes made no sound on the tile floor. The clatter of typewriter keys drifted from somewhere ahead, along with the mutter of quiet conversation. Nothing to concern her. So why was she so nervous? *Play it clean.*

She'd memorized the building's layout years ago. Briefly, she considered checking the prisoner manifests to confirm what Marvin told them, but decided against it. Prisoner records were kept in the south wing, near the cells. Security was tight there; never less than three armed cape coppers on duty at a time, according to standard protocol.

Breaking in wasn't impossible, but she needed to keep attention away from her investigations. If Met Div really was responsible for the kid's abduction, she'd rather they didn't know she was coming.

That left the archives for her to investigate. The basement it was, then. Sticking to the wall, she made her way quickly down the hallway to the stairs. She kept both hand in her jacket pockets to stop herself reaching for her gun.

A copper wandered past the hallway ahead of her, facing away from her and gripping a mug of coffee like his life depended on it. Niobe drew still, pressing herself into the corner. The copper wandered on without so much as glancing at her. When he passed, she pulled open the door to the stairwell and made her way downstairs.

Even now in the beginnings of summer, the basement of the building was cold. She emerged into the dark of the archives, surrounded on all sides by row upon row of filing cabinets and file boxes. From the looks of it, the archives had started out as one large hall, but it had spilled over into the accompanying rooms. Offices and supply rooms had been commandeered as the number of meta-related cases soared in the early sixties. File boxes of old case reports were stacked nearly to the ceiling. But from the dust in the air, she'd bet most of them were at least five years old.

She was alone down here; no one guarded the archives. The clerk who tended the records would've gone home at five o'clock. *I wonder what that's like,* she thought.

She pulled the torch from her utility belt and swung the beam of light around the room. Her footsteps came quiet on the concrete floor as she walked back and forth through the rows. After a few minutes, her torch beam came to rest on a bank of filing cabinets behind the clerk's desk. She moved closer to read the labels. It took her another minute, but then she found what she was looking for. *Officers - Active.*

She picked the lock on the cabinet with ease and flipped through the files one by one, shining her light on the photograph paperclipped to the first page of each folder. If he looked like he might have the strong build of the man from her vision, she pulled the file out and examined it in detail. Each folder had a brief summary of basic information: DOB, height, weight, race, nationality. No need for gender. Every copper was male.

It took her nearly forty-five minutes to go through the files. For each "maybe", she compared the print she'd picked up on the boat to the fingerprint card inside the folder. On the fourth one she pulled out, she found him.

The guy's name was Daniel O'Connor. Caucasian, 44 years old, New Zealander. In the photograph, he sported long sideburns that didn't suit his square face, and two cauliflower ears. His expression was hard, cold. Whoever had done the original inking on the fingerprinting was sloppy, but there was no doubt the two matched. She had her man.

She'd give the file a proper look later, but something bothered her about it. A flip through revealed the same basic forms she'd seen in the other folders—tax records, recruitment scores, his original CV, payroll form—but it was still lighter than the others. She pulled out another file to compare. O'Connor's had no mention of cases or operations he'd worked on. No arrest records. No commendations or accident reports. No recent evaluations.

She frowned, her mask rubbing painfully against the scratches on her cheek. A cover-up? If so, it was sloppy. Why not just take the whole file and be done with it?

As she returned the comparison file to the cabinet, the beam of her torch swept over something at the base of the metal drawer. A leaf of yellow paper poked out from below the rows of folders. She tucked O'Connor's folder under her arm and retrieved the loose piece of paper.

Daniel O'Connor: suspended from active duty, the typewritten letter read. She swept the light down. *Operational reports to be delivered to Senior Sergeant Raymond Wallace and CCed to Internal Affairs.*

The signature was an unreadable scrawl. No date, but it wasn't old or faded. The paper had probably slipped out when the clerk put it back in the cabinet.

"Bloody hell," she murmured. If she was back in the Carpenter's precious golden age, she'd be able to get her hands on this sort of info easy. You didn't say no to the Wardens. Not because they were power-ful. Because they got shit done.

She pushed up the bottom of her mask and breathed in a lungful of dusty air. The name was something, she supposed. There were people who could look into these things. Maybe the copper's suspension had something to do with all this, or maybe he was just generally crooked, and now that he had no job, he found other ways to pay the mortgage.

Bugger it. She tugged the mask down again, slid O'Connor's folder into her trench coat, and closed the filing cabinet. The floors above creaked with footsteps. She kept her ear trained on the stairwell, ready to descend into shadow if someone came, but there was nothing. She couldn't hang around here forever, though.

She made her way through the main stacks, where evidence and case reports were collected, to the metahuman records. She'd had to come here once a couple of years back, to get a lead on a shapeshifter who was blackmailing a local politician with some "sensitive pictures". She had a look the photos before she gave them to the politician. She'd never figured the old guy would be able to bend like that.

Unlike the search for O'Connor, it was a piece of piss to find Avin's file. Out of convenience, metas were listed by primary alias rather than name, since so many metas had kept their identities secret. Avin's file was thicker than O'Connor's. She flipped through reports and newspa-per clippings from the old days. Like Niobe, Avin wasn't officially regis-tered, and no kill-switch frequency was recorded. No reports from the last couple of years. That wasn't unusual; even Met Div couldn't keep tabs on every meta. It was another pain in the arse though.

She glanced through the summary sheet, searching for a last known address.

Alias: Avin

Real name: Unknown

DOB: Unknown

Powers: Flight (winged), enhanced strength, intrinsic weapons (talons), enhanced vision (unconfirmed)

Affiliated Organisations: Wardens (disbanded), Patrolmen

(disbanded), Heroes for Freedom (disbanded)
Known associates: Kid Arrow, Blue Shaman, Screecher

No address, but those were names she hadn't heard for a while. Kid Arrow was definitely part of Heroes for Freedom. The little bugger always had an obnoxious one-liner for the papers. As for the other two heroes listed, she wasn't sure.

She pulled files on all three of Avin's known associates. According to the files, Blue Shaman was sleeping the big sleep after getting hit with leukaemia. Kid Arrow had gone to the lunar colony, and Screecher was presumed dead.

She tucked Avin's file into her coat along with Kid Arrow's and Screecher's. Her trench coat was getting heavy, and the corner of the folder poked into her when she twisted. But that wasn't nearly as frustrating as hitting another dead end. *What the hell is it with this case?* Everything was a black hole of information.

On a whim, she consulted the file index and tried to find something on Frank Julius. Nothing. She'd been expecting that—the name was almost certainly fake—but it was worth a shot.

She turned to leave, then paused. She was running low on time, but she went back to the "D"s. She searched the whole row, found nothing, and searched it again. *Where's Doll Face's file?* Doll Face hadn't ever been sighted in New Zealand, but he was high-profile enough to warrant a file. Hell, he was high-profile enough to warrant a whole bloody police division. She checked with the index and confirmed it should be there. A date was pencilled in beside the index entry—three days ago—along with someone's initials. RW. *Raymond Wallace,* she thought. She wondered if the bastard had felt the floor drop out from under him like she had when she learned Doll Face was in the country.

She checked her watch. Half an hour until the evening shift left and the late nighters came along. She'd like to be out before then, when everyone would be moving around. But she had time, didn't she?

She chewed her lip and tapped her watch with her gloved finger. *Bugger it. I'm here anyway. Let's see what Senior Sergeant Wallace knows.*

———◆———

Wallace's office was on the top floor. She had to waste eight minutes getting there, avoiding the coppers that roamed the halls like caged lions. The lock on his door was solid, but that couldn't stop her turning to shadow and sliding underneath.

Like all the other offices on the top floor, it was empty. She switched on her torch and gave the room a quick sweep with the beam. It was big, but it seemed to be wasted on Wallace. No pictures on the walls, no pot plants, no decorations of any kind. A set of blinds covered the window on the back wall, but it must have had a good view of the Old City. Somehow, she couldn't imagine him ever enjoying the sights.

She padded softly over the carpet to the utilitarian desk. Except for a couple of chairs and a set of the ubiquitous filing cabinets, the desk was the only piece of furniture in the room. All his paperwork sat in neat piles, and for the first time in her life she came across an outbox that was more full than the inbox. If he had a family, there was no picture. Neither was there a memento of his service in the war. With the scar on his scalp and the bullet wound in his arse, maybe he didn't need anything else.

A strangely shaped machine had pride of place next to the telephone. It looked kind of like a cash register, but when she rounded the desk to get a better look at it, she saw it had a small glass screen set into it and a full keyboard, like a typewriter. A Unity Corporation logo was stamped on top.

It's a computer, she realised. She'd never seen one outside a supercriminal's lair before, and those had been a hundred times the size of this one. She recalled hearing that Unity Corp had been racing to ship personal computers before their competitors caught up. But what was the point in it? Probably just a way for Met Div to blow some more taxpayer money.

She tore her eyes from the machine and checked her watch. Twenty minutes until she wanted to be gone. Maybe the computer was full of interesting information, but she didn't have a clue how to get it out. Didn't these things work on punch cards or something? She had no choice but to ignore it and deal with any information she could find in paper.

Doll Face's file was the first thing she found. It actually consisted of three thick manila folders bound together with rubber bands. She unbound the first folder and glanced through. A slideshow of horror greeted her. Crime scene after crime scene was described in meticulous detail, followed by transcripts of interviews with victims. She wrinkled her nose and snapped the rubber bands back in place. She could take the file, but none of the information appeared to be new. The pages ended with Doll Face's supposed death in Ukraine. That wouldn't help her now.

Fifteen minutes. She slipped Doll Face's file back into the pile and continued searching. O'Connor's information wasn't on the desk. She picked the lock on the desk drawer and started rummaging.

She got a glimpse of O'Connor's name under a sheaf of departmental forms when a floorboard creaked in the hall outside.

Her breath caught. She snatched the papers from the drawer, crammed them into her inside pocket, and switched off the torch. Inside, her blood ran cold, but she kept moving.

The shadow of feet appeared in the crack beneath the door, and someone ran a key into the lock. Niobe checked behind the blinds, but the window was sealed, not made for opening. Even as a shadow, she couldn't pass through glass. Shit. The bare office left nowhere for her to hide. Double shit.

She inhaled and held her breath as the doorknob turned. The room's shadow swallowed her and drew her down. The door opened silently, and a panel of dull light leaked in. She fled along the floor away from it, making for the corners. She slipped up along the wall and dropped back down to the floor a few feet behind the figure that entered the room.

A moment before he flipped the light switch, she exhaled and left the shadow. She resisted the urge to suck in air like she'd been trapped underwater.

The orange glow of the light bulb filled the room, and she touched the contrast control on her goggles and blinked against the sudden glare. Simultaneously, she drew the revolver from under her coat and kicked the office door closed behind the man.

"Evening, Senior Sergeant," she said, cocking the gun. The click of cold metal reverberated through the room, and Wallace's breathing stilled. She stayed a couple of feet away from him, but kept the barrel aimed squarely at his back.

This was the closest she'd ever been to the man, and the first time she'd spoken to him. A faint scent of cologne clung to his clothes, but mostly she smelled Wallace's sweat, built up over a long day. He looked even gruffer in person than he did from a distance. He was short enough that she could clearly make out the white scar tissue cutting through his thick brown hair.

He half-turned towards her, arms to his side. He didn't move his muscled arms to the 9mm at his belt. Smart guy. He was in the blue Met Div uniform, minus the helmet, with the tunic buttoned up to his thick neck.

She spun together something that might pass for a plan. She should've left straight after the archives, but there wasn't anything she could do about that now. "Away from the door," she said, waving her gun. Her hands were steady despite the adrenaline pounding through her. "I'll be outta your hair soon. I figured you'd gone home. Burning the midnight oil, eh?"

He edged towards the centre of the room where she directed him. His jaw was clenched, and his moustache quivered. For a moment, they stared at each other, then his eyes narrowed. "You're the one who attacked my men." It wasn't a question.

She thought back to the coppers she'd chained to the apartment building stairwell after they tried to drag the McClellan widow downtown. "I didn't attack anyone. We just had a disagreement on what constituted lawful detainment."

"Lawful…?!" A muscle in his neck twitched. "Do you have any idea what you'll get for threatening officers?"

"I threatened people trying to abduct an innocent woman."

"The woman violated international law, hiding that child. We were obligated to bring her in." His voice was like gravel. "Now get that gun out of my face."

The bull of a man took a step forwards, and the vein pulsing in his forehead looked like it might blow at any minute.

"Easy, Senior Sergeant." The last thing she wanted was to shoot the bastard, stun rounds or not.

"What do you want? I'm a shit hostage, if that's what you're after. I'm just a bloody civil servant. Or is this supposed to be some kind of vigilante justice?"

"All I want is information for a job."

His face twisted into a scowl. "Shove it up your arse."

It's like trying to reason with a gorilla. She fought down a sigh. "You hear of any kids being nabbed lately?"

"What do I look like, Missing Persons? I'm a cape copper."

She studied his face, but it revealed nothing but anger. Beneath her mask, she chewed her lip, then made a decision. "The kid was grabbed by one of your boys. Daniel O'Connor. Know him?"

A pause. "No."

She pulled the handful of crumpled papers from her pocket. "Then why's his name stamped over all this crap I found in your desk?"

His lips formed a line, and he said nothing. The son of a bitch wasn't going to hang one of his people out to dry. It was always the same with ex-military guys. Like a goddamn old boys' club.

"Tell me something else then. What's going on with Doll Face?"

His scowl managed to get even deeper.

The building's intercom system crackled to life, and Niobe almost had a heart attack. *Easy*, she told herself.

"All officers to briefing room one," the intercom said. "Six eighty-five in progress. Repeat: all staff to briefing room one." A hiss of static, then silence.

She didn't take her eyes from Wallace, but her mind tried to decipher the police code. *Hostage situation involving metahumans.* Was that right?

She opened her mouth to confirm it with the Senior Sergeant, but a red light blinked twice on the inside of her goggles. A signal from the Carpenter.

Keeping her gun on Wallace, she dropped her free hand and depressed a button on her belt. "Go ahead."

"Spook, you wanna see this," the Carpenter said through the radio.

"Kind of in the middle of something," she said. Wallace's glare was almost painful.

"Postpone it. I got a feeling you'll be pissed if you miss this."

"Roger," she said, and she released the button.

Wallace licked his lips. She could see every muscle in his body quivering with rage. "I'll get you," he said.

"Not today."

She brought the gun up and fired.

The light bulb shattered, and darkness flooded the room. She caught the sound of metal sliding free of a leather holster, but she'd already drawn darkness around her.

She fled under the door and reformed on the other side. No doubt the gunshot would've been heard throughout the building. She needed an exit, fast.

The door crashed open behind her, and the floor creaked under Wallace's weight. Without slowing, she blew out another light bulb, slipped back into shadow, and fled into another office. Shouts and footsteps reverberated against the surface she travelled along.

She came out of shadow still gripping her gun. With a flick of a switch on the modified cylinder, the revolver hissed and clicked. Live rounds armed.

Still running, she pointed the gun at the window and squeezed the trigger twice. Glass shattered and the blinds shuddered. Her ears rang with the sound of the shots. Once more she inhaled, and then she was a shadow again, slipping over the broken shards of glass and out onto the rough brick surface of the building's outer wall.

She didn't stop when she reached the ground. She was on the wrong side of the building, so she skirted away from the streetlights and fled around the rear of the building. Met Div officers scrambled to their vehicles in the car park. Were all of them searching for her? *No, something else is going on. The hostage situation.*

She kept going, darkness pressing in on her. She was staying in shadow too long. Too long without air. Her senses dimmed.

Finally, she emerged from the alley, back onto the street where Solomon had parked. Her lungs burned as she reformed herself, and she gulped down air. *Too close.*

She holstered her gun, checked her pockets to make sure she had all the files she'd grabbed, and touched the brim of her bowler hat to confirm it was still in place. Where was Solomon? She stayed in the shelter of the alley and scanned the street.

He pulled up a moment later. With another glance around to make sure the coppers weren't following, she dashed from the alley and into the car.

"This better be good," she said, pulling off her mask and goggles and wiping the sweat from her forehead.

The Carpenter peeled away from the side of the road. Sirens filled the air, but they were getting further away, not closer. He flipped open a panel in the centre of the dashboard and switched on the small television concealed there. "Take a look."

The television hummed, and a black-and-white picture expanded to fill the screen. She was about to ask him what channel to switch to, but saw there was no need.

The picture showed the local newscaster's desk at the TVNZ studio, but the man who sat and smiled at the camera was no news presenter. He wore an unusual suit jacket so white it was almost blinding. A few patches of pale skin disfigured his face, disappearing behind a black domino mask. Objectively, she supposed he had the sort of sculpted features that could be considered handsome, but the cold eyes that stared out at her would freeze the hormones of any horny schoolgirl.

He seemed to be reaching the pinnacle of some rousing speech. His accent was faintly British, but it was tainted with so many others she couldn't pick out a region.

"So here we are, in the world you people so desired." His smile was flat, painted on. "The people who used to protect you lie in gutters, drinking wine from paper bags. A generation of superheroes lie in unmarked graves. And the only ones left, the only ones who could save you, live hundreds of thousands of miles away on the surface of the Moon. The only place they could escape your persecution."

Outside the car, the night was lit with flashing police lights. A pair of police vehicles tore past, sirens screaming. Solomon drove quietly past an appliance store, where late-night pedestrians crowded around the televisions in the store window.

"He's been going like this for five minutes," Solomon said, eyes fixed on the road. "Guess what he calls himself?"

She'd already guessed. "Quanta."

"Right on, little lady."

Whoever was wielding the camera was either an amateur or scared out of their skull. It shifted constantly, altering focus and moving Quanta out of the centre of the frame. As it moved, she caught glimpses of other costumed figures in the background. They were shifting something into position. One of the metas caught her eye. A skinny man in a skin-tight suit came into view, a visor covering his face. A pattern of sea-green waves shifted along the surface of the fabric.

"Does that look like Screecher to you?" she asked.

Solomon glanced at the TV. "Hey, yeah, maybe. What's he hanging out with these wackos for?"

She chewed her lip. The file said Avin knew Screecher, and here he was. Too many coincidences. "These are our people. They've got Sam. They've got my picture."

He shot her a look, then returned his attention to the road and shook his head slightly. "We sure can pick 'em, huh?"

Quanta folded his gloved hands on the desk and smiled his dead smile. "My demands are simple. First, all incarcerated metahumans in the Asian-Australasian Union are to be released. All such metahumans are invited to seek me out and join me. You will be richly rewarded for your service. Failure on the part of the AAU to comply with this demand within thirty-six hours would be unwise. Needless to say, the civilian death toll would be significant."

"Can you believe this guy?" the Carpenter said. "I'm getting all nostalgic here. He's playing all the old classics."

Niobe didn't take her eyes from the screen. Something about this guy was off. His words didn't gel with the look in his eyes.

She could hear the faint wail of sirens from the TV now. Quanta didn't take any notice of them. "I have another request to make. I'm looking for a man, someone very important to me. He is currently calling himself Frank Julius."

Solomon grunted, and Niobe's grip tightened on the mask in her hands. *Oh, bloody hell.*

"Frank," Quanta said, "if you're listening, and I'm sure you are, I want you to seek me out. I know you've lost something precious to you. It's safe." *For now*, his smile seemed to add. "All you have to do is return to the place you lost it. I'll find you there. Or you can try to find me another way. If you stay in hiding, however...." He turned his hands palm up and shrugged. "Well, I think I can show you."

He stood, and the camera clumsily tracked him as he moved to the side of the newscaster's desk. In the background, the television studio's crew and presenters huddled, watched by a metahuman in desert camouflage. But the camera continued to track, and a darker sight came into view.

A huge, musclebound man with a pug-nosed face sat cramped inside a cage that crackled with energy. He glared at Quanta as the super-criminal crouched beside the cage. Quanta's pure white suit stood in stark contrast to the huge man's sweat-stained shirt.

"Tell them your name," Quanta said.

"Go fuck yourself, cocksucker," the giant man growled.

Morgan didn't react except to press a button on a panel on the side of the cage. Lightning arced inside the cage, and the man screamed.

"Jesus Christ," Niobe said. She could hear Solomon grinding his teeth together.

Quanta released the button. The screams were replaced by moans.

"Tell them," he said.

The man seemed to be having trouble breathing. "Hayne. Name's Will Hayne. Happy, you motherfucker?"

Solomon's knuckles went white on the steering wheel. "Did he just say...?"

"Yeah," she said. *What the hell's going on?*

Quanta smiled at Hayne. "There might be some viewers out there who don't remember that name. But maybe if you were more recognisable, they'd remember. I've disabled the field. How about you show them?"

Hayne panted and glanced at the button, where Quanta's finger hovered. He licked his lips, staring at Quanta with uncertainty in his eyes. Then he began to change.

It only took a second. The metal scales seemed to slide out of his skin all at once, flattening against his muscles, moving with them. The scales caught the studio lights and shone with a perfect gleam. In an instant, he was covered from head to toe in shimmering steel. A metal war machine, the living tank of the Manhattan Eight.

Quanta turned to the camera. "Ladies and gentlemen, behold one of your greatest heroes. Iron Justice."

Niobe's insides churned. There was only one way this could end. She wanted to switch off the television, go home, and wrap her arms around Gabby, but she couldn't take her eyes from the screen.

Iron Justice threw himself against the side of the cage. It crackled, sparked, but barely budged. Quanta regarded the raging hero. For a moment, he seemed conflicted. Then he returned his gaze to the television, the fake smile gone.

"A caged superhero. You people should be enjoying this. This is what you wanted. Behold your perfect world." He paused, took a deep breath. "Now let me show you what I can do to your perfect world."

Turn it off, she told herself, but she couldn't. Quanta pressed his hand against the side of the cage and closed his eyes. For a moment, nothing happened. Then something seemed to form around him. The studio got darker, but Quanta got brighter. Energy flowed around him like honey, dripping from his white suit. Light flowed from his hand and began to fill the cage.

Iron Justice screamed again, a scream that turned Niobe's spine to ice. The liquid energy filled the cage and flowed into Hayne's eyes, ears, nose, mouth. Anywhere unprotected by the scales. His screams became the gurgling of a drowning man. He thrashed against the side of the cage, but it barely shuddered.

It seemed to take hours. Quanta's face betrayed nothing as the superhero died. The agonizing movements slowly stilled. Vomit pooled in the back of Niobe's throat, but she swallowed it back. Sweat trickled down the Carpenter's cheek. He was shaking a little.

It's over, she assured herself.

Then Hayne's body exploded. Like a bomb had been placed in his chest, he detonated from the inside out. She turned away, covering her face, but not before she saw the hero's flesh and metal painting the cage's shields.

"Oh, Christ," she whispered. "Bloody hell." The Carpenter was a statue.

When she turned back to the TV, the cage was gone from view. Quanta's face filled the screen. In an instant, she knew she hated him. She hated him beyond reason or possibility. *He's got Sam. Jesus.*

"You have thirty-six hours," Quanta said. Then the picture turned to static, and he was gone.

Niobe tried to speak, but her throat wasn't working. Solomon spared her the need to talk first. "Iron Justice," he said hoarsely. He looked like he was driving on automatic. "An entire German armoured division couldn't kill him during the war."

She tried to clear her head, but it was all fuzzy. *He's got Sam.*

"He was supposed to be invincible," Solomon said. "How'd this psycho get his hands on him?"

"The same way he got the kid, I guess."

"Iron Justice," he said again. He didn't appear to have heard her. "He was one of the Manhattan Eight. He was friends with Dr Atomic, for Pete's sake."

Something clicked in her brain. *The Manhattan Eight. No. It couldn't be.* She rummaged through her pockets and pulled out the photo she'd found in Sam's drawer on the boat. Two young men stood in front of a log cabin, one slightly taller and slimmer than the other. She recognised them now. But it was impossible.

"Frank Julius," she whispered. "I know who he is."

"What? Who?"

She studied the picture. "He's Frank Oppenheimer. Bloody hell, Frank Julius is Omegaman."

She fished out the ring she'd found on Frank's boat. A signalling device. The signalling device used by the Manhattan Eight.

Solomon didn't say anything for a moment, but she could see his mind working. If Frank Julius was Omegaman, then his brother, Sam's father....

"Sam's father..." the Carpenter said, "...his father is J. Robert Oppenheimer."

She nodded. "Dr Atomic." *The first hero. The greatest hero that ever lived.* "Sam is the son of Dr Atomic."

"He shouldn't exist."

"He does," she said. "He could be the most powerful metahuman on the planet." *And Quanta's got him.*

The Carpenter nodded. "Told you you didn't wanna miss this."

Silence filled the car. As they drove, the wail of Met Div's sirens grew louder. She switched on the police radio. Chatter came through in an unending stream. She picked one voice out of the noise. "I repeat, we are taking fire. Suspects are making for their vehicles. Three white Bedford vans and one larger van, make unknown. Requesting air support." The voice dropped back into the noise of overlapping chatter.

Niobe didn't like the look of the shaky smile on Solomon's face.

"How do you feel about car chases?" he asked.

She sighed and nodded. "Fine. But I'm driving."

CHAPTER 14

MAY I HAVE THIS DANCE?

Yeah, I seen him. Hell, I was probably the first to see him, after he changed. I was new at Los Alamos, baby-faced and bored as hell. Who wants to be stuck in the middle of New Mexico when all your friends are off fighting the Japs? But then them Nazi bastards blew up the research lab, and things weren't so boring anymore. I never knew what those scientists was making there, but I tell you, when Dr Atomic came floating outta that rubble, naked as the day he was born and without a scratch on him, I thought I was seeing an angel. I just couldn't figure out if it was the Angel of Mercy or the Angel of Death.

—Pvt. Danny Caton, US Army

Morgan sprinted to the vans against a background of flashing lights and a cacophony of sirens. Obsidian and Tinderbox were holding off the first police to respond, giving him and the others time to cross the distance from the shattered TV station entrance. Morgan panted as he ran. His little spectacle with Hayne's execution had sapped his strength, both physically and emotionally. Perhaps he should have just lopped the man's head off with his light blade and been done with it. *No, they needed to see. I needed to make them believe.* And he needed to get what he came for. He could still feel Hayne's innards between his fingers as Morgan had fished through the blood and shit and guts to find an intact hunk of grey, meaty tissue.

His shoes squelched with every step, sweat pooling around his feet. He never relished killing, and that had been a particularly brutal way to kill a man. Even now, over the shouts and coursing fire, Hayne's screams haunted him. It was the sacrifice he had to make. He touched the vial in his pocket, where the grey tissue now sat. *The sacrifice both of us had to make.*

The earth lurched suddenly, and the tortured sound of tearing concrete echoed through the street. He just managed to keep his balance. He made a mental note to ask Obsidian to warn him before she did that. In a glance, he saw that she'd effectively destroyed the street to his right, where most of the police had converged on them. Metahuman Division vehicles toppled over huge cracks in the pavement, and blue-uniformed officers struggled to get to their feet. Tinderbox followed up with a sweeping wave of fire that sent an armed response team scattering. One was too slow, and caught the blast full in the chest. His uniform burst into flame, and he began to scream as his skin turned black.

In response, Morgan's head pounded in agony, but he forced it away, locking the pain deep inside himself. The black splotch that clouded his vision prevented him from seeing more of the carnage, for which he was thankful. He tore his gaze away from the fight and saw that he had reached the vans. With a leap, he pulled himself into the passenger side of the main van and slammed the door behind him. The driver had already started the engine, and as the other metas piled into the back, he shifted into first and peeled away, tyres screeching.

Morgan pressed his gloved palm to his forehead to try to massage the pain away. It had gone well. No casualties so far. He didn't anticipate serious issues from the police. The city only owned two helicopters and a handful of dirigibles, and they were so out of practice dealing with a major attack the response would be slow. The scrambling device Navigatron had developed would keep the kill-switches from being activated in those of his people who had them. And the surprise he'd left at the television studio would buy him more time.

He wound down the window and let the wind whip his hair. An adjustment of the side mirror showed the other vans racing behind him.

He checked his watch. Armed response teams should be storming the TV studio any second to secure it and confirm the safety of the hostages. He didn't anticipate police air support for another three or four minutes. Perhaps he'd encounter a roadblock or two, and some police would try to pursue him, but they were no concern on their own.

Right on cue, a blast of pale blue light lit up the night sky in his mirror, exploding out of the windows of the TV studio. Perfect. The detonator hidden in the base of Hayne's cage contained an odourless gas that caused rapid onset abdominal cramps, nausea, and vomiting. In addition, he'd developed a device that would release a field of virtual particles that would trigger the police's radiation detectors. In a few minutes, everyone in the building would be heaving the contents of their stomachs onto those nice tile floors. It wouldn't be long before the entire place was locked down for fear of acute radiation poisoning. A good twenty per cent of the Metahuman Division's elite troops would soon be out of commission for the next few days. And while everyone was imagining a horrible impending death, Morgan could make his escape.

Despite the pounding in his skull and Hayne's screams weighing on his conscience, a warm glow suffused him. *This is right,* he thought. *One day, they'll understand.* The world knew him now. True, all they heard was some hogwash about freeing supercriminals, but he had to keep up appearances. Frank Oppenheimer was the true target. Morgan would get the supercriminals one way or another, but Frank was going to be more difficult to flush out. Perhaps the challenge he'd issued really would inspire the great Omegaman to throw off his civilian trappings and come face him. Now that would be interesting.

His earpiece crackled. "Screecher reports two helicopters inbound, my lord," came Obsidian's voice through the static.

"Thank you," he said. "Proceed as planned."

The radio hissed twice in an affirmative response, and then the static vanished. A few seconds later, he caught the thrub-thrub of helicopter rotors in the distance, and a pair of spotlights flashed in his mirror, lighting up the street around him. He could hear police cars drawing closer.

He watched in the mirror as the middle van in his convoy threw open its back doors. He could picture Haze drawing in a deep breath.

Thick black smoke suddenly poured from the van, weaving into the sky. Within twenty seconds, the twin helicopters were blocked from his view, and the flickering glow of their spotlights reflecting off the smog was the only thing that remained. Haze would probably need to sleep for a week after this, but he'd seemed eager to do it.

The thumping of the helicopter rotors grew louder. Smoke began to swirl and part as the choppers moved in closer to keep a visual on Morgan's vans.

He watched them approach, and smiled. *Too close.*

Barely shadows against the thick smog, Devil Wing and Black Moth shot out of their respective vans and soared upwards. Behind each of them, Morgan could just make out a thick braided cable glinting in the spotlights. One of the helicopters saw Black Moth approaching and tried to evade, but it was too slow. Devil Wing swooped up and grabbed the landing skid of the left helicopter, while Black Moth took the right. Morgan caught a glimpse of each of them clamping the wire to the helicopters before they dropped back down and glided through the smog to their vans.

One of the helicopters tried to swerve away, and the wire connecting it to the van went taut. The van jerked, but held its course. Struggling would do the police helicopters no good.

A blast of sand flew from the van and collided with the windscreen of the helicopter on the left. Blinded, it tilted wildly. At the same time, a cone of fire shot just to the right of the other helicopter. The panicked pilot swung away from the flame, struggling against the wire.

As far as Morgan could tell, they never even noticed each other until the two helicopters collided. The night was filled with the screeching of agonised metal and the sputtering of rotor engines still struggling to work.

Morgan didn't have to prompt his people to release the cables. The two helicopters crashed to the ground, spouting flame. One smashed through some suburbanite's house. A trio of police cars screeched to a halt behind the wreckage, one of them clipping a tail rotor and taking out a postbox. Morgan's convoy raced on.

Sighing, he sat back and pulled out a couple of pill bottles. *Perfect*, he thought. Their road should be clear the rest of the way. He swallowed down four pills: two for the seizures and two for the headaches. *It's going to work. I'm going to do this.* A flutter of relieved laughter built in his lungs.

He picked up the radio handpiece that connected him to the other vehicles and depressed the button. "Outstanding work, everyone. You can all be proud. When we get—"

Something dark hurtled towards the van. Morgan's breath caught.

"Shit!" the driver yelled, and he tugged hard on the steering wheel.

Time slowed. The van lurched to the side, pressing Morgan against his seat. The huge brown object flew past, scraping the bonnet of the van and missing the windscreen by inches. The van's tyres squealed and the driver kept up a stream of nonsensical screams as he tried to maintain control of the vehicle.

"Was that a tree?" the driver yelled. "Was that a *flying tree*?"

Morgan's headache flared. He grabbed the side mirror and angled it in time to see the tree turn in mid-air and collide with the side of the van directly behind him. The body of the van crumpled, and the whole vehicle went into a squealing spin. The road filled with the smoke of burning rubber.

The next van in line managed to swerve around the wreck and continue on, but then the tree started to shake itself loose. Like a guided missile, it took off and cut through the air root-first, clipping another of his vans. *What in God's name is going on?*

His driver fought the van until it was back under control, but he was pale and sweating. "Fuck! What was that? Fuck!"

"Silence," Morgan said. He swivelled in the seat, trying to locate the source of the tree.

He didn't have to wait long. An old-fashioned two-door Ford sedan tore out of a side street and came skidding into line between his van and the one behind. A purple flame lit up the road behind it. A rocket engine. That was no police car.

A figure leaned out the passenger side, arms outstretched, cloak flapping. A snapping sound came over the whistling of the wind, and a tree branch hurtled at Morgan's van. His driver shouted and attempted to swerve, but the branch hit, smashing one of the headlights.

Metas already. Oh yes, this was getting very interesting. It was a telekinetic. Something squealed behind him, and he caught a glimpse of the tree battering another of his vans in the mirror. Not just a telekinetic. A telekinetic with a preference for wood. *The Carpenter.*

He would have smiled if everything wasn't going to hell. The van's engine protested as the driver accelerated, but the black car kept pace. The radio on the dashboard came alive again with static and voices. "Orders, sir?"

He realised he was still tightly gripping the radio handpiece. Within a second, he sketched out a new tactical plan in his head. "I want Tinderbox in a position to deal with that damn tree. Sand Fury, see if you can slow them down. And have Screecher gathering information on the car. If they've got any special tech in there, I want to know."

Obsidian's voice came back at him. "Sand Fury's vehicle was taken out, my lord. Should we return for them?"

Damn it. He sighed. "No. Leave them." He returned the handpiece to the dashboard. *They won't talk if the police get them. They're loyal. They're brave. And this isn't over yet.* "Get us onto the upper highway," he told the driver. In response, the driver spun the wheel and brought the van screeching onto an on-ramp.

Something pinged off the back of the van. He readjusted the mirror to get a better look at the tailing car. While the Carpenter leaned out the window, hat flapping in the wind, the driver had an arm pointed at the van. A gun flashed, and a crack appeared in the van's armoured windshield, just to the right of his head.

Morgan ducked down in the seat and snatched the radio up again as another round pinged off the rear bumper. "They're shooting. Modified rounds of some sort. Can anyone take them down?"

"No, my lord." There was a roar from somewhere, and orange light filled his mirror. "Tinderbox is occupied with the tree."

He considered his options. Even modified as the vans were, he didn't think they could outpace the car's rocket engine. What was the Carpenter doing? He hadn't heard of the hero being operational for years. The Wardens had disbanded peacefully, if grudgingly.

A bullet cracked his mirror, discharging a small amount of blue lightning. *Who's the Carpenter got with him? The woman from Avin's picture?* He swivelled in his seat and tried to get a look. The figure was small, masked, wearing what looked like a bowler hat. It could be a woman, but he couldn't tell.

It was an admirable effort on their part. He honestly hadn't expected a reaction from metas so quickly.

He depressed the button on the radio. "Who is our best flier? The most dexterous?"

"Avin, my lord," Obsidian said. "But of those present, Black Moth."

"Have him on standby. On my signal, I'll need a pickup."

"My lord?"

"Just get him ready," he said, and he shoved the handpiece back into its cradle.

There was almost no traffic on the highway. Morgan licked his lips and straightened his gloves. Sirens still moaned in the distance, but they were too far away to be any nuisance now. The remaining vans careered along the raised highway while the Carpenter's car pestered them like a mosquito. The pills had done nothing to take the edge off his headache.

"Whatever you do," he told the driver, "keep this thing steady."

Without giving the driver time to respond, he hooked his hands around the window frame and hauled himself out of the seat. He drew in the light from the street lamps that flashed past, feeling the energy build inside him. Then, leaning out the window, he flicked his wrists. Two ropes of light flew out and lashed themselves across the van's roof. With another tug, he pulled himself halfway out the side window and clambered onto the roof.

The wind buffeted him, but the light ropes extending from his hands kept him from falling. The roof was surprisingly slippery, and each tiny movement of the car made his stomach turn. This would be much easier if he could see properly. He brought a shield of light up in front of him just in time to deflect another bullet. It ricocheted off with a flash of sparks, flying into the night.

He got to one knee on the roof, facing his pursuers. They swerved in the lane, trying to get a better shot at the tyres. Over the glare of the headlights, he thought he could see the Carpenter's mouth twisting in surprise.

Carpe omnia.

He released the ropes, took two running steps across the roof of the van, and leapt.

For a moment, everything seemed frozen. His heart pounded even above the wind whipping at his back. He was in freefall, his stomach lurching. He could make out the twisted shape of another modified bullet as it pinged off his shield. Strangely, he was free of fear. His mind was focussed, calculating trajectories, weaving light into the perfect cushion. He was alive.

The car's bonnet crumpled under his weight. The jarring collision brought him back to the present. The light shield he'd created saved him from breaking any bones, but pain still stabbed up his legs as he landed. Despite that, he smiled at the two metas inside the car. The driver's face was completely masked, so he couldn't see her expression—he was sure it was a woman now—but the Carpenter was gaping. It was nearly enough to make Morgan laugh aloud.

Instantly, he lashed himself to the car with new ropes of light. Just in time too, because the woman suddenly swerved, trying to shake him loose. Morgan grinned at her. Holding the ropes with his left hand, he formed the blade in his right.

The Carpenter stuck his quarterstaff out the window and awkwardly tried to swipe at him, but Morgan's blade passed straight through it, slicing it in two. The broken end of the staff fell from his sight. A moment later, it was back. The fragment started swirling around him, battering away at his shield, trying to find an opening. It was a waste of energy. Morgan grinned at the Carpenter through the windshield and ignored the pesky piece of wood, even as it slammed against his shield and dug into his neck and ribs.

Morgan raised his blade in a salute and bowed his head to the heroes. Then he plunged the sword into the bonnet.

Steam hissed up from the hole around his blade. The rocket engine sputtered, valiantly trying to function even as he cut through the fuel lines that fed it. The woman shot at him again and gave swerving another try, but neither were effective. He raised his blade into the air, and it flashed with a sudden beam of light. The next instant, it had vanished.

"Until next time, heroes," he shouted over the wind.

A pair of hands grabbed him under the armpits. Morgan let the light ropes dissolve as the flying meta tugged him suddenly upwards. He caught one last glimpse of the woman slamming her fist against the steering wheel before Black Moth swung him around and carried him away from the slowing car. His other metas spurted fire and lightning as they raced past the damaged car and disappeared into the night.

A *productive evening,* he concluded as Black Moth flapped his wings and carried Morgan over the panicking city.

CHAPTER 15
THE PUPPET AND THE PUPPET MASTER

DOLL FACE

REAL NAME: *Unknown*

POWERS: *Mental manipulation and torture via organic probes (possibly neural cell bundles), enhanced reflexes.*

NOTES: *Likely insane, though never captured for long enough to receive psychoanalysis. He has allegedly murdered several hundred people, including many women and children. Despite his insanity, experts agree his mental capacity is far above most normal humans, and he is able to process hundreds of memories, identities, and sensations simultaneously. Presumed dead following a military raid in Ukraine.*

—Notes on selected metahumans [Entry #0398]

Sam woke to the sound of footsteps approaching his cell. His heart instantly took up a snare drum beat in response, and he jerked up from the mattress, his throat closing.

It's him, he thought. *He's come for me again. God, no.* The creature that called himself Doll Face had visited his cell twice more since that first terrible meeting. Each time he'd yammer his psychotic ramblings, occasionally poking Sam with the point of a kitchen knife. And it only got worse from there.

The footsteps drew closer, and Sam shrank down on his mattress, knowing it wouldn't do him any good. There was no escape from the pain and the fear and the sickness.

He couldn't explain what Doll Face did to him. God, he didn't even want to think about it, but it wouldn't leave him alone. It never stopped haunting him. When the strings touched his mind, he was nothing but Doll Face's plaything. The creature probed his mind, testing things, searching. Every now and then a rush of agony would go through him, and some new energy would bloom inside him for a moment before being locked away. He felt like Doll Face was preparing his mind for something, sweeping away everything that made him who he was and laying down new foundations. He couldn't explain it. All he knew was that there was nothing he could hide from Doll Face.

The creature showed him things, showed him what he'd done to others. The children he'd made eat their own faces. The games he played, the people he'd forced to hunt each other through twisted mazes, like rats armed with daggers. And it wasn't just visions, either. He could taste the blood in his mouth. He could smell the rancid flesh, the burning organs, feel the texture of the maggots as they crawled into his eyes. And above it all was the giggling.

It wasn't just Doll Face's crimes he saw, either. Through the hazy, twisted mind of the creature he saw huge explosions that obliterated hundreds of thousands of lives in an instant. He saw a man with metal skin punch a hole through a soldier. In another vision, a man in a grey costume passed through a wall like a ghost and slit someone's throat with a long silver dagger. He saw men in blue tunics raping women in cells not unlike his own. He felt the loneliness of the world dripping through him. And he saw his father—he knew it was him instinctively—standing over bodies snapped clean in two.

He saw fear, and it smelled like blood.

I'm going to break, he knew. The hallucinations didn't let up now. He'd wake up with a hundred cockroaches burrowing into his arms, but when he tried to pick them out, they crumbled to dust and vanished. His arms and legs were streaked with blood and dying flesh where he scratched in his sleep.

He was going to break, and now Doll Face was coming again. His stomach heaved, and he lurched to the side and retched. The pitiful contents of his stomach spilled onto the concrete floor. His throat burned and his guts tried to force their way out through his eyes again, but only clear liquid came now.

The footsteps were right outside. But something was different about them. They didn't sound the same. And there was no singing. *It's not him! It's not Doll Face.* His heart soared, and at the same time he had to blink back tears. Muscles trembling with fatigue, he pushed himself away from his vomit and tried to get to his feet.

There was a pause, and all he could hear was the rasp of his own breath. *Did I imagine it?* But then the lock clicked, and the door creaked open.

The man who slipped inside was no one he'd seen before. He was tall, with slicked-back dark hair. He wore no uniform, just jeans and a collared shirt.

Without speaking, the man placed the food tray he was carrying on the floor, glanced back out the door, then pulled it closed. He studied Sam, eyes sweeping up and down. Sam tried to hide the wounds on his arms and legs. The man's eyes were warm. Sam could almost believe the man was concerned for him.

The man quickly crossed the distance between them. Suddenly nervous, Sam tried to back away, but there was nowhere to go. The man stopped and raised a hand, as if to show he meant no harm.

"I can't stay long," he said in a low voice. His accent was strange, but the words had a kind of quiet strength to them. "My name's Paul. I'm a friend of your uncle's."

The words gripped his soul and tugged it out of the darkness. The torture, the horror, it was over. Before he knew what he was doing, he'd grabbed hold of the man's shirt and started babbling. "You've come to get me out. We've got to go now, before Doll Face comes back. Please, we have to go."

Gently but firmly, the man removed Sam's hands from his uniform and directed him to sit on the mattress. Sam did so, forcing himself to hold his tongue. He couldn't let anything sacrifice his chance at getting out of here. Not anything.

"We can't leave," the man said. "Not yet."

The fragile hope shattered like glass. He bit back tears, but still they welled in his eyes.

Paul laid a hand on his shoulder and gave it a squeeze. "It's still too dangerous. We'd be shot thirty seconds after leaving this cell. I'm sorry."

Sam picked at the mattress with broken, bloody nails and tried to hold himself together. *I have to be strong.* But he had no more strength left. Doll Face had taken it from him.

Paul gently took Sam's arm and examined the scratches that ran across them. "God," he said. "What have they done to you?"

Sam shivered. "I don't know. I don't know what they want with me."

"You have to stay strong, Sam. Has Doll Face...has he done things to your head?"

The horror flashed through him again, while something black and damp gripped his heart. "Yes." His voice was barely a whisper.

"What has he done?"

Sam swallowed. "He's changing things around. Remaking them. And...."

And showing me things that were already there. That's what scares you most, isn't it?

Paul waited for a few moments, but Sam couldn't finish the sentence. He pulled his knees up to his chest and tried to hold back the tears. "Why is he doing this?"

"I don't know, Sam. I'm trying to find out. But I think someone wants something from you."

"What could I have? I don't know anything! I don't understand."

Paul said nothing for a moment. He rested his hand on Sam's shoulder. The touch was comforting.

"Do you know about your father?" Paul said.

Sam shook his head. "Doll Face called him a wizard."

A sad smile crossed the man's face. "Not quite, but the idea's there. Your father was the first of a new type of human. The first, and the most powerful. A superhero. He called himself Dr Atomic."

Superhero? Dr Atomic? The words meant nothing to him. If his father was so important, why hadn't his uncle ever told Sam about him? Did other people know about these things? Was that why his uncle didn't let him visit the cities or speak to anyone?

"Your father wasn't born as Dr Atomic," Paul said. "He was a scientist. A physicist. Back then he was just Robert Oppenheimer. In the war…you know about the war?"

Sam nodded. "A little." He'd heard it mentioned, and he knew about the Germans. He wasn't sure why it happened, or when.

"Your father ran something called the Manhattan Project. It was a secret weapons program. But there was an accident at the labs." He grimaced. "Not an accident, really. Some German spies attacked the Los Alamos facility. They detonated a bomb, and a lot of people died in the initial blast. But there was more. Some of the radioactive substances the scientists were using were released. In the hours following the attack, a lot of the survivors got sick. Some died. Your father, your uncle, and a few of the others were trapped in the rubble of the main facility for days. Everyone assumed they were dead. The base was miles from anywhere, and it took the military time to pick through the debris. The rescue teams were about to abandon all hope when a light began to glow through the cracks in the rubble. Your father burst out, completely unharmed. Your uncle too. They had changed."

Changed? He still didn't understand any of this.

Paul smiled and squeezed his shoulder again. "I don't have time for the whole story right now. But your father became stronger. He developed powers, powers like no other human had ever seen. He could tear the barrel off a German Tiger tank. Bullets barely grazed him, and he was quick enough to dodge anything big enough to do him damage. And he could fly, Sam."

Fly? Was this man crazy? Sam studied his eyes, looking for a lie. *Is it so impossible?* a voice inside him said. *You saw what Doll Face can do. You* felt *what he can do.*

"If my dad was so strong, how'd he die?" Sam asked.

"Cancer," the man said. "Even the greatest warriors can be crippled by disease."

Sam ripped a patch of fluff from the hole in his mattress. If this man was telling the truth, it meant his uncle had lied to him, kept things from him. *He had no right.*

Paul leaned down in front of Sam, forcing him to meet his eyes. "I don't have any proof to offer you, but you have to trust me. Your father was one of the most loved people on the planet. He was also one of the most hated. I think that's part of why you're here."

Sam made himself meet the man's stare. Trusting the wrong person could get him killed. But so could not trusting anyone. Finally, he nodded. "I believe you. Please, get me out of here."

"I will. Soon. But I'm going to need your help."

Sam frowned, fists tightening around the thin mattress. What was he supposed to do from in here?

Paul glanced at his watch, and his voice sped up. "Your father was the greatest superhero the world has ever seen. The radiation altered his DNA, gave him those powers. Somehow, the mutations seem to affect the germ line as well. They can be passed on to children. To you. Your uncle thinks you have powers."

"No," he said quickly, refusing to believe it, but a voice whispered inside him. *The energy. You felt it.*

"Yes," Paul said. "You know it's true. You've felt something before, haven't you? If you want to get out of here, you have to learn to use your powers."

Something deep in his guts quivered. He released the mattress and glanced down at his palms. "Teach me."

"I can't," Paul said. "Even if I had powers myself, every person is different. But I'm told it first manifests during times of high emotion."

He thought back to when the man attacked him on the boat, and the fight he had with his uncle, when he first sensed the energy. And again during Doll Face's tortures.

Paul checked his watch again. "There is one thing I can offer that might help you. Your father once said that when he was trapped in the rubble at Los Alamos, growing delirious from thirst, a warmth began to form in his chest." Paul touched himself just above his heart. "It was desire, Sam. He wasn't ready to die. He wanted to see his wife—your mother—one more time. He couldn't leave her alone. He was a brilliant man, your father. The world was at war, and he couldn't leave his family to face it alone. He'd protect them, no matter what. Then something touched him, he said. It was the same energy that lived inside the weapon he was creating. It gave him strength. Your father drew the energy together and formed a little ball right here." He touched his chest again. "Like an atom's nucleus. Like the radioactive core of the atomic bomb. And then he wasn't Robert Oppenheimer anymore. He was Dr Atomic."

Sam couldn't find the words to speak. *Father. Dad.* He wanted to talk to him. He *needed* to.

"I have to go," Paul said.

Sam's stomach went cold again. "No. Please."

"I'm sorry, Sam." The man stood and straightened his shirt. "I'll be back for you. I promise." He offered Sam a warm smile. "Find what drives you, Sam. Learn to use your power. Without it, there will be no escape from Doll Face."

The cold chewed through Sam's guts as he watched his only hope open the cell door. Freedom was so close. He could taste the air outside. He would have died just to breathe the fresh sea air again.

"Don't let him break you," Paul said.

The door swung slowly shut, and the sound of the lock clicking into place reverberated through Sam's numb mind.

He was alone.

No. His uncle was out there. And if his uncle couldn't save him, Sam would have to rescue himself. Just like his father had.

He closed his eyes and began to concentrate.

Morgan pushed the heavy metal lock back into place and peeled off the slick-haired wig. He brought his handkerchief to his face and wiped off the makeup that had concealed the pale patches on his skin. It was horrible stuff, slimy and thick. He hated disguises, but he had to see Sam for himself. He had to give the boy the push he needed.

His footsteps were loud in the narrow corridor. The boy was different than he expected. He undoubtedly resembled his father physically, but in temperament he was more like his uncle. More cautious, less charismatic. *Though after what Doll Face has done to him, maybe that's to be expected.*

It had been a long night, so long it was nearly dawn. Between the attack on the TV station and his time as "Paul", his head was pounding again. The flickering light overhead didn't help. He should get a few hours sleep before morning. He'd been surprised today by the Carpenter's interference. He had to be ready for the next phase. No mistakes, no false moves. And there was an important call he had to make when he woke up.

The light flicked off again. When it came back on, he wasn't alone.

"Is the Pretty Man done, hmmm?" Doll Face darted out from the shadows, and Morgan recoiled. "Can Doll Face play?"

For a moment, he considered sending Doll Face away. The creature unnerved him. Morgan was playing a dangerous game, keeping Doll Face so close. If Morgan slipped, even for a moment, Doll Face could butcher him. Besides, Sam looked terrible. Maybe he should let the boy recover before inflicting this insane villain on him again.

What am I thinking? He had no time for conscience. This was the choice he'd made when he started this plan in motion. He knew it would hurt people. *Are you growing soft, supervillain?*

"He's ready," he said. He pulled a vial from his pocket and held it out. The grey tissue inside glistened in the light. "Bring him to the edge."

"Doll Face wants to make the bad boy cut," the creature whined.

"No. Soon." He thrust the vial into Doll Face's hands.

Doll Face's eyes narrowed behind the eyeholes in his mask. A shiver ran down Morgan's spine.

"Go," Morgan said. "Do not disobey me."

Doll Face cocked his head, and the light flickered again, casting the menacing false face into shadow. "It walks a fine line, yes it does," he whispered. "Remember, Pretty Man, Doll Face is no puppet." He giggled. "He is the puppet master."

Doll Face giggled once more, then brushed past Morgan. He skipped down the corridor towards Sam's room, humming a gleeful tune.

Morgan watched him go, feeling filthy where the creature had touched him. *Pain*, he thought. *The world runs on it.*

His dreams would be dark tonight.

CHAPTER 16

A FAMILY MATTER

KINGFISHER

REAL NAME:	*Jacques Rouze*
POWERS:	*Flight, energy shield.*
NOTES:	*Pioneered Skyra, the air-based martial art for flying metahumans, which includes both unarmed and weapon-based techniques. Founding member of the Light Brigade, a supergroup that patrolled the skies over Europe from 1949-1958. Following the signing of the Seoul Accord, Rouze accompanied the Alpha League to the lunar colony. Rouze has not returned to Earth since.*

—Notes on selected metahumans [Entry #0098]

Niobe kicked the van's dented bumper. "Bloody hell."

Empty. Abandoned. They'd missed their chance; that son of a bitch Quanta had stuck his goddamned magic sword in the car and got away clean. They'd lost two hours fixing the damage after they limped off the highway.

The Carpenter sat on the back bumper inches from where she'd kicked, silhouetted by the open doors and the empty back, idly chewing on an apple he'd brought from the car. It infuriated her to see him so calm.

The tracking device she'd shot at the van during the chase had done its job. Trouble was, by the time they got to the underground parking lot, Quanta and his henchmen were long gone. The van was free of prints, free of everything. She'd even scoured the entire car park looking for something—a tyre tread mark, a cigarette butt, anything—but they had no luck. *Story of my life.*

"You look pleased with yourself," she snapped at Solomon. She was being unfair, but she was frustrated. They'd been so close.

He shrugged and smiled below his half-mask. "I got to throw a tree at them. Been a while. Never gets old."

She scowled. The tree had taken out one of the vans, but Met Div had rounded up the metas inside before she and the Carpenter could get them to talk. Now the villains would be locked up deep in the bowels of Met Div headquarters, and getting in again right now was out of the question. The cape coppers would be doing their best to make the bastards squeal about Quanta's location, of course, but that wasn't much use to her. The coppers weren't exactly going to be forthcoming with anything they learned.

"Calm down, Spook," the Carpenter said. He patted the bumper beside him. "Take a load off."

She ignored him and continued to pace. She had to work out how this all fitted together. Quanta dressed like he was trying to sneak into a royal wedding, but there was ruthless logic behind those cold eyes. It didn't make sense. His demands were pure insane supervillain, but her gut told her he was neither psychotic nor a psychopath. Even those dead eyes were an act; she saw that when he leapt onto their car. Then his eyes had blazed with excitement. *And admiration.*

Solomon continued to munch on his apple in silence. She gave the van another kick, half-hoping something useful would dislodge. All she got was a sore toe.

"If you're going to sit there," she said, "at least help me think."

He took another bite of the apple. "All right," he said with his mouth full. "How about the timing? It's all wrong. Sam's what, thirteen? If his dad really was Dr Atomic, the kid should be in his twenties."

She nodded. That had been bothering her as well. Oppenheimer's wife and children were killed by German agents around 1950. Oppenheimer retired and disappeared from the public eye, and died a few years later. It was 1969 now. None of it added up. "But the guys in the picture are Robert and Frank Oppenheimer. No doubt about that."

"Doesn't make the kid Dr Atomic's son."

"So you think Frank Oppenheimer picked up a stray and gave the kid that picture? Why? It doesn't make sense."

The Carpenter grinned. "None of it makes sense. That's what makes it so fun."

"You're a pain in the arse, Carpenter, you know that?"

He finished the apple, tossed the core into a rubbish bin, and rose unsteadily to his feet, leaning on the van for support. Niobe stopped pacing to watch him. *The thing with the tree. It took more out of him than I thought.* She made to help him, but he waved her off. Her frustration faded. He wasn't as strong as he used to be, she realised.

"Oh, don't look at me like that," he said. "I ain't dead yet. But these questions are too hard for me. If you're finished getting huffy, maybe it's time we found someone to ask."

"You have someone in mind?"

"As a matter of fact, I do," he said, smiling.

"Does he happen to be a balding American ex-superhero?" she said.

He tipped his hat to her. "See, this is why you're the brains of the operation."

They got back in the car, Niobe behind the wheel. She lit up a cigarette and drove out of the parking garage.

"I wasn't getting huffy," she said after a minute.

He pulled his hat over his eyes. "Drive, Sherlock."

After an hour dodging the police cars that still roamed the streets, Niobe and Solomon found a good vantage point to check out the television studio. The place was under full lock-down. A radio broadcast they tuned into was buzzing with words like "radiation poisoning" and "suspected nuclear device". Maybe it was true. The only people brave enough to venture into the building were dressed in full-body hazard suits, and they only stayed in for ten minutes at a time.

Whatever he was planning, this Quanta wasn't screwing around.

The radio advised people to remain in their homes, and for the most part, it looked like the public agreed. The sun rose on a city that was remembering what it was like to be afraid.

When they figured there was nothing else they could learn from staking out the television studio, Niobe drove on. A few minutes later, they pulled into an alley near the Starlight Hotel and changed into civilian clothes before getting out of the car. Solomon had stuck on a fake beard and run some white powder through his hair to make himself look older, while Niobe had painted on a thick layer of makeup. She hated wearing makeup, but it was that or masks, and they agreed that appearing in costume in daylight was a good way to get themselves shot right now. The radio said Met Div were already conducting investigations in the Old City, trying to shake out some leads. Niobe's mind went to Gabby, sitting alone in their apartment. If the cops came again....

No. Gabby had probably built new security measures for the apartment already. *She'll be fine,* Niobe told herself for the millionth time. She almost believed it.

She activated the car's security system and they walked the short distance back to the street. No dramatic entrance this time. She peeked in at the hotel lobby. Nearly empty except for the clerk on duty. No chance of sneaking to the lifts unnoticed. They went to the payphone just outside the hotel entrance.

"You wanna do the honours?" Solomon asked.

Niobe peeked through the hotel's revolving door again at the reception desk. "It's a female clerk. Middle-aged, no wedding ring. Do you still have any charm left in your old age?"

He raised an eyebrow and picked up the phone. "I think that was a challenge. Gimme the number."

She dialled for him while he fed coins into the slot. She heard it ringing, then she ducked back to the door and watched as the hotel clerk picked up the phone. She could just make out her lips moving.

"Hello, Rose," Solomon said in the smoothest voice she'd ever heard him use. "What a lovely name."

Niobe snorted.

"I'm Officer Peters from the police," he continued. "Sorry for calling so early. Is it just you on duty this morning?"

Niobe watched the woman speak into the phone.

"That's fine," Solomon said. "I need you to do me a favour. You've heard the news from last night? We're trying to track down one of the vehicles used in the attack, and we've received a tip that it might be in the area. We're a bit busy, as I'm sure you can imagine."

She said something, and Solomon laughed good-naturedly.

"No, no, nothing like that. I just need you to go outside and check the car park for a white van with the plate E-O-nine-zero-five-four." Silence for a moment. "Sorry, I know you're not supposed to leave the desk. I wouldn't ask if it wasn't urgent. You could help me track down some very bad people. Tell you what, you nip outside and have a quick look, and I'll come by tomorrow night when things have quietened down a bit and take you to dinner. It's the least I can do."

The woman touched her hair, and her lips spread in a smile. Niobe couldn't believe it. She shook her head. "The world's gone mad," she muttered.

"You will? That's great. Thank you very much, Rose. I'll stay on the line."

He let the handpiece dangle from the phone and grinned. "Done."

"Show-off," she said. They ducked around the side of the hotel just as the clerk came through the doors and hurried towards the car park. Her cheeks were pink.

"You're going to break that poor woman's heart," Niobe whispered as they snuck through the revolving doors and crossed the hotel lobby.

"I know. I'm pure evil." He winked. "I'll send her some flowers."

Niobe slipped into the lift, pressed the button for the fourth floor, and held the door while Solomon stepped in behind her. The doors slid closed and the lift began to move.

Niobe took off her glasses and pulled on her mask and goggles. Solomon put his mask and hat on as well, tearing off the fake beard as he did so. They didn't have time for a full costume change, but hero or not, she didn't trust Frank Oppenheimer. He'd kept too much from them.

The elevator doors opened. No one in sight, not even cleaning staff.

Silently, they made their way to room 408.

She grew tenser as they approached the door. Frank Julius—or Frank Oppenheimer—had taken on a new persona in her mind. He was Omegaman, the ghost of Los Alamos. In his prime, he'd been the perfect antithesis to his brother, Dr Atomic. In his black and grey costume he went places the rest of the Manhattan Eight couldn't reach, neutralizing Nazis or supercriminals and their minions.

Niobe inserted her pick in the door to room 408 and worked the pins. Next to her, Solomon cracked his neck and pulled back his jacket to touch the handle of the hatchet hanging there. It wouldn't do them any more good than her gun if it came to that. If Omegaman retained even a tenth of his previous speed and power, he could best them easily. But if they knocked, they'd alert him to their presence. And if he fled before they could talk to him, they'd be left with nothing. He wasn't going to give up information easily.

No one ever does.

The last pin gave in to her pick, and she licked her dry lips. She glanced at Solomon, nodded once. He swallowed and gave her a smile. The effect was spoiled somewhat by the twitch in his cheek.

With a twist of the torsion wrench, the lock clicked and the door swung open.

The light struck her like a bomb going off. She flinched and twisted, her hands going to her eyes. The goggles did nothing to stop the searing pain in her retinas. No chance of turning to shadow under the light's onslaught. She heard the Carpenter grunt, but she was too blinded to see where he'd gone. Blinking away the purple afterimage, she took a step back and reached for her gun. Something moved to her right. A figure passed *through* the wall, like a ghost of black and silver. And then it came for her.

The figure was behind her before she could move. A strong arm embraced her almost tenderly, and something sharp pierced the side of her neck. She was falling. By the time she hit the ground, she was out.

Niobe woke to light piercing her eyelids. She could sense it all around her, leaving no room for shadows. A flex of her wrists was all it took to determine she was tied to the chair. Tight, too. They hadn't skimped on the quality of the rope that bound each of her ankles to the chair legs. Without opening her eyes, she tested the range of movement in her hands. There was no way she'd be able to reach her utility belt, if it was still in place. Mentally, she checked herself for any signs of injury. She was still a little sore from her fight with Avin, but no new pains stabbed at her. *That's something, I suppose.*

She opened her eyes into slits, still feigning unconsciousness. Her goggles were still in place; another small mercy. A dozen lamps and torches pointed at her from every direction, propped up on tables and chairs. Whatever wattage the lights were putting out, it was way above the manufacturers' specifications. In the glare, it was difficult to see, but she'd bet good money she was in Frank Oppenheimer's hotel room. A figure was silhouetted in the chair beside her, the brim of his hat drooping over his face.

"Carpenter," she whispered. "You okay?"

He lifted his head an inch, and she caught the glint of his eyes in the reflected light. "You know, I'm starting to think we may not be the master tacticians we thought we were."

She wriggled in her seat. "I think this chair's wood. Can you get me out?"

Something moved in the corner of her vision. Silver flashed, and before she could react, the point of a thin dagger touched her throat. No, not a dagger. A sword-cane.

"Don't try it, Carpenter," a man's voice said. "Who do you think is faster, you or me?"

Her body screamed at her to suck in air and turn to shadow. Not an option. She pushed the urge aside. Bugger it all, she was stuck.

"G'morning, Frank," she said.

The blade stayed in place, but Frank Oppenheimer slowly moved into her line of vision. Squinting through the light, she saw he wore civilian clothes: a grey shirt tucked into a pair of black trousers. His movements were fluid, with none of the creakiness she'd seen last time.

It had all been a damn act.

"Bit early in the day for all this, isn't it?" the Carpenter said. His voice was thin. "We just came for a chat."

For a moment, Frank said nothing. He leaned forwards a little, until he was close enough for her to see that his face was drawn and his forehead was creased with deep wrinkles. He looked like he hadn't slept in a week. Her palms grew damp.

Finally, he spoke, his voice quiet and measured. "I'll ask you this once and once only. Do you work for him?"

Him? "You mean Quanta?" she asked.

"Funny," the Carpenter said. "We were about to ask you something similar. To be honest, you're not exactly doing a great job convincing us you're not."

Frank scowled, and the blade's point dug into her skin.

"Carpenter, shut up," she said. "We don't work for Quanta. We don't work for anyone. We're just trying to find your nephew, Frank. Or do you still prefer Omegaman?"

If he was surprised she knew who he was, he didn't show it. "Those days are over."

"Not for Quanta, apparently," she said.

"How's the TV reception in here?" the Carpenter chipped in. He just couldn't keep his damn mouth shut. "I take it you caught the evening news. Old buddy of yours in the cage, right?"

Frank paused, and a moment later the blade was gone from her throat and his hands were in his pockets. Still, she knew Frank could slit both their throats before either of them could react. Omegaman wasn't a speedster—though he could still thrash any normal in a foot race—but he was agile.

"Hayne was a terrible man," Frank said. He turned away from them. "He always was. Smarter than he looked, though. He never let his guard down when we were active."

She tried again to get enough give in the rope to reach her utilities, but the bonds just dug into her wrists.

"We know who Sam is," she said.

No reaction.

"Ever think some of that information might have been relevant to our investigation?" the Carpenter said.

"It was too risky to tell you," Frank said. "It's always been too risky. I had to protect him."

"And a fine job of that you did," the Carpenter said.

Frank's back stiffened, but he didn't raise his voice. "I still haven't decided if I can let you walk out of here knowing what you know. Don't test me."

"Quanta already knows," Niobe said, trying to suppress a growing frustration. "How much longer do you think your precious secret's going to last?"

"I need to protect Sam," he said again.

"No. You need us to do our jobs. I don't care about you, Frank, and I don't trust you. We've got a bunch of ex-heroes aligning themselves with that supervillain, and for all I know you might be one of them. I'm here for Sam. I don't know what Quanta wants with him, but given what he just did to Iron Justice, I don't think the son of Dr Atomic is going to have a long, fruitful life ahead of him. Not unless you let us go and let us do our fucking jobs."

Her hands had formed fists so tight her nails dug into her palms. With a conscious effort, she forced herself to relax and breathe. She couldn't let her emotions get out of control.

For a few minutes, silence filled the room. Far away, she could still hear the wail of sirens through the city. The coppers were wasting their time. Quanta was way out of Met Div's league.

Finally, Frank turned back to face them. "I think I believe you. I heard how you went after Quanta's people last night. There aren't many metas who throw trees around." He sighed. "And I suppose I don't have any other choice."

"Swell," the Carpenter said. He wriggled his hand beneath the ropes. "If you don't mind…?"

Frank nodded, and he held up the sword-cane. Her stomach clenched at the sight of it, but he just sliced through the bonds around her wrists and ankles and then moved to free the Carpenter. A thousand needles prickled her fingers as the blood rushed back. She pulled back the sleeves of her jacket and rubbed her wrists where the ropes had left purple marks.

She stood up—slowly. Oppenheimer made no move to stop her. Stretching felt good. Whatever Frank had drugged her with was potent stuff. She stepped outside the ring of lights, and for a moment she pressed herself into the darkest corner she could find, avoiding the morning light coming through the window. It was heaven to be out of the glare.

She found her gun sitting on the table. A sudden, insane urge gripped her, telling her to put a stun round in Frank Oppenheimer and get some real answers. But she just slipped the gun back into its holster beneath her jacket. She wasn't going to solve this with violence. Not when Omegaman could kill her before she could blink.

She picked up the Carpenter's hatchet and tossed it to him. It slowed and stopped in mid-air, then settled gently into the loop on his belt. He tipped his hat to her.

"All right, Frank," she said, "here's how I see it. You need us, that much is clear. If you didn't, you would've already gone after Quanta yourself."

He said nothing while he busied himself unplugging a cord from the wall socket. All the lamps and torches went out at once.

Niobe checked her pockets and utility belt to make sure he hadn't helped himself to anything while she was out. Everything was in place. She continued.

"I figure you're afraid to go out. You know Quanta knows too much about you."

Silence for a moment. Then he began to speak. "It's not fear. Twenty-five years ago, when I stopped being a physicist and became a weapon, when I found myself crawling through German bunkers in Berlin, hunting down the last of Hitler's inner circle to put my knife in their spines, that was fear. This is logic. Pure, cold logic. Something happened, and now Quanta has a line on me. If I try to move against him, he'll know, and he'll kill me before I can kill him." His voice dropped almost to a whisper. "Sam needs me more than he knows. If I die, he's lost. I won't die."

"So Quanta already tried to make a play for you," the Carpenter said.

Frank grunted. "I came to New Zealand to meet someone. Someone I'd known for thirty years. We went to college together, for God's sake. He'd moved out here to work in Unity Corporation's agricultural research subsidiary. Their main work was in genetics, improving beef and milk yields, but they'd also been studying the effects of the Auckland bomb on livestock. He got a message to me through a series of old friends, saying he had something I would want to look at. Something that would keep Sam safe forever. We set sail for New Zealand the next day."

"A trap?" Niobe asked.

He nodded, and his thick eyebrows drew down low over his eyes. "They nearly had me. Metahumans, maybe a dozen of them. They'd stunned me before I knew what was happening, before I could phase away through the walls or the floor. There was a psychic there, I think he put a trace on me."

So that was why he couldn't do this himself. The psychic would sense it as soon as Frank came within half a mile of him. Without surprise, even Omegaman couldn't fight all of Quanta's metas at once.

Frank paused for a moment, then continued. "I only got away because one of them tripped when they were putting me in the cage. I fought my way free and went straight back to the boat. I had to get Sam and get out. But something was wrong. I could tell someone was watching the boat. I got in the water a few hundred yards up and swam back, staying underwater as much as I could. Phased up through the hull of the boat. But Sam was already gone." He scowled. "I grabbed what I needed and left."

She was having trouble summoning sympathy for him. He'd dragged the kid halfway round the world for this crap, only to be stupid enough to walk into something like that. So much for all the cautious uncle bullshit. Sam would've been better on his own.

She fished out her now-crumpled cigarette pack and extracted a Pall Mall. Frank frowned at her, but he didn't say anything when she lit up.

"All righty," the Carpenter said. He crossed his arms and perched himself on the edge of a table. "Maybe you should explain to us kids at the back of the class how the heck Dr Atomic managed to get himself an extra son no one knew about."

"Not to mention one apparently born years after Robert's death," she added.

If the subject of his brother's death was painful to him, Frank didn't show it. "It's complicated."

"Simplify it," the Carpenter said.

Frank sighed. "The world considers Dr Atomic to be the world's most multi-talented superhero, as well as the most powerful. Speed, flight, telekinesis, bullet-resistance. The jack of all trades, and master of them all, too. But really, all his powers were manifestations of a single ability. He was a psychic, an impossibly strong one. There was almost no limit to how he could manipulate the world around him." He locked eyes with her. "Like I said, in those early days, we were weapons. Los Alamos, the Manhattan Project, they were military projects, and so were we. No one could kill Nazis like Dr Atomic."

His eyes caught the glint of a lamp's bulb, and she could tell Frank wasn't there in the room with her. She breathed out a lungful of smoke into the silent room, and waited.

"One night in forty-five we were hiding out in a farmhouse a few miles from Berlin. I found him huddled in the corner, crying. I hadn't seen him do that since we were children. It took a while before I could get him to tell me what was wrong. But in the end it came out. He'd been hearing voices. And not just any voices. The voices of those he'd killed. For the last two months, there had been an ever increasing chorus of babbling and screaming and begging inside his head."

"Psychosis?" she said. "Or a tumour?"

He shook his head. "When we were stateside again, the metahuman doctor gave him a psych evaluation and brain scan. No tumour, no atrophy, no simple psychosis. But with Mr October's psychic help, the doctor figured it out. It wasn't a hallucination. Whenever my brother killed someone, their mind left an imprint on his hypersensitive psyche. Like voices on a gramophone record. And each new imprint fractured his mind a little more."

She'd never heard this story. It wasn't impossible. Psychics often had problems with mental instability. But in all the comic books and propaganda films, Dr Atomic was infallible. If there was someone standing in the way of freedom, he could always be counted on for a quip and a fast right hook. Through the haze of her cigarette smoke, Frank started to look old again.

"What do you know of Dr Atomic's retirement?" he asked.

"His wife and kids got caught in a bomb meant for him." It was one of the earliest events she could still remember since the Blind Man had taken her memories. The papers ran the story on Dr Atomic's family for weeks. The assassins were never caught, though the Manhattan Eight had shaken down every major supercriminal they could get their hands on. Dr Atomic withdrew from the public limelight after that. A few years later, he was dead from throat cancer, and the world mourned.

"I never thought everyone would buy the story, but Mr October sold it. They'd left the world in our hands for years by then. They'd believe anything we told them."

"Believe what, Frank?" she said.

"There was no assassin, no bomb," he said. His voice was thin. "It was Robert. Dr Atomic killed his wife and children with his own hands."

Her cigarette had almost burned down to nothing. Ash dropped onto her boots, but she barely noticed.

Frank closed his eyes. "He didn't mean to. To this day, I believe that. My brother was a good man. He was the best of men. But the voices in his head did things to him. Those last few months, he never knew what he was doing, where he was. He screamed through the night. We all tried to help; we thought we could fix him. But after he killed his family, we knew what we had to do.

"It took all seven of us to bring him down. Protos and Mr October were in intensive care at the base for nearly three months after his psy-blast hit them. Protos left the hospital in a body bag. In the end, it came down to me and Iron Justice to bring down Robert. Hayne was the only one tough enough to take his attacks, and I was the only one quick enough to get behind him."

"You killed him?" The Carpenter sounded incredulous. She wasn't sure she believed it either. "You killed Dr Atomic?"

For a moment, he didn't move. Then, slowly, he shook his head. "Hayne wanted to. We probably could have. But when I went before the House Un-American Activities Committee and they accused me of being a Communist, Robert spoke for me. He was the one who brought me onboard at Los Alamos. We shared summers at the family cabin in New Mexico. The world loved Dr Atomic. But I loved Robert. He was my brother."

"What did you do with him, then?" she asked.

"We imprisoned him. We built the strongest prison the world has ever seen, right in the middle of New Mexico, and we left him there. And there he stayed, out of his mind, never knowing what he had done, until the cancer got him." He shrugged slowly. "Perhaps that was all the mercy we could hope for."

She stubbed out the pitiful remnant of her cigarette, flicked it into the kitchenette sink, and stood awkwardly in place, hands in her pockets. She still didn't trust Frank, but she couldn't exactly be angry at him, either. She could barely remember her own brothers, but she tried to picture herself in Frank's situation with Gabby or the Carpenter on the other side. The thought sent ice through her veins.

The Carpenter stepped up and put a hand on Frank's shoulder. "Sorry, Frank. Really. That's rough." Solomon glanced at her and nodded towards the man.

"Yeah," she said. "Condolences."

Once more, the room was silent. She had a head full of questions, but interrogating him now seemed a tad on the insensitive side. She ran through what she knew of Dr Atomic's deeds in her mind. It was around 1950 when he "retired", and maybe '53 or '54 when he died. The accident at Los Alamos that led to the creation of the first heroes was in '44, so Dr Atomic was active for around five or six years.

The Manhattan Eight had their share of enemies back in those days. The Russians weren't too happy to get beaten in the race to Berlin, and there were rumours that at least some of the Manhattan Eight were sent on covert missions in the Soviet Union soon after the war. They were nearly sent to Japan as well, but Truman and his generals decided to show the world their other secret weapon, the atomic bomb. The US was making it clear that it wasn't to be messed with.

But when the war was done, public support for military-backed superheroes waned. The Manhattan Eight—like many of the other fresh-faced heroes emerging at the time—were scientists at heart, not soldiers. Eventually, the government relented, and the Manhattan Eight became independent, dedicated to protecting the world and the innocent, not the interests of any one nation. Or so the comics went. Dozens of corrupt politicians, rogue states, supercriminals, and organised crime rings fell to them.

The Carpenter was the first to break the silence. "Question," he said, raising his hand like a schoolboy. "If Dr Atomic killed his wife and kids, where does Sam come in?"

Frank nodded. "Kitty—Robert's wife—figured out how sick he was long before the rest of us. When she found out she was pregnant again, she came to me. She was so scared. I don't know what he'd done to her, and I didn't understand then, not really, but I agreed to keep the pregnancy a secret. Robert was away for months at a time in those days, on mission after mission. Even when he was in the States, he barely visited her." He shook his head. "God, I don't know why it took me so long to understand how sick he was."

He touched his fingers to his temple and continued. "Kitty had the baby alone, just her and her doctor. All she gave the child was a name before she passed him onto an old schoolfriend. Looking back, I think she knew that would be the last time she saw him.

"After Robert…after Kitty died, I tracked Sam down. Whatever had driven Robert to do those things was still driving him. I think he could sense the baby, even if he didn't know what it was. If we failed to capture him, he'd find Sam. Future Girl had been leading the research on a cryogenics rig, and I went to her. Sam screamed his little lungs out when we put him in the machine. Ten minutes later, he was silent. Flash frozen. I didn't unfreeze him until a couple of years after Robert's death, when I could ensure his safety. I was worried bringing Sam out while Robert was still alive would give his broken mind the incentive he needed to mount an escape. I couldn't risk it."

"And since then, you've been on the move," she finished for him. "Sheltering him."

He nodded.

"You must know something about what Quanta's up to," the Carpenter said. "You saw him on TV. The bugger wasn't wearing much of a mask. You must recognise him. An old enemy. Someone you lot fought back in the good old days."

"No," he said. His voice almost cracked. "I've spent the entire night searching my memory. There's nothing. I've never seen that man before in my life."

"There has to be something," she pressed. "Anything."

"I've told you everything. Everything. Only a handful of people in the world know what I've told you. The rest of the Manhattan Eight are dead, or lost forever, like Future Girl. Hayne and I were the last." Pleading crept into his voice, and he took a step towards her. "Help me find Sam. My offer stands. Fifty thousand dollars. More, if you want. Please."

Niobe met Solomon's eyes. She could tell he was thinking the same as her. This had got more dangerous than they'd ever imagined. Quanta had tracked down Omegaman and the son of Dr Atomic. Sam was in his hands, helpless. And now Quanta knew they were after him. How long before he struck back and hit them where they lived? How long before he came for Gabby?

Gabby's bloodied face flashed before her eyes, and her gut twisted.

No. Niobe wouldn't let him. She'd save Sam, return him to his uncle, and then get Gabby off this goddamn planet forever. She had to protect them. She had to protect everyone.

Or they were all dead.

The two of them were quiet on the drive back to the Old City. The day was growing warm as the morning wore on, but all Niobe wanted to do was sleep. Exhaustion seeped through her bones. Despite their best repair-work, the engine kept up a constant rattle. As long as she didn't push it, she thought it would keep going all right.

The radio spouted a pair of matching statements from the Prime Minister and the Secretary-General of the AAU, claiming they would not bow to any of Quanta's demands. After that, the early morning news reported the events at the TV station in such repetitive detail that she was nearly ready to put her boot through the damn radio. Instead, she settled for changing the station to one that dutifully played a Beatles tune every third song. Solomon stared out the side window. No jokes from him. No nothing. Probably as lost in his thoughts as she was.

They needed to regroup. Find somewhere to sit down and run through everything they knew. She still had the files from Met Div. They'd go through every page with a comb so fine a gnat couldn't escape. There had to be something there that would lead them to Quanta. No one operated without leaving a trail.

A hiss crackled through the radio, drowning out John Lennon.

"Good morning, heroes." The voice that came through the radio was distorted, but she recognized it instantly. She jerked upright in her seat and glanced away from the road to stare at the radio. *No, it can't be.*

"I had Screecher help me connect to your radio," the voice said. It had a strange echo to it, not like any sort of radio distortion she'd heard before. "Don't worry, no one else can hear us. This little conversation is a private chat. Well, I say conversation, but since I'm only transmitting, I suppose I'll be doing most of the talking."

The Carpenter met her eyes. A beat passed, and then he was punching the button for the recording equipment while she pulled into a dark street corner. She killed the engine and a spool of magnetic tape began recording the transmission.

"I assume you both know who this is, but I should introduce myself properly. I am, of course, Quanta. I suppose we are something of adversaries at the moment."

There was definitely something weird about the distortion. Maybe the echo wasn't from the radio at all. Maybe it was on his end.

"Don't worry about introducing yourselves; I know who you are. I couldn't miss the Carpenter's skilful use of that tree. I believe a half-dozen of my people are in police custody thanks to you. And I won't forget you, Gloomgirl. Or is it Spook now?"

Her skin crawled.

"Marvellous work with the tracking device. I confess, I didn't even notice it until we'd parked and one of my associates pointed it out to me. I wasn't expecting such an enthusiastic response to my broadcast from the local meta community. Truth be told, Carpenter, I'd assumed you'd be in the ground somewhere, and as for you, Spook, you weren't even on my radar.

"Now, I'm going to take a stab in the dark here, pardon the expression. You're working with Oppenheimer, correct? You were at his boat, and it's the only reason you could be onto us so soon after we hit the television station. And now I hear someone broke into the Metahuman Division's headquarters and got into a bit of a kerfuffle with the good Senior Sergeant. My, you have been busy."

How did he know all this? He must have people everywhere, or maybe he had a few powerful psychics under his command. *He has my picture*, she reminded herself. Her throat constricted at the thought. He was going to find out her name, if he didn't already know. It was a race now. If they didn't find Quanta before he found them, everyone they cared about was at risk.

"I just wanted to express my delight at having such worthy challengers against whom I can test my skill," Quanta continued in his too-jovial tone. "There's something traditional about all this, isn't there?

Like the old days. But you'd do well to remember these aren't the old days. This is a neo-battle for a Neo-Auckland. War isn't what it used to be."

She could see his dead-eyed smile on the other end of the radio. *I'll make you eat that smile, you smug bastard.*

He laughed like he heard her thoughts. There was a clang somewhere in the background, and then his echoing voice returned one more time. "I'll see you soon. Try to keep up."

Static. Then nothing.

CHAPTER 17

REST MY WEARY HEAD

We never wanted this, but it has become unavoidable. We only wanted to help, to protect, to build, but it is clear that you no longer want us here. We will not submit to the barbaric practice of kill-switching. We will not. Before we leave, we extend an invitation to every metahuman on Earth who wishes to live free of persecution and fear. Join us on the Moon. It will not be an easy life, but it can be a good one. Perhaps one day we will return to Earth and be accepted for who we are, but do not hope for it. This world has given up on hope.

—Statement from the Alpha League, 1961

"No," Niobe said. "No bloody way."

"What's the big deal?" The Carpenter lounged in the passenger seat, unmasked like her. "You said it yourself. We need a place to gather our thoughts and go through all this paper you nabbed from the coppers."

She shifted down a gear and took the corner nice and easy, careful not to stress the damaged car. These abandoned roads wouldn't be doing the old Ford any good, but she sure as hell wasn't going to take the main highway back to the Old City, on this morning of all mornings.

"Your place is better," she said. "More room to spread out. Secure. Out of the way if Met Div throws any more raids in our direction."

"You didn't hear my wife yesterday," he said. "Kate, she…uh…." He paused.

"She doesn't like me."

"No," he said. "Well, yeah. But that's not it. Not all of it."

She was too tired for this. "Spit it out, Solomon."

"She wants me out of the game. Says I should stop playing superhero." He grinned. "She thinks you're a bad influence on me. What'd she call it? Oh yeah, 'enabling me.'"

She snorted. "Me? A bad influence on you? You're the one stuck in the past."

"Lemme finish, will you?" He put his arm out the window and tapped on the car's exterior. "She'll go along with it for now, but she won't have me bringing work home anymore. Doesn't want me exposing the kids to it. She thinks it'll corrupt them or something, you know?" He shrugged. "She's wrong. Those kids are so darned headstrong I couldn't force them into a cape and mask even if I wanted to. And no kid wants to follow in their father's footsteps anyway. But she made me promise that you wouldn't come around anymore. She's serious."

"How serious?"

His mouth formed a line. "Serious enough that if we go to my house now, I'd better learn how to cook meals for one in an awful hurry."

Christ. This was just what they needed. Kate meant well, and Niobe didn't dislike the woman, per se, but you couldn't marry a damn superhero and then try to take the cape off him.

She sighed. *Where have I seen that before?* Gabby was just as bad as Kate. It'd been easier back when Niobe was in the Wardens. She had no family to worry about her then; she hadn't even met Gabby yet. If she got horny, her teammate, Madame Z, was always happy to oblige. Everything was simple.

But in her heart, Niobe didn't want simple. Gabby was more than her lover. She was her best friend, her partner. Niobe wanted to make it work. Hell, that's why she was doing this damn job, so they could make a new life together somewhere they'd belong. But they were such different people in so many ways. Gabby didn't understand that Niobe couldn't just take her pension and live out her days. She didn't understand that Niobe had to protect her.

It had never been a problem before. She loved spending the afternoons reading on the couch while Gabby rested her head in Niobe's lap, puzzling over some new gadget. Niobe could run her fingers through the tight curls of Gabby's hair, and she'd be content. They loved each other, and that was enough. But now....

"Do you love your wife, Carpenter?" she asked.

He shot her a quick look. "Yeah. 'Course I do."

"How much?"

"More than anything."

"How do you know?" she asked.

"Because if I had to choose between letting her die and setting the world on fire, I'd be reaching for the matches. What's gotten into you?"

She didn't say anything for a while. Damn it. Why did all this have to be so difficult?

"You sure we have to go to my place?" she said.

"You got a better idea?"

She didn't. It wasn't that she didn't trust Solomon. It was just that the fewer details people knew about her, the safer they all were. And she had to keep Gabby safe. She had to.

"You can't keep pushing your friends away forever, mate," the Carpenter said.

Oh, bugger it.

"Fine." Her chest grew tight as she said the word. "Just don't touch my stuff."

All quiet on the home front. If Met Div were conducting investigations in the Old City like the radio claimed, they were in another neighbourhood. Niobe parked the car in the apartment building's basement.

Solomon whistled as he stared around at the basement. "So this is where the Silver Scarab does her thing."

Gabby had converted the basement into a workshop that resembled a mad scientist's laboratory. Strange, misshapen tools lay in neatly ordered racks around the room. In one corner, a blue light shone through a porthole in a box-shaped machine that hummed to itself. A clipboard covered in figures and scatter plots hung next to it. Everything was squared away so neatly it almost hurt Niobe's brain to come down here.

"This is it," she said, tucking the files from Met Div under one arm. "Though I wouldn't go calling her that."

"Huh?" He was peering at something that resembled a harpoon gun with a loop of cable running from the spear to a metal coil the size of her thigh. "Oh, right. Not the Silver Scarab anymore. Gotcha."

They took the stairs up. Gabby must've fixed the door to the apartment. Niobe put the key in the lock, then paused and held out the files to Solomon.

"Maybe you should hang back for a couple of minutes. I'll make sure it's okay with Gabby first." Gabby and Solomon had never met, and Niobe wasn't sure how she'd react to having a stranger in the apartment.

"Sure." He slung the bag containing his costume over his shoulder, took the folders, then strolled back and leaned against the wall near the stairwell. He fished a dried plum from some hidden pocket, popped it in his mouth, and grinned at her. Shaking her head, she opened the door.

There was a flash of frizzy blond hair. Before Niobe could react, her cheek blazed with fire. Her head snapped around, and a brief flash of animal anger went through her.

She caught Gabby's wrist before the second slap landed.

Gabby's face was wild. She wrenched her hand free, and Niobe involuntarily took a step back.

"What the hell are you doing?" Niobe asked. She put a hand to her cheek to soothe the heat. She should've left the mask on.

—*No*, Gabby signed, *what are you doing? You said you'd be home last night.*

"I was working," she said, signing as she spoke.

She tried to slip past Gabby. A hand grabbed her by arm and spun her back.

—*Don't*, Gabby signed, releasing her arm. *Don't brush me off like that. I saw the TV. You were out there in the middle of all that, weren't you?*

"Gabby—"

—*Weren't you?* Her finger pointed jerkily, and Niobe realised her hand was trembling.

She hesitated. She was caught. "Yes," she said finally.

Gabby slammed the door and stormed away from her. Niobe wanted to talk to her, call her back, but it was useless. Gabby always dominated their arguments like this. You couldn't argue with the back of a deaf person's head.

Damn it, what did Gabby want from her? She got upset when Niobe went out on jobs, so Niobe tried to keep work separate from their home life. But that just seemed to upset Gabby even more.

Niobe stayed rooted to the floor and watched as Gabby stalked across the room, her shoulders rising and falling with barely suppressed anger. Or maybe she was just fighting back tears. From her spot near the door, Niobe could see Quanta's picture plastered across the early edition newspaper sitting on the table. The picture did nothing to convey the fire she'd seen in his eyes when he'd leapt onto their car.

She was still frantically trying to prepare her counter-arguments when Gabby turned and flew back towards her.

—*You said it was safe. You said it was an easy job.*

Niobe had to make her understand.

—*I did it for us*, she tried.

—*I felt the car getting damaged.* Gabby touched her forehead. *I felt the gun being used. You were fighting.*

Bloody hell, she hadn't thought of that. Gabby was a gadgeteer. She retained a form of psychic link with her creations. Of course she'd know what Niobe had been getting up to.

—*Look, I'm sorry,* Niobe signed desperately. *The car's not in bad shape, you can—*

—*I don't give a damn about the fucking car!* Gabby's arms moved furiously. *That maniac had dozens of metas with him. I watched the news all night, waiting for them to find your body.*

—*I'm fine.* She tried to smile reassuringly.

Gabby pointed to Niobe's cheek, where Avin's claws had raked her.

—*Then what's that?*

Niobe opened her mouth to defend herself, but the door creaked open and Solomon's face appeared. "Uh…you guys okay?"

Gabby followed Niobe's gaze and started.

"Ah, damn," Niobe said. "Solomon, this is Gabrielle." She caught Gabby's eye and signed to her while she spoke. "Gabby, Solomon."

Solomon grinned and nodded to her as he slipped inside. Gabby waved back. *I thought she'd be more nervous*, Niobe thought. But she looked more embarrassed that anything. Embarrassed that he'd seen them arguing.

—*You don't mind him being here for a while?* Niobe signed.

Creases formed between Gabby's eyebrows.

—*Why would I mind? You're the paranoid one.*

—*But I thought….* She let her hands drop. She couldn't work Gabby out.

The sharp corners were going out of Gabby's face, but the pain was still there. Niobe's heart sat heavy in her chest. She bit her lip.

"Maybe you should go get started on those files," she said to Solomon. "We'll just be a second."

He nodded and took the hint, retreating to the kitchen table. Trying to ignore the look on Gabby's face, she led her to the bedroom and closed the door.

—*You're still working*, Gabby signed. Her movements were small, resigned.

—*There's a kid out there somewhere*, she signed. *This Quanta bastard's got his hands on him, and he's got something dark planned, I know it. We're trying to get him back before that happens.*

Gabby studied her face, her grey eyes locked on Niobe's.

—*What's his name?*

—*Sam. He's only thirteen.*

—*What did he do?* Gabby signed. *Why does Quanta want him?*

—*It's a 'sins of the father' situation.*

Gabby didn't drop her gaze. Niobe tried not to squirm. How was it this woman always made her feel like a bloody schoolgirl being reprimanded?

—*There's more, isn't there?* Gabby signed.

Niobe sighed. No point holding anything back now.

—*Cash. Lots of it up for grabs. No, don't look at me like that. It's enough to get us out of here. It's enough to get us a ticket on a lunar rocket.*

A pause. Gabby's face went through emotions like someone flicking television channels. Niobe held her breath and waited to see which one Gabby would land on.

She was ready for the slap this time, but it still stung like all buggery.

—*You knew,* Gabby signed. *You knew right from the start how dangerous this would be. That much money. And you know the worst thing? You didn't even discuss it with me. You promised you'd talk about this, but you didn't. You were too busy playing private fucking detective.*

She started to storm away, and Niobe threw out her arms and tried to pull her into a desperate hug. It didn't work. Gabby pulled away and made for the door. There were tears on her eyes.

Niobe made one more grab for her, pulling her around to face her. "Where are you going?"

—*To fix your car. I'll leave the dynamic duo to do their bloody work in peace.*

Gabby slammed the bedroom door as she left.

CHAPTER 18

Ladies and Gentlemen, May I Have Your Attention?

PROTOS

REAL NAME:	*Neil Finlay*
POWERS:	*Manipulation of gravity.*
NOTES:	*Amongst the most technologically gifted of the Manhattan Eight. The explosion at Los Alamos damaged his larynx, forcing him to rely on an electronic voice modulator to speak. Piloted the Eight's rocket-plane and submarine. Died of undisclosed causes in 1951.*

—Notes on selected metahumans [Entry #0005]

Morgan lashed out, sending the neat stack of typewritten pages billowing across the table. "What is this?"

John lurched backwards and bumped into the used mattress they'd set up for him in the corner of the tiny office. "I…I don't…."

Morgan snatched a handful of papers up and thrust the crumpled wad under the reporter's nose. The portly man's eyes darted to the door, but Obsidian stood there with her arms across her black stone chest, blocking the way.

"I told you to read what I gave you and write your story," Morgan said. His head throbbed in time with his pulse.

The reporter bobbed his head. "I…I did. My lord," he added quickly.

"And you understood nothing! Look at this rubbish. 'Neurotic'. 'Sadistic'. 'Vain.'" He looked up from the paper, and John withered beneath his stare. "Vain? This sounds like a psychiatrist's report. Are you a head-shrinker, John?"

"No...you didn't say...I'm a reporter, you just told me to write the truth."

Morgan balled his hands into fists. Again and again pain flashed through his head. It took all his willpower to keep himself from forming a blade and separating the reporter's idiotic head from the rest of his worthless body. How could the man be so blind?

"You were supposed to understand," he said through gritted teeth. "You were supposed to make *them* understand." His finger stabbed north, towards the city. "You were supposed to help pick up the pieces when this is all done. If you cannot, I have no use for you."

He turned away and tossed the papers to the floor, along with the rest of the rubbish. Everything was too close for it to fall apart now. He massaged his pounding forehead and glanced at Obsidian.

Damn this fool. "Obsidian, take care of John." He paused. "Do it clean."

A low, desperate moan left the reporter's throat. Obsidian nodded and stepped aside as Morgan made to leave.

"No, wait," John said. "I can still do this." Morgan heard Obsidian hauling the man to his feet by his collar. "My lord!"

Morgan was beginning to hate that title. He stepped into the hallway.

"Come on," Obsidian said to the reporter.

"Quanta!" John yelled. Morgan shut his eyes, and then the door.

"You still need me! Morgan!"

His hand froze on the door handle. A memory exploded into life inside his head, a vision of tears and blood and a woman screaming his name. He forced it down. The fires in his head blazed all the stronger.

A muffled scream came from inside the room. *The damn fool.*

He threw open the door again. "Release him."

Obsidian's rock face almost managed to look confused, but she dutifully released John from the headlock she held him in and stepped back.

"You have one chance to save yourself. Or I let her start again."

The reporter clutched his throat, coughing. Morgan waited. Finally, the man pushed himself to his knees and looked up at Morgan, gasping. "Was that how the girl died?" he said between breaths.

"What girl?"

"Your girl. Lisa."

The blade was in Morgan's hand and at John's throat before he could think. He wanted to plunge it into the reporter's mouth and take out his tongue for saying that name. *Lisa*. A flick of the wrist, and it would be done. His hand trembled. His head screamed.

He was close enough to notice the way John's pupils dilated to almost completely obliterate his irises. Sweat rolled down the man's cheeks with every panting breath.

"No," John said, voice cracking. "You did it yourself, didn't you? Like this."

The blade shimmered like honey.

"You don't know anything," Morgan said. "She wasn't in the file."

"You've been talking in your sleep."

Morgan glanced at Obsidian. She said nothing. The man was lying. Wasn't he? John's room shared a wall with the one he'd used to get a few hours sleep. And he had dreamed of Lisa again. He'd dreamed of cutting her down while she cried, while he cried, while each begged the other to forgive them. Morgan's chest felt tight.

"You know nothing," Morgan said.

"If you kill me, no one will know anything."

John kept one hand at his throat, half-poised to ward off the sword. But he moved from his knees to a crouch, and slowly raised himself up. Morgan kept the blade aimed at the man's carotid artery. The light rippled as a drop of John's sweat splashed onto the blade.

"You wanted me to write your story," John said. "This Lisa, I think she's part of that story. A large part."

"She's irrelevant."

"No," John said. He shot a glance at Obsidian, standing motionless a few feet away, then turned his eyes back to Morgan. "I think she's the catalyst. She helped make you who you are. You didn't mention her in the file, but her presence is everywhere. It drives you."

Morgan tried to smile, but it felt like a grimace. "You think you understand me now, John?"

The reporter nodded quickly.

Morgan brought the blade to the man's chin. "Explain it to me."

John licked his lips, and his eyes drifted towards the ceiling. "After the massacre at Cambridge, you fled the country. Made your way through Europe for a few years." He screwed up his eyes, thinking. "Maybe you met Lisa somewhere there."

"Rome," Morgan said. "We met in Rome."

"You fell in love. She was a normal. She...she didn't know what you were, probably. Not at first. You began to forget, as well." Morgan could almost hear the man piecing the fragments together. "But eventually she found out."

He could still remember the look on her face, the way her lips twisted in disgust. They were in Madrid. It was warm that evening, so she wore a golden summer dress as they made their way back to their hotel. He was so busy drinking in the sight and smell of her that he didn't notice the thugs until they were on them.

They were metas, but too weak and stupid to be real supercriminals. Morgan offered them his wallet, but that wasn't what they came for. One of them clubbed him down with a blackjack, and then they started in on Lisa, eyes leering and filthy hands going for the straps on her dress.

Morgan left them alive for Lisa's sake. Well, he assumed they lived. The ringleader, a black-haired Spaniard with a basic electricity manipulation power, was losing a lot of blood from the stumps at the end of his arms.

John interrupted the memory. "Uh...there was a transcript in the files. The letterhead said it was from the Metahuman Control branch of Interpol. The witness's name was blacked out, but it was someone who knew you intimately."

Morgan closed his eyes and nodded. "She was just scared." He'd spent nearly a decade trying to convince himself of that. "The propaganda machine had done its work, and I became a monster in her eyes."

"Interpol turned her. They worked out who you were. She led them to you. And you—"

"That's enough," Morgan said. The blade's glow turned orange, like fire.

Her blood was hot when it left her. For a moment, her cheeks had been the same brilliant pink as when they made love. Then they turned grey, like the rest of her.

Morgan felt Obsidian's footsteps as she approached. "My lord?"

Electricity ran through his forehead. His head felt so tight he expected the arteries in his temples to burst. No. He wouldn't have another seizure. Not in front of the reporter.

He breathed deeply, trying to calm his mind. Slowly, ever so slowly, the pain and flashes of light subsided, retreating back to the part of his brain that kept his demons caged. His blade of light had disappeared. He couldn't remember letting it dissipate.

"My lord?"

He blinked away the fog, until the permanent black splotch was the only thing that clouded his vision. John was staring at him, his forehead damp and his round face pale.

Morgan forced himself to stand up straight and return his hands to his side. *Perception. It's all that matters.* God, this had been going on for so long.

His muscles seemed to creak when he put a smile on his face. "You're on the right track, John. You have one more chance at this story. Don't disappoint me."

He turned and left without waiting for a response. He thought he heard the reporter choke out a gasp of hysterical laughter, but by then Morgan was too far away to hear if it turned into sobbing. With his handkerchief, he wiped the sweat from his brow.

Obsidian caught up to him in the hallway. "My lord." She paused, as if struggling for words. "That…emotion. It is unlike you."

The incident at the TV studio flashed back to him, where he had allowed himself to be goaded by Iron Justice in his cage. He waved away the statement and the memory. "That isn't your concern." He checked his watch. Nearly midday. "Have you heard anything from Tinderbox?"

"Yes, my lord. A transmission came through just before you called me to deal with the reporter. It is done."

He breathed deep and forced himself to smile. It was all going to work out. John would figure out what needed to be done. And now Morgan had reinforcements, of a sort.

"You have command of the base, Obsidian. I'm going to meet our new friends."

As the dusty road rolled past, Morgan listened to the car radio. As he expected, the Prime Minister and the AAU had both been quick to refuse to comply with his demands. Frank Oppenheimer had yet to show his face, but that was no surprise. The time would come for that. In the meantime, there was one more thing he had to do before he moved into the final phases of his plan. His heart felt tight at the thought of being so close. The strain of all this was taking its toll on him. The interference of Spook and the Carpenter had convinced him to accelerate his plan by a few days. He'd given the authorities thirty-six hours to liberate their metahuman prisoners. That time wasn't yet up, but there was no point waiting for something that was never going to happen. So he took the prisoners himself.

Finally, after more than an hour of gravel roads and the rumble of the car engine, Morgan's driver slowed and took a turn into a long, narrow driveway. They were eighty or so miles outside of Neo-Auckland, on an old farm that had been abandoned and half-swallowed up by thick forest. As the Honda sedan topped a rise, several figures came into view at the end of the driveway. The freed prisoners slouched against the corrugated iron of the shed or prowled through the tall grass amongst the sheep droppings. He studied them, trying to judge their powers. *Yes. They'll do.*

His driver slowed to a stop in front of the prisoners, a cloud of dust riding in on their coattails. Morgan forced a smile onto his face as he stepped out. Gravel crunched beneath his shoes. He should have eaten before he came; he'd forgotten to have breakfast with all the excitement. It wouldn't do to have his stomach rumbling when he was trying to make a good impression.

Most of the metas were trying to look tough, which almost amused him enough to take his mind off his headache and his earlier outburst with John. These metas were small-timers, punks and thugs who had played at being supercriminals. A few were strong, even stronger than his people, but they were untrained, and more importantly, undisciplined. An albino with fists the size of Morgan's head and arms to match spat through the gap in his teeth, his thick eyebrows pulled down in a look of barely-disguised disgust.

Compared to the prison break in Siberia, this had been a cakewalk. The police had stepped up security on the small facility since his attack on the TV studio. It hadn't been enough. His man on the inside of Met Div, Daniel O'Connor, was suspended, but that didn't stop the police officer gaining access to the prison.

O'Connor stood off to the side of the metas, dressed in his blue Met Div uniform. A gas mask hung around his neck. He was an ugly fellow. His dark sideburns fell along the sides of his wide face. *A foul man.* Still, he knew how to move, and he knew how to fight. He nodded as Morgan approached him.

"Any issues?" Morgan asked.

O'Connor shook his head. "They let me right in the front door. I slipped your little gas canister into the air conditioning, and everyone but me got pretty drunk." He tapped the gas mask hanging around his neck. "Then I just let Tinderbox and the rest of the lads in, and got these bastards out. Easy. No deaths, and not a shot fired."

Tinderbox and the four metas in his team stood around the prisoners at equally-spaced intervals, watching. They were outnumbered three-to-one by the prisoners, but none looked uneasy. In any case, the threat of force wouldn't be needed to keep the prisoners in line much longer.

"Good work," Morgan said, and he shook O'Connor's hand. "Oh, I nearly forgot." He reached into his pocket and slipped the Met Div officer a thick envelope. "For your troubles."

O'Connor grunted and took the envelope, and Morgan moved away to examine the prisoners.

Most of the thugs tried to look uninterested, but their eyes drifted towards him. There were televisions in the prison facility, he knew. They'd seen him.

He smiled broadly and raised his arms to greet them. "My brothers. And sisters," he added to a pair of lithe twins reclining against the shed, both sets of eyes crackling with green lightning. "Thank you for meeting me. My name is Quanta."

"What kind of name is that, huh?" one of the prisoners called. "Look at those shoes. Prince of Faggots, more like." The rest roared with laughter.

Vulgar creatures, he thought. *But at least they have fire in them.* The smile never left his face. Slowly, the hoots and hollers subsided.

"I've come to see if you can be of use to me and my organisation," Morgan said. "I'm sure such fine people as yourselves would be delighted to change the world forever."

"Go fuck yourself, cocksucker," one of the twin girls said. "We ain't joining no one." The other prisoners added in their jeers. Again, he waited for the noise to die down. They were having trouble keeping up their defiance under his gaze. Pathetic.

He strolled amongst them until he was standing in front of the twins. He smiled at the one who had spoken. "Such a filthy mouth on such a pretty face. But I'm afraid you misunderstand me. We're full up at the moment with better metahumans than yourselves. So our organisation does not have any vacancies, as such."

They stared at him with blank looks on their faces.

"There is one opportunity available," he said. "But the chances of career advancement are, sadly, nil."

Their faces were still twisted up in confusion when he drew up his blade of light and cut the first woman's skullcap off.

One minute later, it was done. A few prisoners had scrambled to their feet in time to try to put up a fight, but they were slow. Now their blood soaked into the soil, and their bodies lay amongst the sheep shit.

He'd lost his appetite. His shield of light had kept the blood and flesh off him, but he could still feel it all over him. He wanted a bath. He could have had Tinderbox or the others do the butchering, but that wouldn't be right. Their deaths served his plan, so the blood should be on his hands.

Even O'Connor and the others were quiet, their eyes carefully sliding over the bodies. While Morgan caught his breath and went back to the car to retrieve his bag, O'Connor and Tinderbox approached him.

"Why?" O'Connor demanded.

Morgan took his bag and made his way back to the bodies, O'Connor and Tinderbox keeping pace beside him. "Why did I send you in to get them out if I was just going to butcher them?"

They nodded.

"Sometimes, the dead have more use than the living." He crouched and rolled one of the bodies over. Leaning close, he examined the spot where his light blade had sliced the top of the prisoner's skull off. The slice was so clean he could make out the tiny network of fibres that ran through the bone. The blade had partially cauterised the brain matter as it passed through. The smell of cooked brain tissue was not unpleasant, which only made it all the worse.

He brought up a thin layer of light around his hands to keep the gore off his gloves while he took a small specimen jar from his bag. With a tiny, scalpel-like blade of light extending from the tip of his index finger, he sliced out a marble-sized chunk of brain and dropped it into the jar.

When he turned back, Tinderbox's flames had dropped to candle-strength and had a sick, green tinge to them. O'Connor turned and spat. Morgan smiled.

"If this makes you ill," Morgan said, "gather your team together and congratulate them on a job well done. Then have them dig us some graves. O'Connor, you'll be staying here with C team. Prepare the airship. I'll be in touch in a few days."

O'Connor nodded. Tinderbox swallowed and retreated to the rest of the metas, who stood huddled and whispering. After a moment, Morgan let the strained smile drop and moved onto the next body.

If the dead cared, they didn't complain.

CHAPTER 19
THE LAST DOMINO

I was on the eighteenth floor, getting dangled out the window by Suicide Prime, and I figured I was a goner. The coppers couldn't do a damn thing. I was looking down on all the sirens and flashing lights below, and the crowds looked back, trying to get a good view for when I got splattered on the footpath. And then I saw her. Madame Z. Christ, she was a beautiful lass. She came floating up outta nowhere, just floating in thin air. Without breaking a sweat, she blew Suicide Prime away with some kinda psychic blast and magicked me safely back inside. It wasn't right what everyone said about her when they found out she was a dyke. She can screw the Circuit's robots for all it matters. She was the best damn hero I ever saw.

—Witness report from the Doom Corps hostage crisis, 1955

Niobe woke to the sound of sizzling and a spicy scent filling her nostrils. Her stomach growled and knotted. Bleary-eyed and groggy, she pulled the bowler hat off her face and sat up on the couch, putting a hand against her spine. That had been a bad place for a nap. Her back felt like a sumo wrestler had done a tap dance on it.

She plodded to the kitchen. *Gabby?*

Her heart sank when she saw Solomon stirring the sizzling vegetables around the pan. Solomon gave her a too-cheerful grin as she sank into a seat at the table and propped her chin up on her hands.

"Why so glum?" he asked.

"Bite me," she said. "Where's Gabby?"

Solomon shovelled the vegetables into piles on two plates. "Still in the bedroom."

Niobe put her face in her hands. Gabby hadn't so much as looked at them when she came back up from the basement, her clothes streaked with engine grease. She went into the bedroom, shut the door, and then Niobe heard the shower running. That was the last she'd seen of her.

Solomon shoved a plate and a big glass of water in front of her, and forced a fork into her hand. "Eat, kiddo."

She wasn't so hungry anymore. She glanced at the bedroom door, but no matter how much she willed it, it didn't open. She could just go in, but that might cause more problems than it would solve. Or maybe Gabby was in there waiting for her to come apologise. This bloody thing was too complicated.

Solomon sat opposite her, putting his plate down on top of an old police report about Daniel O'Connor's team taking down some metahuman kidnappers. He chowed into his food immediately, but Niobe poked a piece of broccoli with her fork. "What's this supposed to be?"

"Stir-fry," Solomon said with his mouth full. "I thought you were supposed to be Asian."

"My folks cooked Japanese food, not Chinese. And I spent most of my time at boarding school." She could barely remember her mum cooking. But the food did smell good. "Aren't you supposed to have rice or noodles or something with this?"

He shrugged. "Quit your complaining and eat. You can't go hunting supervillains on an empty stomach."

Her hunger returned as soon as she started eating. Her stomach rumbled with satisfaction. "What's the time?"

He checked his watch. "Five in the afternoon."

Crap. Her nap had gone a few hours longer than she intended. No wonder she was hungry. She drained her glass of water and went back to the food. They'd spent until midday poring over the documents she'd taken from Met Div, trying to piece everything together, find connections. They'd got nowhere. They were working with too few pieces of the puzzle. They needed to work out how everyone fitted together, but more importantly, they needed a location on Quanta. She'd lost count of how many times she'd listened to his smarmy voice on the recording, but the background noises were too distorted to be of any help.

The midday radio news said there had been reports of a breakout at the Metahuman Correctional Facility, but the cape coppers had lips as tight as their arses. It must've been a hell of a breakout. All the meta prisoners would have kill-switches, so any guard who caught them escaping would be able to blow the back of their head out in seconds.

Everyone who had a hint of authority had been quick to assure the public that the AAU wouldn't bow to Quanta's threats. The media called him a terrorist, not a supercriminal, like they were trying to play down the fact that he just executed one of the world's greatest superheroes on live television. Still, that didn't stop the reporters from snooping around the Old City, trying to get comments from ex-heroes. So far, they'd failed miserably.

Other than that, Met Div were floundering. Some were suggesting the radiation bomb Quanta left at the TV studio was a trick—real radiation poisoning didn't completely wear off after a couple of days. The cops had evacuated a mile radius from the studio, and had hazard teams cycling in and out to monitor the contamination. If it had all been for nothing, some people at Met Div would have red faces.

That said, she and Solomon weren't doing any better. Her eyes hurt trying to make out the handwritten reports. Solomon looked as shattered as she felt. Thankfully, he avoided asking any questions about her fight with Gabby. The situation was awkward enough as it was.

While she chewed, her eyes drifted over the paper scattered across the table. Avin and Screecher were definitely connected. They'd communicated and even worked in the same teams a few times back in the old days, and they were both active in Heroes for Freedom. Avin was a prominent member, while Screecher was a behind-the-scenes guy, but the organisation hadn't been large. It wasn't hard to picture them becoming friends and following the same causes.

What could entice them to fall in with Quanta, though? And what about Daniel O'Connor, the Met Div officer who'd snatched Sam from the boat? Judging from some of the reports in his file, O'Connor seemed to have links in the meta community. Was that how he'd encountered

Avin and Screecher? He'd started out as a beat cop in New Zealand, but he got friendly with some AAU bureaucrats and was promoted to some unspecified international government work in Europe in the '50s. Interpol, maybe, or some sort of special unit, the documents weren't clear. When he came back to New Zealand, he got tasked on some of the higher-profile stuff. Supercriminals and hostage situations and the like. He volunteered for Met Div when the unit was set up after the Seoul Accord was signed. He'd had a couple of brutality complaints, although nothing stuck. But then there was something interesting. The report of his dismissal was vague, but "indiscretions" were mentioned, along with veiled accusations of corruption. It wasn't conclusive, but she had a pretty good idea what'd happened. He'd been leaking departmental information. He'd been spying for Quanta. And by the sound of it, it had been going on a long time.

But how did he get to know Quanta in the first place? And where was the link she needed? It was here somewhere. There was something in these files that could help her find Quanta and Sam. There had to be. *Sam. He's alone with that bastard.*

She gobbled down the last bit of carrot and sat back in her chair. She'd never felt so satisfied. The Carpenter was giving her a funny look.

"What?" she said.

"Got any answers for us yet? I can hear your brain working from here."

She opened her mouth to tell him she was fresh out of ideas. A knock on the door cut her off.

He raised his eyebrows at her and frowned. She met his look, heart racing, and gave a tiny shrug. She didn't entertain visitors. Ever.

They stood silently. She reached for her gun before she remembered she'd left it in the holster in her bedroom, along with her mask. The Carpenter pulled on his mask and hat while she quietly padded to the bedroom and opened the door. Gabby was lying on the bed in a bathrobe, eyes puffy from tears. She sat up when Niobe entered.

Niobe pressed a finger to her lips, grabbed her gun from its holster, pulled the mask over her face, and slipped back into the living room.

The gun was loaded. She deliberated for half a second, then switched to stun rounds. The knock came again, louder. She went to the window and pulled the curtains closed. The Carpenter stood by the door, hatchet in one hand and a small, crazed smile on his face. She came alongside him and held up a fist. *On three,* she mouthed. He nodded.

She held up one finger. *One.*

Who the hell could it be? *Two.*

She sucked in a lungful of air and slipped into shadow. The comforting dark embraced her, and she became part of the faded carpet. She sped through the crack under the door and got an image of the sleek surface of someone in a full bodysuit. She darted between his legs and emerged from the shadow behind him.

Three.

The Carpenter jerked the door open, and at the same time she shoved the barrel of her gun against the stranger's back. The man jumped, but before he could react, the Carpenter's hand darted out, latched onto his shoulder, and hauled him inside. Niobe followed, gun pressed against the white bodysuit that covered every inch of skin.

She kicked the door shut behind her as the Carpenter pressed the man against the wall. The suited man was so tall she had to stretch to press the gun barrel against the side of his head. The masked man raised his arms, palms out, and said, "Jesus Christ, don't shoot!"

It took her a moment to recognise him. "Quick-fire?"

"Bit far from the Blind Man's territory, aren't you, speedster?" the Carpenter said, the man's suit fabric scrunched in his fist. "Get lost on your way to buy a pack of smokes?"

There was a patch on his suit covering the spot where Niobe's stun round had hit him. That felt like years ago.

"Talk quick," she said. "How do you know where I live?"

"The Blind Man." His voice was clipped. "He knows all that sort of stuff."

That son of a bitch. What else did he get when he was rooting around in her brain? Were her bloody memories not enough?

"What do you want, Quick-fire?" the Carpenter said.

The speedster reached to his neck and pulled the mask off his face. Christ, he was just a skinny little kid himself. The Māori boy couldn't have been more than twenty. Dark fuzz peppered his upper lip, and his head was a mop of black curls. His wide eyes darted between them, but they kept coming back to the gun she aimed at him.

"Jesus, lady, take it easy with that thing. I got a message for you from the Blind Man. Information."

She growled and he looked even more scared. Taking pity on the kid, she uncocked the revolver and let her arm fall to the side. The Carpenter glanced at her and eased up his grip, but he didn't let go completely.

"Yeah?" the Carpenter said. "How much is he charging for it this time? I got a soul I'm just dying to sell."

"No charge. Mates' rates."

She shared a glance with the Carpenter. "Bullshit."

"No, really," Quick-fire said. "You guys have got a common enemy."

Ah, so that's it. "The Blind Man's taken a disliking to Quanta then," she said. "He wants us to do his dirty work for him."

Quick-fire nodded. "Something like that."

"Piss off."

"No, wait. The Blind Man says it will help you get the boy back."

She frowned beneath her mask. It smelled fishy, but then everything attached to the Blind Man did. She could see the same thought going through Solomon's brain. His grip tightened on Quick-fire's white suit.

"Think I should let him go?" he said.

She tapped her cheek with her free hand and considered it. A dark part of her was enjoying watching the poor kid squirm. But finally she nodded. "Go on, then."

He let go, brushed the creases out of the kid's suit, and stepped back. Quick-fire eyed them warily for a few seconds, then he seemed to breathe a bit easier.

"This information," she said. "How'd your boss come by it?"

"A guy came around looking for new recruits. One of Quanta's boys. The Blind Man didn't like that. We got hold of him, and the Blind Man poked his mind to see what came out."

She couldn't see a lie on his face, and it seemed like the sort of thing the old man would do. "All right. Talk."

His gaze flicked over them again, and he took another couple of breaths to calm himself. "The guy, Quanta, his real name's Morgan Shepherd."

Niobe grabbed a pen and paper from the table. "S-H-E-P-H-A-R-D?"

"Nah, —H-E-R-D. I think."

Quanta = Morgan Shepherd, she scribbled. "What else?"

"He's definitely got the boy you're looking for. The boss wasn't sure, but he thinks they're trying to mess with his brain."

"His brain? Why?"

Quick-fire shrugged. "Dunno. But Doll Face is the one doing the messing."

Her heart dropped into her intestines. She'd been blocking out that particular thought, hoping Quanta had some other use for Doll Face. What tortures had Sam already been through? *Jesus Christ, he's just a kid!*

"Spook?" the Carpenter said quietly.

She realised her fingers were trembling around her gun. Hot anger pulsed through her in time with her heartbeat. She forced herself to breathe. Getting worked up wouldn't help anyone.

Did Quanta think he could control Doll Face? Supercriminals had tried it before, and they always regretted it at the end, when the end was a long time coming.

"If we're gonna stop this guy, we need a location," the Carpenter said. "Tell me you've got that for us."

Quick-fire's lips formed a line. "Not exactly."

"What's that supposed to mean?" she said.

"The boss could only get an image. He drew a picture." Quick-fire pulled out a slip of paper from a hidden pocket.

Niobe was skeptical about an old blind man's artistic ability, but when she unfolded the paper, she had to stifle a gasp. The picture could've passed for a photograph. It depicted part of the Neo-Auckland skyline. She could make out the Peace Tower standing tall above all the other buildings. But it was far away. The picture had been taken from a fair way south.

Solomon pointed to the other side of the picture, away from the skyline. "Are those chimneys? Industrial chimneys?"

She studied it for a moment, then nodded. There were two bigger than all the others, far in the distance. From their tips, steam rolled into the sky. She'd seen them before.

"The power station," she and the Carpenter said together.

The Carpenter swept a bunch of documents off the map of Neo-Auckland on the table. He stabbed the point with his finger. The power station was a few miles south of central Neo-Auckland, a little way past the edge of the industrial district. It was a coal and gas station that provided power for most of Neo-Auckland and the surrounding towns.

Solomon looked at the picture again, then back at the map. "The land's flat there. You can see those chimneys for miles around."

Damn it, he was right. She glanced back at Quick-fire, who stood forgotten in the corner. "This is all he's got? He can't pinpoint it more closely?"

Quick-fire shrugged. "Sorry, lady."

She put a hand on her forehead and tried to think. "It's no good. There's too many places for him to hide."

"When he was yakking to us on the radio," the Carpenter said, "there was all that noise, and that echo. A factory, or a warehouse maybe."

A warehouse. Something dim sparked inside her head. She snatched a pile of documents off the floor and started rifling through them. *Where was it?*

"Spook?" the Carpenter said.

"Daniel O'Connor was involved in a raid back in the late fifties before he joined Met Div. A kidnapping. There were these three low-level supercriminals doing ransom jobs. They got busted, and their hideout was a warehouse in the industrial district. They'd outfitted it for holding captives. Just the place for a budding supervillain." She dropped the stack and moved to another. *Where the bloody hell was it?*

Her hands seized the report. "Got it." She scanned the page and flicked through the summarised case notes. "The coppers seized the warehouse. It doesn't say what happened to it, but after the trial it would have had to be returned to the owners or auctioned off to a private party." Maybe O'Connor himself bought it. He'd get it for a song, and who would be better placed to know it was available?

"Private party, eh?" Solomon tapped the address of the warehouse. "I think we just scored ourselves an invitation."

Her heart was doing a trapeze act in her chest. She matched the address to the map and circled the spot with her pen. "We have to move. No telling how long he's going to stay there."

The Carpenter nodded, his face split with an infectious grin.

Quick-fire hadn't moved. She put her hand on his shoulder and firmly directed him towards the door. "Thank the Blind Man for us."

"Sure."

"One more thing," she said as she pushed him into the hallway. "Tell him the next person he sends to my house gets returned without knee-caps."

The boy's eyes widened. Niobe shut the door in his face. She heard a rush of air as he streaked away.

"Poor kid," Solomon said. "Sounds like he's running fast enough to set the stairs on fire."

"They've gotta learn somehow." She pulled off her mask.

Solomon folded up the map and shoved it in his pocket. "Meet you downstairs?"

She nodded and put the note with Quanta's real name on the table. *We're coming for you, Morgan Shepherd.*

Solomon opened the front door, checked outside to see if Quick-fire was gone, then turned back. "Hey. Good work, mate."

She smiled, and it felt good. "Yeah, you too, partner."

He tipped his hat and disappeared into the hallway.

Gabby was standing when Niobe went back into the bedroom. The tearstains on her cheeks were gone, but her eyes were still bloodshot and rimmed with pink. For a moment, they stared at each other. Niobe's excitement deflated when she saw the lines straining Gabby's face.

—*It's okay*, Niobe finally signed. *It was a friend. Kind of. We've got a location on the kid.* She tried another smile, but it was harder this time.

The corners of Gabby's lips twitched upwards as well, just for an instant, but her eyes didn't match the smile.

—*Tell the police. Stay.*

—*Gabby....*

"Stay," Gabby said.

Niobe's heart dropped into her toes.

—*I can't. The kid's a meta. Maybe a powerful one. If Met Div gets their hands on him....* Her hands fell. She pictured McClellan lying stretched and dead in the street, his baby in the hands of those arseholes.

Gabby took her by the front of her coat and pulled her close. "Please don't go alone."

"I'll have Solomon with me."

"That's not what I mean."

Niobe tried to kiss her, but Gabby turned her face away. God, she felt like such a piece of shit. She settled for giving Gabby a peck on the cheek. No reaction.

Niobe sighed, took her holster from where it hung on the bedpost, and strapped it over her shoulder.

—*I'll be back soon*, she signed.

Gabby turned away and put a hand across her eyes. All Niobe wanted to do was take her in her arms, pull her close, kiss her, tell her she was sorry, she'd stay, she wasn't going anywhere. She reached out a hand...

...and let it drop. She had a job to do.

"I love you," she said, knowing Gabby wouldn't hear her with her back turned. "More than anything. I'll get you out of this place. I promise."

She slipped her gun into its holster and went out of the room.

CHAPTER 20
PACKAGED AND DELIVERED

GRIM

REAL NAME:	*Kang Shen*
POWERS:	*Danger sense, luck.*
NOTES:	*The most controversial member of the Wardens. Claims to have become metahuman in 1941, a full three years before Robert Oppenheimer became Dr Atomic. Whether he was actually metahuman or not was hotly debated. During the battle against the Nagasaki Horrors, Grim developed a reputation amongst Japanese civilians as an infallible good luck charm. When mandatory metahuman registration began, he fled the country, always escaping pursuing police officers by minutes through improbably lucky circumstances.*

—Notes on selected metahumans [Entry #0556]

It rang once, then he picked up. "Senior Sergeant Wallace."

"Do you know who this is?" Niobe said into the phone.

There was a pause. "Vigilante bitch."

"Spare me." Niobe leaned against the wall of the public phone box and stared at the rows of chimneys billowing smoke into the evening sky. "How are those metas we took out for you? Any of them squealed on Quanta yet?"

Silence.

"Didn't think so," she said. She cradled the phone against her shoulder, put a Pall Mall between her lips, and lit up. "Look, I didn't call for a pissing contest."

"Could've fooled me. Want to turn yourself in?"

"Not particularly. I'll send you a cheque for that window I broke when all this is done. Then we can call it even."

The grunt he gave was probably the closest he ever came to laughing. "What about the light bulb you shot?"

"Add it to my tab."

Neither of them said anything for a moment. The Carpenter was leaning on the car, a pair of binoculars pressed to his eyes. Nothing moved at Quanta's warehouse, but that didn't mean nobody was home. Old shipping crates and a simple chain-link fence surrounded the building. Unlike the rest of Neo-Auckland, the industrial district didn't take much design advice from *Flash Gordon.*

"We've got a common enemy," she said. "Quanta."

"That right? Here I was thinking you two might be good friends."

"I don't care if you believe me or not." She took a long drag on the cigarette. "But if I were you, I'd want to come pay a visit to thirty-three Hakea Avenue. I'd want to bring a lot of guys."

He grunted. "I'll find you, vigilante."

"Until then, Senior Sergeant." She hung up.

A few more puffs of the cigarette, then she stubbed it out half-finished and pulled her mask back down. She made her way back to Solomon and the car. Gabby had done a fine job on the Ford. It ran better than ever. Niobe wished she'd remembered to thank her properly.

"Met Div will be here in twenty," she said. "See a way in?" She adjusted her goggles to get a better look at the warehouse in the darkening evening. The main warehouse had a handful of smaller buildings attached to it, all painted a horrible not-quite-pine-green colour that had never been fashionable.

He lowered the binoculars and pointed. "There's a couple of roller doors there, the kind you back a truck up to. And when we were driving past, I saw another entrance that you could get a forklift through. I don't know about you, but I'm not too keen to try opening any of those."

She shook her head. They looked like they were locked down tight, and besides, Quanta and his goons would poke them full of holes the instant they went in. "What, then?"

"You see there, on the south-west corner?"

She adjusted her magnification. Just peeking around the corner she could see…. "Stairs."

"I figure it'll take us up to an office," he said. "Maybe even a switch-box if we're lucky. Then we just do a top-down sweep. Easy-peasy."

She drew her gun, checked the rounds, and tugged her bowler hat down. "Still remember how to do this, old man?"

He grinned and brandished his freshly-grown quarterstaff. "Kids these days. No respect, I tells ya."

They broke into a run, sticking to the shadows. Solomon led the way down the side of the chain-link fence, taking them away from the road. Nothing else moved.

The Carpenter sped up to a sprint, raised his quarterstaff, and thrust it onto the concrete in front of him. The wood bent like a pole-vaulter's pole for an instant. Then something in his eyes flared, and the staff snapped straight. She got a last look at him launching himself over the fence, cape flying behind him, before she sucked in a lungful of air and slipped into shadow.

She went through the fence and kept moving for the stairs on the warehouse's exterior wall. The concrete shuddered as Solomon landed behind her, hatchet and staff at the ready. A moment later, she exhaled and came out of the shadow, gun aimed up the metal stairs, scanning for threats. *Clear.*

She glanced at the Carpenter and jerked her head. He nodded and silently backed towards her, guarding their rear. A floodlight cast the side of the warehouse into sharp relief, which wasn't doing it any favours. The green paint was faded and peeling, and the concrete bore half a hundred dried oil stains. Nothing fresh, though. It didn't look like anyone had bothered to show up here in a decade. *Is this really Quanta's hideout?* It had to be.

She led the way up the stairs. The door at the top said *NO ADMIT-TANCE* in scratched red. She put her ear to the door. Voices. A lot of them. She couldn't make out what they were saying. *Oh yes, this is the place.*

The door was locked. Her picks saw to that. Out of the corner of her eye, she watched the Carpenter bounce on the balls of his feet. Her stomach was doing a similar dance. For a moment, doubt crept into her heart. Gabby was right. They shouldn't be doing this alone. In the old days, they'd have half the Wardens along to deal with someone as crafty as Quanta and his band of metas. Avin and Screecher were classically trained. God knew how many others were pros. It wasn't quite a suicide mission, but it wasn't far off.

Then she thought of Sam, of the chill that ran through him when O'Connor elbowed him in the throat. She thought of him sitting alone in darkness, at the mercy of Quanta. Screw the old days. She wasn't a hero anymore, but she still had a job to do. She could still save this one kid, do this one last good thing, before she left Earth. Frank had fucked up. She couldn't.

"Remember the old oath?" the Carpenter whispered. "We are the masked, the hidden, the endless watchers. We are the strangers who guard the world through the night."

We are every man, the words came automatically.

Their fate is our fate.

So we will stand,

And we will hold back the storm,

Until the light shines through,

Or the night takes us.

She glanced at the Carpenter. He grinned and gave her a thumbs up.

"Shut up and fight." She cocked her gun and threw open the door.

Morgan closed the false wall in the rear of the warehouse and turned to face the stacks of crates and rusted industrial shelving. He wiped his forehead with a handkerchief. It was done. All the pieces were in place, bar one, and that one would come to him eventually. Sam was looking even worse this time. It wouldn't be long now.

He stretched his arms above his head. The level of chatter in the warehouse was low. He could hear Tinderbox in the corner boasting about his part in the prisoner extraction, and by the sound of the laughs, he'd attracted quite a crowd. They deserved time to relax after a hard couple of days. Perhaps he'd skip dinner and get an early night himself. Yes, that'd be just the ticket.

A muffled sound came from the other end of the warehouse. Darkness struck the room like a club.

In an instant, Morgan had formed his blade. He used it like a torch, holding it ahead of him to guide his path in the thick blackness. Shouts echoed around the warehouse.

"Standard units," he yelled as he ran. "Check your targets before you attack. Tinderbox!"

"My lord." His flames flickered as he trotted towards Morgan, three other metas in tow.

"The main switch bank is in my office. Get these lights back on."

Tinderbox nodded. "Come on, you lot. At least try to look fearsome, you sacks of meat."

This wasn't a power outage. Navigatron had built generators. Those wouldn't just break down. Morgan's heart pounded as he moved.

Two cracks echoed, and he thought he caught a tiny muzzle flash on the upper balcony before the darkness swallowed everything again. His people responded with lightning and fire. Someone heavy—Knuckles, maybe—leapt a full story through the friendly fire towards the attacker. He came crashing down on the catwalk above, his shadow flickering against the steel wall. But the attacker was gone. A moment later, the gun barked again from somewhere else, and Knuckles staggered backwards, slumping against the wall. Lightning crackled again, and purple afterimages blinded Morgan for a moment.

"Obsidian!" he called, before he remembered she was off with Navigatron and O'Connor preparing *Hyperion*.

"Aw, hey now, don't look so glum," came a voice from behind him. "All couples fight, but I'm sure she'll be back before you know it."

He spun, bringing his blade up to guard. The cloaked man just stood there, his smile half-hidden by shadow, his eyes glowing behind his mask. Morgan returned the smile.

"Too honourable to strike a man while his back's turned, Carpenter?"

"Not really."

The corner of something heavy slammed into Morgan's lower back. An explosion went off in his kidney that matched the one in his head. He stumbled forwards. The Carpenter seemed to flash, bringing his staff streaking towards Morgan's face.

He got his shield up. Sparks flew as the staff rebounded. Morgan gritted his teeth against the shockwave that rolled through him. He ducked another strike and lunged, but the Carpenter planted his staff and leapt backwards.

The Carpenter's eyes crackled. Morgan caught movement out of the corner of his eye. He twisted and sliced another flying wooden crate in two before it could strike him. Another two came at him from opposite sides. He slashed at them and dived back. The sliced fragments flew at him, pelting him from every side. He put his reserve energy into his shield and let it take the hits.

The Carpenter grinned at him, and he couldn't help but smile back even as the wood hammered at his shield. "You're quick, Carpenter."

"Cheers. You a fan? Want me to sign that fancy magic sword of yours?"

"You should've killed me while my back was turned."

He shrugged. "Old dogs, old habits, all that."

"You'll come to regret that, you know. I told you that on the radio. These aren't the old days."

They moved in a lazy circle. Every now and then a gunshot or a shout would punctuate their silence, but back here in the stacks they had a degree of privacy. He could smell the stink of panic in the air. He hadn't had time to properly train his people on defensive operations. They were warriors, barbarians, not soldiers. No matter. Once the lights came back on, Spook and the Carpenter would be no match for their numbers.

"So, where's Sam?" the Carpenter said.

Morgan let his smile grow. "And here I thought you came to stop me taking over the world."

"Nah, that's the B-plot. Give us the kid, maybe we'll put in a good word for you when you get arrested."

Morgan laughed, and he didn't even have to fake it. "I'm sure your Metahuman Division will appreciate your earnest testimony."

The Carpenter jabbed high. His staff sizzled when Morgan batted it away with his shield. In return Morgan feinted left, sweeping right at the last second. The Carpenter darted back, sending another three crates flying to block his retreat. Morgan cut them from the air. Stillness returned.

"Carpenter," came another voice from up above. Morgan sidestepped away from the voice to bring the speaker into view without putting his back to the Carpenter.

"Yeah, mate?" the Carpenter said.

Morgan spotted her now. She crouched atop a crate, her trench coat draped around her like a crow's wings.

"I've searched every bloody room," she said. "Nothing."

A twitch of the Carpenter's mouth was the only expression he gave, but it was amusing nonetheless. "Ah," Morgan said, "the esteemed Spook. But you don't mind if I call you Niobe, do you?"

In the glow of his blade, he could see the Carpenter's eyes widening behind his mask. Morgan shifted his feet slightly, preparing for the Carpenter to lunge. Spook disappeared and reappeared on the ground. Her goggles gleamed in the light.

"Not at all, Morgan."

His throat closed up for a moment, and the muscles in his cheek froze. Then he laughed. There was nothing else he could do. "Oh, you two are good. This is more fun than I could ever have anticipated."

Spook raised her gun and fired. His shield was up, but there were no sparks. *She missed at this range?* Then he heard the choked cry of one of his people collapsing behind him. She turned the gun on him.

"There's a secret room," she said. "A trapdoor. Something like that. Where?"

"Are you going to shoot me, Spook?"

Car tyres screeched outside.

"Where is it?" she demanded.

Doors slammed, and he heard someone trying to wrench open the loading bay's roller doors. His people wouldn't stop shouting.

"Mate, we gotta go," the Carpenter said.

"You invited your friends?" Morgan asked. "I thought we were going to keep this personal."

The Carpenter took a step back and glanced at her. "Spook."

"Not without Sam." Her gun hand never trembled. "Where is he?"

Morgan smiled at her.

"We can't find him if we're banged up," the Carpenter said. "We'll come back when the coppers are gone. We'll find him. But we gotta get lost, and it's gotta be now."

"Where is he?" she screamed.

Sam pressed his ear to the door of his cell. It had gone quiet. There had been banging. Shouting. Then nothing.

"Help!" he hollered, his throat raw and aching. He hammered on the steel again and again.

Pain. He hurt everywhere. His hands were streaked with blood. It was the only way to get the blackness out. It stuck to him; it was everywhere, in his veins, in his flesh, in his soul. He no longer noticed the taste of blood when he gnawed through his skin.

He was so alone. He'd always been alone. He couldn't remember what was outside anymore, but he had to get there. Something deep inside told him that. Maybe it was a hallucination. He had those a lot. Maybe this whole room was a hallucination. Maybe *he* was a hallucination.

"Help," he said again, but his voice was quieter now. Who was he calling to? He couldn't remember. But the noises outside meant something. Outside. Yes, outside. There was sunlight, he knew. Sunlight that smelled like sweat and salt and wind. And there were people there. Family. His uncle, yes. And people he could meet. Pretty girls swimming in the ocean.

Remember. Remember Dantès. Remember your father.

Something deep in his chest shifted. It spread through him like boiling water. *The energy.* He shivered. Dimly, he recalled a tale about his father. No one came to save his father when he was trapped and dying. But he'd wanted to see his family again. So he'd concentrated on the energy running through him, the energy given to him by the weapon he'd created.

A far-away wrenching sound shattered the silence. Boots stomped somewhere above his head. They wouldn't find him. He was somewhere hidden, that much was obvious. Some of the fog began to clear from his mind.

He stepped back from the door and let the energy drip through him, just like his father had. He could feel it in his skin, in his fingers, warm and tingling and electric. With a little push, it began to flow inwards, towards his chest. It began to build, slowly filling him up drip by drip.

The pain faded as the warmth grew. It almost made him sleepy. When was the last time he truly slept? But no, he couldn't sleep now. Not now. He had one chance to get out of this hole, to see the world again. One chance. The energy filled him to the brim. And it kept flowing.

The pressure built in his chest. *No, wait. Stop.* It was too much. He couldn't handle it. He felt like he was swelling, expanding. The energy needed to escape. It should be pouring out his eyes and ears and mouth. *No. I can't take more.* He tried to stop the energy flowing, tried to push it back out to his extremities. But it was like trying to turn back a river with a teaspoon. Shivers ran down his spine, through every inch of him. The world swayed, and he was on his knees. Too much. It's too much. *I can't take it!*

The energy exploded inside him. He was on fire, burning, burning forever. He was a pile of embers, he was ash.

He lived.

His skin parted in a thousand places, but there was no pain. Just power. Through the cuts in his skin came sheets of shining metal, gleaming beneath the fluorescent light. The extra bulk shredded his shirt and coated his skin, forming a layer of interlocking scales. Strength rippled through him. He knew what to do. Someone had shown him.

The metal plates in his cheeks clinked together as he smiled.

His fist struck the steel door with the heat of a thousand suns. It screamed, glowing red, and flew off its hinges, shattering the concrete of the opposite wall. The building groaned. His mind had been murky as the sea, but not now. Now he could see.

He stepped out of the cell. No, he didn't move; the world moved beneath him. He was invincible. Shouts and movement came from upstairs, but there was no hurry. He was going to see his uncle again, and the sun, and the sea. He was Dantès. He was free.

Spindly fingers wrapped around his throat. Something sharp drove itself between the plates in his side and kept driving. The metal scales screeched and retreated into his skin. His back arched as the strength slipped away from him. *No. Oh God, no!*

"Did it forget me, hmmm?"

Doll Face's stench filled Sam's nostrils. His hands went to his throat, trying to pry away the fingers. *Please.* He groped for the energy, but it was gone. Something worm-like crawled along his cheek and touched the corner of his mouth.

"They're taking the Pretty Man away. It's just Doll Face and the boy, now." The creature giggled, and Sam's vision blurred.

More worms on his face, in his mouth. As one, they began to slide down his throat. He gagged, eyes stinging, but he couldn't move.

"Did it hear that? Nothing to stop Doll Face now. Doll Face will enjoy the cutting."

Somewhere deep in Sam's mind, something cracked. His eyes rolled back in his head.

CHAPTER 21

Always in the Last Place You Look

It's easy to condemn when you've never been through the same thing yourself. I'd just buried my husband and my daughter. Or I would have, if there'd been anything left to bury after Magnon shrunk them down and crushed them. So yeah, I tracked Magnon down, and yeah, I killed him. And now you're asking me how I got through all his henchmen and took down the supercriminal himself when I'm just a normal? I'll tell you how. I hit them harder and faster than anyone else had. I was willing to go further than any hero. I had no time for mercy.

—Court transcript from the trial of Pamela Jenkins
(aka the Lioness), 1958

Even from the shadow of the alley, Niobe could see the smug way Quanta strutted out of the warehouse. It made no difference that a hood covered his face and energy cuffs bound his hands together. The squad of Met Div officers surrounding him could have been an honour guard, escorting him from his limousine to accept an award for supervillain of the year.

She tapped the dashboard with her finger, trying to hold back the magma inside her. Sam was in there, she knew it. But the cape coppers were swarming around the place like ants, loading metas into vans and high-sec transport trucks under half a dozen floodlights. It didn't make it any easier that she was the one who called them in the first place. She'd had to; it was Quanta's territory. She could only have given his gang the run-around for so long before they got their act together and brought their numbers to bear. She needed the cavalry.

She could see Senior Sergeant Wallace barking orders at men a good head taller than him. The coppers obeyed without question. It was probably the moustache that did it. His mouth kept moving, but his gaze never left Quanta as his men loaded him into the biggest truck they had. The vehicle was armour-plated with a field generator on the roof, and by the looks of it, the bastard had the whole thing to himself.

The Carpenter lowered his binoculars and slouched down behind the steering wheel. "I count thirty-one arrested so far. No bodies. You didn't kill anyone, right?"

She lifted her mask and jammed a cigarette between her lips. "Stun rounds only. I got maybe nine or ten of them before I came to talk to you." She clicked the button on her auto-lighter, but the damn thing was on the fritz. Bloody hell. "Surprised none of them killed their mates, the amount of firepower they were putting out." One of them had sent a throwing knife her way, and it would've got her if she hadn't gone into shadow the same instant.

"He sure went quiet." Solomon sounded like he was talking to himself.

She banged the auto-lighter against the dashboard and tried again. Nothing. "Bugger it," she grumbled, snatching the unlit smoke from her mouth. "What did you say?"

The Carpenter pushed his hat back. "Quanta. He's fast, Niobe. And I'll bet my life savings that shield of his is bullet-proof."

"You don't have any life savings."

"None that you know of." He put the binoculars back to his face. "Maybe the coppers would've got him eventually, but he could've served up a nice helping of decapitations first."

She didn't give a damn what the bastard did. She wasn't much enamoured of Met Div or the AAU's metahuman laws, but they'd throw the book at him for what he'd done, and it would be a big bloody book. That was some kind of satisfaction.

Quanta knew her name, though. That grated. But she couldn't see how he could use it against her now. Even if he sold it to Senior Sergeant Wallace for a deal, she and Gabby would be sitting cozy in a lunar rocket by the time he came knocking.

"Come on," she said. "They're not leaving here for a few hours. I'm starving. Let's come back when they've shipped everyone off."

"Wait," he said, peering through the binoculars. "Who's that guy? Doesn't look like much of a supercriminal to me."

"Is it Daniel O'Connor?" She switched up her magnification.

"Not unless he shrunk in the wash."

It took her a moment to figure out who he was talking about, then she spotted him. The man was young, less than thirty, shortish, and a bit flabby. All the metas being led out around him were in costume, but this guy was dressed in slacks and a button-up shirt. A single cape copper escorted him.

"I got bells going off in my head," Solomon said. "Do you know him?"

"I saw him in there when I was searching for Sam. Just hiding in an office. He didn't see me, so I left him alone. Can't say he looks familiar, though."

It was a curiosity, but she couldn't see what the Carpenter was getting so worked up about. She switched off her magnification and glanced at him while he chewed his lip.

"I got it," he said, snapping his fingers. "He's a reporter. British guy. Uh...somebody Bishop. John Bishop, that's it."

"Friend of yours?"

"I saw him on TV once. He's a newspaper kid, I think, but he was in the spotlight for a while for some stories he did on a coup in Syria."

She looked again, but he still didn't seem familiar. Then again, she and Gabby didn't own a TV. "He doesn't look happy about being hauled away. Hostage?"

"Could be."

The copper helped John Bishop into the back of a marked car. After a few minutes, some of the full vehicles formed a convoy and rumbled back towards the city. Eventually, the Carpenter lowered his binoculars again and smiled at her.

"How about that grub?" he said.

———·———

They changed into civilian clothes and found an all-night truck stop and diner on the main road at the fringe of the industrial district. Apart from a single trucker sitting in the corner, they had the place to themselves. The mashed potato was lumpy and the steak was tough, but Niobe gobbled it down all the same. At least it was hot. She'd forgotten how hungry combat made her.

She expected Solomon to be more excited. He got to play superhero again, and they caught the bad guy. Well, someone caught him, anyway. When she'd finished her meal and he was only halfway through his burger, she tried asking him what was wrong. He just grinned and said, "That guy was fast. He'd give Omegaman a run for his money." But the grin faded quickly.

She was finishing off her second glass of lemonade when the Met Div vehicles started going past in convoys of three or four. The trucker in the corner noticed them too. His wide face furrowed all over as he squinted out the window, but he stayed silent until he finished his meal, waved goodbye to the waitress, and walked back to his truck.

Niobe kept count of the vehicles. After another half hour, she downed the last of her drink. "That's all of them. Let's go."

When they got back to the warehouse, it was nearly deserted. Most of the floodlights were gone, and police tape covered the entrances. They parked a block away, changed back into costume, and walked the rest of the way. No traffic on the roads, not even a bird perched on the power lines. While the Carpenter climbed to the rooftop opposite to observe the front, Niobe did a quick circuit of the compound, popping in and out of shadows.

She emerged from the shadow and crouched beside the Carpenter on the rooftop. "Four coppers in two pairs, patrolling. Each pair's got a radio. Looks like their plan is to call for backup and run like hell if any angry supercriminals show up."

The Carpenter lowered his binoculars and nodded. "Got us an entrance?"

"Same as last time."

They stayed clear of the streetlights as they crossed the road and moved silently along the fence line. The pair of cape coppers on the other side of the chain links weren't the most diligent on the force; one of them had slung his rifle over his back to better hold his cigarette, while the other was so nervous he looked ready to put a round in the first stray cat unlucky enough to wander past. Niobe and Solomon waited until the coppers rounded the corner, then he pole vaulted the fence and she slipped through the shadow. Quiet as roaches, they scrambled up the stairs, cracked the lock on the door, and went inside.

The darkness inside was almost complete. Even through her mask, she could smell ash and dust and melted plastic from the fight.

The door they entered led to the head office, probably intended for a manager or foreman. Earlier in the evening she'd been too preoccupied to notice the map of Neo-Auckland pinned to one wall. She ran her fingers along the paper. Holes from thumb tacks or pins were left all across the city's surface, but all the pins themselves were gone. She puzzled over it for a moment, tapping her cheek with her finger, but there were too many holes to make out any sort of pattern. It didn't matter. Quanta was locked up; it was over now.

The Carpenter half-heartedly checked the desk drawers and filing cabinet.

"Anything?" she asked.

He shook his head. "Cleaned out."

By Quanta or Met Div? she wondered. Never mind. Whatever Quanta's plan was, he'd have a hell of a time trying to conduct it from a prison cell. "We need to find Sam. There's got to be a secret room somewhere."

"A basement, maybe," he said.

It was a good thought. She went out onto the catwalk and increased the contrast on her goggles. At the far end of the warehouse, she could make out a set of shelving lying toppled over like a wrecked ship, spilling its crates onto the cracked warehouse floor. Before the fight, most of the metas had been scattered around this end of the warehouse, near the loading bays. But she'd found Quanta and the Carpenter fighting near the far wall, amongst the stacks.

"Was Quanta down there when you found him?" she asked. "Away from the others?"

"Yeah. I just jumped him where I saw him."

She put a finger to her lips and tapped them through her mask, thinking. "Let's see what the bastard was doing down there."

It was easy enough to find the scene of the Carpenter's brief fight. Several crates had been bisected as if by a laser, complete with scorch marks. Now they spewed outdated, boxed kitchen appliances across the floor. Niobe and Solomon split up and tried to trace Quanta's steps. Their footsteps echoed lightly through the warehouse.

If there were any trapdoors, they were well-hidden. She made her way around the stacks, careful to inspect any crack or crevice in the floor, but there was nothing. She wanted a cigarette. She looked around with her contrast on the highest setting, trying to picture the warehouse's layout. If they'd had time, getting blueprints of the place would've been a smart idea. She'd already searched the smaller build-ing adjoined to the main warehouse; just offices, bathrooms, that sort of thing. But Quanta had been here, amongst the stacks. *Maybe he was getting away for a cigarette too.*

Her eyes fell on the back wall, where a ladder with wheels sat against a huge dusty chalkboard. When she got close, she could make out a crack in the wall behind. She tapped it with her knuckle. The sound resonated. Hollow.

"Carpenter," she called. She shoved the ladder out of the way, put her shoulder against the wall and pushed. It gave a little, but not all the way. "There must be a release or a button around here." She felt along the wall to the side.

"Here's your release," he said.

"What?" She turned and found a crate hovering in the air in front of the blackboard. The Carpenter's eyes glowed, his mouth split in a grin. "Wait a minute. Do you think that's a good—?"

The crate crashed into the blackboard. Something snapped—maybe a few somethings—and the false wall rotated, leaving a gap a few feet across. Niobe cringed at the noise as it echoed around the warehouse.

"Bloody hell, Carpenter, you trying to get us caught?"

He shrugged. "We won't be if you stop yakking and get on with it." He stuck his head in the gap. "It's pretty dark, but there's stairs here."

Now she really wanted a cigarette. *Goddamn man-child.* He disappeared down the stairway. She followed, pulling her mini-torch from her belt. The beam illuminated concrete stairs and walls streaked with damp.

The stairs looped back on themselves and brought them to a basement underneath the warehouse. The air was thick and stale. Somewhere, water dripped. A shadowed opening sat in each side of the grey corridor. Nothing moved. Niobe's spine crawled. She freed her gun from its holster and crept forwards.

She shone her beam down the end, where one of the steel doors stood open. The room inside was empty. This door was wider than the other, the steel thick enough to stop a tank. What were they keeping down here, a war elephant? *No,* she realised. *Iron Justice.*

She swept her torchlight across the other door, where it lay crumpled and dented against the wall. Her palms grew damp and her heart raced. What the hell could've done that?

Never mind. *I'm here, Sam.* It was over. She raced ahead of Solomon, the torchlight bouncing with every step.

She shone her beam into the cell. A mattress in one corner, stained and leaking springs. No window. No furniture.

And no Sam.

She flicked the beam around the room again. "No. Where...?" Someone had sucked the butterflies out of her stomach and left a hole in their place.

Then she saw the blood, a streak of dark red in the doorway. She bent down to examine it, heart thumping.

"It's fresh," she said, trying to keep her voice steady. "A couple of hours old, max." Her pulse pounded in her ears. "He was here. He was fucking here!"

She didn't remember picking up the mattress, but the next thing she knew, she was hurling it across the room. It slammed into the wall with a hollow thud and slowly toppled to the floor. She shouted wordless screams that echoed around her.

Arms enveloped her, and Solomon's earthy scent blocked out the thick, musty smell of captivity. She struggled, almost putting her elbow into his stomach, but he held her tight. "Easy, mate. Easy."

She wanted to cry. She wanted to smoke every cigarette she had. She wanted to go home and climb into bed with Gabby and pretend none of this had ever happened.

But most of all she wanted to feel Morgan Shepherd's smug face breaking beneath her boot.

CHAPTER 22
HOME, WHATEVER THAT MEANS

MADAME Z

REAL NAME: *Keira Hall*

POWERS: *Mental projection, telekinesis.*

NOTES: *Joined the Wardens early in their history, and quickly made a name for herself when she removed the mind-control effects of the Mind Spider from fellow supergroup the Patrolmen. Once her homosexual relationships became common knowledge, fundamentalist religious groups began a smear campaign in the media. After the Wardens disbanded, she left Earth for the lunar colony established by the Alpha League.*

—Notes on selected metahumans [Entry #0229]

"It's not over yet, mate," Solomon said as he drove. "With Quanta out of the picture, it's only a matter of time until we find Sam."

Niobe had burned through three cigarettes since they started making their way back to the Old City. Now she twirled her last one between her fingers, glaring at it. "We got nothing. That was our one lead, and we blew it. I blew it."

The night was cooling quickly, but she left the window open a crack to help her think. That goddamn false wall. If she'd found it the first time, before Met Div arrived, Sam would have been there. Someone had taken him while they flew away like frightened pigeons. Maybe it was Met Div, but she didn't think so. No normal had ripped that door off its hinges.

"We didn't blow a thing," the Carpenter said. "You think Met Div could've tracked down Quanta and his gang without our help?"

"Yes."

He paused. "Well, all right, eventually. But how many more people would die before they did? We stopped the clock. Saving lives, catching villains. This is what we're meant for, Niobe."

She slammed her fist down on her knee. "Enough, Carpenter. You see those people out there?" She jabbed her finger towards the manicured suburbs. "They don't want heroes anymore. They hate us. They want to pretend that bad things don't happen. They want to pretend they're safe. They want to believe in their shopping malls, and their four-door imported cars, and their bright economic futures. They don't believe in us anymore, Solomon. They don't need us."

He shook his head slowly. "You don't understand. I don't think you ever understood." He reached over and picked up the goggles sitting in her lap. "You've always looked at the world through these lenses, but they distort things. Sure, the world is dark sometimes. The world's not a four-colour comic book. But there's still good, mate, and there's still things we have to stand up for."

"There's no 'we'. Not anymore."

"Of course there is." He gave her goggles back and rested one hand on the gear stick. "There always will be. You know why those people think they're safe behind their picket fences? Because most of them are. When superheroes first came along, the world was at war. We were a bright light in a dark room. Metas helped change the world, Niobe. We made it better. And then when peace came, they began to doubt us. And worse, we began to doubt ourselves. They decided there was no more room for superheroes. And we began to believe it too."

He stared out the windshield. The lights of the skyline reflected off his mask.

"They don't hate us," he said. "They just think that if heroes exist, then villains do too. That scares them. But villains exist whether we're here or not. Someday they'll realise that. There will always be room for us in this world. Sure, we'll screw up sometimes, and some of us will do bad things. We're only human. But we have to keep trying to be better. We can do good, mate. We can *be* good. Because if we aren't, who will be?"

We are the strangers who guard the world through the night. No. She shook her head, ridding herself of the thought. She had been good. She'd saved lives, fought villains. She'd stood side by side with some of the greatest heroes of her generation. And what had that got her? The normals had loved their heroes. Until they got scared. Until those superpowers started to cost normals their jobs. Her old teammates had all given up, retiring injured like Gabby or just sucking down so much booze they couldn't fight off the flu, let alone Suicide Prime or the Manhunters. She and the Carpenter were no more than mercenaries now. They couldn't hold back the darkness on their own.

"I'm leaving Earth," she said, quieter now. She put the cigarette between her lips, but didn't light it. "Me and Gabby. We're going to the Moon."

He pulled onto the highway, and the industrial district fell away behind them. "Oh."

"Oh?" she said. "That's all you've got to say?"

"I'm thinking. Gimme a break." She could see him turning the words over in his mind.

The silence grew thick. He had the look of a disappointed parent. Finally, she couldn't take it anymore. "I know what you're thinking. But there's nothing here to stay for. We'll be safer up there. It'll be easier to protect Gabby. And she won't have to worry about me getting into trouble."

He gave her a sideways glance. "Is that what you guys were arguing about?"

"Something like that."

"Because she worries about you?"

"Yeah," she said.

"Are you sure?"

"What are you, the love doctor?"

He smiled and gestured in front of him. "Look around you."

She stared out the window. "What? The city?"

He shook his head. "This car. Who put it together for us? Who fixed it?"

"Gabby, but—"

"Those goggles. That gun. All them gizmos on your belt. Who made them for you?"

"You know damn well who made them," she said, pulling her goggles close to her stomach. "Make your point."

He shrugged. "Just doesn't seem like the sort of thing she'd do if she didn't want you out here doing this." He switched lanes to overtake a late-night driver. "My wife doesn't like me going out, 'cause she doesn't get it. She was never a hero. But Gabby was the Silver Scarab. You really think she doesn't understand why you're out here every night?"

She chewed her lip. "That doesn't mean she's not worried about me."

"I never said it did. Heck, I was worried about you a couple of hours ago when we were about to walk into Quanta's hideout. We're pals. But that's not why she's upset."

"Oh, so you're not a love doctor, you're just a psychic," she said.

"Let me guess," he said. "You've been keeping things from her. Not telling her what the case is about, or how dangerous it's likely to be. You've tried to insulate her. Stick her in a box full of cotton wool. Don't let her worry her pretty little head. Am I warm?"

Niobe realised she was chewing the end of her cigarette. The Carpenter's grin grew wider when she didn't say anything.

"She's not upset because you go out," he said. "She's upset because you're leaving her behind."

No. Gabby didn't want to be a hero. The nightmares she had were bad enough. "That was all a long time ago," Niobe said. "Before Kiloton nearly killed her."

"So she's a little broken. We all are. You, me, Quanta. Even Senior Sergeant Wallace. She doesn't need you to protect her from the world. I reckon all she wants is your love and respect."

She turned the cigarette in her fingers.

"Take it from me," he said. "She's no different from half the metas in this city. In her heart, she's still a hero. She wants to help you. But if you keep pushing her away...." He shrugged.

She stared out the window, where a sliver of the Moon hung above the lights of Neo-Auckland. It was safe up there. No matter what Solomon said, that was what they wanted. Right?

The memories came back to her one by one, every fight, every hurt look in Gabby's eyes. Every miscommunication. She touched the goggles in her lap, crafted with such care by the woman who loved her. Her beautiful, brilliant Gabby.

Goddamn it. He was right. And he'd never let her forget it.

"When'd you become such a goddamn guru, Carpenter?"

"Us old guys gotta have wisdom," he said. "How else are we supposed to impress the ladies?"

They were silent for a while, but it was a peaceful silence. She'd been so dumb. But she'd make it up to Gabby. The city had gone quiet again, everyone sleeping safe and sound. At the top of the tallest towers, red lights blinked to warn off aircraft. Aside from the police dirigible hovering near the Old City, the night sky was clear. By now, Quanta and his gang would be in chains. The news would be filled with celebrations, and people across the city would be breathing sighs of relief.

She tried to summon some pride, but it didn't come. She'd been wrong too often to pat herself on the back. She'd made Gabby cry too many times. And she hadn't saved Sam yet.

Solomon must have read her thoughts. "We've done all we can tonight. Go home, get some rest. Talk to Gabby. Make up with her. That's what I'll be doing with my wife. God knows if I don't spend some quality time with the family, Kate's gonna string me up by my toes."

"By your toes, huh? You're into some weird sex, Carpenter," she said.

Solomon threw his head back and laughed harder than the feeble joke deserved. She didn't know whether it was the sleep deprivation or the aftereffects of the adrenaline, but a second later a laugh bubbled up inside her too, and soon they were both cracking up like a pair of drunks. The giggles washed over them, subsided, and then came again for no reason. The harder they tried to stop, the harder they laughed. Christ, it felt good.

Twenty minutes later, they pulled up behind her apartment building. Solomon wiped the tears from his eyes. "I'll come pick you up tomorrow."

"Yeah." She opened the door.

"We'll find him, mate," he said.

She glanced back at him and smiled. "Yeah." She shut the door and waved. He blinked the lights once, then pulled away and headed back towards his house.

She walked up the stairs, put her key in the door of her apartment, and opened it. As soon as she stepped inside, a wave of exhaustion washed over her. Part of her was telling her to get back out there and find Sam. But she knew she couldn't walk another step without falling asleep on her feet. Besides, the Carpenter was right. In the morning, she had amends to make.

She went to the kitchen and drained two glasses of water, then opened the door to the bedroom. It was dark inside. Gabby would be asleep. Turning on the light would wake her, so Niobe kicked off her shoes in the darkness, dropped her coat to the ground, peeled out of her bodysuit, and snuggled beneath the covers. It was a little cold. She reached over, feeling for Gabby.

She wasn't there.

Blinking, Niobe sat up in bed and flicked on the bedside lamp. The bedroom was still as a tomb, and the duvet on Gabby's side was crisp and unwrinkled. There was no light creeping out from under the bathroom door. Gabby was nowhere.

Niobe threw back the covers and padded naked to Gabby's wardrobe. Her heart felt like lead as she pulled open the doors. All Gabby's favourite clothes were missing. "No," Niobe said to the empty room.

She flicked on the light to the bathroom. There should have been two toothbrushes in the cracked mug by the sink. There was only one. "No."

Niobe came back into the bedroom, and her eyes fell on Gabby's bedside table. A quarter inch-thick sheaf of paper and a small plastic box sat next to her old clock. Niobe's legs shook like a rag doll's as she crossed the room.

She looked at the box first, shaking it as she picked it up. Ammunition. The bullets looked like her charged rounds, but with a sharpened tip and a thick black coating. There was something scribbled on the box lid. *Prototype shield-breaker rounds.*

She put the ammo box down and turned her attention to the pile of papers. A note was paperclipped to the top page. Trembling, she picked it up and perched herself on the edge of the bed.

N,

I loved you, but you haven't let me into your world for so long. I can't take the lies. Not anymore.

The rounds might help against Quanta. This is the last thing I'll do for you.

I'm sorry.

G

She read the note again and again, until she could picture the delicate curve of every letter even when she closed her eyes. Her throat was tight. A breeze blew against her skin and made her shiver, but she made no move to pull the covers around her.

When she couldn't bear to look at the note anymore, she picked up the rest of the papers. She recognised her own handwriting on the first page. It was the note she wrote to herself when Quick-fire came by, the note giving Quanta's real name. Beneath it was clean, white paper, typewritten and annotated with Gabby's flowing script. Courtesy of the Metahuman Division's new computer filing system, it recorded every known fact about a certain Morgan Shepherd, wanted throughout Europe, last seen in Madrid in 1962. On the second page was a sketch Gabby had done based on a photograph. The drawing was near-perfect. The boyish Quanta stared out of the page, grinning.

Niobe hurled the pages at the wall. They broke free of the paperclip and flew apart like a snowstorm, slipping under the bed and behind the bedside table. The first sob caught her by surprise, but soon they were tumbling over each other on the way out of her throat. Niobe curled up on the bed and let her tears trickle onto the sheets.

CHAPTER 23
THE DEVIL IN THE DETAILS

SKINWALKER

REAL NAME:	*Unknown*
POWERS:	*Doppelgänger/shapeshifter.*
NOTES:	*The only Manhattan Eight member whose original identity is unclear. It is possible that he himself cannot remember. Skinwalker infiltrated Hitler's inner circle near the end of World War II, and later did the same in several supercriminal groups, often simultaneously. Distrusted by the American public and even other metahumans, he was the only member of the Manhattan Eight never to be interviewed by the media. Following their disbanding, rumours began to surface that he engaged in deviant sexual practices, including impersonating women to sleep with their unsuspecting husbands. Whereabouts unknown, but presumed dead.*

—Notes on selected metahumans [Entry #0006]

Solomon picked Niobe up just before noon. The daylight was harsh, and even the birds were hiding from its heat. She wore civilian clothes—the gun in a holster beneath her jacket—and carried her coat, mask, and bodysuit in a bag. She felt like a corpse. She looked like one too, if the mirror had been any indication. Her eyes were sunken, her cheeks marred by deep wrinkles. She'd never felt so old.

Solomon eyed her as she pulled the passenger door shut. He looked like he'd actually managed to get some sleep. Lucky bastard.

"I thought you might've convinced Gabby to come along with us today," he said as he started the car. "Would've been fun to actually work alongside the Silver Scarab."

Her stomach tied itself into a knot, and she stared straight ahead. "Not today. Let's go."

She could feel him looking at her, but he kept quiet and drove. They headed out of the Old City, the hot wind blowing through the open windows.

"I talked to my guy at Met Div," he said. "The reporter, John Bishop, he's at St. Helen's."

"The hospital? He didn't look injured."

He shook his head. "Physically, he's fine. Just a couple of scrapes, probably from some overzealous arresting on Met Div's part. They gave him a Stanley test to make sure he wasn't a doppelgänger or anything, then sent him off to the quacks to give him the once over. Probably worried about a repeat of the Cobraman incident."

She nodded. That had been just before she left the Wardens. After the coppers locked away the supercriminal Cobraman, they started to debrief his hostages. It wasn't until the hostages started screaming that the coppers discovered Cobraman had surgically implanted vials of acid under the hostages' skin, set to release on a timer. Only one of the hostages died. He was probably the happiest of all of them, by the end.

"Have Met Div talked to Bishop yet?" she asked.

"Only an initial debriefing, I think. As far as they're concerned, this thing's wrapped up. They're supposed to be talking to him at three in the afternoon to get a formal statement once the head-shrinkers have made sure Quanta didn't steal his marbles."

She checked her watch. That didn't give them much time. Why'd they always have to do this stuff during the day? "Guards?"

"Just one copper posted on the door. Private room on the ward. Sounds swanky."

"They always did like to impress the media." She sighed. "Disguises again, I suppose? I don't think you understand how much I dislike makeup."

"It gets better." He leaned over and reached into the backseat, fumbled for a minute, then dropped a paper bag in her lap. "*Pour vous, mademoiselle.*"

She unwrapped the top and peered inside. "Carpenter, I think I hate you a little more every day."

The wig was blond, permed, and hideous. The net inside felt like sandpaper coated in itching powder. She turned it back and forth in her hands, trying to see if the light made it any better, but she couldn't shake the feeling someone had skinned a Yorkshire Terrier and stuck it in curlers.

Solomon grinned like an idiot. "Aren't you going to try it on?"

"One of these days…." She sighed, pulled her own hair into a loose bun, and slipped the wig over the top. She'd underestimated the itching. It felt more like a nest of army ants crawling across her scalp.

"You know," he said, "you look a bit like my wife when you wear that."

"I swear to God, you get fresh with me and you'll find out just how painful ten thousand volts can be."

They'd switched seats partway to the hospital so the Carpenter could fix his false beard to his face. By the time they pulled into St. Helen's hospital car park, Niobe's skin was several shades lighter, her lips were pinker, and she wanted to throw the wig into the Black Golem's bottomless pit. Her sunglasses would cover the shape and colour of her eyes, and with a bit of luck she'd be able to pass as a white woman—or at least half-white—from a distance.

They got out and crossed the car park. Whoever designed St. Helen's must've had something against corners, because each edge was rounded with a series of curved glass windows. The only concession to flat space was the north end of the roof, and that wouldn't have been there if the architect could figure out a way to make helicopters land on a slope. Knots of patients in gowns stood on the lawns outside, enjoying the fresh air in a cloud of cigarette smoke. The smell made her hand clench around the new packet of Pall Malls in her pocket, but they didn't have time to sit around while she indulged herself.

The doors slid open on an automatic mechanism as they approached. The lobby looked like it belonged in a hotel, not a hospital.

The effect was spoiled by the old people shuffling along holding IV poles.

"Wait here a sec," Solomon said. He disappeared into a gift shop while she hovered awkwardly near the wall, watching people come and go. A fat security guard stood near the doors, but he looked half-asleep, and he hadn't taken any notice of them. The hospital's ubiquitous antiseptic smell had seeped out here, and it was giving her a headache. She checked her watch again. More than an hour until the cape coppers were supposed to talk to the reporter, if Solomon's man was right. Should be plenty of time, but no one was stupid enough to rely on the timetables of public servants.

Solomon emerged a minute later, carrying a huge bouquet of gerberas and chrysanthemums. "Think our patient will appreciate them?" he asked.

"You're a thoughtful soul. What floor?"

"Eighth."

They went straight to the lift like they knew where they were going. She pressed the button for eight, and jabbed the button to close the door before they had to share the lift with anyone else. It started moving upwards with barely a shudder.

He passed her the flowers. "Want to do the innocent family member routine?"

"I don't suppose we could switch roles this time?" she said.

"You're not strong enough to do my bit."

He was right, but that didn't stop her scowling at him. He winked and patted his fake beard to check it was still in place. The elevator bell rang once, and the doors slid open on the eighth floor. Solomon stuck his head out. "Clear."

He went out first, strolling down the corridor to the left. She gave him ten seconds while holding the door open, then followed. The corridor was the same clean white as hospitals everywhere. Judging from the leisurely way the nurses and young doctors moved, this wasn't a high-pressure ward.

She spotted the Met Div officer in the corridor a few doors down from the nurse's station. There was a chair beside the door, but he'd taken the more professional option and decided to stand. He wasn't carrying a rifle, but she could make out the bulge at his hip where his sidearm was concealed. He gave Solomon the hard eye, his fingers flexing, but he relaxed when Solomon went right on by and continued towards the four-bed room at the end of the hall.

Niobe felt ridiculous in her get-up, but at least the heels gave her an extra inch or two. She cast a quick glance around as she walked past the nurse's station, but only two nurses were there, doing paperwork. Neither took any notice of her. She peered at the holders outside every door that listed the patients' names, furrowing her brow as she did so.

The officer saw her, but he didn't tense up the way he had when the Carpenter passed. He was young, lean, with a haircut so straight he must have used a spirit level to get it right in the morning. Holding up the flowers so they partly obscured her face, she stared at the empty name holder beside the copper.

"Excuse me," she said, putting on the sweetest voice she could manage. "Is this Michael Kane's room?"

"No, ma'am."

"Are you sure?"

He frowned. "You'll have to move along, ma'am. This man is in police custody."

"Oooh." She stood on tip-toes to try to peer through the glass in the door. "Is he dangerous? Could I just have a quick peek? It sounds exciting."

"Ma'am—" His voice cut off as a hand snaked out from behind him and clamped around his mouth. He went bug-eyed and tried to turn, but the Carpenter's other arm appeared around his throat and started compressing the arteries in his neck.

"Little help?" Solomon said. He'd slipped on his mask, but she could still see the strain in his face as the copper struggled.

She snatched her plastic cuffs from her jacket pocket and grabbed hold of the man's hands long enough to slip them over his wrists. With a jerk, she pulled them tight.

She glanced over her shoulder, but the man's muffled grunts hadn't roused any of the nurses. While the man's movements grew slow and his face became drowsy, she took off her glasses and the hated wig and pulled on her mask.

Solomon nodded at her, and she bent down to get a hold of the copper's ankles. The man went floppy. The only movement was the slow rise and fall of his chest. She tucked the flowers under her arm and hefted his legs while Solomon backed into the door, and together they carried him into the room.

It was swanky all right. A huge window covered the entire wall, bathing the room in the early afternoon light. There was only one bed in the room, with a curtain running around it. A pair of comfy chairs and a table with an unfinished lunch tray sat in the corner.

"Who's there?" someone called from behind the curtain. They ignored him and dropped the unconscious copper into a chair. The Carpenter stuck his head into the corridor, then ducked back inside and quietly closed the door.

Niobe pulled back the curtain to find the portly young reporter reaching for the call button hanging from the corner of his hospital bed. She snatched it away before he could get to it and tossed the flowers in his lap. "We couldn't find you a vase," she said.

John Bishop shrank back on the bed, raising his hands as if to fight them off. A curious mix of bravery and cowardice. He wore hospital pyjamas; his normal clothes sat in a neat pile on the set of drawers beside him.

"I'm not done." John spoke with a Yorkshire accent. "You can't kill me yet."

"Relax, kid," the Carpenter said. "We don't work for Quanta."

"What?"

"I thought reporters were supposed to be good listeners," she said, a little harsher than she intended. "We're the good guys."

Solomon shot her a look. "Maybe we should give the kid a break. He's been through a lot."

She opened her mouth, then checked herself. She must be more tired than she thought. Her thoughts kept wandering back to Sam's blood on the floor of that cell, and Gabby's perfect handwriting as she tore her heart in two. *No, focus. One thing at a time.*

The reporter stared at them for a few moments, then his gaze went past them and his eyes widened. "What did you do to the policeman?"

She glanced back at the copper. His head hung to one side, mouth partly open. "He'll be fine. Look, he's breathing."

John didn't look entirely convinced. Given the circumstances, she supposed she couldn't blame him.

"You're metas, aren't you?" he said.

"See," the Carpenter said, "told you he was smart. I'm the Carpenter, this is Spook. We're looking for something that Quanta stole. Someone, to be more precise."

The reporter licked his lips and sat up higher in the bed. "You're not working with the police?"

"We just knocked one out. What do you think?" she said. Solomon gave her another look, and she shut her mouth before she could snap again.

"We have nothing against the coppers…" Solomon said.

Speak for yourself, she thought.

"…but they tend to try to arrest us when they find out what we are, and we don't really have time for that," he said. "Anyway, here's the point. Quanta kidnapped a boy, a kid named Sam, and we're trying to return him to his family. Quanta's in jail now, but we can't find the boy. Do you know who we're talking about?"

John stared at them for a long time. After what he'd been through at the hands of metas, she guessed his hesitancy was unavoidable. It didn't make the seconds ticking away any less painful, though.

Finally, he seemed to make up his mind. He put the flowers on his bedside table and swung his legs over the end of his bed to face them properly. While Niobe ground her teeth, he poured himself a cup of water from a jug and took a sip.

"I never saw any boy," he said slowly. "I heard them talking about him, though."

The Carpenter went to the man's lunch tray and plucked a couple of raisins from the opened box. "Them?" He popped the raisins in his mouth. "Who's them?"

"Quanta, and…." He licked his lips again and took a long drink.

"And?" Solomon said.

She saw the fear on the man's face, and it clicked. "Doll Face."

John's knuckles tightened around the cup, and he nodded, a small, jerky motion.

"Shit," she said. "The coppers didn't get him. He's with Sam."

Solomon's face had gone tight, and he looked like he'd aged thirty years. "All right. John, we need your help. Where would Doll Face go if the warehouse was compromised?"

"I…I don't know. I didn't talk to the freak."

"Did you get taken anywhere else aside from the warehouse?" she asked.

He shook his head. "It's the only place I've seen since I got off the airship."

The airship. Their informant at Met Div had mentioned an airship. She glanced at Solomon, and she could tell he was thinking the same thing.

"Airships aren't exactly stealthy," she said. "It must've landed somewhere secluded."

"It's more discreet than you think," John said. "It's got some sort of camouflaging cloak. But I couldn't tell you where we landed. They kept me locked in my quarters for the descent, and then they blindfolded me for the journey to the warehouse."

Damn. Still, cloak or not, an airship couldn't land too close to the city. The population got spread out a few miles outside the city limits, so-called civilization giving way to farmland and forest. "Did they take you in a van or something to the warehouse?" she asked.

He nodded.

"How long was the journey?"

He put his hand to his chin and chewed his lip. "An hour, maybe longer."

That was a big area to search. And in what direction?

"What time of day was it when you arrived?" the Carpenter said.

"I don't know. Morning. Ten a.m., maybe."

"Was there sun on your face while you were driving?"

"What?"

"The sun," Solomon said. "What side of your face got hot?"

Of course. She watched while John chewed his lip again. Then he pointed. "My left."

They'd come from the north. They would have had to circle the Old City on their way into Neo-Auckland. There wasn't much left up north; few of the farms were still running. There'd been concerns over radiation in the soil since the bomb hit, and most people living there had moved somewhere less isolated.

Think. There had to be something that would narrow it down. "Is there anything else? Anything else you can remember that might help us?"

"Uh…we went inside a building soon after we got off the airship. I think they were shifting supplies. They left me blindfolded in the corner." He screwed up his eyes like he was trying to recall the place. "I could feel…grates or something on the ground in some places. Concrete in others. And it smelled."

"Smelled?" she said. "Smelled of what?"

He screwed up his face. "Rotten meat."

Meat? Most of the livestock had died or been shifted from the area years ago. What then? A butcher's shop? Did butcher's shops need grates in the floor? She could see the appeal a butcher's might hold for Doll Face.

No. Not a butcher's. "A freezing works," she whispered to herself. She looked at the Carpenter. "There's a few old meat works up north. Most of them have been shuttered for years."

"Just the place for the budding psychopath and his victim," the Carpenter said while he wandered towards the window. "Still a lot of ground to cover."

"You afraid of some old-fashioned footwork?" she said. She turned back to John, crossed her arms and leaned against the table. "Thanks for this."

He ventured a small smile. "My pa was a reporter too, for a little local rag. Stories about local council members and the effects of the recent downpour on the local livestock, that sort of thing. But one day he got a tour of the Light Brigade's Sun-base, and an interview with Kingfisher. He said it was the proudest moment of his career."

She made a noncommittal noise. She didn't want to tell him how distant those days were. "What did Quanta want with you anyway?"

"He wanted me to write a story about him."

He did seem to like the limelight. "What'd he want you to say?"

"He's dying. A brain tumour. But before he dies, he wants to make the world understand why he did all this. He's insane. He's hung up on the woman he murdered, his lover. He blames the world for turning her against him. I think he thinks he's some kind of avenging god."

She opened her mouth, but the Carpenter cut her off before she could speak. "Time to go, mate." He turned away from the window. "Now."

"Met Div's here already?" She checked her watch. *Bloody public servants.* "How long have they been here?"

"Dunno. The cars are there but no one's in 'em."

Ah, hell.

"Hey, wait!" the reporter said, his voice rising. He pointed at the unconscious copper. "What about him?"

The Carpenter grabbed her by the arm and hauled her towards the door.

"If you can, give us thirty seconds to get out," she said. "Then press the button to call the nurse. Tell them what you have to tell them." She paused. "But if you can, keep the thing about Doll Face quiet. Met Div's out of their depth here. If they go chasing him, a lot of coppers are going to die."

He nodded and got back into bed. "I think I was asleep the whole time. I didn't see or hear a thing."

Solomon stuck his head out the door and nodded at her.

"See you round," he said to John.

They ducked out the door, pulling off their masks as they went. She shoved the wig back on her head and they strolled quickly towards the lift bank. A pretty young nurse smiled at them, but they didn't stop to chat.

Solomon pointed at the numbers lighting up above the lift doors. One of them was steadily approaching their floor. Heart thumping, she opened the door to the stairwell and ducked inside, Solomon close behind. She just got the door closed when the elevator bell rang and the doors slid open. She watched through the window as three uniformed officers came out and marched down the hallway towards John's room.

Wiping the sweat and makeup from her forehead, she allowed herself to breathe. The Carpenter grinned at her from beneath his false beard.

"Road trip?"

CHAPTER 24

A Drop of Blood

The Carpenter

REAL NAME:	*Solomon Doherty*
POWERS:	*Telekinetic control of wood, communication with plants.*
NOTES:	*One of the founding members of the Wardens. Relatively famous even overseas, but always preferred to stay out of the public eye. Instrumental in the defeat of the Nagasaki Horrors. His teammate Battle Jack once said in an interview: "Didn't matter how many pricks were trying to kill you, didn't matter how shit things got. You could always look back and see the Carpenter standing like a kauri tree in a thunder storm. If you had him at your back, you weren't going down. No way."*

—Notes on selected metahumans [Entry #0165]

Niobe went into the petrol station to get a pack of smokes while Solomon filled up. It was an independent station, not one of the big chains, and it showed. The guy behind the counter looked like he'd had every bone in his face broken at some point, and he had a zit on his cheek that was ready to blow. She put a couple of bottles of Coca-Cola, two mince and cheese pies, and some potato chips on the counter. The Carpenter had picked the wrong place to stop if he wanted fresh fruit.

"Give me a pack of Pall Mall twenties," she said, fishing some cash out of her pocket. The guy sniffed and limped away to the cigarette cabinet.

The Coke would be a godsend. They needed the caffeine. It was morning, 8:27 a.m. according to the clock hanging behind the counter, a good twenty hours after they'd left the hospital. Twenty bloody hours of searching. Well, they caught a few winks in the car when they quit at two in the morning. The sun came up at six, which put paid to any ideas they had about sleeping in. She'd tried to call Frank Oppenheimer before they left, but there was no one home. They had to do this alone.

The station attendant threw the packet of cigarettes onto the counter and sniffed again. "You paying for the petrol as well?"

"Yeah." She handed him the cash, and he rang it up. She'd abandoned the wig. No amount of secrecy was worth the itch.

She pocketed the smokes, slung the fizzy drink and food under her arm, and walked out. The morning was cool and cloudless, so bright it stung her eyes even through the sunglasses. She tossed the supplies into the car and got in next to the Carpenter. He was starting to smell pretty ripe. She knew she needed a shower as well. But this wasn't exactly the sort of place to find motels, not anymore. Plenty of bushes if you wanted to take a piss, though.

The Carpenter was poring over a map, stroking his stubble. He'd given up the false beard. The map was covered in pencil scratchings, mostly circles with crosses through them.

"How many we got left?" she said as she ripped open a bag of chips and offered him some.

"Three." He pointed them out on the map, then took a handful of chips. "What if we're wrong?"

She pushed her sunglasses out of the way and rubbed her eyes. That wasn't something she could think about now. Getting Sam back was the one thing she was clinging to, the one thing in her life that still had meaning. She shoved a couple of chips in her mouth, but she could barely taste them. "Start the damn car."

They rolled down the narrow roads, spewing dust into the air behind them. The roads were unsealed and bumpy as hell. The country was wild here, mostly farmland reclaimed by Mother Nature when the farmers left. A few towns still hung on, more like villages now. The petrol station they'd stopped at was the last one for miles. Occasionally, a car or ute would come winding along the road towards them, but for the most part the only vehicles they saw were rusted tractors and the odd motorcycle. A few miles to the east, the sun would be climbing above the South Pacific, but she couldn't see the ocean through the hills and trees.

They were thirsty by the time they got through the first packet of chips, so they took turns swigging the Coke. It cleared the spiders from her mind, at least for the moment.

The first meat works they hit that day was another dud. It was much too close to the nearest village for any feasible use as an airship landing field, and half the roof had caved in. They got out and circled it half-heartedly, but it was clear this wasn't the place. The Carpenter scratched it off on the map and they went on their way.

While he drove, Niobe checked her gun and belt for the twentieth time, taking stock of her armoury. Six rounds of live ammo and six stun rounds in the modified revolver, and another thirty-six of each in her belt. Gabby's shield-breaker rounds were in the glove compartment, but they wouldn't be any use against Doll Face. Four smoke pellets. A mini-stunner capable of delivering several thousand volts, but it required physical contact. If Doll Face got that close to her, she didn't rate her chances. Might be useful if any more of Quanta's minions were lurking around, though. She had a handful of other non-combat items: torch, modified lenses for her goggles, miniature first aid kit, plastic cuffs, a thin but high tensile strength rope. She might as well be going into battle naked.

"Say we find Doll Face," she said, breaking the silence. "What's the plan? We can't go calling Met Div in on this one." Doll Face would see the flashing lights coming a mile away, and she didn't fancy cleaning copper blood off her hands.

He shook his head. "This is our fight. We should've taken him down years ago, back when we still had the numbers. But he moved around so fast, going to ground straight after one massacre and then popping up on the other side of the world. And the supergroups were too reactionary, waiting for something to happen instead of tracking him down."

"There were other things to worry about," she said. "The Nagasaki Horrors in your time, the Syndicate in mine."

"We're paying the price now. But we'll learn from this. We'll do better next time."

She frowned and checked the charge generator on her gun. "There's not going to be a next time. We're it. The last bloody superteam."

He just smiled. Fine, let him have his fantasies. Let him dream of a world where people still need heroes. They both knew what they were going into, chasing Doll Face like this. If they had to die, at least one of them could leave a smiling corpse.

Solomon spotted the dust-caked sign on the side of the road and pointed it out to her. *Schuster Meat Solutions.* He slowed and took the bend in the road. The building emerged from behind a hill. As soon as she saw it, she knew this was the place.

The smile on Solomon's face faded, replaced by a look of hardened determination. Without exchanging a word, he pulled over in the shelter of a small copse of trees. They pulled on their costumes. If she'd been religious, she would've said a prayer, but instead she just checked her gun once more. Live rounds armed. With Doll Face, there'd be no second chances.

They crept up a small mound, crawling as they approached the top to avoid making silhouettes against the skyline. The freezing works was a brick building topped by two side-by-side slanting roofs. It sat in the centre of a wide basin, with overgrown roads leading up to both ends. Once, it would've been a big operation, probably supplying most of the jobs of some nearby town long since abandoned. From her position atop the hill, she could make out native forest reclaiming the surrounding farmland and a few sheep still managing to scratch out a life on the land. The air was still, silent. No birds sung. Goose bumps crept along her arms.

There was no sign of Quanta's airship. If the cloaking was as good as the reporter said, they'd have a hell of a time finding it. But that didn't matter. It was the bodies that marked Schuster Meat Solutions as Doll Face's new home.

Doll Face had skinned the three bodies from the neck down. Their muscles had gone dry and brown in the sun. Pools of dried blood stained the concrete beneath them. They dangled near the entrance, strung up on long ropes by hooks that pierced their arms and legs.

"Like puppets," she whispered. She swallowed back bile.

Solomon's eyes were closed behind his mask. His hand had gone to the pouch on the right side of his belt. She knew it held a small silver cross his wife had given him. She'd only seen him do this once before. The day the Syndicate had left Battle Jack's severed head outside the Wardens' headquarters.

Niobe gripped her gun so hard her fingers ached. She looked up at the sky. Why did they always have to do this in the daytime? She laid her free hand on Solomon's shoulder, and he opened his eyes. Without a word, he slipped the hatchet from the loop in his belt. With the quarterstaff in one hand and the axe in the other, he didn't look so much like a peaceful farmer.

Without speaking, they slipped from their cover and made their way silently down the hill. Aside from a low wooden fence, there was no cover, no way to approach unseen. Two dozen boarded-up windows covered the side of the freezing works. *There's no eyes in those windows*, she tried to convince herself every time she thought she saw a flash of movement.

The air became a wall of buzzing flies as she approached the bodies. She pushed through them, grateful that her mask kept them from crawling into her ears and nose. Still, that didn't block out the stench of rotting flesh. The bodies were peppered with wriggling maggots. Her stomach rebelled, but she swallowed down the nausea before it could overtake her. *You can't afford to lose it.*

With all her strength, she forced her eyes upwards to look at the faces of the dead. Doll Face had left the skin there intact, but the eyes had been replaced by staring plastic with grotesque false eyelashes glued to them. It took her a moment to notice that lines of stitching ran around the tops of each of their heads, like they'd been scalped and then sewed up again. She knew one of the faces. He'd been on the front page of the paper yesterday morning. One of the small-time meta criminals that had broken out of prison a couple of days ago. Somehow, she didn't think this was how he intended to spend his freedom.

Through the cloud of flies, she signalled to the Carpenter. He nodded, flies crawling across his unprotected chin, then carefully ducked under one of the bodies to reach the freezing works' brick wall. She followed, suppressing the urge to shudder when she got a close look at the hooks that pierced the dead prisoners' tendons.

They pressed against the wall on opposite sides of the wooden doors. She peered through one of the cracks in the battered wood, eyes straining, but even with her contrast turned up, she couldn't see any movement. She blinked the sweat out of her eyes and glanced at the Carpenter.

"Do it," she said.

He thrust his arms out, eyes pulsing with light. The doors flew off their hinges, blown inwards. Before the first crash, she was moving, her gun leading the way.

A tiny flash of movement was the only warning she got. Fear hit her faster than logical thought. She dived into shadow. It saved her life. The three circular blades embedded themselves in the door frame with a sickening crunch, right where she'd been standing.

She released the shadow. She brought her gun up, squeezed the trigger twice. Her rounds pinged against something metallic. An eerie giggle shrieked in response. She ducked behind a rusted conveyor system as another pair of blades came flying at her. *Jesus Christ.*

The Carpenter threw himself in beside her as another spinning blade soared past, taking a slice out of his hat. Panting, he pushed himself up against the machine. "I'm starting to think the element of surprise is overrated."

A figure moved on the far side of the room. She squeezed off another two shots and ducked back as a blade answered. Doll Face giggled louder. "Doll Face has a new plaything!" The high-pitched voice echoed through the meat works. "It will be pretty like the others once it cuts off its own skin."

Every hair on her body stood on end. Her mouth had gone dry. The stench in here was even worse than outside. She crept along the side of the conveyor, licking her lips. "Sam!" she called out. "We've come to get you out. If you can hear me, stay down."

Another wave of giggles rolled across the room. "It's a funny one, yes it is. Did the boy hear that? Maybe Doll Face will string the boy up with the others and make it dance for the funny one. Or maybe Doll Face will skin the boy himself. Hmmm, yes." A muffled groan came from somewhere behind him.

"Shit," she whispered to herself while she broke open the revolver and slipped in some fresh rounds. "Carpenter." He wasn't looking at her. His eyes were fixed on the ceiling. "Hey, Carpenter."

"Mate." He pointed up, and she followed his finger.

"Oh, fuck," she said.

More than a dozen bodies hung by their feet from the ceiling. The meat hooks went through their ankles and left their arms pointing towards the floor. She could make out rivers of dried blood on their fingers. The ones closest to the door were naked and skinned like the ones outside, while the ones further back were still dressed.

One of the bodies twitched. Her breath caught. It had a plastic mask stitched to its face, but she recognised the build and the blue uniform. Daniel O'Connor, the Met Div officer who'd captured Sam. A long, agonised groan came from him as he dangled, blood matting his hair. *Oh God, he's still alive.*

"Help…" O'Connor said in a rasp, his voice muffled by the mask. "P…please…."

Jesus. She'd hated the man since she saw him in the Blind Man's vision, but no one deserved this. She raised herself up an inch to reach for him, but another pair of blades flew at her, forcing her back down. He was too far away.

"Carpenter, can you get to him?"

Doll Face's giggle rippled through the room.

"Not a chance," the Carpenter said.

A scream tore through the room. Niobe's attention snapped back to O'Connor. He was moving. His muscled arms jerked up and down. Was he trying to pull free? No. There were strings in his arms, like the bodies outside. The ropes went up to little pulleys set in the ceiling, then disappeared into the back of the meat works. Doll Face was putting on a puppet show for them. O'Connor's tortured screams grew louder.

One by one, the bodies began to dance. Clumps of coagulated blood shook loose and rained down on her as she huddled for cover. One chunk landed on her knee. She slapped it away and forced herself to keep her eyes open. Closing them was death. More pulleys started grinding, and the bodies slowly dropped to eye level, never stopping their inverted, macabre dance.

Niobe blocked out the sound of O'Connor's screams. To get him down they had to take out Doll Face. The Carpenter had his sleeve across his mouth. He glanced through a space in the conveyor. "Can you see the kid?"

She took a look herself, trying to get a clear view through the darkness and the bodies. Shafts of light slanted in through cracks in the boarded-up windows, but all they illuminated was flies and dust. "Hang on."

She sucked in a lungful of air and drew the shadow around her. The rusted surfaces of the benches were thrown into high contrast, and she could sense the slick layer of blood that coated the concrete floor. The dancing bodies turned everything into a confused mess of movement. At least the screams were dulled. She darted across the floor, trying to get closer. Rows of conveyors and benches filled the space between her and Doll Face. On the far wall she could just make out a set of open doors, probably leading to the cold storage area. A figure was dragging something out of there. No. Someone.

She slipped out of the shadow next to Solomon. "Carpenter. He's taking the kid to the meat cutting area."

"Why can they never take their dates to the pictures like normal folk?" His voice was as strained as the joke. "If I give you a distraction—"

"I'll get him. See you on the other side, Carpenter."

"Good luck, hero."

She slipped back into shadow just in time to sense the Carpenter stand and fling back his cloak. In one movement, he ripped open a pouch on his belt and flung the contents into the air. Twenty balls of petrified wood flew like bullets, curving around the dancing bodies to head straight for Doll Face.

She didn't wait to see if they hit. She was already moving up the wall, darting around the boarded-up windows, making her way to the back of the room.

A shrieking laugh rattled the walls. She couldn't tell if it was because the Carpenter had hit, or because he'd missed. She was close enough now to make out Sam's bound and struggling body as Doll Face lifted him one-armed onto a steel preparation bench. The masked creature picked up a cleaver, casually hurled it at the Carpenter, then picked up a smaller knife and turned his cocked head towards Sam.

Niobe slid back to the floor and darted closer. The improvised wooden bullets were still harassing Doll Face, crashing into him, but he didn't seem to notice even when they broke his skin and cracked his ribs. Behind her, she could see the Carpenter running amongst the dancing bodies, the remnants of one of the doors hovering in front of him like a shield. Doll Face continued to toss knives at him even as he brought his own blade down on Sam's bare chest.

Now. She dropped the shadow and rose shooting. Six rounds flew at Doll Face's torso.

He dodged them.

No. It wasn't possible. No one was that fast. The creature turned to her, a pink grin painted across his plastic mask. She didn't notice the flick of his hand until the flying blade pierced her thigh. With a grunt, she dropped to one knee, pain lancing upwards. *He's so fast.* Her vision blacked for a moment.

The Carpenter's cry brought her back. She saw him topple, a trickle of blood coming from his shoulder where a blade had found a gap in his shield. He was up again in a second, scrambling for cover.

With a grunt, she ripped the knife from her thigh. The blood didn't pulse out. No arterial bleeds. But as she tried to get back to her feet, she knew she was already too late.

Sam's half-naked body was blue from the cold storage area, his skin torn in a dozen places across his arms and legs. His arms were bound behind him. He looked so small, so broken. He grunted and flopped from side to side. Above him, Doll Face stood giggling, a knife inches from Sam's chest. Somewhere, a humming stopped. The bodies on the ceiling stopped dancing. O'Connor's screaming finally ceased.

"Let's make the toy sing," Doll Face said. "Yes, let's."

The point touched Sam's skin. That was as far as he got.

A sonic boom exploded from Sam's mouth. Doll Face reeled backwards, screeching. Niobe went down on her back, trying to keep her brain from leaking out her ears. The ropes that bound Sam's arms vanished in a burst of smoke, leaving ash in their wake. With an animal ferocity, Sam leapt at Doll Face. It might have been the ringing in her ears, but she swore Doll Face was screaming.

Sam's body wasn't blue anymore. It wasn't flesh at all. The skin rippled once, and then the boy was covered head-to-toe in chrome. The floor cracked beneath him. The metallic behemoth advanced on Doll Face, the ground shaking with every step.

Niobe told herself to move, but her legs wouldn't work. She couldn't even feel the knife wound in her leg. What the hell was going on?

Doll Face pounced, blade flashing. It struck Sam's metal skin and turned. Again Doll Face attacked, and again Sam shrugged off the blow and took another hulking step forwards. In a voice loud enough to shatter glass, Sam screamed something incoherent. Doll Face took a step back.

Sam's fists crashed together with Doll Face's skull between them. Niobe turned away as a splatter of gore fountained out of the villain's crushed face. *Oh God. Bloody hell.* When she had the stomach to look back, neither of them had moved. Doll Face twitched like a dying insect. After an eternity, Sam slowly moved his hands apart. Doll Face drooped to the ground. Sam stared at the body, motionless. His metal skin shivered, and then he was just a boy again. O'Connor's moans were the only sound in the room.

Niobe tore her eyes from him and glanced around in search of the Carpenter. He stood amongst the dangling bodies, eyes wide behind his mask, face pale. Her gaze went to the knife wound in his shoulder, but it didn't look too bad. He was okay. They were all okay. She breathed.

When she looked back, Sam was on his knees next to Doll Face's body. He was dragging his fingers through the gore leaking out of the villain's skull.

She took a step forwards. "Sam?"

He started and turned his eyes towards her. They were blank, his face expressionless.

"It's okay," she said, edging closer. She holstered her gun and raised her palms. "Your uncle sent us to help you. We're going to take you home, Sam."

His lip twitched, but he remained frozen. O'Connor moaned again, and Sam's gaze shifted to the cape copper hanging by his ankles in the centre of the room.

"You," Sam whispered.

"Ignore him," Niobe said. "You don't have to be scared anymore, Sam."

She saw the madness behind his eyes. Sam's face twisted into a snarl.

He raised his arms, and lightning left his fingers. The blue light crashed across Niobe's vision, blinding her for a moment, and the taste of ozone covered the stench of death. But it couldn't cover the strained screams leaving O'Connor's mouth.

Smoke poured from O'Connor's body as the lightning ripped through him. His uniform turned black, and so did his skin. Niobe could smell his flesh cooking. The copper jerked and shuddered like a puppet once more.

The lightning disappeared as quickly as it had come. O'Connor slumped, no longer screaming. He stank like charred meat. Niobe wanted to spew.

Sam turned his eyes on her. The metal plates covered his body again, just like Iron Justice. He charged.

"Spook!" the Carpenter yelled. "Get out!"

She tried to back away, but she couldn't. Something invisible was holding her limbs in place, crushing them, keeping her from becoming shadow. She couldn't even close her eyes. *He's a telekinetic. He's got me pinned.*

Sam ran at her, his fist growing to the size of a bowling ball, lightning dancing in his eyes. He screeched. Some invisible force hit her, throwing her down. Her head slammed against the metal grates in the ground. The boy bore down on her, and she knew she was dead.

A body tackled Sam, throwing him off balance. She tried to track what had hit Sam, and then she saw. The Carpenter. Only he wasn't the same Carpenter she'd seen before.

A hundred fragments of wood gathered around him, meshing together. They moved as he moved, sticking close to his body like plates of armour. The largest pieces of wood sloped down from his shoulders and protected his chest, while the smaller bits coated his arms and formed a helmet around his head. *Like a samurai*, her dazed mind marvelled. He gripped his quarterstaff in two hands, holding it like a sword. A moment passed as Sam and the Carpenter stared at each other. The Carpenter opened his mouth to speak.

Sam attacked.

Solomon swept to the side, bringing the quarterstaff down on Sam's shoulder. The boy screamed.

Niobe tried to stumble to her feet, but the signals from her brain were misfiring, making everything spin. A blast of lightning shot from Sam's hand, lighting up the warehouse again. The blast slammed into a panel of wood guarding the Carpenter's shoulder, sending it spinning free for a moment before the Carpenter brought the scorched wood back into place. Solomon planted his feet and leapt forwards. The cut turned into a feint, and the staff took Sam's legs out from under him. The whole building shuddered as the boy hit the ground.

I have to help. She tried to get up. The aftereffects of Sam's psychic attack were wreaking havoc with her body. She tried again. This time she got as far as her knees before nausea went through her and her legs turned to rubber. *No. Get up, damn it!*

The wooden struts that supported the building cracked and groaned. The Carpenter stood, hands in front of him, limbs shaking. Every unattached piece of wood in the building flew at Sam, slamming into him and forcing him against the ground.

"Spook, get to the car," the Carpenter said. He sounded strangely calm. "I can't hold him."

Sam screeched. A shockwave rippled through the air, sending the fragments of wood flying away. The Carpenter crossed his arms in front of him, trying to ward off the force of the sonic boom. It was useless. He went down on his back, the quarterstaff knocked from his grasp. And then Sam was on top of him. The boy snarled and raised his fist.

Before he could strike, Solomon grabbed his wrists and pulled him into a stranglehold.

"Sam, stop," the Carpenter said through gritted teeth. "We're trying to help."

Sam snarled and kept fighting. The Carpenter's quarterstaff flew into the air and hammered the back of Sam's head. As the boy tried to shake it off, the Carpenter shifted his weight and rolled, putting himself on top. Even through her dizziness, she could see the muscles in Solomon's arms bulging as he tried to hold the boy down. Niobe finally got to her feet.

"He's getting stronger by the second," the Carpenter yelled. "You've gotta—"

Sam wrenched an arm free of the Carpenter's grip. She saw it coming, but she was too slow. Solomon's eyes widened behind his mask.

Sam drove his fist deep into the Carpenter's chest. The wooden plate shattered, and she heard the Carpenter's ribs crack. The rest of his armour dropped away in an instant, nothing more than useless fragments of timber. Sam clambered to his feet, snarled once more, and tossed the hero aside like a doll. The Carpenter fell with a thud against the wall.

"Carpenter!" Her head pounded.

There was something sticking out of a crack in Sam's armour. A sliver of wood dug deep into his shoulder, blood trickling down the metallic skin. Sam clutched at it, a stream of nonsensical whispers tumbling out of his mouth. "They want to put me in boxes, cages, they want me to be alone, alone forever. Run, run, have to run."

Niobe stumbled forwards, drew her gun, switched to stun rounds. *Doll Face drove him mad. Totally mad. I have to knock him out. I have to get him help.* She didn't get to fire the first shot.

Sam turned to Niobe and screeched out another sonic boom. Her ears popped. She fell back, her head striking the corner of a preparation bench. Black spots floated in her eyes.

There was another scream, and a whoosh of displaced air. Something crashed; the whole building shook. The place was going to collapse, she was sure.

But when she blinked away the static in her eyes, the building was still standing. It was brighter now. It took her a moment to notice the crumbling hole in the centre of the ceiling, directly above where Sam had been standing. For a moment, she spotted a dark spot silhouetted against the sky. He was heading south. *He can fly as well? Jesus Christ.*

She struggled to her feet. Her thigh screamed at her, but she pushed the pain aside. Coughing up dust, she stumbled along, using the benches to support her weight. "Carpenter." Her voice was thin. She coughed and tried again. "Carpenter, we gotta get to a phone. He's going for the city. We gotta warn Met Div. Carpenter."

The Carpenter was slumped against the wall, his mask askew. But it was the bloody, open wound in his chest that drew her attention.

No no no no no no no.

She dropped to her knees, ripped off her gloves, and touched her fingers to his carotid artery. Nothing. His wrist. No pulse there either. *No, God, no.*

She grabbed his ankles and pulled him away from the wall, his torso thumping on the floor. He was limp. His wide-brimmed hat dropped into the pool of blood. "Carpenter, hey." She slapped his face. "Hey!" He didn't move.

She pulled off her mask and put her ear to his lips. *Breathe. Please.*

Nothing.

Okay. Okay. She tore off his shoulder-cape and tried to wrap it around him to cover the hole in his chest. She couldn't get it under him; he was too heavy, and her fingers kept slipping in the blood.

"Hey," she said. "You can't be dead. Remember what you said? You have to be alive, you have to be a hero. 'Cause if you aren't, who will be?"

He didn't reply.

There had to be something else. She couldn't do CPR, his sternum was shattered. There was no way to do chest compressions. She slapped her forehead again and again. Think!

Cardiac massage. They'd taught her that in the Wardens. His chest cavity was already open, broken and torn as it was. She didn't hesitate. The shattered ribs scraped her hand as she reached through the hole and searched inside his chest. Where was his heart? Goddamn it, where was it?

There. Her hand enveloped something wet and tough and meaty. She squeezed it. Squeeze. Squeeze. Blood spurted from his chest. Her hand slipped, she couldn't get a good grip, her fingers kept slipping into shadow. Her cheeks were wet.

She didn't know how long she knelt there, with the cold concrete biting her knees and her hand in Solomon's chest. His face didn't flicker, not once. The sun shone through the hole Sam left in the roof. She wasn't cold, but she shivered.

When she finally removed her hand, her coat sleeve was sodden with blood. She straightened the Carpenter's mask, bent over his face, and pressed her lips against the stubble on his cheek.

He was the masked man, the hidden man, the endless watcher.
He was the stranger who guarded the world through the night.
He was every man.
He held back the storm,
And he made the light shine through,
Until the night took him.

"Sleep well, hero," she said.

CHAPTER 25

There's Always a Way

OMEGAMAN

REAL NAME: *Frank Oppenheimer*

POWERS: *Enhanced reflexes, able to phase-shift through stationary or slow-moving objects.*

NOTES: *Younger brother of Dr Atomic and second-in-command of the Manhattan Eight. Despite his pacifist tendencies, he acted as the supergroup's assassin during World War II. Brought before the House Un-American Activities Committee for alleged Communist ties. Later acquitted. Whereabouts unknown following the death of Dr Atomic.*

—Notes on selected metahumans [Entry #0002]

For thirty-six hours, they kept Morgan in darkness. Not what usually passes for darkness, where after a while your eyes adjust enough to make out shapes and movement. This darkness was so thick he could almost feel it drowning him with each breath.

He had the cell memorised by now. Six foot by eight, thick concrete all around, with an approximately six inch thick steel door. If he stretched while lying on the mattress, he could touch one wall with the top of his head and reach the other with his feet. A metal toilet and basin were the only other fixtures in the cell.

He pressed his palm against the cool wall. He'd known it would be hard if he got caught, but he hadn't known how hard. They brought him food and drink, but that wasn't what he needed. It was light that sustained him, that gave him his power, and they gave him none of that. Granted, it would have been immensely foolish for them to do so, but that knowledge did nothing to quench the hunger in him. They'd even used some Unity Corporation tech to drain him of his reserves after they captured him. The hypocrisy annoyed him. Most of that technology had been developed by metas. Now the authorities sought to use it against them.

At least his headaches had dulled in here. It was the quiet, he thought. The only sounds here were the ones he made himself. It was peaceful, in a way. *I'll miss that if they grant me bail.* The ludicrousness of the thought made him smile into the darkness. The Senior Sergeant said he wouldn't be taken to the courthouse for his hearing. A telephone system would be set up to allow him to give statements and hear the case against him from the comfort of his cell. A gross breach of his legal rights, of course, but the Chief Justice, the Prime Minister, and the heads of the AAU had all agreed that it was for the best.

No matter. If it came to trial, he had no hope of ever being acquitted, whether he was physically in court or not.

His lunch had arrived an hour ago, but it lay beside him uneaten. It was decent fare; most meals came with potatoes or bread, and a good range of fruits and vegetables: tomatoes, peas, apples, bananas. He was having trouble summoning an appetite, but he knew he should eat. The winds of fate could change quickly, and you had to be ready to put up sails. He prodded a tender spot in his top gum with his tongue, and reached for the tray.

It wasn't a noise that alerted him, so much as a feeling of presence. He smiled. "My dear Dr Oppenheimer, I was beginning to think you had forgotten me. You never write, you never visit."

Something struck his cheek, and his head snapped around. Purple spots swam through the darkness, accompanied by lightning bolts of pain shooting through his bones. He tried to reach out, and realised he'd fallen onto his side. Blood filled his mouth. He pushed himself up on shaky arms. A hand closed around his throat and pulled him the rest of the way.

"Where is my nephew?" Frank Oppenheimer's voice hissed in his ear.

Morgan couldn't speak if he wanted to. His windpipe screamed in agony as Frank's palm crushed it, and his lungs started to burn. The purple spots returned, the only colour in a room of black. For a moment, his confidence slipped, and doubt entered his mind. *He'll kill me if I'm not careful.*

The hand relaxed, and air rushed in to fill the void in his lungs, along with the scent of Oppenheimer's sweat. Spasms wracked Morgan's chest, and he coughed again and again.

"Where is he?" Frank demanded again.

Something slammed into Morgan's stomach, and the coughs doubled in intensity. "Frank," he managed to gasp before another coughing fit struck him.

"Tell me where Sam is!"

"I will," he choked out. "Don't…don't hit me again."

He waited for another blow, but it didn't come. He forced himself to take deep breaths, suppressing the spasms in his throat. Frank's hand had left him. He wanted to curl over and vomit, but he suppressed that too.

"Sam's safe," he said when he could speak again. "He's fine."

"Where?" The voice was coming from his other side now. Omegaman could still move silently, no matter his age.

"I figured you'd come, Frank. I'm glad we finally have a chance to talk. I always admired you."

The noise that came from Morgan's right was more of a growl than words. "Why? Why did you do this?"

"Because someone had to."

He could feel Frank moving around the cell. He wondered if the man was in costume. *If it still fits.* Omegaman used to have goggles that let him see in the dark, but even those wouldn't be much use down here. You couldn't amplify a photon if it didn't exist.

"Did you know how powerful Sam could be?" Morgan said. The movement stopped. "You must have had some idea, or you wouldn't have come to see your friend, the one who worked at Unity Corp."

Frank grunted.

"I was surprised you fell for it so easily," Morgan said. "But you were eager, weren't you? A medicine to suppress metahuman powers. You couldn't get here fast enough."

He said nothing.

"Were you afraid Sam was going to go mad and try to kill you like your brother did? Or did you just want to spare him this life?" Morgan heaped scorn on the sentence. "Tell me, Frank, are you ashamed? Do you regret being Omegaman?"

"I'm ashamed that I share an origin with you, monster. With people like you to represent us, no wonder the normals hate us."

Morgan laughed. "Oh, come now. You and I both know that super-criminals had nothing to do with what they did to people like us. Like many metas, I thought for a long time that it was economics. We were taking their jobs and doing them better. But it was more than that. We lost some part of ourselves. We didn't fight this, because we didn't believe in ourselves anymore."

"Stalling won't save you."

Morgan prodded his sore gum again. It was becoming a compulsion. "I just want to make you understand, Frank. Do you remember that old saying? A hero's greatest power is his mind. It turns out that's true. Well, not the mind, but the brain. We did some research. There's a protein that builds up in the neocortex of the brain, especially in more powerful metas, and especially in psychics. A collection of proteins, really. Your brother would have been swimming in it. Perhaps that's what drove him mad."

He made out the sound of steel leaving a sheath.

"The protein complex is incredibly elaborate, and unique to the individual. And recently, we discovered something very special. It retains an imprint of the meta's powers, even when removed from the brain in question. Of course, this is useless for the most part, a curiosity. But there are ways of conducting a transfer. Ways of giving someone another's powers. All you need is a powerful psychic stimulus, and a metahuman malleable enough to take the transfer. That part is the tricky one. Such a metahuman is exceedingly rare. It needs to be a tier zero meta. Someone like Sam."

A palm slammed into Morgan's sternum and shoved him back against the wall.

"Enough," Frank said. A blade whistled as it cut the air. "Enough of your talking. You will tell me now. Where is Sam?"

"You were a scientist," Morgan said. "I thought that bit of information might interest you. Maybe you're out of practice. Should we should start with something simpler? Perhaps the sort of experiments children do in school. Do you remember the chemical reaction that you get from putting zinc and copper electrodes into certain fruits and vegetables?"

The point of a blade pricked his neck, but he didn't stop.

"Potatoes and tomatoes, for example." Morgan's hand groped to the side, until it touched the metal tray. "The zinc is oxidised, and hydrogen gas is produced. And along the way you get a nice little flow of electrons." He prodded the spot on his gum again, where the false tooth used to sit, waiting for this day. "The whole reaction only gives less than one milliamp of current, of course. But you know, it's just enough to generate..." He pressed the tiny bulb into the tomato's flesh, and it began to glow. "...a little bit of light."

Morgan could see. And in the dim red light, he made out the realisation in Frank Oppenheimer's eyes. Each time Morgan had done this over the last two days, he'd savoured every morsel of light he could drink up. Hoarding it. For just this occasion.

He smiled.

Oppenheimer was fast, but Morgan had surprise on his side. The blade of light he formed in his hand was a pitiful thing, dull, not much longer than a bread knife. But when he passed it across Frank Oppenheimer's throat, it sliced through just the same.

The old man toppled. His silver dagger clattered to the ground. Morgan had to dart forwards to catch Oppenheimer before he hit the ground. Gently, Morgan lowered the ex-hero the rest of the way, while the man's wide eyes stared at him. The spluttering was awful. Again and again Frank tried to take a breath, only to draw more blood into his lungs.

God forgive him.

"I'm sorry, Frank," Morgan whispered. He cradled the man's head in his arm and used his sleeve to wipe the blood from around Frank's mouth. "I wish you could understand. I'm going to make a better world."

The old man was looking at something Morgan couldn't see. Oppenheimer's eyes glistened in the dim light of the blade. His mouth made gulping motions, and his hands gripped helplessly at the grey and black fabric of his bodysuit. He was wearing his old Omegaman costume after all. At least he'd die as a hero. A small comfort, but a comfort nonetheless.

Morgan waited with Frank until the man's eyes glazed over and blood stopped squirting. The blood was all over Morgan's face, he knew, but for once he didn't concern himself with his appearance. There'd be time enough for that in a few minutes, when he'd gather his captured metas and escape this prison. But first, he had something to do.

Finally, when everything stopped moving, he laid Frank's head on the cold concrete and shifted his weight. The headache was back, and it was trying to make up for the last two days. Morgan wouldn't complain, though. The price was far cheaper than the one Frank Oppenheimer had paid.

"You deserved better than this," he said to Frank. "We all did."

He brought his blade down on Frank's skullcap and began to cut.

PART THREE

He aha te mea nui o te ao?
He tangata, he tangata, he tangata.

What is the most important thing in the world?
It is people, it is people, it is people.

—Māori proverb

CHAPTER 26
THE LONG WAY HOME

BATTLE JACK

REAL NAME: *Jack Kingi*

POWERS: *Super strength, rapid healing.*

NOTES: *Noted close-quarters combatant and ranged weapons expert. Often operated as the Wardens' shock trooper, distracting villains and keeping them occupied while the rest of the group manoeuvered into flanking positions, rescued hostages, disabled bombs, or achieved other secondary objectives. In 1957, supercriminal group the Syndicate uncovered Kingi's secret identity and kidnapped his wife. Kingi was lured into a trap and executed.*

—Notes on selected metahumans [Entry #0310]

The Carpenter was too heavy to carry, so in the end Niobe had to fashion a sled out of the bits of broken wood and drag him out of the meat works. She left Doll Face for the flies.

Once she got him to the car, she used the first aid kit to clean and dress the wound in his chest. She stripped off his shirt and did her best to clean off the blood. When she was done, she covered him with one of his spare cloaks he kept in the car boot and laid him down in the back seat. The car was a two-door, so it took her ten minutes of awkward pushing and pulling to get him in. The sun beat down on her, but she didn't stop to remove her stained trench coat.

The wound in her thigh wasn't bad. It'd stopped bleeding by the time she peeled off her bodysuit enough to expose it. She didn't mind the stinging when she applied the rubbing alcohol. It'd leave a scar if she didn't get stitches, but she couldn't summon the urge to care. She covered it in gauze, wrapped a bandage around, and zipped up her bodysuit.

She didn't know what time it was when she finally climbed into the driver's seat. Her watch had broken sometime during the battle, but she guessed it was mid-afternoon by the look of the sun. Solomon had been driving last. When she had to pull the seat forwards so she could reach the pedals, she nearly broke down then and there.

She barely noticed the overgrown landscape as she drove south along the gravel roads. Every now and then she looked up at the sky, but she never spotted Sam. Logically, she knew she needed to find a phone, contact someone. People needed to know. But every time she passed through a village that looked like it might have a phone line, she kept driving.

When the Neo-Auckland skyline came into view an hour and a half later, it was no comfort. She thought about going straight to Met Div headquarters and trashing the place. No, that wouldn't solve anything. Something dark was building inside her, and it needed a target, that was all. She had to stay calm. Cold. A shadow.

She turned off the northern highway and took the back streets to the Old City. Everything was quiet. A few people moved on the streets, utterly unconcerned about the world around them. They didn't understand, none of them. Christ, she wished she was one of them.

After ten minutes, she pulled up outside their usual phone booth. How many times had she or the Carpenter used this phone? *Stop it.* She closed her eyes and forced the thoughts out of her head. She fished her cigarettes out of the glove box and lit one. Not even that helped. She turned to the Carpenter. She wished she could say that he looked like he was just taking a nap in the back seat, but that would be a lie. His cheeks had gone grey, his limbs were fixed in a way that no living human could replicate.

"I'll be back soon," she said around her cigarette.

By now, she knew Senior Sergeant Wallace's extension by heart. She stepped into the phone booth and punched in the number, expelling a lungful of smoke as she waited.

"Yes?" a strange voice answered.

She frowned. "Where's Wallace?"

"He has important business elsewhere at the moment. This is Constable Hinerau. Can I help you?"

"Yeah. Tell him if he visits a Schuster Meat Solutions up north he'll find the supercriminal known as Doll Face. He's dead. But that can wait. A meta called Sam Oppen…Sam Julius may be a risk to the public. He's just a boy, and he's not himself, but he is extremely powerful. I don't think he'll be hard to find. Tell Wallace that the boy needs to be taken into custody. But if Wallace harms the kid, he'll have me to answer to. Tell him I'll be contacting him again. Tell him I want to help him in this."

There was a long pause on the other end of the line. "Uh…who can I say is calling?"

"The vigilante bitch."

She hung up.

She knew what she had to do now, but her stomach clenched at the thought. After one last puff, she stubbed out the cigarette and returned to the car. The Carpenter hadn't moved. She got behind the wheel, turned the ignition, and pulled back onto the road.

The drive was nowhere near as long as she wished it was. She'd give anything to delay the moment. But all too soon she was pulling over again in an isolated cul-de-sac. She left Solomon in the car again and walked with heavy feet up to the door of the weatherboard villa, pulling on her mask as she went. Three knocks on the frosted glass. Then she waited.

Kate Doherty looked as beautiful as ever. Her blond hair was full-bodied, her beige dress crisp and clean. The polite smile on her face cracked the instant she saw Niobe. "What do you want?" she asked, crossing her arms.

"Kate. I…." Her tongue felt three times its normal size.

"What?" The annoyance in Kate's face faded. "Where's Solomon?"

The words wouldn't come. *Bloody hell.*

Kate's face dropped, and for a moment it looked like her legs would follow. But then the woman straightened. Kate took Niobe by the lapels and shook her. "Where is he?" she said, her voice sharper than Doll Face's knife. "Where is my husband?"

Niobe never felt the strikes that Kate landed. The woman was no fighter. She was just a girl who'd married a superhero.

It took both of them to get his body inside. Kate broke down sobbing as soon as they had him laid out on the bed. Tears ran down Niobe's face as well, but they were swallowed up by the fabric of the mask. Kate had nothing to hide behind. Grief and hate took turns swallowing her features. Niobe couldn't do anything but stand by and watch.

They say kids don't understand death, but these ones did. Riley, the oldest at ten years, tried to be brave for his little sister and his mum. But she knew the pain in his heart. She still remembered how she felt when she found out her parents had been killed in the blast that destroyed Auckland. The Blind Man hadn't taken those memories from her.

After a while, she left the family she'd broken to its grief. She returned to the car and sat behind the wheel without starting the engine. The street was quiet. The garden that Solomon had tended so lovingly still stood, but it seemed colourless, empty. Bloody hell, she couldn't stand this silence. She switched on the radio, hoping for music. She got a news bulletin instead.

"...man found murdered in the cell wearing the costume of the Manhattan Eight superhero has been confirmed as the original Omegaman, Frank Oppenheimer. Oppenheimer was the brother of J. Robert Oppenheimer, also known as Dr Atomic. The Metahuman Division is refusing to offer any more details at this time."

For a moment, she wondered if she'd heard it wrong. *It's all a sick joke. It has to be.*

The radio droned on. "For those just joining us, the police have confirmed that the supercriminal Quanta and his gang have escaped from an undisclosed holding facility less than forty-eight hours after their apprehension by the Metahuman Division. The body of ex-Manhattan Eight superhero Omegaman was found in Quanta's cell. Whether Omegaman was involved in the escape is still under investigation. In a press conference less than an hour ago, a Metahuman Division spokesman warned the public to stay indoors and not to use the phone lines except in the case of emergency."

Escaped? She and the Carpenter had served them Quanta with a bloody apple in his mouth, and Met Div let him escape?

She slammed her fist down on the steering wheel. Again. Again. Pain shot through her, but she didn't stop. It was all for nothing. The Carpenter was dead, Frank Oppenheimer was dead, Sam was broken and gone, Gabby had left her, and it was all for fucking nothing.

Slowly, her rage abated. She slumped down in the seat and put her face in her bruised hands. The car wasn't a good target for her anger. It didn't shout, it didn't fight back. She wanted to hurt someone, and she knew who. But she had no leads on Quanta. Doll Face had obviously killed several of Quanta's people back at the meat works. She could drive back out, spend hours looking for Quanta's airship. If he hadn't already taken it and left, of course. Even if it was still there, there were miles of abandoned farmland to search, and it would undoubtedly be well hidden.

The caffeine she'd guzzled to compensate for her three-hour sleep had faded long ago. Someone had scooped out everything inside her, and now she was just an empty bag of skin. There was nothing else for her to do here.

She took a few deep breaths to gather herself together, then drove the short distance back to her apartment. The sun slowly dropped behind the Old City's skyline, and the world went grey.

The apartment was as empty as she'd left it. The dirty dishes from the meal she'd shared with Solomon still sat in the sink. She ignored them and opened the refrigerator door. Her stomach protested at the sight of food, so she shut the fridge again. She tore off her mask and tossed it on the floor. For a while, she stood in the middle of the kitchen, lost. What was she even doing here?

Finally, she limped out to the living room, pulled a chair up to the window, and lit a smoke. Gabby always made her open a window when she was smoking. She tried to smile at the memory, but her lips wouldn't work. While the smoky cloud drifted around her, she stared out at the city. *I'm staying on Earth now, I guess.* Frank Oppenheimer wouldn't be sending her a paycheque anymore. Even if she could afford the lunar rocket ticket, she couldn't go by herself. There was nothing on the Moon for her. There was nothing here for her either.

She took a shower. The wound on her thigh stung in the scalding water. The steam made her dozy. Slowly, ever so slowly, the aches in her body subsided. Sometimes, she and Gabby would share a shower, taking turns with the soap, laughing as they tried to manoeuver in the tight space. Most of the time they'd barely even get dry afterwards before they collapsed onto the bed and made love. If she closed her eyes, she could picture Gabby lying naked on the bed, the blinds letting shafts of sunlight fall across her curves.

But when Niobe opened her eyes, she was alone again, and the water had gone cold. She shut off the shower, dried off, and returned to the bedroom. She could still smell Gabby's scent in the air. Or maybe it was just her imagination. Barely able to keep her eyes open, she crawled under the covers, leaned over, and switched the bedside lamp off.

She switched the light back on. Something had been poking out from under the bed, something that had taken her mind a moment to register. She blinked at it, trying to get her vision in focus. Then she realised what it was. A sheet of paper from the file on Quanta.

For a good ten minutes she stared at the paper, and it stared back. She should just turn off the light and go to sleep. Maybe things would be clearer in the morning. But the paper had a hook in her mind, and it was tugging her.

"Oh, bugger it," she said. She clambered out of bed and picked up the paper. Most of the other bits were still behind the bed where she'd thrown them. Ignoring the pain in her leg, she put her back against the bed and shoved it aside.

The pages were numbered, so it didn't take her long to gather them together and put them in order. Without bothering to return the bed to its place, she climbed back under the covers and started reading.

Morgan Shepherd had a short rap sheet, but it was bloody. Wanted for a riot at the University of Cambridge in 1958 where he murdered twenty-six anti-metahuman squad officers, with another nineteen dead at the hands of the metahuman mob he'd incited. According to all reports, that was the first time anyone was aware he was a meta. There were a few more counts of assault and wounding with intent throughout Europe, mostly involving police and special agents sent to capture him. The list ended with the murder of his lover, Lisa Neve, in Spain. After that, he vanished into the ether. The son of a bitch should've stayed there.

His biography was sparse: a few sentences about his family and early life in a town near Birmingham. Did extremely well at school. Accepted into Cambridge University. There was no psychological report, nothing to suggest madness. The report laid the riot at Cambridge squarely at his feet, but she could remember the way the world was turning in those days. If the anti-metahuman squad didn't open fire first, they were itching for the excuse.

But why was he here? And why had he taken Sam? Had he meant to unleash that power in Sam when he inflicted Doll Face upon him? "Why did you do this, you bastard?" she asked the picture of the young Morgan Shepherd.

Her eyes were drooping again, but she kept flicking through. The rest of the document consisted of reports by the teams that had tracked him through Europe. Interpol had taken a special interest in him. They'd been tracking him for two years before Shepherd's lover sold him out to them. But when they went to arrest him, Shepherd escaped, leaving half the team dead. Along with Lisa.

She skimmed past the list of Interpol officers involved in the operation. Then she paused. Gabby had underlined two names: the lead investigator and the squad leader. She went back, forcing her tired eyes to read. She knew the names. One Daniel O'Connor, and Met Div's beloved Senior Sergeant, Raymond Wallace.

"You knew," she said to Wallace's name. She didn't feel tired anymore. "You knew who he was all along, didn't you? You fucking arse-hole. He's here for you, isn't he?"

The paper didn't respond. She threw back the covers and got dressed. She had places to be.

CHAPTER 27
NO LIGHT WITHOUT DARKNESS

There are two main ways to become a superhero: through a supergroup, or through an apprenticeship. Many young metas wish to be accepted for a training position in one of the world's prestigious supergroups, such as the Light Brigade or the Alpha League. But spots are highly limited and usually only open to tier two or higher metahumans. Therefore, for many superhero hopefuls, the best way to learn the ropes is to take an apprenticeship as an existing hero's sidekick. Trying to become a superhero without supervision or training is not advised. Every year, dozens of young, solo metas are killed when they take on a threat they are not equipped to handle.

—Educational pamphlet from the Metahuman Advisory Board, 1954

Niobe pressed her palm against the wall of the phone booth. "What do you mean he's not there?" she said into the phone. "You have supercriminals running around free out there, and he's taking a sick day?"

"I can take a—"

"I don't want to leave a damn message," she said. "I need to talk to Senior Sergeant Wallace. Now."

She could practically hear the constable grinding his teeth. "The senior sergeant went home to take care of an urgent matter. If you have information for us, I will pass it on to Sergeant Hawthorne."

"Sergeant Hawthorne can go...." She paused. "He's at home? Wallace is at home?"

"Yes, but I can't give you his home number."

"Don't worry," she said. "I know his address." She slammed the receiver down before she could get the constable in any more trouble with his superiors.

She got back in the passenger side of the car and pulled her address book from under the seat. As far as address books go, it wasn't much to look at. The black folder was crammed with so many index cards and scraps of paper the thing was damn near overflowing. But it was in perfect alphabetical order. If you needed these things, sometimes you needed them in a hurry.

She'd picked up Wallace's address a couple of years back. It was a kind of insurance; an *In Case of Emergency* type thing. She only hoped the son of a bitch hadn't moved.

She kicked open the passenger door. She started to climb out, but something glinted on the floor behind the seat, catching her attention. Frowning, she stood up and slid the seat forwards so she could reach behind.

The object was smooth and hard beneath her fingers. She held it up to the light. It was a small circular pendant, black-rimmed with a white circle inset, a bit bigger than a bottle cap. The string attached to it looked like leather, but she knew it was a synthetic rope, far stronger than a tacky-looking piece of jewellery deserved. She recognised the pendant. She used to wear one just like it around her wrist. She'd turned in her signalling device when she left the Wardens, but the Carpenter....

She shook her head, and a smile touched her lips. The Carpenter had never really quit being a superhero. It must've fallen out of one of his pouches when she laid him down in the back. It was a relic of another era, when she was part of a team. But that was a long time ago. It was just her now. This thing was useless.

She tied it around her wrist anyway.

At least she'd determined one thing as she pulled over to the side of the suburban street: Senior Sergeant Wallace wasn't taking bribes. His house was a piece of shit.

It had a lawn and a fence and everything, but the lawn was threatening to engulf the doghouse in the corner and the fence was missing half a dozen pickets. The lights were off inside. Outside, a Border Collie cross was running back and forth in the garden as far as his chain would allow him, barking his head off.

She sat in the car in full costume, eyeing the house. She'd just come to talk to Wallace. Well, maybe more than talk. She wanted answers, and she wanted them bad.

But something wasn't right. The dog shouldn't be that excited. Quanta was inside, she could feel it in her gut. Every now and then a curtain moved in one of the neighbouring houses, but no one ventured outside. They seemed to be taking the radio warnings seriously. *Do you feel safe now?* she silently asked them.

Something moved just outside the front door. Someone doing a bad job of hiding in the shadow of an overgrown bush. Not Quanta, but a tall, slim woman. Nothing about her outward appearance immediately gave her away as a meta, but it didn't take a rocket engineer to pick out a henchman on sentry duty.

Niobe brushed her fingers against the Carpenter's pendant and got out of the car. She strode quickly across the road, hands in her pockets, hat down across her goggles. She headed straight for the door, pretending not to notice that the woman had noticed her. The woman growled, crouched like a cat, and leapt.

Niobe slid into shadow. An instant later, the woman landed awkwardly where Niobe had been standing, viscous ooze dripping from fangs, claws extending from her fingertips. The confusion on her narrow face was almost comical. But Niobe wasn't in the mood for laughing.

Niobe came out of the shadow behind the woman, drew, and fired. The electric crack of the gunshot broke the night's silence. The woman grunted and went down in a heap. Whimpering, the dog backed into its doghouse. Now Quanta would know she was coming. Good. She hoped he felt a shiver go through his heart.

Niobe retrieved the rope from her utility belt, tied up the unconscious woman, and shoved her into the garden. Done. *Now it's your turn, Morgan Shepherd.* With a deep breath, Niobe pulled the shadow back around her and slipped beneath the front door.

She reformed herself inside, gun drawn, with her back to a corner. It was quiet. She'd come out in a tiny kitchen with a linoleum floor and food stains on the tile counter. Grey light flickered from the next room; a television, maybe. Her boots made no sound as she moved forwards, hugging the wall and adjusting her goggles to the low light.

She swept through the opening into the next room. A busted-up old couch sat in the centre of the carpet. Behind it, a seated human silhouette was outlined by the flickering television. She moved without thinking, putting the couch between her and the figure.

The light in the room suddenly bloomed. Another man stood behind the seated figure, a halo of light surrounding him. "Spook," Quanta said, smiling. "A pleasure, I'm sure."

She flicked a switch on the side of her revolver. It hissed and clicked. Shield-breaker rounds armed. It might not kill Quanta, but it should put a dent in that pretty smile of his. She pointed her gun at him.

"Oh, come now," he said. His right hand swept forwards, a golden blade in his palm. He played the sword against the throat of the broad-shouldered man sitting tied and gagged on the chair in front of him. "We've both done this dance enough times to know the steps."

She licked her lips. Raymond Wallace managed to look like a copper even tied to a chair, wearing a singlet and missing his boots. His teeth dug into the fabric of his gag like he intended to gnaw his way through it then bite Quanta's throat out. The light radiating from Quanta cast the scars and grooves on the copper's face into shadow, aging him.

Niobe considered her options. The lounge was cluttered. Between the flickering television and the light Quanta was throwing off, there were one or two shadows she could hide in for a second. But she wasn't sure she was fast enough to flank him before he slit the leathery skin of the copper's throat.

"The cape copper's no friend of mine," she said, keeping her gun raised. Wallace grunted.

Quanta smiled. A black domino mask covered the top half of his face, turning his eyes into glowing orbs. He'd managed to find himself a pretty new white suit since his escape. She supposed his prison uniform would be soaked with Frank Oppenheimer's blood.

"You're alone tonight," he said. "Or is the Carpenter planning on sneaking up on me and throwing a few more boxes in my direction?"

"Just me," she said. No point lying.

"Hmm." He cocked his head. "I'm sorry to hear that."

Her trigger finger itched.

"Well, I must say you've surprised me again," Quanta said. "Unfortunately, you've interrupted something rather private."

"Private? Seems to me like you've been trying to get as many people as possible to pay attention to you. And this is your masterstroke? Tying up a middle-aged man because he spent a couple of years chasing you around Europe?"

Quanta tilted his head back and laughed. "Oh, Spook, I really thought you were smarter than that. This...." He brought the blade close enough to Wallace's throat to shave him. "This is just a private piece of revenge. Nothing to do with my true plan. I wanted to make sure the good Senior Sergeant saw the man he'd created, that's all. I wanted him to watch what I could do to his city." He grinned down at the copper. "Wallace and I played the cat and mouse game for years. But you know all about that, don't you? Then you'll know what he did. This man drove me to kill the woman I loved. He let me see exactly what the world needed. He's like a father to me, in some ways." Wallace's lip curled and his muscles bulged, but the ropes that lashed him to the chair held him tight.

"And what about Daniel O'Connor?" Niobe said. "Did you get your revenge on him by throwing him to Doll Face to torture?"

"I didn't mean for that to happen. Doll Face would have remained under control if I hadn't been imprisoned. But don't shed any tears for O'Connor. He was a thug, through and through. Do you know what I had to give him to convince him to kidnap Sam for me?" He paused, shaking his head incredulously. "Money. Not even very much. How uninspired."

Niobe adjusted her grip on her gun. Every muscle in her body told her to shoot him now, while he was still prattling on. She might not get another chance like this. But if her shield-breaker rounds didn't drop him instantly, Wallace was a corpse. The copper was an arsehole, the cold weapon of a corrupt government, but she'd seen too many bodies today. She couldn't be responsible for another one. While she kept him talking, Wallace lived.

"Your reporter hostage says you fancy yourself some sort of vengeful god," she said.

Quanta looked almost wistful at that. "Does he now? And what do you think, Spook?"

He was certainly vain enough for it. But her gut still told her there was something more going on here. If he'd been trying to make himself into a god, he'd been far too brutal. Did he know about Sam? Did he know about the boy's power?

His eyes danced with satisfaction. Of course he knew. He'd arranged everything; he'd used Doll Face to do god-awful things to the kid. Sam's rage, his power; that was no accident. But did Quanta really think he could control the boy? She'd seen Sam's eyes. He was no easily-manipulated child anymore. He wasn't even a minion. He was a force of nature. He was destruction itself.

"What did you do to Sam?" she asked. "He did nothing to you."

"No. That was an unfortunate necessity. But tier zero metas are impossibly rare. As Dr Atomic's son, Sam is probably the only tier zero in the world right now. His potential—most especially his psychic potential—make him a sort of sponge, to use a poor analogy. Harvesting neural tissue from other metas is a simple enough task, if gruesome. At first, I had him ingesting other metas' brain matter, slipping it into his food."

He couldn't be serious. Her stomach turned at the thought.

"I understand your disgust," he said. "I felt the same way. But as his absorptive capacity grew, it no longer became necessary. By now, he'll be able to absorb a dead meta's powers simply by coming into contact with their neural tissue. Doll Face manipulated Sam's mind to accept the transfer, wiping him clean. And voilà! We have the most perfect destructive force to ever threaten the world. Sam was always destined to be one of the strongest metas ever to exist. But now he's unstoppable. Beautiful, isn't it?"

That sick son of a bitch. She remembered the metal forming on Sam's skin. Just like Iron Justice. How many metas had Quanta butchered so he could feed their brains to Sam? No wonder Sam had gone mad.

So much power in the hands of a madman. Not even a man, a boy. And he'd only grow stronger. Who could stand up to that kind of power? Even if the greatest metas on the Moon returned, they might not be able to stand against him. Quanta had put the entire world at risk. Everyone she cared about. She'd hated supercriminals before, but Quanta...Quanta deserved death. Her finger trembled over the trigger.

"You're getting angry," Quanta said. "Since you're here, and I don't have to be anywhere quite yet, how about a game to calm you down?"

"Bite me."

He grinned, grabbed Wallace by the hair, and roughly tugged the copper's head back. The cape copper grunted and squirmed, but Quanta slammed his elbow into the side of the man's head, and Wallace's eyes went out of focus. Before Niobe could blink, the blade grew narrower and sharper. Her grip tightened on the gun, ready to fire. Quanta brought the blade's tip within half an inch of Wallace's eye. He crouched down, shielding himself with Wallace's face.

Niobe froze.

"Here's the game," Quanta said. "You've got one minute to work out why I'm doing what I'm doing. Why I'm here. Or else...." He waved the blade's tip at Wallace's eye. "Well, you know. Sound fun?"

She licked her lips. "Why are you asking me this?"

"Tick tock."

She could see the sweat dripping down the side of Wallace's cheek, and the look on his face as he watched the blade. *I've got no choice. All right, think.*

Something Quanta said before clicked in her mind. *Threaten the world.* "I read your file," she said slowly. "The riot. The murders. You had to have trained yourself to carve through that many coppers. But you didn't start out as a supercriminal. You always thought you were going to be some sort of hero, didn't you?" She paused, studying his face. "I've seen metas just after they've killed for the first time. It changes them. Killing those anti-metahuman officers swept away everything you thought you knew about yourself."

He smiled at her and said nothing.

She licked her lips. "So you had to build a new identity for yourself. A misunderstood fugitive. Not a hero, not a villain, just a man. Not even a meta. You tried so hard to be that person. But it didn't work out, did it? Lisa found out what you were."

Quanta's smile grew fixed, but his eyes glowed brighter. "And she turned me in."

"Yes. And to escape, to live, you had to kill her." She nodded towards Wallace. "They *made* you kill her. Or that's what you tell yourself. And your new persona, the one you'd worked so hard to create, shattered. So you rebuilt yourself once more. This time as…"

"…a villain," Quanta said. "A monster." He looked at her like a proud parent.

Those eyes. It fell into place. "You actually want to be hated, don't you? That's what this is all about. That's why you did those things to Sam. You want him to be a threat to the world."

"And why would I do that?"

She chewed her lip. Her arm was growing tired, but she kept it outstretched, the gun aimed at the spot between Quanta's eyes. How had he attracted so many followers with this madness? Were there that many metas out there who just wanted to bring pain? No, that wasn't it. Avin, Screecher, they weren't psychopaths. Heroes for Freedom had been radical, but they were no terrorists.

Heroes for Freedom. That was it. She met Quanta's eyes, and his grin widened. Had there really once been an innocent boy behind that mask?

"You want to create a threat that the normals can't handle on their own," she said slowly. She didn't want to believe it, but as she said the words, she knew they were true. "That's why you hit the TV station, and why you publicly executed Iron Justice. You needed everyone to see, both normals and metas. By making Sam what he is, you wanted to create a threat that only metas could defeat." Her palms were slick with sweat. "You mean to bring back the superhero."

He beamed at her. Bloody hell, she felt sick. All this, all these people dead, was a ploy designed to convince the world that they needed superheroes to protect them. *Christ, the blood's on my hands now as well. It's on every meta's hands. This bastard has painted it there.*

"People like us protected the world for two decades, Spook." His voice was calm and maddeningly cheery. Wallace's eyes widened as the blade drifted back towards his throat. "But those heroes were too good. They locked up almost every supercriminal. They pushed the world back from nuclear war. They worked their way right out of a job. And when the doomsday threats came fewer and farther between, the normals started to forget. They got concerned that we were going to steal their jobs, or turn rogue. Their love for us turned to fear. And the hero forgot who he was. So be it. I'll use that fear."

"The reporter was right," she said. "You really do fancy yourself a god."

"If gods exist, we're not them," Quanta said. "Metas aren't superior to the normals. I don't mean to rule anything. But I will not stand by while everything we stand for is forgotten."

"How noble," she said, letting her words drip with sarcasm. "But this plan's a bit crude, isn't it? You really think you're saving metas by doing this?"

"This is real life, Spook. Sometimes crude works better than elaborate schemes." His face twitched. She noticed for the first time the lines running down his face, the strain in his neck.

She shook her head. *He's mad.* "You've just made things a million times worse. Every life you take is another reason for them to hate us. You've doomed us all, Morgan."

"No. I'll take all the hate on me. Me and Sam, we'll be the pariahs.

The world will see how much they need their heroes. Why do you think I chose to do this here in Neo-Auckland?"

"Because Wallace is here. You wanted to show him what you could do."

Quanta shook his head. "He was the reason I had the original idea, but there's more to it than that. Since the bomb hit, New Zealand has always had one of the highest metahuman densities in the world. Only Japan and Poland are greater. Combine that with your country's pitiful excuse for a military, and…." He shrugged. "It's a perfect site to wreak havoc. The normals stand no chance here without heroes to defend them."

He stood slowly and met her eyes.

"There's just one thing I need you to do for me," he said.

"You really think I'll help you?"

He laughed again. "Spook, Spook." He shook his head, chuckling to himself. "Tell me, what do you believe?"

"What?"

"Do you believe in goodness? Kindness? Do you believe that some things are self-evidently right? Do you believe that there are bad people who will hurt others? Kill them? Torture them? Do you believe those people need to be stopped, no matter the risk to yourself?"

Solomon's voice came to her, so clear he could be standing right next to her. *There's still good, mate, and there's still things we have to stand up for.*

"Yes," she said.

Quanta smiled. "Then I'll see you on the battlefield, hero. Let's put on a good show."

Light flashed from his body, so bright it overwhelmed her goggles. Blind, she threw herself behind the cover of the couch, her ears tuned to threats. Something smashed. Glass. Then Wallace's grunts were the only noise in the room.

When she could open her eyes, the bright light was gone. She came up gun drawn, blinking away the afterimage. Quanta had disappeared. The window behind Wallace was broken. She rushed past the cape copper, her boots crunching on broken glass, but when she stuck her head outside, there was no sign of Quanta.

"Shit," she said, kicking the skirting board. She had the son of a bitch in her sights. She was too knackered for these goddamn goose chases. With a sigh, she shoved her gun back in its holster.

The bastard was slipperier than a trout. She'd known he was dangerous when she saw him on TV, but this was something else. Even if Sam didn't end up destroying everything, the world's governments were going to come down harder on metas than they ever had before. It was going to be a bloodbath one way or another. *And with Frank dead, there's no payday. And no way off this planet.*

She forcefully unclenched her fist, moved in front of Wallace, and crossed her arms. "Are you going to try anything dumb if I untie you?"

By the way he glared at her, she knew he was considering it.

"Bugger it." She undid his gag.

Wallace spat the wet fabric out of his mouth. "You should've shot him," he growled.

"That'd be vigilantism, wouldn't it?" She stomped behind him to untie his hands. "Bloody hell, hold still, will you?"

The cape copper stopped wriggling long enough for her to get the ropes off. He worked his shoulders back and forth for a few seconds while he rubbed his wrists, then he went on to untie his legs. He kept his eyes on her the whole time.

She paced around the room while she thought. There were no books in the lounge, but the copper had a collection of Coltrane records on a shelf in the corner. She didn't take him for a jazz fan.

"Do your colleagues know that you knew who Quanta was the whole time?" she asked.

He got to his feet and shrugged back into his blue tunic. "I didn't know right away."

"Yeah?"

"He was wearing a mask."

She snorted. "That little thing barely covered his eyes. You knew damn well who he was."

Wallace grunted and said nothing.

She wanted a cigarette, but she wasn't going to reveal even a small amount of her face to this guy. Instead, she continued her pacing. "He's going to move, and soon. Are your people ready?"

"Yes."

"I don't know if you can handle Sam. The boy, he's strong."

Wallace shrugged. He hadn't moved from his spot near the chair. At least he wasn't going for a gun. "We've put down strong freaks before," he said.

She ignored the jab. "Not like this." She inspected a framed photo of a brunette woman and a young girl tucked away in the corner. The colours were all turning red. The girl looked a little like the Carpenter's daughter.

"Maybe…maybe you should call for aid," she said.

"Aid?"

She untied the pendant hanging from her wrist. "A long time ago, there used to be a special transmitter in the basement of the police headquarters. In case of emergency."

His eyes hardened. "I won't play his games."

"You're already playing, and you're losing wickets." She held out the pendant to him. "This has all the frequencies that were in use in New Zealand. There might still be a few receivers out there. Someone might come."

"No," he growled.

"This is no time for your bloody prejudice—"

"This is about the law! This is about order."

Her hands formed fists inside her pockets. "Law? Is this the law that lets you break up families and kill babies? Fine. Go defend it. I'll be defending everything else." She tossed the pendant on the floor at his feet and made for the door.

"Hey," he yelled. "We're not done here." She could hear him stomping after her as she went back through the kitchen.

"I am."

"The McClellan baby," he said.

She paused with her hand on the doorknob.

"The baby's alive," he said. "Got a kill-switch, but alive. With a foster family in Favona. Good folks."

Alive. Alive with a goddamn kill-switch. Like that meant something.

"Get your people together, Senior Sergeant, and start getting the civilians to safety. Lie to them. Tell them you'll keep them safe. They like that." She slammed the door behind her.

The Border Collie had gone quiet. Niobe's rope sat coiled on the ground, but the fanged woman had disappeared. Sighing, Niobe shoved the rope back in her utility belt. She pulled up the bottom of her mask, tapped out a Pall Mall, and put it between her lips. The street was so still she could've believed that she was the only person left on Earth.

She missed the Carpenter. He'd know where to go from here. Even in defeat, he was always the one pulling them through. He helped push back the Nagasaki Horrors. He fought at her back in a hundred different battles. She tapped the auto-lighter against her head to get it working, then brought it to her cigarette. *You're all alone now, Spook. Deep down, isn't that what you always wanted?*

Then she looked up and saw the white airship floating above Neo-Auckland, and her muscles froze. Even in this light, she could make out the cannons on each corner of the gondola. A pair of rocket engines flamed orange, bringing the airship in a slow, banking turn towards the centre of the city. The barrels of the cannons began to glow with a blinding yellow light. A second later, a whining sound reverberated through the air.

The cigarette dropped from her lips as she sprinted for the car.

CHAPTER 28
CAN ANYBODY HEAR ME?

RIGEL VII

REAL NAME: *Victor Lorenzen*

POWERS: *Able to "surf" on streams of light (especially starlight) and use light as an energy source.*

NOTES: *Although an American by birth, he rarely spent time in the US after he became a metahuman. Lorenzen became known as the "Wandering Star" as he travelled the world, aiding other supergroups when they required help or using his powers to do civilian work. His lifestyle was funded by the licensing fees he was paid for the comic books based on his adventures. Retired following the Seoul Accord. Died in 1965 of testicular cancer.*

—Notes on selected metahumans [Entry #0051]

Not for the first time, Morgan wished he could fly. Not if it came with hideous wings, of course, like Avin, but a psychic-based flight would be convenient. It was one of the few things he envied Sam.

He popped the clutch on the rocket bike and zipped past a truck and trailer, the tyres screaming against the road. Driving the contraption with his limited vision was one of the riskier things he'd done today. A bubble of perspex kept the wind and the bugs off his face, but it had a nasty habit of distorting the light from the street lamps as they strobed above him, pulsing in time to his headache. Serpentessa was taking the van back on her own. There was only room for one on the rocket bike. Besides, the woman had been careless to let Spook interrupt him. He would have enjoyed leaving Wallace trussed up in front of the television, watching his city die.

Overhead, Morgan's airship *Hyperion* continued its slow circuit of the city, ray cannons charging. Navigatron and the skeleton crew could handle the aircraft without any trouble. It looked beautiful against the backdrop of stars.

Morgan glanced down at the flashing dot on the rocket bike display. It pointed to the centre of the city, where the Peace Tower's needle pierced the sky. *Yes, this would definitely be easier if I could fly.* High-powered rocket-packs were dangerous if you weren't in an armoured suit, and he found the suits inconvenient and impractical. The needle on the speedometer climbed slowly higher.

The radio piece in his ear crackled. "We await your pleasure, my lord." Navigatron's modulated croaking sounded more like one of the Circuit's robots than a human.

So this was it. The end. Morgan could feel the weight pressing down on him. It shouldn't have had to be like this. He paused for a moment, then thumbed a button on the handlebars. "Three minutes. Acquire your targets to maximise panic."

"Understood." Another crackle, then there was only the sound of the bike's rocket engine.

The highway swept beneath him. He checked the display again. The dot hadn't moved. Doll Face had done well, implanting the rendezvous location deep in the boy's subconscious. He just had to meet with the boy one more time before the end. And up there would be a good spot for the boy to contemplate.

The speedometer beeped twice. Critical speed attained. His head pounded as he hit the thruster. He only hoped the bike didn't burn up on launch like the prototype had.

Something whirred behind him. A new wave of heat pressed against his legs. His white shirt stuck to the sweat on his back. The bike coughed twice, and Morgan held his breath. Then the bike jerked suddenly forwards and upwards, pinning him against the seat. His gloves slipped on the handlebars. For a moment, he lost his balance, and the bike lurched like a drunken sailor. But the tips of his fingers caught the grip. He twisted the throttle, and the hum of the tyres on the road was replaced by the incessant roar of flame.

He wiped his forehead against his shoulder without taking his hands from the controls. As he did so, he glanced out the side of the bubble. The road fell away beneath him, obscured by the heat waves from the rocket engines. The wheels retracted to gain protection from the heat.

That was not pleasant, he thought as he brought the bike fully under control. Perhaps wings wouldn't be so bad after all. He gunned the throttle, and relaxed as the rockets carried him upwards through the night. The streetlights had turned to pin pricks now, mirroring the stars above. The air whistled against the side of the bike as he raced towards the Peace Tower.

The tower was narrow at the bottom and swept out into a wide observation deck in the middle. Higher still, the tower tapered back in until it formed a needle that continued a further three hundred feet into the air. A red light blinked atop the tower, but tonight there was something else there as well. A tiny shadow balanced on the needle's tip, looking down over the city. Morgan slowed his approach, and the shadow turned to regard him.

Sam showed no sign that he noticed the cold wind that buffeted his hair. His arms hung loosely at his sides, and as Morgan approached, he saw the boy wasn't actually standing on the needle. He hovered a foot or so above the tip, his toes pointed towards the earth. The night shrouded his eyes. Red scratches marred Sam's bare chest. Some were narrow—knife wounds, perhaps—while others were thick. They all looked more healed than they should, though. Perhaps one of the prisoners Morgan had butchered had an accelerated healing power.

Are you proud of yourself, supervillain? he asked himself as he eyed the boy's wounds and saw the madness in his eyes.

Morgan brought the bike into a holding pattern ten feet from the boy. If Sam decided to attack him, the bike would offer him no protection. The boy was powerful now, and soon he'd be stronger than the most optimistic of his models had predicted. The combination tracker/sensor he'd had implanted in the boy when O'Connor first brought him in had reached the maximum detectable power level twelve hours ago, and Morgan had no doubt Sam had grown stronger since then. Morgan could practically feel the air bend around the boy.

With the flip of a switch, the bubble around him began to retract. His heart thudded as the flimsy perspex barrier moved aside, leaving nothing but the roaring wind between him and Sam.

The boy slowly raised his head. His eyes were pure white.

—*I remember you. Are you here to kill me?*

Sam's lips never moved, but Morgan heard the words anyway, as clearly as if Sam was inside his head. Maybe he was.

"No." Morgan had to shout over the wind. "You are unkillable."

Sam appeared to consider that. His head drooped to one side, as if the muscles in his neck were incapable of supporting the weight of his brain. Dried dirt gathered on the slack flesh of his face.

—*Are you here to save me?*

Morgan gave a strained smile. "No, Sam. I'm here to tell you how to save yourself."

Sam turned his head to the side, and Morgan followed the boy's gaze. *Hyperion* hung above the city, ray cannons glowing. Almost invisible against the night, dozens of ropes dangled from the loading bay. Every now and then, a tiny dot of a human zipped down to the rooftops of the city below. His people were moving into position. Sirens rang through the night. Soon, battle would be joined.

"I have something for you." Morgan reached into his front pocket and tossed a small vial towards Sam. It stopped in mid-air and hovered close to the boy's face.

—*What is it?*

"It belonged to your uncle."

The vial shattered and the glass plummeted to the street, but the grey fibres inside floated. Sam slowly raised his hand and touched the brain tissue. It dissolved as it touched his skin.

Sam sighed deeply and floated in place for a few seconds. Then his head turned slowly towards Morgan.

—*I can hear everything*, the voice said. *EVERYTHING. I hear sirens. I hear screams. I hear pain to come. So much pain.* The voice cracked, and Sam's body shivered.

Morgan nudged the bike closer. Gently, gently. Sam's skinny body twitched, his fingers rolling like an ocean swell.

"You've always been alone, Sam. Your uncle kept you away from the world, didn't he?"

His eyes flickered.

—*I don't remember. Maybe. Maybe he did. I don't remember.*

"He did it to protect you. Do you know what happened to your father? Look into your uncle's memories."

A shiver ran through Sam, and he fell silent. The wind whistled in Morgan's ears, cutting through his jacket, but he waited.

—*They trapped him. Put him in a box. My father. They never let him see the sun again.*

"They're coming again, Sam. The boys in blue. And others. They'll do the same to you. If you don't stop them."

Sam's white eyes rolled back towards Morgan.

—*How? How do I stop them?*

"Control them."

His body convulsed, and his head snapped back and forth.

—*No no no. No. I can't.*

"I know it's scary," Morgan said. He touched the throttle again, just enough to bring the bike alongside Sam. Blood pounded in his ears. He swallowed his heart back down, stretched his arm out across the abyss, and gently laid it on Sam's shoulder. "But you have to. Or you'll be alone forever. They're killers, all of them."

—*Killer. I'm a killer. I killed two people. Or did I?* He pressed his hands against the side of his head. *Why is it so hard to remember?*

Morgan could feel the icy coldness of the boy's skin seeping through his glove. "It's time. You don't have to be alone anymore. You can keep yourself safe."

—*Safe and sound.* Sam nodded slowly.

"Did you ever learn Latin, Sam? Do you know the phrase, 'carpe omnia'?"

I know. Yes, I remember. He held his hands in front of his face. The skin twitched and stretched, and then a hundred tiny strings wormed their way out of every fingertip. He opened his mouth for the first time. "Seize everything."

Morgan trembled.

Senior Sergeant Wallace stuck his head out the car window to get a better look at the figures zip-lining down from the zeppelin. Dozens of freaks. The flashes of fire and lightning were starting, and so were the screams. God help them.

The fuckers were coming down right in the middle of the city. Dense civilian population, hundreds of apartment blocks and commercial buildings. The monorail would be the first thing to go when people panicked. The streets were narrow; getting people out would take time. Time those freaks wouldn't give him. Goddamn it, this was going to be worse than the house-to-house fighting in Italy during the war. He put his foot down harder, letting the siren clear the way for him.

Wallace jerked the radio handset off its cradle. "Unit one to unit four. Talk to me, Hawthorne."

There was a brief pause, then a voice spoke. "Unit four to unit one. Sir, where have you been? We've been calling—"

"Save it, Sergeant. What's happening out there? Have you got people on the ground in the CBD?"

"Two teams, sir."

"Two? I'm counting..." He glanced out the window again. "...eighteen metas so far, with more still jumping out of that damn balloon. They're going for maximum panic. You don't need the rest of the division handling evacuation. Let the regular police handle that."

The radio crackled. "Evacuation, sir?"

His fist tightened around the handset. The scar on his scalp twinged. "Yes, Sergeant, evacuation. Getting the civilians the fuck out of what is about to become a battleground. You are evacuating them, aren't you?"

"Sir—"

For a second, night turned to day. He slammed on the brakes, filling the air with the smell of burning rubber. A flash of light shot from the airship overhead, punctuated a moment later by a high-pitched screech. The yellow beam crashed into an office block to the east of the Peace Tower. Fire instantly erupted through the midsection of the building. The tower started to tilt to the side like a block of butter left out in the sun.

"Sweet Jesus," he said. The office block should be empty at this hour—or as close enough to empty as he could hope for—and maybe there was no one on the street below. Maybe. But the next shot....

His eyes darted around at the spires of apartment buildings, symbols of a bright new future that had never come. Thousands lived there, and soon they'd all be crowding the streets on foot and in cars, trampling each other, trying to escape the carnage, and running right into the paths of Quanta's metas. If a blast didn't kill them first.

He depressed the handset button. "Hawthorne! Are you there?"

"Y...yes, sir."

"Our primary objective is to get the civilians into the bomb shelters. Then we need to figure out how to take that aircraft down. Do you understand me?"

"Sir, our helicopters are still being repaired after the television station attack."

"Then get on the line with the Army and the Air Force. Find something, damn it."

"Yes, sir. We...." Something burst across the radio, and the car filled with static.

"Hawthorne!" Wallace shouted into the handset. There were smaller flashes of light coming from the buildings ahead. "Sergeant!"

The static dropped away, replaced with hisses and pops. "We're taking fire, sir." Hawthorne's voice had gone up an octave. "Oh God. Mauger, above you, the fliers! Do something about them."

Damn it, damn it, damn it. Wallace gunned the engine again, and the car took off. He didn't have the people to deal with this. "Fuck the court orders, activate their kill-switches, Sergeant."

"I'm trying, sir, I'm trying. I think they're using those scramblers again."

Wallace slammed his palm against the steering wheel. They'd grown complacent, and now they were paying the price. As he neared the central city, department stores and chic restaurants closed in around him. Civilians ran screaming in front of his car, dragging children and suitcases with equal carelessness. He leaned on the horn, but neither that nor the siren cleared his way. The car had to slow to a crawl to fight through the churning mass of humanity. A woman brushed against his car wearing her nightgown and every piece of jewellery she owned. There were still curlers in her hair.

He shielded his eyes as the airship let out another blast. He couldn't see where it hit, but even from here he could make out the wrenching sound of cracking concrete. Something caught his eye, illuminated against the fading light. It hovered up in the sky, a tiny dot glowing faintly. Another of Quanta's criminals? But the figure was all on his own. Something about the way he stared down at the carnage made Wallace's skin crawl. *What the hell is he doing?*

Wallace slowed the car and fumbled for his folding binoculars in the glove box. *It's just a boy*, he realised as he pressed the lenses to his eyes. His thoughts went back to Morgan Shepherd's gloating conversation with the vigilante woman, while he sat bound up like a goddamn wild pig. This couldn't be what she was afraid of. The kid looked like nothing.

Another beam lit up the boy, casting shadows across his face. Wallace caught sight of something else. A cloud was emerging from the boy's hands. No, not a cloud. A web. Like fibres being spun out of freshly-shorn wool. The fibres snaked down towards the street. Wallace brought the binoculars down to follow them. Some of them disappeared straight through the walls of buildings, while others continued their descent. Something in the way they snaked made his stomach ache. He'd never seen Doll Face's powers, but the descriptions in the few survivors' reports were hard to mistake.

He shoved the car door open against the crowd and leaned out. Too many people. He couldn't get them all out. Instinctively, he reached for his sidearm, but at this range he had no chance of hitting the boy. His forehead grew damp as the fibres plunged into the crowd.

The change was subtle. Most people were too panicked to notice a few unlucky souls stopping in their tracks. But when he stood up on the lip of the car door and stared over the crowd, he could see the strings slipping inside a dozen civilians' open mouths and noses. Their eyes went blank and their legs stopped moving. The crowd shoved past them, but the captured civilians stood as solid as a mountain in a storm. Then, as one, they started to float into the air.

"Goddamn it," he said. He ducked back inside the car and got on the radio. "Sergeant. Are you still there?"

"Yes, sir. I've sent half my team to escort a couple hundred civvies to the Greene Street shelter. The freaks are still pressing us, sir. We've got three dead and another five seriously wounded. We're falling back."

Shit. "Hawthorne, that is a negative. You have to hold. The primary threat is a Caucasian male teenager flying above..." He tried to work out where the boy was closest. "...Mayoral Street. Probable psychic. He's targeting civilians." He watched as another wave of strings came floating in. Behind them, the captured civilians floated slowly upwards, forming a loose sphere around the boy. Damn it. How the hell were they supposed to mount an attack on the kid with civilians in the way? "Hawthorne, do you have a visual?"

There was a pause. "Sir, it's too hot on the surface. Beech just got frozen solid by some sort of ice beam, sir. We're moving underground."

"No, dammit! You can't mount a defence from there. We need every man trying to put this kid down."

The pause was even longer this time. Then the radio cut out. The son of a bitch had switched off his radio. *He switched off his fucking radio!* Wallace slammed the handset down hard enough to break the cradle. He was going to tear that insolent boy a new arsehole when this was over.

He gripped the steering wheel in both hands, trying to force himself to be calm. He needed a plan. He needed weapons. And he needed men.

Static hissed from the radio again. Had Hawthorne come to his senses? Wallace snatched up the handpiece again and depressed the button, but the static remained. What the hell?

A voice boomed through the speakers. "People of Neo-Auckland. I'm sure you know who this is by now. And I'm sure that deep down you always knew this would happen."

Wallace ground his teeth together hard enough to make his jaw ache. Morgan Shepherd. This was supposed to be a secure frequency. The fucker must be broadcasting across every band.

Quanta's voice continued. "One day you will understand why I'm doing this, if you survive tonight. Do you see the boy above your city, taking your loved ones away? He could have been the greatest hero the world had ever seen. But you didn't want that, so I gave him a new purpose. There will be no negotiations. No ransom. If you don't break us here, we will move onto another city, and another, and when this country is nothing but a burning ember we will start on the next."

Quanta paused, and the screams of the city filled the gap. Damn this bastard. Damn the government for not giving Wallace the men he needed. Damn everything!

"I just have one question for you all," Quanta said. Wallace could hear the smile in his voice. "Is there anyone out there who can stop us?"

The radio hissed once more, then went dead. Wallace switched it off before he was tempted to put a round through it.

He turned his attention back to the crowds scattering around him. More and more people were starting to rise into the air, fibres slipping into their ears or their noses. Others phased straight through the walls of apartment buildings, still in their pyjamas, and drifted slowly up towards the boy. On the street, some civilians were grabbing hold of ankles and trying to pull the hostages back down. He could taste the sweat and fear in the air.

Half a block down the street, a fibre dropped down and slipped into the nostril of a young Polynesian girl getting dragged along by her father. She stopped, the terror in her eyes fading, and jerked her hand free of her father's grip. The man stopped, buffeted by the crowd, and yelled something at his daughter, gesturing frantically. She didn't even glance at him as she turned away.

"Son of a bitch," Wallace said. He squeezed out of the car and fought through the press of bodies. The air was stifling. Elbows jabbed at him as he shouldered his way onwards. For a brief, mad moment he considered firing his 9mm into the air just to clear himself some space, but that might turn this into a stampede.

He caught sight of the girl again a moment later, three feet above the ground. Her father was battling against the current as well, but he was too slow, too timid, and he wasn't gaining ground. Wallace grunted and shoved past him, following the glimpses of black hair he got through the elbows and dresses and suitcases.

"C'mere," he said as he got close enough to lay his hands on her shoulders. He could feel something pulling her upwards, but she made no move to fight him. Wallace elbowed aside a man and tugged on the girl, pulling her down.

The string looked like fishing line, but when he touched it, he could feel it quiver with soft fleshiness. It disappeared into the girl's left nostril. He gave it a tug, but it was anchored on something. He didn't want to think about what that something was. He'd seen these strings disappear straight through solid walls, so he might only get one chance at this. Holding the limp girl with his left arm, he pulled his multi-tool from his belt and used his teeth to open up the wire cutter.

This better not fucking kill her, he told God. No response from Him. Typical. Wallace put the string between the blades and cut.

The fibre split with an electric buzz. The girl continued to dangle limply from his arms for a moment. He took her in both hands and shook. "Wake up."

She gasped and blinked. Her muscles went tight, regaining their tone. She stared at him with horror in her wide eyes. Then she began to kick.

"What are you doing?" a man's voice yelled. The girl's father finally came stumbling through the crowd.

Wallace shoved the flailing girl into the man's arms. "Police. Get her out of here, and don't stop."

A scream ripped through the night, louder than humanly possible. Wallace's gaze snapped up to the figure of the boy hovering above the city. The multi-tool was slippery in his palm. The boy was facing towards him. Staring at him. Bugger. The boy had felt the fibre being cut. *That was reckless.*

"Move!" he shouted at the crowd. A new wave of strings flew towards him. With his ears still ringing, he plunged through the crowd, moving perpendicular to the flow. A dozen strings snagged civilians around him, but he couldn't stop to help. He pressed onwards, making for the shelter of an elevated monorail station.

The crowd thinned, allowing him to break into a run. The kid's screams still echoed around the street, drowning out those of the civilians. He ran until he was breathless and his bad hip stabbed at him with every step. He was going towards the danger area, where Quanta's metas were wreaking havoc, but as long as it was away from the boy, he didn't care.

Finally, he pressed his hand against a brick wall in the shadow of a shoe-store's awning. His moustache was drenched with sweat, and his breath came in short, sharp pants. How was he supposed to fight something like that? He didn't have the men he used to, and the ones he did have were probably all cowering or running for their lives now. He could still hear a few scattered gunshots popping in the distance, but he couldn't tell if they were friendly. How was he supposed to do his job?

The vigilante woman's words came to his mind. He tried to force them away, but they clung to his brain and dug their claws in. No. This was still his city. He wouldn't play that madman's games. He wouldn't.

The screams hammered against his skull. His city. His fucking city. And it'd be his to enjoy all on his own once everyone was dead.

"Son of a bitch." He clenched his fists and started running again. This time, he ran south.

The main police headquarters wasn't far, but his joints had nearly locked up by the time he got there. During the war he'd done a forced march all the way from the Sangro River to the Gustav Line, and now he couldn't run two bloody miles.

Silhouettes moved in the windows of the police station. He stepped off the street through the main doors into a hive of panic. In the tiled entrance hall, uniformed officers desperately tried to fend off the attention of desperate civilians. Most of the officers were unarmed. He'd have to take the best men from here and get them some rifles from Met Div before there wasn't a city left to defend. But first, there was something he needed to do.

No one challenged him as he shouldered his way through the officers and panicking civilians. Like Met Div headquarters, the basement was used for archives and evidence storage, but he knew this building had a sub-basement as well. The elevator didn't go down that far, so he had to take the stairs, his hip aching with every step. He was panting again by the time he reached the bottom.

The thick black door at the bottom was locked. He pulled his key-ring out of his pocket. Even though it'd been years since he'd used this particular key, he found it with ease. Grudgingly, he slid it into the lock and worked the rusted hinges.

The musk of a different age assaulted his nostrils. He flipped the light switch, but the bulb had probably given out years ago. He switched on his torch and crossed the room. As he swept the light around, he was greeted by the smiling faces of a hundred heroes. Their pictures adorned the walls, everyone from the big shots like Battle Jack to two-bit heroes like Weeping Willow. Away from the sunlight, their pictures were unfaded. His heart grew heavier as he looked on them, so he flicked the beam away. This was a stupid idea. This was what Quanta wanted. But as sick as it made him, he had no choice.

He stopped in front of a radio transmitter that covered the entire wall. Countless dials and switches glinted in the torchlight, dust coating the upper surfaces. There were no instructions and half the labels had peeled away or faded, but he still remembered. He was still good for that, at least.

The pendant that the vigilante left him was heavy in his pocket. He took it out and held it up to his torchlight. It looked like such an innocent thing. "Goddamn it."

He placed the pendant into a recess in the machine and flicked a couple of switches. The machine reluctantly whirred to life. A panel lit up, and a needle jumped to attention. Static hissed through the speakers.

Damn it. How had it come to this? It was pointless anyway. Even if the transmitter worked, there was no reason to think any of the receivers still did. He'd be doing more good out on the street with a rifle in his hands and a supercriminal in his sights. He wouldn't save the city, but maybe he could get a couple more people to safety. Maybe he could put a few of those bastards down.

He glanced once more at the pictures around the room and sighed. "Goddamn it." He'd lost control of his city. There was no bloody choice. The chair creaked when he sat down. Sighing, he pulled the mouthpiece up to his face, covered his forehead with his palm, and depressed the button. The static went silent, and the faces on the walls waited.

"Calling all heroes, calling all heroes...."

CHAPTER 29
ONCE MORE INTO THE NIGHT

There's always something. No matter how much you want to rest, there's always a death ray or a bank robbery or a tsunami or a doomsday machine. There's always more people to save. So you run and you plan and you dive through the fire and sometimes you fight when you have to but mostly it's running, always running. Always trying to outrun the next crisis, always trying to be faster because you weren't fast enough the last time and if that little girl had just hung on a second longer you would've been there, but she couldn't, and you weren't, and now she's dead, so you run, trying to beat destiny. And you're tired, always tired, but you run anyway. Because you chose this life, and there's nothing else you'd rather do than see the smiles of the ones you save.

—Memoirs of a Speedster

Neo-Auckland burned, and Niobe watched. She sat on the roof of the Starlight Hotel with her feet dangling over the edge, taking long drags from her cigarette. It kept trembling in her fingers; she'd nearly dropped it over the edge once already. A portable radio sat next to her, barking one horrible fragment of information after another. She'd nearly tossed it over the side when Quanta had his little speech. The fighting was still a few blocks from her, but it would come. Every few minutes, the night lit up with another blast from Quanta's airship, and a new wave of screams rolled across the city.

With her goggles and the aid of the radio, she tracked the progress of the battle, looking for something—anything—that would allow her to get to Sam. Met Div and the police were in tiny units scattered across the city, being ambushed and picked off by Quanta's metas. The radio said the AAU was sending in military support, but they'd be lucky if there was anyone left to rescue by the time they arrived.

Over there to the south, she saw Avin leading an aerial attack on a pair of rooftop snipers; and there, a fire-based meta sent a column of flame into a building, flushing out the Met Div officers who were then struck down by some bestial creature as soon as they reached the street. And all the while, Sam hovered above the city, snagging civilians and pulling them around him. He already had close to two hundred people forming a near-impenetrable meatshield. And she'd stood by and watched, because there wasn't a bloody thing she could do.

She stubbed out her cigarette and lit another. At least the fighting hadn't touched the Old City. If Gabby was still there, she had time to get out. Part of Niobe screamed at her to rush back home, that Gabby would surely be waiting there, ready to accept all her apologies and take her back. Even if she wasn't there, maybe Niobe could leave a message for her. It was so clear now, so clear what was really important.

But she couldn't. Her place was here. *Sorry, Carpenter. We were too slow. I wasn't smart enough, and you...you were too damn heroic for your own good.* She was alone against a psychopath now. No, not a psychopath. Worse. An extremist. A zealot. A man who could rationalise the torture and exploitation of a boy whose only crime was having the wrong father. How could she fight that kind of dedication?

Quanta's airship slowed again. Half an hour ago she'd seen the flash of a miniature rocket engine as a small vehicle landed in the airship loading bay. It was Quanta. It had to be. He was sitting up there, watching the carnage he'd unleashed. And now he was using the airship to transport groups of his metas from one part of the city to the other. It made sense; the streets were so packed with cars and civilians that moving by ground was damn near impossible. She upped the magnification on her goggles and watched five supercriminals as they clung to the ropes that dangled from the airship. The rocket engines flared, carrying the airship up to float above a department store rooftop half a mile from her. The metas disembarked and disappeared from view, probably regrouping and gathering their strength.

Wait a minute. They'd dropped metas off on that same rooftop before, maybe twenty minutes ago. That meant they were using specific
roofs as dedicated staging areas. The airship moved on, with a pair of
fliers in support. She ran back through the movements of the ship in
her mind. It had definitely stopped there before, and before that, at the
offices for the Bank of Australasia. They were moving in a pattern. A
circuit. *The next building....* She pushed her hat back and pressed her
fingers to her forehead, picturing the airship's movements in her head.

The Unity Corporation building.

Ice hardened her heart and cooled her fear. She drew her gun,
checked the cylinder, and pulled the darkness around her. The world
went flat, split into easy divisions. Light and dark. Black and white.
Safety and danger. She darted down the side of the Starlight Hotel and
onto the street. The airship let out another blast, but it was far enough
away that the light only prickled her. She slipped out of the shadow
running, tossed away her cigarette, took another breath, and dived
back into darkness.

She could feel the vibrations of ten thousand panicking civilians
running from their doom. Off to her right, the surface of a building
became indistinct as it crumbled. On she went, slipping up walls and
creeping along windows to go places no normal human could reach.

Her lungs started to burn again, so she threw off the shadow on an
apartment balcony and breathed deep. She was in the heart of the city
now, her view of the surroundings cut off by tightly-packed towers, but
she could still glimpse the majesty of the airship as it tracked across
the city. It was nearly in position. She took a lungful of air and let the
shadow take her again.

She slipped off the building, crossed a street littered with the rubble
of a fallen tower, and zipped up the side of the thirty-floor Unity Corporation building. The light from the airship's rocket engines stung,
but she steeled herself and continued up. The Auckland arm of Unity
Corporation had designed their office building as a twisting glass behemoth, the upper floors rotated forty-five degrees with respect to the

bottom floors. The roof tapered to a tall spire on one side with the Unity Corporation logo displayed in huge glowing letters. The other end of the roof was flat, dotted with exotic plants and paved with tile walkways. It was probably a lovely place for the corporation's workers to take their smoko break, but more importantly, the rooftop gardens gave her cover.

She came out of the shadow behind a short row of hedges just as the group of battle-worn metas touched down on the roof. She pressed herself flat against the ground to keep out of sight and wriggled forwards, gun in hand. The ropes hanging from the airship's gondola each ended in a small metal platform, wide enough to allow someone to stand. Three male and two female metas rested on the ground. She recognised two from the attack on the warehouse: a man with fire licking his skin and another with smoke seeping from his lips. None of them so much as glanced in her direction. They'd be tired; shooting fire around in combat was no cake-walk. The airship's engines roared again as it started to move away. Now was her chance.

She dropped back into shadow, the dim light stinging her, and raced past the exhausted metas. The platforms at the ends of each rope scraped along the tiles and started to lift as the airship gained altitude. She raced after it as the ropes neared the glass barrier that surrounded the edge of the building.

Now. She slipped out of the shadow, planted a foot on the top of the glass barrier, and leapt. There was nothing but a thirty-floor drop below her. Someone shouted behind her, and she could hear the metas scrambling to their feet. Everything sounded hollow compared to the blood rushing in her ears.

Her free hand looped around the rope and her foot hit the platform. The momentum carried her forwards. Her stomach lurched as her foot slipped and the rope twisted out of her grip. Her muscles clenched instinctively. That was the only thing that kept her from dropping her gun. She caught the rope again in her elbow, and her knee came down heavily on the platform. The rope stretched and recoiled a little under her weight, and for a moment, she was sure it would snap. *Don't be stupid. It's held heavier people than you.* Then she was steady, kneeling on the platform with the city spread out beneath her.

She blinked the sweat out of her eyes in time to see a flutter of wings bearing down on her. A screech pierced the air. For a split second, she froze like a mouse being hunted by a hawk. Then she saw Avin's face against the night, and suppressed rage bubbled up inside her. The bird-woman stretched her claws in front of her.

Niobe fired from the hip. The stun round struck the meta just below her left collarbone. Her eyes went wide and her wings stiffened. Niobe shifted her weight on the platform and rocked herself out of the way just as Avin went soaring past her. With a strangled groan, the bird-woman glided past and slammed into the rooftop garden, wings twisting and popping as she hit. For a moment, guilt touched Niobe's heart. She hadn't meant to cause Avin that much damage. Then Niobe put her hand to her cheek, where the scratches still hadn't healed. *Bugger the bitch. She took my goddamn picture.*

The wind whistled around her as she perched on the platform. She could make out flashes of gunfire and blue light against the glass buildings. The streets surged with civilians. Heights didn't normally bother her, but the adrenaline was still pumping from the jump, and a slick sense of nausea sloshed in her stomach every time the rope twisted in the wind.

She shook her head and looked up. The ropes hung down from an opening at the rear of the airship's gondola. *I guess asking them to winch me in is out of the question.* She holstered her gun and pushed her hat down tight on her head. *I'm coming, Morgan.*

It had been a long time since she'd practiced climbing a rope, but she fell back into the rhythm quickly. *Pull yourself up, press the rope between your insteps, repeat.* The wound in her thigh stabbed at her with every movement. She was breathing hard by the time she was halfway up. She'd gotten used to using shadow to slip up walls, but a rope by itself didn't hold enough surface area to contain her entire shadow. So she pulled herself up, inch by inch, only looking down to make sure the airship hadn't yet picked up any more passengers.

Finally, her hand touched metal. Panting, she dug her fingers into the grooved floor of the bay and hauled herself up. Her arms protested, but then she was on her hands and knees in a loading bay stacked with crates and webbing. A white motorbike with a bubble of glass to protect the rider was strapped to one wall. Scorch marks marred the floor beneath the bike. She could smell the rocket fuel from here.

She touched her goggles to adjust for the brighter light. A figure stood motionless in the centre of the loading bay. Niobe had seen this meta before, sitting in one of the getaway vans from Quanta's raid on the TV station.

"My lord has been expecting you," the figure of glistening black stone shouted over the sound of the engines.

Niobe drew her revolver and fired twice. Two spots of blue sparks flared up in the meta's chest, dead centre. Kill shots. Except they didn't even make her stumble.

The stone woman charged, and the bay shook with every step. Niobe's vision narrowed, her breathing shallow. Behind her, the bay doors stood open to the air. She couldn't back away.

The meta swung a fist. Niobe threw herself forwards, feeling the fist skim past. She rolled and came up behind the meta. The stone woman stood at the edge of the loading bay, her back to Niobe.

Now! Niobe planted her feet, changed direction, and threw her shoulder into the small of the meta's back.

The woman didn't budge.

An elbow came out of nowhere and connected with Niobe's sternum. Something cracked, and she went falling back, gasping. Spots swam in her eyes. *No, get up!*

She blinked. The meta's foot loomed above her, poised to strike. With a surge of adrenaline, Niobe rolled to the side. The foot slammed into the bay floor, denting the metal. Niobe scrambled to her feet and backed away. There wasn't enough room to manoeuver in here. And there was sure as hell no way she could go toe-to-toe with this woman.

The meta charged and swung again. Niobe grabbed hold of a tall crate and pulled herself on top an instant before the fist landed. The crate splintered beneath her, but by that time she was leaping to the next one along, trying to put some space between them. The loading bay was too bright. It was time to do something about that.

She fired at one of the lights, shattering it, then leapt to the next crate before the meta could catch her. Two more lights to go. She fired again, and another bulb shattered.

Something hard and cold gripped her ankle for a second. She kicked and got free, but it was too late. Her stomach lurched as she slipped off the crate and landed hard on the ground.

"You can't get away," the meta said. Her footsteps clanged as she approached. Niobe scrambled along the ground, away from the woman. "The door is sealed shut. There's nowhere to run."

"Who says I'm running?"

Niobe fired once more, and the loading bay fell into darkness. Now it was her turn.

A fist came for her, but she was already part of the shadow. In one quick move she slid across the floor of the loading bay.

"My lord respects you, you know," the meta said as Niobe came out of the shadow and adjusted the contrast on her goggles.

"Your lord is bonkers, you know that?" *Where was it? There.* She slipped her pocket knife out of her utility belt and sliced through a pair of loading straps.

The footsteps turned back towards her and started approaching. "He is a great man."

"Yeah?" She holstered her gun and tried to judge the position of the footsteps while she searched for an on-switch. "You believe in his cause?"

"I'd die for it."

"That'll make this easier."

Niobe turned the ignition, and the rocket-bike's engine rumbled to life. Perfect.

"What is...?" The footsteps stopped.

Niobe flicked the switch, and blue flame lit up the loading bay. The meta's stone features displayed nothing as she stood silhouetted against the open doors.

Niobe pulled the clutch, stomped on the gear lever, and twisted the throttle. The rocket-bike shot forwards like a missile. Niobe dived out of the way to avoid the heat of the rocket engines.

The bike slammed into the meta. Without slowing, it went flying out the open door and into the darkness, carrying the stone meta with it. The woman's shouts were drowned out by the screaming engines.

Niobe put her back against a crate, panting. The woman looked like she'd be tough enough to survive the fall. She certainly packed a hell of a punch. Niobe prodded herself just below her left breast and winced. Cracked rib, probably. Most likely it hadn't punctured anything vital. She needed to keep moving.

The ropes the metas were using for transport were attached to a set of motorised winches set into the ceiling. After a few moments of searching, she found the panel that controlled them and punched buttons at random until she figured out how to reel them in. She had no intention of letting anyone climb up behind her. When she'd set all the winches going, she moved quickly to the only door out of the loading bay, using the walls and crates to give her cover in case someone came to investigate.

The door resembled something off a submarine, with a locking system that sealed the entire door in place when the handle was turned. She wrenched the handle down, pain stabbing through her chest. The door didn't budge. Damn it, the stone woman was telling the truth. It really was sealed.

Plan B it was, then. *Fucking great.* Sucking in another breath, she dived back into shadow and made for the bay doors. Pricks of light from the city stabbed at her as she slipped out the door and over the outer surface of the airship's gondola. *This day's getting worse by the minute.*

She couldn't feel the wind as a shadow, but she could sense the way the airship shuddered, and it did nothing for her confidence. She'd had enough heights already this evening. She slid along the outside of the gondola, looking for a good place. She stopped by a window. *Here, this will have to do.* For a moment, she mentally prepared herself, trying to ignore the blackness creeping through her.

Then she came out of the shadow and grabbed hold of the vertical handrail with both hands. The wind started buffeting her immediately. The iciness of the metal handrail cut through her gloves, straight to the bone. She dug her toes into a tiny gap in the outer surface, praying she wouldn't lose her grip. Her teeth chattered.

Trying to still the screaming in her head and the butterflies going berserk in her stomach, she peered through the window, trying to see if anyone was inside. Clear. It looked like some sort of sleeping cabin, with rows of bunk beds crammed close together in the tiny room. This would have to do.

It took all of her courage to let go of the rail with one hand. Awkwardly, she broke open her gun and fed a live round into the cylinder. She snapped the revolver closed, pressed it against the glass, and turned her face away. *Here goes nothing.* She squeezed the trigger. The glass shattered.

Cringing at the noise, she used the butt of her gun to clear the jagged shards sticking out of the frame, then she holstered her gun and looped her leg over the window. Using her arm to steady herself, she adjusted her balance and fell ungracefully onto the floor of the barracks room. She figured she deserved a moment to get her breath back. She reloaded, checked her hat was still in place, and exhaled sharply.

All right, time to move. Still shaking, she got to her feet and made her way to the heavy door on the other side of the cabin. She put her ear to it. No shouts of alarm. With a bit of luck, the sound of the airship engines had covered the noise she was making. One way to find out.

She pulled the heavy door open and ducked back into cover. Nothing came flying at her, so she peeked out. A narrow corridor ran perpendicular, with a spiral staircase directly opposite. She considered for a moment, chewing her lip, and then made for the staircase.

The air smelled vaguely of oil and metal. Her boots clattered lightly on the metal steps. She emerged into another corridor. She was facing towards the bow. If Quanta was on the airship, he'd be watching the battle. He wouldn't be able to resist. She made for the bridge.

She held her gun ahead of her as she moved in a silent crouch. She glimpsed starlight from the wide glass windows in the room at the end of the corridor. Beeps and hums punctuated the rumble of the engines, covering the sound of her steps.

This was it. It was time. Heart hammering, she stepped onto the bridge.

"What…?" A skinny man in a blood-red bodysuit stared at her with wide eyes from his position at the door. She fired once, and he dropped like a stone.

She swept to the right, using a bank of control panels and flashing lights for cover. The dark skyline spread out before her through the viewing windows on the far side of the bridge. For a moment, she thought the thing sitting in the centre of the room surrounded by monitors and keyboards was a corpse. She could see his bones jutting against the brown leather of his skin.

But then his head rolled slowly towards her, and his husky breath quickened. The pilot. Just the pilot. But where was…?

She sensed the flash of light coming from behind her. Too slow, too late. Pain exploded through her cheek and she went down hard. Blood filled her mouth. She spat it against the inside of her mask and tried to shake away the fog in her head. The next blow hit her in the gut. No pain this time, but the air fled her lungs and she gasped for breath.

Fight back fight back fight back.

She rolled. Half a second later, a lance of light struck the ground where she'd been lying. Her goggles were slightly askew, but somehow she'd kept hold of her gun. With the flick of a switch, the gun hissed, switching to the shield-breaker rounds. She squeezed the trigger twice, firing half-blind at the blazing figure of white. The rounds left green streaks and the taste of copper in the air.

The shield-breaker rounds struck Quanta and sent him reeling back. *I hit him!* He staggered, his shield of light cracking. His eyes went wide as he sank to one knee. She wanted to kiss Gabby. *She'd done it. Jesus Christ, it worked!*

Then the crack in his shield began to fade. He put his hand on a railing and pushed himself back to his feet. He stumbled back a few steps. And he smiled.

Her heart felt like it was made of stone. Nothing stopped him. Nothing. *No, don't think like that.* It had bought her breathing room. She rolled again and stumbled to her feet, using a bank of display monitors for support. Quanta watched her, his fingers touching the points where her shield-breaker rounds had struck. The golden shield had reformed completely, as solid as ever.

There had to be something she could do. She looked at the lights set into the bridge's ceiling. Too many to take out, and besides, Quanta was so bright it might kill her to go to shadow. He was watching her now, his teeth as white as his suit, his golden blade in his hand at his side.

She touched the shoulder of her trench coat and found a scorched hole in the seam separating the sleeve from the torso. Bloody hell. Too close.

"I can recommend a tailor for that," Quanta said. "To be frank, you could probably do with a whole new costume. The trench coat look's a bit nineteen thirties, isn't it?"

"Excuse me if I don't take fashion advice from a guy who looks like he took a dip in a bucket of white paint on the way to a business meeting." She swallowed some of the blood in her mouth and tried to straighten without wincing.

She aimed the gun from her hip, but the wheezing husk of a pilot and the rows of control panels didn't allow her a clean shot. *Not that it would stop him permanently.* Still, maybe it could buy her a few seconds if she needed it. The red-suited man twitched on the floor in the corner.

Quanta moved with a dangerous grace, never putting himself in the open but closing in again. "Have you seen the admirable job Sam is doing? My people tell me he's got nearly a thousand people under his control now. I've been listening to your police on the radio scanners. You should hear the panic in their voices."

She had to get him in the open. "You've got the city hostage. No one's going to be able to beat you now. Contact the AAU. They'll have no choice but to give you what you want."

"What I want?" There was something strained in his eyes, something desperate.

She stepped closer to the pilot and the huge windows that looked out over the burning city. "You can make them give metahumans their rights back. You've beaten them, Morgan."

He raised his eyebrows at her. "You still don't understand, do you? This isn't about legislation." He chuckled, the light of his sword throwing shadows onto his face. It made him look old. "Is that really what you think happened? You think the most powerful people in the world accepted kill-switches and poverty because of *legislation*?"

The skeletal pilot watched her as she edged closer, his eyes glowing faintly green.

Morgan pointed his sword at the window. "Those laws are still in place, and look what I and a couple of dozen metas have done. The superhero wasn't beaten by authority or force. He was beaten by public opinion. They broke his will. And the superhero, more than anyone, is a creature of will. It's what drives us. It's what drove me and you to meet here today. It's what I mean to give back to metahumans. We're the exceptions, Niobe. The few who bent but didn't break."

"You look pretty broken to me," she said.

He prowled closer. "Maybe you're right. But I know what makes a man into a hero. And it's not superpowers. It's belief. It's knowing what needs to be done."

She lurched forwards and grabbed the pilot by his folds of skin. "Stop." She pressed her gun against the hairless head. "Can you fly this thing, Morgan? Or if I knock out your friend here, will we all go down like the damn *Hindenburg*?"

"We'll hit the city," Quanta said. "You don't want that, do you?"

"What city? Looks to me like you burned it down. Maybe I can't save Sam, but I can screw with you pretty good."

He smiled. "I'll give you one thing. You've got spirit."

She blinked, and he was in the air. *So fast. Everyone's faster than me.*

His blade grew longer and narrower in his hands. The spear of an angel. Her finger started to squeeze the trigger.

The spear of light pierced her gun hand. The metal of her revolver turned to liquid in an instant, splashing across her coat, melting through to the skin beneath. Fire and ice and jagged knives bit into her hand. Her vision blurred. She screamed like she'd never screamed before.

The bridge went black for a moment. When she came to, she was on her back, acid mixing with the blood in her throat. Her stomach spasmed, and she rolled to the side and retched. But the burning in her throat was nothing compared to the pain in her hand. She glanced down at her right arm and then looked away again before another wave of nausea could take her. Her hand was a mangled mess of blood and bone and blackened flesh with the fabric of her glove burned into it. She thought she was missing fingers. She wasn't willing to check.

A foot landed on her chest, and her shallow breaths became difficult. Her eyes watered. She'd lost her hat. She spotted her gun—or what was left of it—ten feet away.

Quanta wasn't smiling anymore. His mouth was a tight line, his forehead knitted with wrinkles. "You fought hard, Spook. There's no shame in that. You and the Carpenter, you were true heroes." He shook his head sadly. "You shouldn't have had to do this alone. Your people let you down."

She blinked away the cloudiness and looked up at Quanta. She could see the smoke from the burning city rising behind him, and beyond that, the dot of Sam and his mind-control strings, lit up by spotlights. She'd lost. The torture going on in her hand didn't stop, but her mind felt strangely clear. She'd never been this clear.

"Since this is just a show," she rasped, "I don't suppose you want to accept your victory and let me live?"

"I would if I could," he said. The night glittered behind him. "But I can't pretend to be a supervillain. I have to actually be one. You understand." He brought the blade down to hover above her mouth. "I'll sever the brainstem. It'll be quick."

Silver and fire flashed outside.

"Then you'd better hurry," she said.

The viewing windows exploded in a rain of glass. The night air whipped Morgan's hair. There was a whirring scream. And then a hail of lead burst through the bridge. Sparks flew from the control panels and smoke filled the air.

Quanta's foot left her chest. She was too busy covering her face with her good hand to see where he'd gone. *Move, damn it!* She scrambled back, using her legs to push herself along the floor while she clutched her ruined hand to her chest. The hail of gunfire stopped, and Niobe looked up. The most beautiful sight of her life filled the shattered viewing windows.

The figure looked like a glorious medieval knight, the huge, bulky armour polished like silver. Twin streams of fire poured from the back of the armour, keeping the figure afloat. A chaingun was slung under the right arm, still spinning down, and a massive cannon was mounted on the left shoulder. The helmet bore huge black eyes and antennae that swept back, like some sort of insect.

Niobe could hardly breathe. It was the Silver Scarab.

"Gabby," she whispered.

Quanta leapt from a cloud of smoke, blade flashing, straight towards the armoured figure. As strong as the armour was, Niobe knew it couldn't take a strike from that blade. Her stomach clenched.

The chaingun screamed again, the sound pounding at her ears in the confined space. A storm of bullets sparked off Quanta's shield. He crashed to the floor in mid-jump. He went to one knee, his teeth gritted and bared.

The whole airship shuddered when the Silver Scarab landed inside the bridge. The rocket-pack cut out, and without stopping the relentless fire, she launched herself at the supercriminal on actuator-powered legs.

"No!" Quanta shouted. He forced himself forwards against the torrent of bullets.

The cannon on Gabby's shoulder let out an electric boom. A spike flew across the room, crashing into Quanta, lodging in the golden shield. Green lightning arced down the cable that connected the spike to Gabby's cannon and spread across the surface of Quanta's shield. His eyes widened as the muscles in his neck pulled his jaw down into a silent scream. The golden shield rippled and splashed off him like it had been made of water.

Niobe's ears rang. Quanta went down on his hands and knees, blood streaming from his ears.

Quanta clutching his head, grunting. His whole body convulsed, legs straining, veins bulging at his temple. *The brain tumour.* Was he having a seizure?

"Pills," Quanta moaned through gritted teeth. "P…pills."

With slow, stomping steps, the Silver Scarab closed the distance between her and Quanta. With all the energy she could muster, Niobe got up and shuffled towards the defeated supervillain.

The convulsions stopped in an instant, and Quanta's hands flashed. Something small and white slipped from his sleeve into his palm. He flicked it at Gabby.

"No!" Niobe dived, stretching out her left hand. Her fingers wrapped around the smooth object. She hit the floor, fire shooting through her as her mangled arm stopped her fall. Adrenaline surged, and she fought back unconsciousness. Through bloodshot eyes and snarling teeth, Quanta grinned at her.

Throw it!

She hurled the object out the shattered viewing windows. A second later, a quiet pop split the night, along with a splash of fire and blue lightning.

"Nice catch, hero," Quanta said, still grinning.

Gabby's huge metal arm swung above her and slammed into Quanta's head. The grin didn't leave his face as he fell to the side, eyes rolling back in his head. Niobe slumped down on the ground and allowed herself to breathe.

The Silver Scarab stepped around her and rolled the supercriminal onto his stomach, pulled his arms behind his back with her bulky power-armoured hands, and slapped a set of energy cuffs on him, similar to the type Met Div used. She put another pair on his ankles and then pulled what looked like a crown from a compartment on her leg. She shoved the device over Quanta's hair and touched a button on her wrist. The crown began to glow with blue light.

Niobe couldn't tell if the light-headedness was from blood loss or relief. She pulled off her mask, forced herself up into a sitting position with her good arm, and rested her head against the cool metal of a panel that had escaped the carnage.

"Gabby." Her throat was raw and her voice came out thinner than she was expecting.

Maybe the suit could help Gabby sense sound, because the armoured behemoth turned towards Niobe immediately. Gabby knelt, her faceplate swinging aside. Christ, she was beautiful. Her eyes were as silver as the armour she wore, and her cheeks were flushed with an excitement Niobe had never seen before.

Niobe held up her injured hand. She was missing all but her forefinger, and even that looked broken. The flesh of her palm was torn and burned, most of that gone too. "I might have trouble signing from now on."

Tears rolled freely down Gabby's cheeks, but that only made her more beautiful. She reached out an armoured finger to Niobe's face, but stopped short. "We need to get you to a hospital," she said in her odd, quiet voice. In that suit, she wouldn't be signing either. Gabby retrieved a small auto-syringe from a compartment in the suit and pressed it into Niobe's left hand. "For the pain."

Niobe nodded, turned off the safety, and injected herself in the thigh. A slow warmth went through her. A few moments later, the pain began to fade.

Gabby began to retract her hand, but Niobe dropped the empty syringe and grabbed the cool metal fingers. "I'm sorry. I was coming home to apologise. I didn't understand, I thought I was protecting you, I thought I could do it all on my own, but I…." She glanced down at her blood-stained costume, then back to her hero. "I'm sorry."

Gabby's huge arms effortlessly swept Niobe up and pulled her close against her armoured torso. Gabby's lips were wet from tears, but Niobe kissed her hungrily, desperately. A warmth spread through her stomach as Gabby's teeth nipped her lower lip. Maybe it was the adrenaline, or the morphine, or just coming so close to death, but she'd never wanted anyone more. Bugger Quanta, and bugger her hand. She wanted to drag Gabby back to bed and never let her leave.

But Gabby broke the kiss and pulled back a little. There was still hurt on her face, still confusion. Niobe pressed her left hand against Gabby's cheek and wiped the tears away. "Don't give up on me yet. Please."

Gabby smiled, and Niobe's heart fluttered. She reached out with her good hand and touched a red scratch running across Gabby's cheek. "You're hurt."

Gabby shook her head. "There were metas waiting for me when I went home to get the suit. They tried to take me."

Niobe's stomach knotted, a flash of cold anger going through her. Quanta had finally linked the photo and the name to an address. *The son of a bitch had tried to kidnap Gabby, use her against me.*

"Don't look so worried," Gabby said, her face more alight than Niobe had seen it in years. "I got to the suit in time. And I showed them what I could do."

Niobe stroked Gabby's cheek and kissed her again, hard.

When they broke the kiss, Gabby gently lowered Niobe to her feet. Her thigh stung like all hell when she put weight on it; the wound had probably broken open again. Her hand was starting to go numb, which probably wasn't a good thing. Awkwardly, she slipped her mask and goggles back on with her good hand, leaving her mouth bare so Gabby could still lip read. She found her hat by the unconscious red-suited man.

The withered pilot had somehow escaped Gabby's rain of bullets. His laboured breathing was fast, scared. Niobe turned back to Gabby and jerked her head towards the pilot, signing as best she could while she talked.

"Can you take over for him?"

Gabby nodded, strode across the room, and lifted the skeletal man out of his seat with one hand. He didn't resist. He didn't look like he had enough muscle to even blink. A series of wires snaked out of the Silver Scarab's pointer finger and found ports in the control panel. A few moments passed. Then the engines shuddered, and the airship began to bank.

"The ship will land itself just outside the city," she said.

Niobe smiled and limped over to her. "My genius." She ran her fingers down the armoured plates. How long had she been building this? Even in the old days, she never had anything this magnificent. "My hero. How did you find me?"

"Your gun, stupid." She frowned and cast another concerned look at the mess of flesh that was Niobe's hand. "At least until you got it killed. We got here as fast as we could."

"We?"

Gabby put a hand against Niobe's back and helped her to the shattered windows. Glass crunched under her boots and the wind threatened to take her hat as she approached the edge. The night was still dark, and the fires still burned, but she could see new flashes across the city. Coloured streaks flew through the air. Blasts of energy shot back and forth amongst the streets. Niobe's breath caught in her throat. *It's not possible.*

The heroes had returned.

CHAPTER 30

How Do You Stop the Unstoppable Man?

GLOOMGIRL

REAL NAME: *Niobe Ishii*

POWERS: *Able to transform into shadow.*

NOTES: *Youngest member of the Wardens. Following their disbanding, she took on a new identity as the metahuman detective Spook. Due to her complete refusal to interact with the media, she was often painted as cold and uncaring. The Carpenter refuted this in a television interview: "She'll kill me for saying this, but she's by far the most compassionate of all of us. She was the first to respond to the 11B monorail collapse of '57. The train was shattered, dangerous as heck, with live electricity and falling bits of track everywhere. She went in again and again, getting the injured out first, then everyone else. And you know what she did when she got 'em all out? She went back in for a kid's toy aeroplane. Just to stop the little guy crying. Can you believe it?"*

—Notes on selected metahumans [Entry #1086]

G abby carried Niobe and the prisoners through the ash and smoke clouding the city and set them down on the outskirts of a war-zone. When she finally had solid ground under her again, Niobe's legs could barely hold her upright. Gabby held out a metal arm to steady her, and Niobe gratefully accepted it.

As for Quanta, the red-suited man, and the pilot, Gabby tossed them into a pile against the wall. She'd produced a black fabric that turned into a box that resembled a coffin when she ran an electric charge through it. It'd keep Quanta from absorbing any light if he woke up and her disabler device failed.

Flashes of energy and lightning crackled in the air above Niobe. She stood in the middle of a four-way intersection, each road blocked off by a makeshift barricade of ruined cars and bits of crumbled masonry. She spotted a knot of people huddled along the side of one barricade, facing down Kent Street. The light from two huge spotlights stung her eyes, and the rifle fire made her ears ring. She could make out brightly costumed figures through the smoke as well, but through the blinding light she couldn't resolve the details.

"Gimme a minute," Niobe said. She slumped down with her back against the wall of an office building and fished out her miniature first aid kit from her belt. It wasn't made for injuries like this, but it would have to hold until she could get someone to look at it.

The Silver Scarab settled protectively in front of her while Niobe worked, weapons trained in the direction of the fight. Niobe slid a knife under what remained of her glove and started to slice it away. The bits that were burned into her flesh stung like all buggery when she tried to peel them out, so she gritted her teeth and cut around them. It was hard going with her left hand, but she managed it. The hand itself was a write-off. Maybe she could get Gabby to build her a robotic claw.

She unscrewed a bottle of rubbing alcohol, braced herself, and poured it over her hand. Fire screamed through her skin. She screwed up her eyes and bit her lip to keep from crying out, but a strangled grunt still left her throat, and her eyes prickled with tears. When the pain finally faded enough for her to move again, she got some gauze and bandages out of her kit and awkwardly wrapped the mangled mess as best she could with her left hand and her teeth. With another strip of bandage, she fashioned herself a crude sling. It sure as hell wasn't pretty, but it might keep her from bleeding out.

She tapped Gabby's armour to get her attention. "Do you have water?"

Gabby produced a plastic bottle from a compartment in her chest and handed it to her. Niobe washed the taste of blood and smoke out of her mouth, spat, and then guzzled the rest.

"All right." She readjusted her mask and struggled to her feet. The thigh wound would have to wait. "Let's do this."

Gabby hauled the prisoners on her shoulders, and Niobe walked. Her hand didn't jar so bad with every step now. She glanced back once and saw Quanta's airship making a slow turn away from the city. Then the smoke covered it, and it was gone.

She turned back to the group firing over the barricade and stopped. "You?"

Senior Sergeant Wallace fired another three shots from his L1A1 and then took a look at her. "Where the hell have you been?"

"Uh, trying to get myself killed, I guess," she said, holding up her hand.

He glanced at it and grunted, then fired off another couple of shots as a streak of purple energy crashed into the barricade.

Niobe looked around at the rest of the group. A couple of coppers— not Met Div, just regulars—were shooting as well. But what drew her eye was the greens and reds and blues of the others there. She dredged some of the names up from her memory. Negabeast. Ballista was there too, firing a dozen bolts at a time from her huge crossbow. Brightlance, shooting beams of brilliant blue from his hands. She recalled the last time she'd seen him in that yellow bodysuit and red cape, when the man was too broken to help them get the McClellan baby back. It seemed so long ago. But now here he was, fighting for the city. Had he kept a signaller all these years, waiting?

There were others she didn't recognise, younger metas. A girl in a pale blue bodysuit who couldn't be older than fifteen hovered a few feet above the ground. Every time she flicked her wrist, a piece of building masonry took on a blue glow and flew through the air towards the supercriminals taking cover down the street. And overhead, a pair of fliers with matching purple uniforms streaked past, whirling chains in hand.

"How...?" Niobe couldn't believe what she was seeing. "How are they here?"

Wallace slammed another magazine into his rifle and pulled back the slide. "I called them." He leaned over the bonnet of the ruined car and fired. "Goddamn typical. Bloody superheroes never could take the fucking initiative." He reached into his pocket and tossed her something. "You can have this back."

She caught the Carpenter's signaller and turned it over in her hand. It had worked. How had so many of them responded? Two days ago these metas cowered in the Old City like rats. But now there was something new in their faces. Or rather, something old. What the hell had Wallace promised them?

"What about civilians?" she asked when the booms of Wallace's rifle took a break.

He jerked his head towards the hotel on the corner. Shadows moved inside the darkened doorway.

"We got a couple hundred rounded up there," Wallace said. "And I've got every copper who can still walk getting people to safety. A few metas are helping too," he added grudgingly. "Probably another thousand got out of the city before the shit hit. I don't have a clue how many are hiding in their homes. Or dead. But the shelters, they got hit worst."

Underground, Neo-Auckland was dotted with bomb shelters, she knew, built in the days when everyone feared another nuke.

"I was watching from the rooftops," she said. "Quanta's people seemed more interested in causing havoc than trying to cut their way into concrete bunkers. What happened?"

"What the fuck do you think happened?" Wallace pointed into the sky. "Your boy."

The controls for her goggles were on the wrong side of her face, so upping the magnification was awkward. But once she did, she couldn't miss Sam. Her heart dropped into her gut. The strings still left his hands, so dense now it looked like he was floating on a grey, pulsing mountain. And in a loose sphere around him were the floating civilians that had become his shield.

"He got into the shelters?" Then she figured it out. "Omegaman's phasing power."

"We figured the shelters would at least slow him down. But he walked straight through the walls and took everyone at once. All we did was save him some travel time."

"Bloody hell," she said. "Mind control? He's making the civilians fight?"

"I'm afraid not." The voice came from behind her, but she knew it immediately. She turned to regard the Blind Man's dark, lined face. He was the only meta present not in a costume, unless you counted the carved walking stick he leaned on. "It's worse than that."

At the sight of the Blind Man, grief and anger swirled inside her. The Carpenter had still been alive the last time she'd spoken to the psychic. There was still hope for Sam, then. She still had her memories. But she suppressed the feelings. "What, then?"

"Come." He turned and shuffled slowly towards the hotel, heedless of the blasts still raining around him. How did he know where he was going? No matter. Gabby must've been following the conversation, because she nodded her insectoid helmet at Niobe.

"I'll stay here and deal with this lot," Gabby said, the voice slightly robotic through the speakers. She gestured to Quanta and the other prisoners. Niobe touched her armoured chest, smiled, and followed the Blind Man.

Inside the hotel, civilians huddled in the lobby, crammed together on couches and mattresses raided from the rooms. They spoke in whispers in the gloom, and the sharp scent of sweat pervaded everything. The Blind Man moved to the back of the lobby. It was nearly empty back here. Hine-nui-te-pō hovered in the corner, still dressed in the same woollen garments Niobe had last seen her in. The woman nodded at Niobe as she approached.

"Spook," Hine-nui-te-pō said. "I'm sorry about the Carpenter. He was a great man."

"How did...?" She shook her head. "Yes. He was."

The Māori woman tended to a pot-bellied man lying motionless on a couch. His eyes were open, but they stared at nothing. His jaw was slack, his breathing slow. At a motion from the Blind Man, Niobe approached the man. She waved her good hand in front of his face.

Nothing.

Her stomach knotted, but she had to know. "Sam did this?"

"Those we get free quickly are fine." The Blind Man shuffled along-side her. "Especially if the victim is young. Then the psychic damage is minor. The mind is remarkably capable of regeneration. Quick-fire and some others have been trying to free who they can before they're taken out of reach. But it seems that those we are slow to retrieve from the boy's grasp are…" He seemed to struggle for the right word, which was so unlike him her stomach grew tighter. "…empty."

She remembered what she felt like after the Blind Man had taken her memories, and her thoughts grew dark. "Amnesia."

"More. I've searched these people's minds, and there is nothing left. No memory, no personality, no will. They will eat, breathe, drink, walk if you guide them, but they no longer retain anything that makes them human."

Jesus. "Why's Sam doing it? Just to shield himself?"

The Blind Man was quiet. The loose skin around his neck wobbled, and she realised he was shaking a little. "Perhaps. He has only used this technique on non-combatants. Perhaps it's just to protect himself. Perhaps he gains energy from them as well, using them to fuel his powers. But I believe there's something else. I believe deep down he's trying to keep them safe, away from the fighting. And then he takes them inside himself, so he'll never be alone."

What the hell did Doll Face do to you? What's going on in your head? She sighed. She could still remember being inside that scared little boy's head as O'Connor attacked him. She still wanted to save that boy.

She couldn't look at the man's blank face anymore, nor those of the others gathered around the room. She turned away from the Blind Man and Hine-nui-te-pō without another word and strode back out into the night, where the battle still raged.

Sam was getting closer. She could feel his energy in the air. How many people were under his control now? Five hundred? Six?

She recalled an old story device from the comics. They called it the

Hero's Dilemma. The villain kidnaps both the hero's sidekick and the girl he loves, and puts them in two separate death traps. There's only enough time for the hero to save one. So which is it going to be?

Of course, in the comics, the hero always cheated. That was the answer to the dilemma. The hero couldn't let anyone die. He had to save everyone. And he was always smart enough, or strong enough, or fast enough to do it.

But this was real life. She couldn't cheat against Sam. He was too strong. So she had to choose. She'd promised to save Sam. She'd promised Frank Oppenheimer, and she'd promised herself. But he was killing people, or worse. It didn't matter that he didn't know what he was doing, that it wasn't his fault. He was sick, he was out of his mind, but he was a threat. With his uncle's power, he could fly through any wall in the world. If someone tried to nuke him, he could dive into the earth itself, letting hundreds of miles of rock and soil shield him from the blast. No one would be safe from him. He'd only grow stronger as the hours passed, until no one would be able to stop him. She couldn't let him keep doing this. How many lives was a promise worth?

And if someone had to stop him, it should be her. She owed him that much.

If she was going to act, it had to be now, while her adrenaline was still up. The bandages on her hand were going red. She couldn't keep this up forever. Her eyes fell on the spotlights pointing down the street, where the supercriminals continued to fight even as more heroes swooped in to join the battle. A plan took hold in her mind. It wasn't the best she'd ever had, but against Sam, nothing would be.

She looked up into the sky once more, finding him amongst the stars and the bodies. With her goggles on maximum magnification, he was close enough that she could make out the pain in his face.

I'm sorry, Sam.

"Wallace," she shouted over the gunfire and blasts. "We need to get Sam on the ground."

"Kinda busy here," he growled. Gabby was next to him, adding her own firepower to that of the others.

"It's not a bloody suggestion, Senior Sergeant. Can you do it?"

"I can." The voice was so quiet she barely heard it over the noise of battle. Niobe found the young girl in the blue bodysuit floating beside her, still telekinetically hurling rocks down the street. "I think," she added, not meeting Niobe's eyes.

Niobe chewed her lip. Bloody hell, the girl was young. "What's your name?"

"Dancer."

Niobe smiled behind her mask. "Dancer, eh? I like it. Where'd you get the costume?"

"It was my mother's."

"You really think you can get him to touch the ground? Or a roof?"

Dancer straightened her back. "Uh-huh. Um, I might need some help, though."

"I reckon that can be arranged." Niobe glanced around at the other heroes. "Hey, Brightlance."

"Yeah, yeah, I'm in," he said without turning away from the barricade.

"Okay. Wallace. You think your people can hold here with only a couple of heroes? I need you to give me a hand with something."

His scarred face betrayed nothing. "This better be good, vigilante."

"You might wanna tell your people to keep an eye on Quanta and the other prisoners too."

"Fine." He barely stopped shooting to glance back at her. "I'll tell 'em to put holes in the bastard if he so much as twitches. Just stop yapping."

"One more thing." She pointed to the spotlights. "I need to borrow those."

She took her time, letting the cigarette smoke play on her tongue, drip down her throat, and slowly exit her mouth again. No one had offered her a blindfold or a last meal, so she was sure as hell going to enjoy this.

From her position back on top of the Unity Corporation building, she had a good view of the city, or what was left of it. The blasts of light in the streets were slowly dying off. Without the airship to extract them, Quanta's metas were isolated in small groups. And as more and more heroes joined the fray, the villains were slowly being picked off. All the supercriminals who had been resting here on the roof had fled or been captured, so she had the place to herself. Well, almost.

"How's that?" Wallace said. She exhaled a cloud of smoke and turned back towards the rooftop gardens. The pair of spotlights stood on either side of the stairwell door, casting a wide shine on the centre of the tile walkway.

She pushed her goggles up to study it with her own eyes. The lights were bloody bright. "That's the low setting?"

"Low as it goes."

Jesus. Her skin was already burning at the thought. She slipped her goggles back on and looked out over the city, where Sam and his shield of civilians drifted slowly closer. The rest of the city had gone quiet, like it was holding its breath. She took a last long drag of her cigarette, then flicked the smouldering butt over the side.

"I need you to do me a favour," she said.

He came alongside her, his rifle at rest in his hand, and watched the city with her. His face was dark. "I've been doing you a lot of favours lately."

"You'll like this one," she said. "If I'm not out in three minutes, I need you to crank up those lights to full power."

He was quiet for a moment. "Is that safe? For you, I mean."

"What do you think?"

Streaks of light began to dart across the city sky. If Sam noticed them, he didn't give any sign. Niobe pulled her mask down to cover her lips. The pain in her right hand was really starting to hit her. She hoped the second dose of morphine she'd taken would kick in soon.

"My wife and daughter are somewhere out in this," Wallace said.

She glanced at him. He could have been talking about the rugby game he'd watched in the weekend.

"Yeah?" she said. "You see them much?"

"Not much."

At maximum magnification she could make out Gabby burning through the sky. To either side of her were the twin fliers in purple, weapons whirling. Dancer, Brightlance, and a dozen more heroes would be in position by now as well.

Wallace spat over the edge. "It was never personal, you know."

"Fuck you, copper."

The lines on his face became less jagged for a second. She could've sworn he smiled.

"You'll do what I asked?" she said.

He nodded. "Three minutes."

"I hope your wife gets out all right."

He shrugged. "I'm not fussed either way."

A boom exploded across the city. Even from here, she could see the flash of Gabby's shoulder cannon. The blast passed between a pair of floating civilians and crashed into Sam's side. His skin shimmered for a second, and then he was covered in steel. Lightning crackled around him.

The purple fliers darted in from the other direction. Each of them grabbed a pair of the smallest bodies under their arms and sliced at the fibres. An instant later, they came free.

Sam's scream put shivers down Niobe's spine. He spun away from Gabby and raced towards the fliers, his hostages following like balloons. Damn it, he was fast.

"They're not going to make it," Niobe said. Her fist clenched in her pocket.

Sam struck. One of the purple fliers flitted away clean, but the other caught a fist that sent him into a spin towards the earth. The civilians under his arms came loose as he fell. A flash of fire came from Gabby's rocket-pack as she zipped through the night to grab the civilians before they hit the ground. But the purple flier wasn't so lucky. Niobe imagined she could hear the sound of his bones crunching as he hit the concrete.

"Was that part of your plan?" Wallace said.

She bit the inside of her cheek so hard she tasted blood. Every death was on her. And if Gabby fell....

Come on, baby.

Gabby and the remaining purple flier released their civilians on the roof of a building and jetted backwards. Sam didn't even seem to feel the bursts of chaingun bullets that hammered him through the holes in his human shield as they retreated. His scream of rage rolled over the city like thunder, and he gave chase.

He was faster than the heroes, Niobe knew at once. The Silver Scarab and the flier broke ranks and went into evasive manoeuvers. A crackle of lightning shot forth from Sam's hand and hit Gabby's armour. The fire of her jets fizzled out. For a moment, she hung suspended in the air. Then she began to fall. Niobe couldn't breathe.

An energy beam shot from a rooftop, catching Sam in the chest before he could chase Gabby into the earth. *Brightlance.* Sam changed course and swooped towards the rooftop, his civilians forming a solid wall in front of him to protect him against any more blasts. The remaining purple flier trailed after, managing to snatch another civilian away.

But Niobe's eyes were fixed on Gabby's falling form. She dropped through the sky, limbs still flailing.

No. Niobe couldn't move. Knives stabbed her heart. Her stomach was a burning oil spill in the middle of a sea storm.

Then a flash of fire sparked from Gabby's back, died, and sparked again, stronger this time. *Come on.* Niobe's fingers fumbled with the focus on her goggles. *Please, let it be....*

The rocket flame caught. The Silver Scarab changed direction at the last minute, soaring upwards, leaving a jet stream behind her as she raced back into battle. A choked noise escaped Niobe's throat, and the burning ocean in her stomach settled.

"It's working," Wallace said. She'd nearly forgotten he was there. "He's coming this way."

He was right, she saw. The purple flier had rescued another pair of civilians, and Brightlance was picking his shots, cutting through fibres. Each time a civilian began to fall, Gabby swept in to catch them, all the while firing on Sam.

The clouds began swirling above Sam, and gales buffeted the civilians. That'd be Ms Typhoon, standing on an apartment balcony six blocks away. The distance between Sam and his hostages grew larger and smaller and larger again as he played tug-of-war with the storm winds assailing him. They might just do this.

Wallace pulled back the slide on his rifle, checked the round in the chamber, and glanced at her. "However this goes…."

"Don't go getting sappy on me, Wallace."

More lights flashed across the sky. More heroes moving to engage. Sam howled, and another hero flickered and burned out like a failed rocket launch. But five more hostages got free in the arms of flying superheroes. Little by little, they were dismantling his human shield.

Sam caught an energy beam in the side and went careening through the supports of a billboard advertising disposable razors, his civilians trailing behind him. For a long moment the billboard swayed one way and then the other, as if it wasn't sure whether to fall or not. Then the support finally gave. Instinctively, Niobe plotted the trajectory of the falling debris, and her eyes fell on the fleeing civilians below. Her stomach knotted again.

The billboard fell, and the civilians below screamed. But before it hit the street, the billboard slowed and came to a stop in mid-air. A shower of dust rained down. Slowly, the billboard rose again and flew back towards Sam. Brightlance fired another energy beam through a mass of fibres. A dozen hostages began to fall. The billboard glowed blue and changed direction again. *Dancer.* The billboard zipped beneath the falling hostages, catching them like a fielder in cricket.

Dancer drifted above the rooftop ahead of Niobe, her blue bodysuit nearly invisible against the night. She looked tiny, and Niobe couldn't help but think once again about how young she was. *Almost as young as Sam.*

Wallace put out his right hand. "Fight well, vigilante." He grunted. "Spook."

Niobe made to shake his hand, then realised she'd put out her own mangled stump. He grinned at her and switched hands. His grip was strong.

"Fight well, Senior Sergeant."

A dozen bits of masonry the size of cars floated into the air around Dancer, then the tiny telekinetic hurled them across the sky. At the same time, Sam's remaining hostages glowed blue and parted like the Red Sea. Sam was too busy trying to shoot lightning at Gabby to see the rocks coming. The first one hit his back, while the others swirled around him to slam into him from all directions.

Deep in the pit of her stomach, she felt every blow.

Sam screamed, and the sonic boom was so powerful that Niobe had to take a step back. The boulders exploded into dust. His head swept around, ignoring the chaingun rounds that continued to pepper him. Niobe saw his gaze fall on Dancer.

"Move, girl," Niobe whispered.

Dancer swam through the air towards Niobe and Wallace like she was doing backstroke, throwing up more debris and the broken husks of cars as she went. Every time Sam got close, she hurled something else at him, slowing him just enough for her to escape the range of his fists or his lightning. And all the while, Gabby and the other fliers snatched more civilians away from him.

"Here we go," Wallace said. He moved to his position on the side of the rooftop and raised his rifle, but Niobe's legs weren't moving. She watched Sam throw aside one attack after another. She'd thought this was possible, but look at him. Even if they got all the hostages away, he was more powerful than all these heroes put together. Did she really think she could stop him? *Bloody hell, why couldn't I have been faster? It never should have come to this.*

"Spook!" Wallace called. "Get in position, damn it."

Dancer slipped by overhead. She spun in the air, gave Niobe a wave, and threw one last boulder at Sam. She was close enough to hear him grunt as he swatted it away.

He's so thin. She could see his ribs pressed against his metal skin. She could even make out the scabs peeking out of the cracks around his ears and mouth. The mind-control strings left his fingers like cotton unravelling from a shirt, moving where he moved. But it was his eyes that drove ice down her spine. They were pale, mad, filled with rage and sorrow. The worst bit was she could still see the same scared boy deep inside them. Some part of the real Sam still existed. And she wondered if that was the most dangerous part.

Wallace opened fire. The sound cracked her reverie, and when she blinked, everything was clear.

She darted across the rooftop for the centre of the lighted area, glancing behind her as she went. Wallace's shots were on target, but Sam didn't even look at him. Niobe slowed. Her heart thumped as she took in the glowing eyes staring back at her.

"Shit," she said. "Wallace, I think he recognises—"

Sam's scream knocked her back several feet. She stumbled, rolled, and got back to her feet. Her hat skittered away across the rooftop, but she didn't stop for it. She had to get him on the ground. That was her only chance. A burst of gunfire skimmed over her head so close she swore she could feel the air sizzle.

"Get down!" Wallace shouted. She caught a glimpse of him charging in her direction, rifle blazing.

Then something exploded in the air behind her. She knew she was on the ground when pain blazed through her teeth. A whistle screamed in her ears. She tried to move, but her limbs weren't getting the message. Groaning, she tried to make her eyes focus on the figure standing in the garden in front of her.

Sam's feet were trampling a clump of lilies. His metal skin was dented and scorched and his breath came in short, measured movements. He was fatigued, but even dazed she knew damn well he still had enough energy to wipe this whole city off the planet if he chose.

She grasped at the tile walkway. Something in the back of her mind was screaming at her to act, but she couldn't remember what to do. Nausea rolled through her in waves. A hollow noise tried to fight through the ringing in her ears.

—*I know you.*

Sam's mouth wasn't moving, but she could hear him speak. His head hung limply to the side, but he was looking at her, she knew.

—I remember. You tried to save me. I killed your friend. And I tried to kill you. But I want to save you. I don't know. I don't remember anymore.

"Sam...." It came out as a croak. He wasn't making any sense.

—It's okay. You won't be alone now.

The remaining civilians floated above, staring down at her with blank eyes.

Sam raised his hand and pointed a finger at her. A fibre crept towards her. She watched it with a sort of detached fascination.

Three loud cracks rattled through her brain. Sparks bounced off Sam's metal skin and his head snapped around.

"Get up!" someone shouted through water a million miles away.

I can't. I can't breathe.

Another burst of gunfire. "Get up and fight!"

A squat figure dived to the side, avoiding a blast of lightning. His face was lit up by the flash of his rifle. Wallace. But his bullets did nothing to Sam. The armoured boy stepped off the trampled garden and into the beams of the spotlights, his weight cracking the tiles beneath his feet.

His feet. He was on the ground. She remembered. She wrapped her good hand around a thin tree trunk and pulled herself up.

"I could do with a fucking hand here, hero!" Wallace shouted. Sam brought his fist back, his snarl fixed on the cape copper.

She tried to leap, but it was more of a lurch. It was enough. She slipped her stump out of the sling and wrapped her arms around Sam's icy torso, tightening the fingers of her left hand around the edges of his steel plates. Beneath the glare of the spotlights, she pulled him into a tight embrace, like her mum did to her on her first day of school.

Then she dragged him into the shadow with her.

The spotlights burned like scalding water. The shadow wasn't smooth and flat this time; it bubbled and boiled with movement. A shape screamed beneath her, flailing, drowning. She held her breath. The clock started in her head. Three minutes.

The black shape scrambled beneath her. She clung tight, dragging him back into the fire of the spotlight beam with her. She was half-blind, burning all over. The shape pulled away from the tile walkway, like a screaming face pressed against the surface of a black plastic bag. His mouth gulped like a fish, but there was no air in the shadow. She grabbed hold of his head and pushed him back down, flattening him against the tile. Somewhere, she thought she could make out Wallace shouting.

Thirty seconds gone. *I can't take it.* Every photon pierced her like a dagger. She could feel Sam's agony as well. Something was melding between them, their shadows mixing. Stray thoughts intruded on her own, and they were full of panic. Images of blood and torture ran through her head, the sound of Doll Face giggling and the stench of fear. Her consciousness flitted across the barrier between their two minds at will, tipping one way and then the other. And all the while, she drowned in a burning sea.

—*Dying I'm dying.* Sam's voice was half gibberish. *Dying burning crushing killing blood oh God blood everywhere. He's inside my head again!*

A minute gone. She could feel Sam trying to use his powers, but there was nothing here for him to get a hold on, and the lights made him weak. He clawed at her, trying to roll her away from the light with him. But here, she was stronger. She wrapped her shadow around a thousand tiny imperfections in the tile and held tight.

As their minds mixed, she sensed more presences. *The mind-control strings.* Still grappling with Sam, she followed the fibres to the edge of the shadow. It seemed like she was underwater, the strings piercing the surface and disappearing into the glare of the lights. *No more, Sam.* She focussed her energy, took hold of a handful of fibres, and tugged. Sam screamed as they snapped. She hoped that out there somewhere, Gabby and the others would catch the hostages before they fell.

Two minutes down. Sam's movements were slowing. Even a tier zero meta needed oxygen. She could feel the life leeching from him, evaporating. It was nearly over. He was nearly gone.

But so was she. The lights were becoming faded halos. Her sense of grip on the tile was going numb. At least the burning was starting to fade. She kept cutting strings. Sam's screams turned to whimpers. Pleading started to flow across the barrier between their minds, and heaviness clung to her heart. His thoughts were mad, disjointed, afraid, but without malice, like a wounded animal who didn't yet realise it was dying. On the edge of consciousness, she could sense Wallace moving to the controls for the lights. *Not yet.* Her thoughts were sluggish. *I've nearly got him.* When Wallace turned the lights up to full, the fire would take them both. There would be nothing left.

—*No!* Sam's thoughts intruded on her own. *I won't be alone!*

Without warning, a desperate fury erupted from Sam. He spun and struck her, gaining a fraction of solidity for a moment. Her grip slipped. He wriggled from under her.

Damn it. She grabbed hold of the edge of his shadow and tried to hang onto the fluid shape. He tugged against her, the edge of him nearly outside the beam of the spotlights. She couldn't let him go. She couldn't. If he got free, she'd be too weak to try again. With the last of her strength, she pulled him back. His screams echoed inside her head.

She pulled him back into her embrace. She could sense the last of his energy leaving him. His struggles turned to feeble flailing. *It's okay,* she told him. *It's going to be okay now.*

The movements grew slower, and slower still. Everything was dark. Then Sam's shadow slumped, and he was still. The fire on her skin and in her lungs had faded. She was so tired. *I'll just rest. Just for a moment.*

"Three minutes, vigilante." Wallace's distant voice jerked her awake. "If you're still alive, get the hell out now."

Time. Through the darkness, she felt Wallace's hand move to the controls.

She threw off the shadow like a heavy blanket. A moment later, the lights blazed. Her retinas burned. She turned away, her stump across her face. Every inch of her skin felt like it was scorched black. She could only manage a strangled grunt before she collapsed back onto the tiles. Something limp was resting on her belly. Sam. He was so quiet now.

Like a little boy.

Her lungs sucked in the air greedily. She couldn't tell if Sam was breathing. His metal armour had disappeared, and now he lay bloodied and pale and nearly naked, his eyes closed. The fibres had vanished. Dimly, she was aware of movement around her, of someone heavy landing next to her, and more brightly coloured figures floating overhead. But she could barely see them. She pulled Sam close, embracing him like a mother once more. And with her good arm wrapped around him, she drifted away.

Dawn bloomed over Neo-Auckland.

CHAPTER 31

IT NEVER ENDS

Dr Atomic changed everything. The world was ready to collapse, un-able to stand under its own weight. And then superheroes appeared and helped shoulder the burden. Whatever happens, society will never go back to the way it was before the heroes came. They are part of us now, inseparable. There is no "us" and no "them". There is just humanity, and all the good and bad and horrible and beautiful things that come with it.

—Superheroes: A Retrospective

Niobe and Gabby sat on the roof of their apartment building, watching the Moon hang in the sky above Neo-Auckland. For two hours they talked. And then they went back to their bedroom and made love.

They were timid at first, like it was their first time together. Gabby was so afraid of hurting Niobe that her touches were like whispers against her skin. It felt strange to be on the other side of the over-protection. Frustrating, even. Niobe stripped off both their clothes—using her teeth when she had to—and kissed Gabby hungrily, wounds be damned.

The doctors couldn't save Niobe's hand. After getting a good look at the damage, she couldn't blame them. They'd scraped away the dead muscle and bone and stitched a skin flap in place. If it didn't hold, they were going to have to take her back into surgery and do a skin graft. They weren't happy about her intention to leave the hospital, but after they'd finished stamping their feet they bandaged her hand up tight, stitched up her thigh, and gave her a form to confirm she was discharging herself against medical advice. She signed it clumsily with her left hand and went home with a course of antibiotics in her pocket and sunlight falling across her mask.

Now Niobe lay in bed, her good hand travelling over Gabby's belly, her lips brushing Gabby's neck. She tasted sweet. They held each other close, nestled together under the covers. Niobe felt the softness of Gabby's thighs, ran her fingers through the curls of Gabby's pubic hair. And then Niobe loved her with her hand and her mouth.

When they were both finished, Niobe lay down with her head in the crook of Gabby's shoulder and enjoyed her smell and the slow movement of her chest. Gabby's eyes were half-closed, but despite everything, Niobe wasn't tired. She gently played with Gabby's small pink nipple, enjoying the way it puckered, while she let her mind wander.

Neo-Auckland had taken a hell of a beating. They were still digging bodies out of the rubble. But worse than the corpses were the blank, soulless shells Sam had left behind. Hundreds of them, maybe more than a thousand. When she left, they were still counting. At least most of the young ones looked like they'd come right. The hospitals all across the rest of the country would be soaking up the overflow. Met Div was facing criticism from the politicians in Wellington, and they were hurling it right back. Quanta's people were under guard in high security prisons across the country, waiting for their time in court. Most were expected to enter guilty pleas and be remanded in custody until their sentences were handed down.

But it was the superheroes that were still dominating the TV and papers. Everyone had their opinion, and they were all too ready to tell everyone about it. Superheroes were a menace. They'd caused all this. No, they were saviours. Without them, Neo-Auckland, the rest of the country—hell, maybe the world—would be buggered. Some called for the Seoul Accord to be strengthened, further limiting metas' powers. Others called for it to be scrapped, and new legislation drafted. Legislation that would bring cooperation between metas and normals, to form new groups that would stand alongside conventional forces to defend the world against those who would harm it. All further kill-switching was on hold until the dust cleared and the world figured out a new way forward. There were even talks about resurrecting the old superhero comics, bringing those bright colours to a new generation.

As for the metas themselves, most were remaining quiet for now. A breeze blew in through the bedroom window. Outside, Niobe could hear the Graysons packing their belongings into their beat-up old ute. Already, metas were beginning to leave the Old City to seek a real life elsewhere.

Niobe leaned over and drew Gabby's nipple into her mouth. Gabby sleepily opened her eyes and smiled down at her.

—*Having fun?* Her fingers drooped the instant she finished signing.

Niobe released the nipple and rested her cheek on Gabby's breast. "I was thinking about the future," she said, signing as best she could.

Gabby raised her eyebrows. "Oh?"

Niobe nodded. "We've got enough money now. If you still want to...."

Met Div had found the cheque amongst Frank Oppenheimer's things, with a note attached. Fifty thousand, just as he'd promised. She'd given Carpenter's half to his widow. As for her own share, Niobe still didn't know how she felt about it. Sure, she'd found Sam, but she hadn't brought him home safe. She hadn't completed her job. But Frank's note told her to take it, no matter the outcome. Once he'd got the measure of Quanta, he'd known the chances of getting Sam home unharmed. He knew how hard she'd tried, all it had cost her. So she'd pocketed the cheque, her conscience still nagging her.

—*The Moon?* Gabby signed.

"Yeah. It's still waiting for us."

Gabby pursed her lips, cocked her head to the side, and ran her fingers through Niobe's hair. Sighing slightly, Niobe stroked Gabby's belly and listened to the sound of her heartbeat. A few moments later, the fingers left her hair. Niobe opened her eyes.

—*Let's stay here a bit longer,* Gabby signed. *And see what happens.*

Niobe pressed her lips against the spot where Gabby's ribs met her tummy, then reflected Gabby's smile. "I was hoping you'd say that."

Her kisses drifted lower again. Gabby gasped.

The sun was setting by the time they were finished again. They cuddled for a while then took showers. Gabby was wrapped in a dressing gown and reading a novel in bed when Niobe came out, towelling her hair with her good hand. She sat down naked on the bed and touched Gabby's leg to get her attention.

"I have to go out. I've got one more thing to do. Wanna come?"

Gabby laid the book down, saving her place, and smiled.

—*I think I'll stay here and have a nap.*

"You sure?" Niobe said.

Gabby nodded.

—*Don't be long. I'm not done with you yet.*

Niobe grinned. She nearly got back into bed, but she really did have one more thing to do. She kissed Gabby, got dressed, kissed her again, and closed the bedroom door behind her.

When she got to Met Div headquarters, Wallace was waiting for her. One wall of the building had been smashed in during the battle, but most of Met Div was still intact. Wallace looked her up and down, eyes narrowing a little at the mask, and grunted.

"You're late," he said.

"Yeah."

She followed him inside.

When Morgan woke, he was in darkness again. After a few minutes of feeling his way around, he determined the cell was not the same one he was placed in before. It was cooler here, and when he tapped the walls with the knuckle of his middle finger, he could detect no sense of hollowness. He couldn't even find a door. A row of tiny vents let in fresh air. They were too small to even get his fingers in. After half an hour, he settled back down on the thin mattress and exhaled.

The silence was good. No more headaches. He checked himself for injuries. A bandage covered his chest where the Silver Scarab's charged bolt had hit him, shattering his shield. He could still feel the emptiness as the light had drained from him, until he'd felt like a set of walking bones. If he wasn't mistaken, it was a modified version of the same tech he'd used to keep Iron Justice under control.

Morgan lay down and rested his head against the pillow. It was done, for now at least. He'd always known he would lose eventually. That was the whole point. He allowed himself a smile. He didn't know how much longer he would last, with the time bomb in his brain, but that didn't matter. As long as the reporter did his job, everything would work out. He'd done all he could. It was up to them now.

For three days he sat there. The tap gave good water. Food came in packages through some sort of pneumatic tube in the corner. No tomatoes, potatoes, or citrus fruits this time. Not that it mattered. They must have found the second false tooth and the miniature radio transmitter hidden under the fingernail of the fourth finger of his left hand, because both were gone. They sent pills along with the food, keeping him alive, keeping the seizures at bay. And that was it. So he munched the carrot sticks they sent him, drank the water, and pissed in the toilet, using the sound to help him aim. And he waited. They could have at least played him some music.

He thought the sound was a dream when he woke one morning. Well, it could have been any time of day, but he decided it might as well be morning. A hissing sound came from above his head. He sat up in bed and cocked his head to one side, listening.

"Hello?" he ventured.

"Hello, Morgan," the voice crackled after a short pause.

He smiled. "Niobe. I didn't think you could stay away. You like me too much. Though I suppose you're not really here, are you. Radio?"

Another delay, like the words hadn't reached her. "Don't stretch that criminal genius too much."

"Criminal genius, hmm?" He put his hands behind his head. "Nice of you to say."

For a while there was nothing but the hiss of the radio. Morgan closed his eyes and pictured the sun.

"If you're waiting for me to express remorse," he said, "you might want to get a cuppa and a book to pass the time."

"You're evil, Morgan. A kidnapper and a torturer and a mass murderer. A lot of people died because of you. Great men died because of you."

"Tell me," he said. "Did it work? Did the heroes return?"

There was a click. A lighter, perhaps. "It's too early to tell." But the hesitation before she spoke was all he needed to hear. Relief flooded him. He grinned in the direction of the speaker. The world had heroes again. That was worth any cost. Whether or not it lasted, that was up to them. All they had to do was be brave and do what was right.

"So the superhero saved the world," he said, and smiled. "But I saved the superhero."

"Your vanity is showing," she said. "Do you truly think they'll remember you? You think this will last?"

Morgan laughed. "I didn't bring a reporter on board for no reason. I can't lose. If John paints me as a monster, the world still has a threat to fear, a reason to need superheroes. If he makes them understand why I did it, they'll know that it can happen again. And even better, some will sympathise with me. It doesn't matter if you're God or the Devil, as long as people fear you."

"There's another option," she said.

"Oh yes? Do tell."

"Your reporter told us about the tumour," she said. "He told us you're dying."

His head throbbed once in response, but he pushed it aside. "I'm sure the thought is cutting you up inside."

She exhaled. He could imagine the cigarette smoke leaving her mouth. "It's a sad story. Very sad."

Something about the way she spoke made his chest tighten, but he said nothing.

"I've read John's piece on you. He's a brilliant writer. He really made me feel for you. The tragic tale of a pathetic, confused man."

"What?"

"That's right," she said. "It seems your tumour's been causing all sorts of paranoid delusions and hallucinations. Your illness drove you to all sorts of evil acts, but you can't be blamed. You were dying. You were sick. You shouldn't be feared. You should be pitied."

No. The word bounced around the hollow in his chest. *Pity.* They couldn't do that. They needed to remember him. One way or another, they needed to know it was him.

"You still there, Morgan?"

He composed himself. It wasn't over yet. "That story won't fly when they find out it was me at Cambridge."

"I don't think there's any need to drag up the past like that. Besides, Interpol has decided that those cases are classified. You're not Morgan Shepherd to the public. You're Quanta. That's what you wanted, right?"

He slammed his fist against the wall of his cell. "They will learn not to pity me."

Her laugh cut through him like a thousand tiny daggers. "And there it is. You think you had such a noble goal, don't you? But it wasn't enough for your plan to have worked. No, you wanted the world to know it was you. In the end, you're no different from any other super-villain. And you'll spend the last of your days the same way they did."

"Laugh, hero. My tumour hasn't killed me yet. I've escaped one prison. I'll escape this one."

"Where do you think you are? Some sort of standard high security meta prison?"

He said nothing.

"You hear that delay each time we speak?" Niobe said. "You're a long way from home. Me, I'm sitting in Met Div headquarters in the heart of sunny Neo-Auckland, and you must be…what would you say, Wallace? Seven thousand miles away?"

A gruff voiced grunted his assent. Raymond Wallace. At least Morgan could still smile about that. They could hide the truth from the public, but Wallace had seen with his own eyes what he'd created by chasing Morgan back in Europe. Wallace hadn't been holding the blade Morgan plunged into Lisa's chest, but he might as well have been. He wanted a monster, and when Lisa's hot blood spilled across the carpet, he got one.

"Amongst Frank Oppenheimer's things," Niobe continued, "we found some documents related to his brother. I suppose you know about Dr Atomic's madness. You're nothing if not well-informed."

"How kind of you to notice."

"One of those documents had a set of coordinates centred in the state of New Mexico. As soon as we realised what it was, we bundled you up and sent you on the first rocket-plane to America. Can you guess where you are now?"

He licked his lips. He knew, but he wasn't going to say it.

"You're in the prison that the remnants of the Manhattan Eight built. You're in the prison that held Dr Atomic until his death." The radio crackled. "Still think you can escape?"

"Ways and means, Niobe. Ways and means."

"Your voice is shaking," she said.

She thought she could goad him, but she was wrong. He'd face the long dark willingly if he had to. Others had already paid the cost. Now it was his turn. But he didn't think it would come to that.

"Tell me," he said. "What of the boy? What happened to poor Sam Oppenheimer? Did you manage to save him after all?"

The delay was so long Morgan wondered if the connection had cut out. But finally she spoke. "Sam's alive."

"But he's not the same, is he?"

"He will be. The best psychics and psychiatrists in the world are going to treat him. We'll undo the damage that you did."

He smiled. "Where is he now?" Then he realised. "He's in this facility with me, isn't he? Where else would you restrain the son of Dr Atomic?"

"Where else," she agreed.

"I saw him once, you know. Dr Atomic. I must have been about ten at the time. I spent all my pocket money on Dr Atomic comics—"

"Fuck you, Morgan," she said. "This isn't a comic. Enjoy your darkness. It's all you'll be getting for the rest of your life. Don't expect a bloody Christmas card." The transmission went dead.

Morgan settled back down in bed. The darkness was absolute, but it didn't feel as oppressive anymore. He'd done what he set out to do. And the world would know it was him, one way or another. A plan was never really finished.

Perhaps the woman was right. Perhaps he was no different from all the other supervillains. But was that such a bad thing? He shook his head and smiled. Somehow, a peace had settled over him.

"Thank you, Spook," he whispered into the darkness. "Thank you for helping me understand myself."

This prison may have held Dr Atomic, but he'd been a madman at the end. No prison was impenetrable. Somewhere on the other side of these walls was a young boy with more power than the world had ever known. If the world forgot that, they could be reminded.

And Morgan Shepherd wasn't dead yet.

It was a week before they held Solomon's funeral. There were a lot of bodies to deal with, and not enough people to deal with them.

The news reported Solomon's death, of course, but it was just one name in a long list of normals and metas who'd died. Some called for a state funeral, but his wife—widow, Niobe supposed she was now—insisted that it would be small. He would be buried as Solomon, not the Carpenter. A father and husband, not a superhero. It made it easier for Kate that way. Niobe didn't think he'd mind. But really, he was all those things. He was the best man she'd ever known. He'd always been a hero. He always would be.

Niobe stood apart from the small crowd of people gathered on the windy hilltop outside Neo-Auckland, watching as they lowered the casket into the ground. It wasn't a proper cemetery, but he wouldn't have wanted that. It smelled good here, like grass and flowers and a hint of salt coming off the sea in the distance. It was perfect for him. Well, almost.

The other guests threw glances at her dressed in her mask and hat, but she wasn't the only one in costume. Brightlance and Ballista stood amongst the group, heads bowed as the minister spoke in monotone.

Somehow, it didn't look strange.

When the tears came, she let them come. Her goggles grew misty. Her missing hand tingled in her pocket. That was the hand she'd massaged his heart with, trying to bring him back. She still wanted to. But she couldn't, and that was okay. Eventually, the tears dried.

She left before they'd finished piling the dirt on top of him. She walked down the hill and sat in the car. It was only five in the afternoon, so she had some time to kill before nightfall. She opened the glove box and pulled out the latest psych report Wallace had got for her. Sam had good days and bad days. Mostly bad days. And the nights were worse. The microphones in his cell picked up the screams and mutterings of his nightmares. She'd tried to listen to one recording. She'd shut it off after thirty seconds. Some instinctive part of her wanted to sit on the edge of Sam's bed and stroke his hair, tell him it was okay, everything was all right. That was madness, of course. He was thousands of miles away, and he'd still snap her in half as soon as he saw her. But the feeling remained.

It wasn't hopeless, though. His lucid periods were becoming longer and more frequent, and his violent outbursts were lessening. In those times he seemed to enjoy talking to the psychiatrists, even if it was only through an intercom. There was even word from the metahumans on the lunar colony that several of their psychics would return to Earth to aid in the boy's treatment, including Niobe's old flame, Madame Z. Niobe couldn't figure out if she was happy about that or not.

The Blind Man had examined Sam before they'd sent him to America. Niobe had stood beside him, still weak from the fight, and watched for six hours as the Māori man sat with his palm against the boy's forehead. And then the Blind Man opened his eyes and said there was hope. "He has great *mana*," the old man had said. "He may yet wash away what he has done." Maybe he'd even be a hero one day. Even greater than his father. *There was hope.*

When the sky turned pink, she got out of the car and walked back up the hill to the Carpenter's grave. He was alone up there now, everyone else mourning somewhere else over pastries and stories. The wind had died down a little, and now the grass barely whispered. She knelt down near the upturned soil and removed her mask.

"You were right," she said. "Damn you, you were right."

She didn't have a spade or a trowel, so she used her remaining hand to dig a small hole over his grave.

"You'll never guess what I spent the morning doing," she said. "Running goddamn try-outs. A new superteam. The money I got from Frank Oppenheimer is more than enough to get us started. There's a lot of us oldies out there remembering what it's like to be a hero. And I'll be buggered if some of these new kids aren't even better than we were. This one girl, Dancer, she's pretty much a shoe-in for the team."

She fished in her pocket for a few seconds until she found what she was looking for. The totara seed looked like a tiny red berry with a green stalk attached. She dropped it into the small hole and shuffled the upturned dirt back over it.

"We're still deciding what to name the new team. The current favourite is 'The New Wardens'. Original, eh?" She patted down the earth, sat down, and faced the sea. "Of course, we don't even know if it's going to get off the ground yet. Lots of variables to factor in. But I'm hopeful." She almost laughed. "You hear that? Hopeful. Me."

The evening was warm. She sat silent for a while, watching the fading sky. It made her smile. She liked the night. It always comforted her. It made her think things might be all right. She glanced at the signaller dangling from her wrist. The Carpenter wouldn't mind if she held on to it.

"Oh yeah, I nearly forgot. Mrs McClellan got her baby back. They dropped the charges against her, so we tracked her down to tell her it was okay to come out of hiding. The kid's got a hell of a pair of lungs. By the sound of it she's gonna be a banshee-type meta by the time she's five."

When the last of the daylight vanished and the stars appeared, Niobe stood and brushed herself off. She had places to be. Gabby would be waiting for her.

"I'll come back next week," she said. "I'm sure I'll have some more stories by then. Everything's changing so fast. It's a new world, Carpenter." She smiled. "See you round, mate."

The first totara shoots had already started to poke their way out of the dirt. She pulled her mask back on and returned to the car.

She was right; Gabby was waiting for her. A light was blinking on the dashboard when she got in the car. She flipped open the panel to reveal the screen and small keyboard.

—*Everything okay?* the readout said.

Niobe had to search and peck at the keys to type the response. It was a great system Gabby had come up with, but it'd be easier if Niobe had paid attention in typing class at high school. Another hand would've been useful too. She couldn't wait until Gabby put the finishing touches on the prosthetic hand she was building.

—*Yeah,* Niobe finally responded. *I'm ready. Where are you?*

—*Look up.*

Niobe leaned over the steering wheel and looked up at the sky through the windshield. There, amongst the stars, was a speck of orange flame, and above it, the glinting of silver armour.

—*Looking good, babe,* Niobe typed.

—*We've got something coming in. Pile-up on the southern highway. Four cars, a bus, and a fuel tanker. We'll be faster than the firemen. You up for it?*

Niobe turned the ignition and shifted the lever of the new automatic transmission. The car rumbled to life, good as ever.

—*Race you there,* Niobe typed.

—*You're on.*

The fire streaked across the sky. They were the strangers who guarded the world through the night. And they had work to do.

Niobe gunned the engine.

Author's Note

I love superheroes. There's something pure and uplifting and primal about the idea of superpowers and saving the world and good and evil. When we live our entire lives in a place where nothing is certain, where everything is a shade of grey, sometimes we need to escape to a world where there are people who are just good, without a reason or a motive or an agenda. I love being able to visit a world where good people have the power to change the world for the better.

For too long, the superhero genre (whatever that is) has been portrayed as nothing more than a power fantasy for young males. But as Kurt Busiek so eloquently put in the first Astro City trade paperback, *Life in the Big City*, the superhero is, above all else, a symbol, a metaphor. (By the way, if you're not already familiar with Astro City, check it out. It's a fantastic comic and requires no prior knowledge of the major superhero universes.)

The superhero is incredibly versatile. He can be a symbol of whatever the hell you want him to be. Superhero stories can be about living gods destroying and creating on whims, like the gods of ancient Greek myth, or they can be normal people like us, just trying to get by. They can be stories of young people, old people, male, female, gay, straight, bi, human, non-human, or anything in between. They can be stories of love, terror, hope, action, or wonder. And they can be all of those things at the same time. Are superheroes simplistic and juvenile? Sure, to some degree. But that purity is what makes the superhero such a powerful metaphor. A story about a superhero can be as simplistic or as complex as the writer chooses to make it.

While this book may be gritty, I never intended to write a "realistic" superhero story. Alan Moore's *Watchmen*, Nolan's Batman movies, and many other stories have already explored what happens when you put a superhero in a relatively realistic environment, and they've done it better than I ever could. I think it's pretty clear that in real life, superheroes would break the world. If people with the power of Superman, Green Lantern, Iron Man, or Professor X existed, the world would change completely, and probably not for the better. But I don't believe that means there's no room for unrealistic superhero stories. On the contrary, I think one of the strongest drivers of the superhero mythos in the public consciousness is that sense of wonder, that sense of strangeness. And I don't think superheroes are going away anytime soon.

I had a blast writing this book. It took me a bit longer than I thought it would and the total word count was greater than I expected, but I'm proud of the finished product. It has been incredibly satisfying to inject a bit of myself and my Kiwi culture into the superhero genre. Whether you guys enjoy reading the book as much as I enjoyed writing it remains to be seen. I owe a great debt of gratitude to all those who helped this book come to fruition. I want to thank Nen and Diana for all their hard work in helping me improve the book. This book wouldn't have been possible without them. I take full responsibility for any and all errors, at least until I can figure out how to pin them on someone else. I have to offer a big thanks to Kitty for her mad art skillz. Thank you to my friends and family who encouraged me on this crazy writerly quest. And of course, a huge thank you to everyone who helped make the superhero such a powerful figure in popular culture, from Jerry Siegel and Joe Schuster, the creators of Superman, to modern day creative geniuses like Joss Whedon, whose big screen take on *The Avengers* is currently tearing up the box office.

None of the heroes or villains mentioned in this novel are intended to be direct parallels of any existing characters in superhero fiction, but with such long, rich histories across dozens of different companies and writers and universes, some characters have acted as inspiration for my own. There are, of course, many nods to classic superhero tropes throughout the book. The only characters in this book who are based on real people are Robert and Frank Oppenheimer. J. Robert Oppenheimer really was the physicist in charge of the Manhattan Project, and his brother, Frank, was among the many scientists at Los Alamos. Their lives make for fascinating reading, and biographies of them are well worth seeking out. Of course, there was never an explosion at Los Alamos, and the brothers never became superheroes. I have taken a number of other liberties with regards to the brothers and their lives, and nothing in this book is meant to reflect in any way on their real life counterparts.

Thank you very much for reading. I hope you enjoyed *Don't Be a Hero*. If you feel like recommending the book to a friend or leaving a quick review on Amazon, Goodreads, or any other site you can think of, I'd be extremely grateful. I sink or swim based on the kindness and enthusiasm of readers like you.

Stay tuned for more stories set in the Atomverse. Niobe's story may be over, but there are a few billion other people out there trying to make it in a world where superheroes and supervillains exist, and they've all got stories to tell. Let's see how many I can get through before the writer's life catches up with me.

Until next time.

Chris Strange

About the Author

Chris Strange is a writer of urban fantasy and other fantastika. He is especially fond of writing hardboiled stories with a noir influence. His goal is to deliver intense, humorous, and sometimes dark stories to his readers.

In his spare time, Chris is an unapologetic geek, spending far too long wrapped up in speculative fiction books, watching old zombie movies and playing computer games. He lives in the far away land of New Zealand, and occasionally he goes to university like he's supposed to.

He doesn't plan on growing up any time soon.

Want to be the first to hear about new releases from Chris Strange? Sign up for the email list at: **http://bit.ly/StrangeList**

Contact Chris at: **chrisstrangeauthor@gmail.com**

www.chris-strange.com

Made in the USA
Lexington, KY
20 June 2014